ATTACK OF THE BOGEYMEN

The solid reality of the weapons were holding the bogeymen at bay, for now. The horde was handicapped by their own experience: killing and kidnapping frightened children does not prepare you for armed adults fueled by pent-up rage and frustration. Yet for every bogey that disintegrated before a notched blade, two more changed their tactics. Now there were the voices.

Voices everywhere, shrieking, babbling, cursing, laughing wild gulping laughter and mocking every slip or misstep. Abby's fingers grew numb on the wood as they chuckled in her ear, whispering all the little things that nobody was supposed to know about. Secrets and shames slipped past into the darkness, leaving each of their lives laid open....

John shifted the sword to his left hand and emptied four shots in the taunting face of a wizened spirit with bear teeth. The shape flashed and fell apart, dissolving into clayed mud. John's foot slipped again on the slick substance, and the bogeymen pounced, ready to be in at the kill.

"You *feel* Chicago in Catherine Butzen's writing. She pulls you into the slushy streets and the city's dark heart to accompany her amazing mix of characters, human and not-so. You feel for Abby, root for her, and appreciate the detail and depth in the supporting cast: John, Keith, El Cucuy, Likho, and more. *Thief of Midnight* is a book to be appreciated and savored for its moody prose... and to be read with the doors locked by those who still believe in the bogeyman."

JEAN RABE, BESTSELLING AUTHOR
OF *The Stonetellers* TRILOGY

Thief of Midnight
Catherine Butzen

STARK
HOUSE

Stark House Press • Eureka California

THIEF OF MIDNIGHT

Published by Stark House Press
2200 O Street
Eureka, CA 95501, USA
griffinskye3@sbcglobal.net
www.starkhousepress.com

ISBN: 1-933586-31-1
ISBN-13: 978-1-933586-31-1

Text set in Figural and Dogma.
Cover illustration by gak, © 2010, WWW.GAKART.COM
Design and layout by Mark Shepard, WWW.SHEPGRAPHICS.COM
Proofreading by Rick Ollerman

First Stark House Press Edition: July 2010

0 9 8 7 6 5 4 3 2 1

For Carolyn (1926-2005)

Chapter One

Abby Marquise didn't like guns, as a rule. Not that she had any moral objection to them; she'd grown up in rural Montana, where they were as much a fact of life as winters well below zero. But at the end of the day, the idea of being able to spontaneously end a life unnerved her.

Unfortunately, not everyone—or everything—in the world was bothered by that kind of thing, and personal scruples had to bow to practicality. On the day Abby went to help kill the doppelganger, she carried a Beretta Tomcat in an inside pocket of her jacket.

It was four o'clock in the afternoon on a gray November day. Winter was still toying with Chicago, and the gutters were filled with slush tinted charcoal by sidewalk runoff, but the streets were mostly clear. Abby's long parka hung open, padded out by a couple of sweaters and a fringed yellow pashmina, but the brisk wind had turned her round cheeks bright pink and tangled her dark blonde hair. The Beretta's bulk was easily hidden under the parka. If asked, Abby wouldn't have bet on being able to reach it quickly. Her fingers were stiff with cold.

Hidden in another inside pocket was the grainy photograph that had brought her and her friends outside in that weather: a black-and-white still from a hidden camera, one of several dozen scattered across the city. The photograph was less than twenty-four hours old, but already, Abby was worried about the time gap. Doppelgangers had to eat at least once a day in order to maintain their shape-shifting mass, and a doppel as small as the one in the still had to be fairly desperate.

A tall thin man was sitting on the newspaper box outside the door of the Goodwill, cradling a green glass jar in his lap. His name was John Sawyer, and unlike Abby, he had no qualms whatsoever about carrying concealed weaponry. There would always be a Desert Eagle pistol hidden under his brown leather jacket, but that certainly wasn't all: she had seen him slip a packet of road flares into his pants pocket before they left the office, and she was prepared to bet that there was more she hadn't seen.

Even better than guns, though, was the glass jar. The angry gray mist swirling inside was a genie—although, to be fair, he preferred to be called a djinn. His name was Harvey.

Abby pulled the photograph out and examined it again. As far as she could tell, the doppelganger had taken the shape of a—

"Pinstripe?" she said.

"Pinstripe," John confirmed, sliding off the newspaper box. His London accent had faded a bit after years in the States, but Abby knew that it would thicken the instant a suspect or a pretty girl came into view. "Looked like a suit jacket. Probably in the men's section." He fished in his pocket and pulled out his cell phone, checking the display. "I've got you on speed dial."

"Me, too," Abby said. "How's Harvey?"

John tossed her the glass jar, which she fielded easily. (Years of Junior Sports League, bless it.) None of the passing people paid any attention to the impromptu game of catch; the first rule of life in Chicago was not to get involved, in case someone might try to attack you or tell you about Jesus.

Abby cradled the jar and listened carefully. Inside, two malevolent yellow eyes opened, and she heard the voice of the djinn in her head:

Ready and waiting, mein Führer. I can give 'em ten minutes of blank memories. Try not to kill anybody, m'kay?

"He's fine." Abby tucked the jar under her arm and shot a look at the door of the Goodwill. The wind picked up, whipping her hair into her eyes. Annoyed, she slipped a rubber band off of her wrist and pulled her hair into a rough ponytail. "Shall we?"

"Best get on with it."

Abby nodded and turned away. The Goodwill was bordered on its north side by an alley, wide but dimly lit and dingy, where the delivery trucks could drop off their loads of donated clothes; it was a perfect place for what the Society for the Security of Reality (dear God, they needed to change that name) had called the djinn drop. The gaseous form of the djinn was vulnerable to the high winds now sweeping down the street, but the alley was protected, and the delivery bay doors stood slightly ajar as the workers inside piled up the mounds of secondhand clothing. With the pickle jar under her arm, Abby walked briskly towards the alley, eyes focused on the copy of the Red Eye newspaper in her hand. Nobody paid any attention, and she paid no attention to them.

She slipped a hand under her left arm and loosened the lid of the jar, shielding her actions from the street with her back and from the other end of the alley with the casually fanned Red Eye in her left hand. There was a quiet hiss, like a release of steam, and thin smoke dribbled out from under the lid. She feigned a yawn and breathed out heavily, and her breath clouded in the air with Harvey's form, masking his passage.

In a moment, the jar was empty. If she looked carefully, she could just see a tendril of gray slipping around the open doors of the shipping bay.

At that moment, her cell phone vibrated inside her jacket. Despite the cold, Abby was sweating a little, and her fingers slipped on the plastic case before she managed to get a grip on it. It was a text message from a contact called "Sudo the Dentist," but it was blank. Abby smiled and tucked away the phone again before tightening the lid again and tucking the jar behind a stack of cardboard boxes. It still seemed funny to her that everyday technology—wireless headsets, pocket computers, and text messages—was so much more advanced than anything she'd seen in the super-spy films when she was growing up. John was telling her he was inside, and that it was safe to follow. She loosened her pashmina and stepped out of the alley, heading for the front door of the shop.

A musky smell rose from the disheveled racks of clothes. Toy bears missing their eyes and dolls with inexpertly cropped hair stared hopelessly at the browsing shoppers. Old teapots and broken crockery—which the store's sign termed "valuable antiques at incredible prices"—were ranged on steel shelves, gathering dust. The customers who browsed among the racks often seemed as worn as the things they purchased: clumsily-dressed women with downcast expressions and shriveled men with V.F.W. badges and Purple Hearts pinned to their worn sweaters. The heating was on far too high, giving the store a thick, stale atmosphere.

John headed straight for the men's section, browsing vaguely through the racks of suits and coats on hangers. Knowing that nobody would remember her, Abby loitered near the front, turning over the various secondhand necklaces and earrings that hung from the rack by the cashier. She watched the reflection of the moving line in a mirrored pendant, examining the clothes in each person's arms for pinstripes. When the clerk glanced suspiciously at her, she picked a long earring shaped like a skull and crossbones off the rack and held it up to her ear, frowning at the reflection in the mirror. The picture she made—sensible sweater, leering piece of chrome—made her laugh.

She didn't feel it was out of place to enjoy herself a little, even in the middle of a mission. Catching doppelgangers was always a lot of hurry-up-and-wait, and the butterflies in her stomach could easily develop into full-on panic if she didn't do her best to stay calm. Some of the other agents had different methods, with drink being the one they all shared. John couldn't indulge that way as often as the rest of them, though; not when he was medicated to the eyeballs to control his fits of temper. He kept a little bottle of yellow pills in his pocket, ready and waiting in case he started to go off the rails again. He'd described it once as a sensation like ants walking around under his skin.

He'd put something else under his skin as well. Mottled, blue-gray lines on the knuckles of his left hand spelled out a homemade message of adolescent defiance: ACAB, All Coppers Are Bastards. It was the mark of a middle-class boy who had had downward aspirations, and who even as a young teenager was able to withstand some pain. Home tattooing was not a phenomenon that Abby's hometown had seen, and the idea of stabbing yourself with an inked needle gave her chills. But John hadn't been home in almost fifteen years, and he seemed to see no need to hide his India-ink mistake; Americans weren't likely to know what message a rebellious kid from Muswell Hill was trying to convey.

There—a flash of pinstripes. A woman was approaching the counter, her arms full of clothing. A jacket was draped over the top, clearly a last-minute impulse buy. Abby's heart began to beat faster. It was an odd choice for a stocky woman, buying a jacket fit for a small man.

Putting down the earring, Abby fumbled for her cell phone. She dialed "Sudo the Dentist" and let it ring twice, then closed it and began moving towards the woman. A wisp of gray smoke flicked past her: Harvey was in position.

She stepped briskly up to the woman and tapped her on the shoulder. "'Scuse me, miss," she said hurriedly. "We've been looking for that coat. I have to take it back—it needs to be disinfected right away."

The woman blinked her heavy-lidded eyes slowly. "What?" she said in a low voice. Her arms protectively tightened on the pile of clothes, and Abby felt a nervous shudder in her stomach: the doppelganger's pheromones were already taking effect on their new host. The woman might have been sleepwalking.

"Ma'am, that coat was put in with the clothes by mistake. Its owner had virulent tuberculosis, and we have to get it disinfected—"

"Fuck off!" The woman's voice was unnaturally loud, and squeaked oddly. She clutched the jacket closer, dropping all the other items but using that little pinstriped bundle to shield her broad belly. Abby drew back slightly, alarmed by the violent reaction, and fumbled in her pocket for the ID she knew was there. Over the woman's shoulder, she could see John hurrying through the racks of clothes. His eyes were fixed on them.

Abby pulled out the badge: Illinois Department of Public Health. "Ma'am, please. There could still be extremely dangerous germs on that jacket."

The woman's grip tightened, and the jacket began to flex and twitch. Her eyes were glazed. Other shoppers were beginning to notice; a heavyset man in sweatpants was eyeing Abby's ID distastefully. (She didn't blame him. It had been cut the day before yesterday, in the basement of the office.) John was a few yards away now, slipping his hand inside his jacket for the Desert Eagle.

Looking into the woman's lifeless eyes, Abby knew that she was already dead. The bundle curled in her arms shuddered again, twitching slightly as it began to expand. Its camouflage flickered as its mass increased. The pinstripes slid apart as it sucked the life out of its new host.

The time for subtlety was long past. Abby lashed out. Moving with the energy of long experience, she plunged forward and seized the doppelganger, digging her fingers into its mushy skin and jerking it as hard as she could. The bundle screeched in rage as it was yanked free of its host's arms, and a long chitinous spike slid out of a wound in the woman's stomach with a damp slurping noise. The victim slumped to the floor, her face a pale blank. Blood, thick and glutinous, was already staining the front of her shirt.

"Pull!" John yelled, shoving the last of the surprised shoppers aside. Without hesitating, Abby flung the flailing doppelganger. It struck the side of the counter, making a noise like a furious cat, and Abby ducked and clapped her hands over her ears. Two gunshots echoed through the store.

Even before the creature's lumpen corpse splattered to the floor, Harvey was on the job. A gray mist flooded the store, muting sounds, freezing the panicking people, wiping minds and smoothing memories over. Amidst the chaos, Abby rose from her crouch, head still ringing with the echo of the gunshot, and hurried towards the counter. The clerk stood blank-faced as his memory was wiped clean; he made no move to stop Abby, who jerked a large plastic bag from between his stiff fingers and knelt to scoop the remains of the doppelganger into it. A smell like rotting vanilla arose from the sloshing corpse.

Footsteps sounded odd in the suddenly silent room. Moving stiffly, John stepped over the slumped form of the doppelganger's host, tucking the Desert Eagle away with shaky fingers. His face was pale. "Cutting it a bit close," he said, mechanically taking the bag from Abby. His knuckles were white, and the ACAB stood out blue-black against his skin.

"John," Abby said cautiously. "Are you all right?"

He twitched, and she knew he was restraining himself. He never took well to killing, and Abby had seen, more than once, that pulling the trigger took him to someplace strange and feral. She stepped back, not saying anything more.

The doppelganger's host was dead. She had been only half alive before, puppeted by the creature while it drained every last erg of life out of her. The stab wound made by its spike would have always been fatal—but nevertheless, Abby wished that she could have done something. It made no sense to blame herself for this anonymous woman's death, yet the guilt would always remain.

She welcomed it, to some extent. The day she stopped feeling guilty was the day she grew accustomed to writing off the deaths of her fellow humans, and the thought terrified her. She had no more regard for the doppelganger than she did for a rabid dog (there had been too many injuries from fights with that kind of creature—the broken ankle, the scars on her back), but she had never enjoyed the act of execution.

But there was nothing she could do right then that could make it right, so she leaned down and closed the dead woman's eyes.

Abby heard the shuffle of footsteps, and the rattle of pills in a plastic bottle. John... well, he did enjoy the act of execution, and enough to worry even him. He wouldn't want her staring, though, so she kept her eyes on the floor and whispered one of the little Latin prayers from her childhood. For whom, she wasn't quite sure.

It only took a moment to dig the bullets out of the counter and fill the holes with chewing gum. They left, and no one would remember they'd even been there. Witness accounts stated that a woman in line had suddenly clutched her stomach and collapsed, apparently the victim of a covert stabbing by a fellow shopper. A sticky gray stain near the counter tested as hemolymph, the compound which spiders and insects have instead of blood. The coroner guessed that it was the result of some careless person spilling a chemical sample; a spider capable of generating that amount would weigh ten pounds or more.

The office of the Society for the Security of Reality was a small, one-story building just off Western Avenue, in a small defunct mercantile park. The office had been built as a free clinic back in the '70s by a group with more idealism than common sense; when the SSR moved in, they had had to rip out several tottering walls and completely rewire the building. Some of the original owners' idealistic enthusiasm still remained, mostly in the form of posters that had been hung in what was now the main office. Nixon, Che Guevara, and the Cook County Peace & Freedom Association stared down at the agents, festooned with years' worth of Post-it notes and irreverent marker graffiti. A dry-erase board had been hung between Che and Nixon—allegedly for office announcements, but currently displaying a scribbled conversation between the two political icons.

Four desks and several bookcases had been crammed into the main office, which had once been two examination rooms. Three of the desks were outfitted as workstations, with a variety of obsolete computer equipment; the fourth held a mess of unwashed coffee cups, the official SSR printer, and a guinea pig in a cage.

There were two people by the desks when Abby and John walked in. One was a teenage girl, dressed in trendy clothing, with a variety of bead loops and feathers braided into her red-gold hair. The other was a broadshouldered, imposing man in gray, who was seated at the nearest computer and typing briskly. The man's name was Marotte, and he was a Shakespearean actor at an awkward stage—too old for Hamlet and too young for King Lear. The girl's name was Mary, and she was a psychic. She waved briskly at Abby and John with the severed hand she was holding.

"Hey, guys!" she sang out. The hand—bone white, with blue-tinged nails—began to rapidly sign a greeting. Mary set it down on the desk and it skittered away, followed a second later by its mate. The second one held a pinkish eyeball clenched between two knuckles. "Didja get it?"

John raised one arm, letting the sloshing bag dangle free. "Got it. One death."

Mary's face fell. "Oh," she said, looking away quickly.

There was the scrape of a chair, and Marotte stood up. On his feet, he was the tallest person in the room by at least half a head. "Requiescat in pace," he said. His voice was slow and deep. "Abigail, there was a telephone call for you."

Abby didn't pay much attention: she had taken the bag from the stone-faced John and was heading towards the basement steps. "Was it Terry?" she called over her shoulder. "I told him I'd only talk with my lawyer present!"

"It was the police. They wanted to speak to you about your son."

She stopped. For a moment, her face went red, but she forced her expression to remain unperturbed. She could feel her heart sink. "Is he hurt?" she managed.

"He is in custody," Marotte said. "Uninjured."

Abby turned away and, without another word, stepped down the staircase to the basement.

There, the tone of the office was much different. Long fluorescent tubes illuminated a stark scene, with uninsulated pipes bulging from the ceiling and gray concrete floors pitted and marked with years of water stains. But there was a brand-new sewer hatch in the floor, and the coffin-sized metal tubs that lined the walls had only minimal wear and tear. Each tub was open, and the glistening mounds of salt sparkled like uncut diamonds as the lights blinked overhead.

Abby's movements were briskly mechanical as she worked. Open the bag and the hatch. Dump the hemolymph into the sewer. There was an empty tub halfway down the row, its salt raked back into ungainly lumps from the removal of what had been there before. She turned the plastic bag inside-out, and with a squelch, the doppelganger corpse landed in the tub. Quickly, she raked the salt with her fingers, burying the squishy body.

The salt would drain the fluid from the body and dry it out. Slowly but surely, like leeching poison from a wound. Then the dried corpse would be soaked in a vat of caustic astringents until it fell apart, and could be safely poured into the sewer. Quick, no, but clean and relatively painless. Problems like that could be solved in the end—with just a little salt and a lot of time. It was too bad all their problems couldn't be solved like that.

Her eyes were beginning to burn. She mopped them on the back of her sleeve, doing her best to ignore the incriminating dampness of tears. It should be nothing. She'd gotten the calls before, and it could always be cleared up. Truancy, a fight at school. The usual teenager stuff.

Maybe she should have let him stay with his father.

A shuffling noise distracted her from her increasingly bitter thoughts. A particleboard wall separated the salt tubs from the rest of the basement, and through the connecting door came a queer, ungainly creature. It was at least seven feet tall, topping Marotte by five or six inches, and had the off-white skin of an albino. A fall of bone-colored hair failed to hide quizzical pinkish eyes, although one was missing at the moment. The loose shorts and tank top revealed deep indentations around every joint, and both hands were absent as well. It smiled and waved one stump at Abby.

"Hi, Dummy," she said, forcing herself to smile back. Dummy could not speak, but he was very far from stupid, and his smile changed to a worried frown when he saw her expression. He raised one eyebrow, and it spoke volumes.

"I'm fine," Abby replied. She wasn't in the mood to be faced with the gentle giant. Dummy had the knack of staying silently neutral, and letting the distressed person incriminate themselves by projecting their fears onto him. Besides, no matter how long she had known him, the polished gleam of that empty eye socket unnerved her.

Without another word, she turned away and began to climb back up the steps. She could feel Dummy's gaze on her back as she went.

A doppelganger was not a real problem. All it took was a couple of bullets, and it went away. Her son was something else entirely. Sometimes, during long bad nights working in the office or staking out a house, she wished there was a quick fix. A bullet, never. That was the kind of thing John would suggest.

She could let Jimmy go with his father, of course. That was the logical course. But some hard little nugget of pride refused to let her admit defeat—state to the courts that she was insane, acknowledge to her ex-husband that she was an unfit mother—and she stubbornly kept Jimmy with her. Silently, she promised herself that this time, she would discipline him properly. He had to learn who was in charge.

Chapter Two

Since the very beginning, humans have told each other tales about what is, what could be, what never was and what hopefully will never come to be. Even history is just another story: people telling their idea of what might have happened, their narratives populated with fantastical characters and unlikely events. Much of what the human race *knows* is simply more stories, passed on by other equally fallible humans in a ten-thousand-year game of Telephone. And over time, the stories change.

Of course, there are constants in even there. Like islands in a stream, some few things remain solid while the worlds of the stories change and rage around them. Most of them are the undeniable fact: mankind has four limbs, and the sun shines in the sky.

Take the example of the bogeyman. Throughout the world, parents try to control their children by telling them stories about the monster in the night. It might be the Mitten-Snatcher, who will grab their legs if they step out of bed during the night. Or sometimes it's the Old Hairy Man, who pursues runaway children through forests and gobbles them up. Parents see these stories as a way to ensure good behavior, but the children see it as gospel truth. So they hide, curled up in their sheets, hoping fervently that the monster won't get them.

They believe in the stories their parents tell them. What they don't know is that belief has a certain power of its own. Believe enough, and you will begin to see evidence of your belief everywhere—in miracles, in signs, in seemingly impossible recoveries or unusually timed accidents. And when enough people believe in what they are told, dreading the possibility and *knowing* that a gruesome fate is just around the corner, their bogeyman comes to life.

Once, thousands of years ago, an old woman told her disobedient grandchild a story. She said that the gods of Night and Fear had two sons: one was a cruel thief, the other a vicious animal, and both would steal bad children. This was the first story of the first bogeymen, and that child believed. Those first creatures have changed, but they are no longer the only ones. Their kindred flourished, and where bad children fear the night, the Family of bogeyman walks.

Once every hundred years, the Family meets and plans for another century. Their ranks have changed over the years, growing and shrinking in accordance with human belief. During the Dark Ages, when a man might go to a priest to be relieved of the evil spirit which caused his toothache, there were so many of the Family that they seemed more like a legion of soldiers than a group of brothers and sisters.

On that warm Thursday night, in a warehouse on the water's edge in Sydney, Australia, the Family was still strong and large. Not so strong as they had been, but strong enough.

If someone wanted a place to get more than fifty specters together, an unused warehouse was as good as any. The watchman had been handled, and the members of the Family were streaming in. Flying, running, crawling on the ground, they came from all four corners of the earth and sported all manner of shapes. But there were always the two breeds—derived, though none of them knew it, from the two brothers of that first ancient story. There were the hairy men, huge shuffling monstrosities. And there were the bag men, clever and vicious thieves.

The hairy men came first. They were the most openly monstrous— nothing but tangled masses of fur, fangs, rags, and gleaming eyes. Some were noticeably beastlike, some were almost human, and several seemed trapped between. Lacking elaborate legends to define them, most of their rank simply faded into existence, lurking in the shadows. Their leader was Sacauntos, a giant with a flensing knife in one hand: the second-in-command of the Family.

After them, wary of their more powerful brothers, came the bag men. Most of them took the forms of withered old men, dressed as wanderers, with rough bags or cages in their arms. Despite their similarities, there was a wider variety of myth to be seen there; El Nadaha, an Egyptian woman draped in water weeds, came paddling up to the dock in a little reed boat, while the Czech Hastrman drove himself in a cart pulled by twelve cats.

Two of the last to reach the warehouse were a pair of bag men, Likho and L'uomo Nero. Likho, the shorter of the pair, was a Ukrainian-Russian spirit; there, he took the form of an old man, dragging a burlap bag in one hand and pulling L'uomo Nero behind him with the other. His companion was much taller than he, swathed in black, with eyes hidden behind a fall of dark dirty hair and a pallid, vacant expression. He trailed behind Likho like a cruise liner being towed by a tugboat.

As the last of the Family passed by, Likho and L'uomo Nero slipped into intangibility and walked through the walls of the warehouse. Their leader, El Cucuy, liked to see things done in a traditional manner, and Likho had already been reprimanded once for smoking like a human. No sense in taking chances, and especially not at the centennial meeting.

The warehouse was an old, sturdy building, a relic of the 1940s pasted with decades' worth of graffiti. Inside, it was all one huge room, stacked with crates. Small windows set high in the walls let in the vague orange light of the street lamps which lined the pier.

The Family gathered together, lining the walls. Some crouched in the corners, and a select few hung from the ceiling. Eyes glittered from every rat hole and in the slightly deeper shadow under every bench. There were a few patches of color—the white shroud of a skeletal woman, and the faint glow of a ten-foot giant made of blue light. But in most places, the darkness was liquid.

A match flared. A small boy flickered into existence in the center of the floor, dressed in shapeless gray clothes. His eyes were closed, but his hand never wavered as he put the match to the flame of an old oil lamp.

Then he smiled at his assembled brethren and opened his eyes. They were very pale and entirely white, except for a brilliant red dot glowing in the center of the blankness.

"Brothers and sisters, we are all here again," he said. His words had the high, soft fluting sound of a little boy with a gentle disposition. But everybody in this watching crowd understood that this creature was nothing like any other little boy in the world. Boys don't suck the marrow from babies' bones.

"Though the centuries march on, I am still El Cucuy out of Mexico. I have the responsibility as leader of the Family." He did not blink or breathe; the physical form was mostly for show.

His unimpressive appearance didn't mean he lacked power. The other creatures instinctively gave him a wide berth.

"Since we last met, so much has happened. Humanity has surged forward. Now, people spread across the globe quickly, traveling as fast as sound itself. Like deities, they fly high above and work miracles without and within." El Cucuy folded his small hands. "My dear family. Another century has gone. And once again, we remember those who have been forgotten by the living."

The lamp flame danced and flickered. Its light couldn't touch El Cucuy; even the tiny spark had more existence than he did. "We come together to remember, as we must," he said. "Wicked Coyote."

A rumble came from the assembled ranks of the bogeymen as dozens of voices spoke. "We remember," they intoned.

"The Old Hairy Man," the child continued.

"We remember."

"The Babaw."

"We remember."

The boy's eyes were fixed on the lamp. "And why do we remember them, O my brothers?"

"For they were forgotten, and we too shall follow in the end."

As the last word hung in the air, the darkness seemed to grow lesser. El

Cucuy raised the candle and gave the assembled bogeymen a long, know-ing gaze. They were waiting for the next part of the litany. After what seemed to be an interminable length of time, their leader moved. "Brothers," the little voice said gently. The red eyes caught the light of the lamp, and they burned like the wick. "My dear family. A hundred years ago, we moved on. We remembered the children, and our duty. That will not be so tonight. Three of our best have been forgotten."

"The children be hanged," rumbled a hair-draped figure, one of the tallest present. "*We* remember them." It shifted uneasily in the shadows, clearly reluctant to let light fall on it. When a single ray illuminated the shine of greasy paws, they were quickly snatched back.

El Cucuy turned to the speaker. "And you are?" he said sharply. "Do I know your face, or has your story changed again? Say your name."

There was another rumble, this one resembling a sigh. "I am Talasam, born of Bulgaria," it said in a deep croak. "I am the barn-lurker, shadow-lover, attic-haunter, child-eater. And, seeing what I see, I do not think that we will meet again when another hundred years have gone by. "

"Why say you?" one of the bag men said, his voice heavy with phlegm. A strange, bent creature shifted into the light, his bag slung over his hunched back; the lank hair was white, and there was an unhealthy cast to his withered face. There was more strength there than in any other old man, for just like the creatures around him, he wore his body as casually as a cheap coat.

"Bonhomme Sept-Heures, man with the bag out of Quebec, seven o'clock man, I is," he said. "I's one of many and I's never forgot, for all they wants to make us nicelings. We's not to end, even if they's tryin' to turn us on our ears."

"Changed too much." Talasam's paws clenched, and there was a shine of teeth in the shifting shadows. "We continue to shrink, because they do not believe in us. We've had their children's minds for thousands of years, but now their minds will not have *us*. All of us have felt it, I'm sure. Even the Mörkö is affected—look at him. His shape's been changed by what the children see on their television screen!" He shot a glance at the wavering blue shape, which gave a mournful bow. Talasam growled at the move-ment of the glimmering form and bared his own rot-flecked teeth like a dog. "The world's not what it was. Their belief is... it's *wrong*. It feels wrong. It *tastes* wrong. And yet, every meeting, all we can do is remember the for-gotten ones?"

El Cucuy nodded gravely. His manner was as calm as a parent reaching reassuring a crying little boy, even though the Cucuy was less than half the size of the hairy man. "Talasam, calm down," he said soothingly. "I have things well in hand." The words fell flat.

Ignoring the tense silence, El Cucuy looked around and spotted the smile of Bonhomme Sept-Heures. "Brother, is there something you wish to add?"

"I, I says fear is forever." The old man grinned a horrible grin, displaying crooked teeth turned shiny and brown. "All of us, every single one, all of us, we're all of us fear—one form or another, bags or cages or hairy pelts like bears. Spritelings will always be afraid. Every time one hides his head under a blanket, we're there. And we go nowhere. They go nowhere."

"They go with me."

The seven o'clock man aimed another grin at L'uomo Nero. "But they don't wants to, do they?" he asked as specks of spittle coated his withered lips. "You just step forward, Old Hannibal. No need to lurk about in the shadows like you was a tooth fairy."

In the dim light of the single candle, L'uomo Nero looked like a cadaver. The shine of light on his deep-set eyes was like the glimmer on a piece of dark flint. Like most of them, he appeared human; he wore a long black coat, dusty with the dirt of the road, and a wide-brimmed Spanish priest's hat which shadowed his face. He, too, carried a bag. The hem of his coat was damp from the salt spray and the waves that had lapped against the dock.

"L'uomo Nero, the Black Man, am I," he said. "Ghost of Italy, shade of the conquering Hannibal Barca, the ghoul of Carthage that still hides at their shoulders when they've been bad. Seen across the walking mountains. They fear to go with me. They go, and they do not know why and where, and I do not know where or why. Will they always fear me so? I do not know. They do not wish to go, but it may not always go so. Mothers knock on the table, and fathers open the door."

"He's gone," the voice of Likho grunted perfunctorily. Seen in company of the others, his little figure was practically invisible alongside the horde of hunched old men and hairy monsters.

"Name?" El Cucuy said.

His tone was getting sharp, and Likho ducked his head hurriedly in acquiescence. "I'm Likho, sometimes called Babay, man with a bag, takes children and might eat them up, depends on the legend and who's doing the translating. They never decided. From Russia and the Ukraine, and so forth. All those little countries that tend to have lots of wars and kill each other way too much." He rattled through the list of his information hurriedly, ignoring the disapproving stare from the ghostly dead child. "El Cucuy, I have to appeal—"

Likho grabbed hold of L'uomo Nero's shoulder, his fingers turning white with the grip. "His mind's gone to the happy place again. I wouldn't trust anything he says; you know how he is these days. Sorry if he's disrupting the meeting, I'll take charge of him for you—"

El Cucuy grinned a bit devilishly. He was clearly enjoying Likho's visible discomfort, and didn't seem to mind the interruption. "No need to appeal," he said calmly. "L'uomo Nero isn't gone, Likho, even if he sounds like it." A low rumble of laughter reverberated around the room. El Cucuy liked it when they laughed with him. "He says, 'Will they always fear me so?' And *this*, brothers, is what concerns us today.

"Talasam has been long in the mountains, but he brings to us a problem that I have been watching ever since our last meeting. Fear today is not what it once was, nor do I believe it will ever be as it used to be. How much longer will a man with a bag, a creature under a bed or in the closet, or even a dead child—" he glanced briefly at his own small hand "—inspire fear in the young ones?

"Not long ago, I came to take a young one in the care of his grandmother. Six years old, he was. A simple mark. But when I moved to spring upon him, he looked straight at me and said 'I don't believe in ghosts.' So simple a thing. It stopped me."

Now there was dead silence in the room. El Cucuy was by no means the eldest of them, but his power had always been unquestionable. To think that he would be halted in a kill or a taking was impossible; of all of the Family, he had always had one of the strongest bases of power. Nobody would ever bet on El Cucuy losing a catch.

"With surprise, you mean?" Likho said after a moment. "Some kids are like that these days."

"No." The small figure's eyes narrowed ever so slightly. "I'm afraid, Likho, that it was worse than that. I couldn't take him. He didn't believe."

There was a hiss from the ranks. A foul exclamation came from Babaroga, who wore the form of a short and hideous old woman with a horn protruding from her forehead. Babaroga had seen many children, and picked more than a few out of her teeth. "He *did not believe?*" she shouted. "Where is his fear?"

"It's very simple." El Cucuy raised his hands. The murmuring died down again. "These children have nothing to fear and no reason to fear it. Many today are safer and in better care than ever before. But without fear, we have no power over these children." His eyes moved over the ranks of the bogeymen, picking out the marks of apprehension in their masklike faces. "And if we have no power over them, then it would be worse than simply being unable to carry out our mission. Without their belief, we will not survive."

The seven o'clock man looked up sharply. "You can't be meaning that, young one. No work, no belief—the work's got to be done, whether the spritelings wants it or not!"

There was a warning growl from Talasam. "Do you think we don't know that?"

"You don't seem to," the hunched figure snapped. "Work's got to be done, young ones got to be taken. That's the way it goes. We don't work, the kids don't get good, we don't live. And El Cucuy knows it, too, so sit down and be quiet before I put you in my bag!"

"Do you think your bag could hold me?" Talasam snorted. "Little bag man, *you* will be quiet, or I'll bite your head off!"

"Hey, hey, cut it out!" Likho interjected quickly. "Keep this up, and the humans will be wondering what the noise is, and then we've got a whole other fish to fry. Look, El Cucuy—" his voice contained a note of pleading that made even himself wince "—we've always known that the stories, the ones they tell about us, those stories *change* what we look like. Isn't that why the naming-yourself-at-the-meeting bit got started—so we could recognize each other? Can't this be just another change happening? Maybe that kid's mom was telling him you look like a big tentacle creepy-crawly or something."

The blue shadow was next to speak. "I AM MÖRKÖ, THE GROKE OF FINLAND. AND I AGREE. THIS IS JUST A CHANGE OF SHAPE."

"A change of shape never meant a change in power. If El Cucuy was merely being reimagined, then the child would have still feared him for being a strange creature. But 'I don't believe in ghosts...'" Talasam bared his teeth at the thought. "There's always been a balance. We make the children good, and their belief feeds us. That's always been the *rules.*"

L'uomo Nero's voice was low, but Likho could still hear him. "The time is out of joint; o cursed spite, that I was ever born to set it right. Do you like clocks, Likho?"

"Ssssh!"

The hairy men liked Talasam; among the less human, he was their natural leader, second only to Sacauntos and El Cucuy himself. Now the huge creature was pacing back and forth, flexing his gigantic paws, and it was making them all uneasy.

"We have to survive. Sitting here remembering is one thing, surviving is another. Do you remember Wicked Coyote?" Talasam snorted, and a cloud of steam wafted into the cool air of the warehouse. "A master. A leader, one since the old days. Forgotten. Less than a voice on the wind. We have to do something."

El Cucuy nodded approvingly, shielding the candle flame from the wind of Talasam's passing with one small hand. "So I believe, Talasam. There is much to be done."

"Much agreed to that." Talasam growled deep in his throat. "We need to bring Bavbav back."

There was a moment of frozen silence. Pairs of glinting eyes turned towards each other, exchanging glances of surprise. Was he really going to say *that?* Here and now, in front of El Cucuy?

The dead boy turned ever so slightly, and his voice was low. "Bavbav left us, Talasam. We did not choose to leave him. His name is not mentioned here."

"He was the first!" Talasam said. His clawed feet scratched uncomfortably at the concrete floor, leaving deep grooves. "Not just the first bogeyman, the first *fear*. He must have seen this on the horizon. He saw everything. What would he—?"

"Enough, Talasam." The childlike creature narrowed his claret-colored eyes. Deep in his own little patch of shadows, Likho glanced up at the angular outline of L'uomo Nero, who stared back a little confusedly. *He's done it now,* Likho mouthed. *Friggin' hairy men, always opening their big hairy yaps.*

"But, El Cucuy—" Talasam began. It seemed to dawn on him that the other hairy men were no longer crowding close around him, and that he was alone in a widening circle of withdrawing spirits and ghosts. El Cucuy stood stiff, a little white-and-gray shadow before the huge black form of Talasam, and the look in those small red eyes shook Talasam to his core.

The leader of the Family was the most powerful of all the bogeymen—strongest in belief and wielding it over every other unreal creature. His form made it all too easy to forget that.

"And *need I remind you* that when he left, you all agreed to abide by my leadership?" El Cucuy's voice never rose; it didn't need to. Likho and L'uomo Nero drew back a little bit further. The wash of power from the small spirit danced like sparks over them, and Likho found it hard to maintain his physical form. There was a lot of rage in that childish body, however flat the facade might be.

"We will not speak about Bavbav here," El Cucuy continued. "Perhaps he was the first, but he also refused to change. And when he left us, he didn't give us any warning or leave us with guidance. We were headless, bodiless, leaderless. Is this loyalty to the Family? No."

"But—"

"You agreed to *abide*, Talasam." There was a definite hint of warning in the tone now.

"I never did—!" Talasam snapped, a little desperately. The circle around him was quite wide now, and perhaps he sensed the draft; he looked around at the others, and an expression of terror crossed his face.

"You did. And when the Svarta Mannen—we remember him as well—objected to my placement, you said 'He eats the souls of children. And who fears like a child?'"

Talasam snarled through his fear. "We all take children, El Cucuy. Don't let your child-form make you think like them!"

"They fear me because I am one of them!" El Cucuy's voice was steady, but there was a tinge of wrath in it. "You, *barn-lurker* and *attic-haunter*, are barely a figment of their imagination. I am the unexpected."

"You're a psycho," Likho muttered. Nobody seemed to hear him; almost all the other creatures were focusing intently on the building confrontation between the hairy man and the dead child. Only L'uomo Nero stood by his elbow, smiling the faint smile of a man whose mind has gone to some other place. Likho sighed and glanced up at his thin friend, who grinned down at him in a vaguely cheerful manner. "And you're a psycho too, you poor bastard."

L'uomo Nero swayed slightly, his eyes now fixed on the crumbling plaster of the wall. "I hear a mamma knocking, hearing it through the noise and mess of the solid world. The mamma thinks what she thinks. She asks me to come and take her child to the new world." His voice was slightly sad. "She doesn't believe in me, Likho. She uses me to make her son fear her instead."

His friend just shook his head and silenced the taller man, eyes fixed on the confrontation at hand.

"The first thing Man feared was the unknown," El Cucuy was saying. Likho twitched, clearly unsure if the strange child-ghost had heard their conversation, but El Cucuy's eyes were focused on the growling Talasam. "And Bavbav was the unknown. The second thing Man feared was other men. Perhaps I am *only* a bogeyman, but I am a child, and the children fear me for it. Talasam, you are a collection of rural superstitions. What makes you think you can even speak out of turn at this meeting, let alone dictate to me—and to the rest of the Family, who have to listen to you whimper— how I should proceed in such a difficult matter?" The child's lip curled. "Is this abiding by my authority?"

Talasam rose to his full seven-foot height, glaring through the mat of filthy hair as if he would dearly love to murder the ghost before him. "I'm given the right by my existence, El Cucuy," he snapped harshly. "I'm one of the Family, and I have a stake in this as well."

"That need not be." El Cucuy's high voice was deadly soft. "There are other hairy men, you know."

The creature's jaw dropped. "You can't—"

"Sacauntos!"

Something rumbled in the back of the room, and there were shuffling noises and the tread of heavy feet on the boards. The huge figure, draped in greasy rags all tied together with bits of string, pushed his way through the crowd. He stared at Talasam through his own fall of matted hair.

"You called, El Cucuy?" he said throatily.

"Sacauntos," El Cucuy said, "you're unique, are you not. There's a bit of the monster in you, and a bit of the bag as well. What do you do that makes them fear you?"

"I take the children, and I kill them, and I cut out their fat to sell at the market."

Sacauntos stared at Talasam. His brow was wide and sloping, like a cartoon caveman's, and his lips were fleshy and cracked. Through a hole in his raggedy garb, the glint of the flensing knife could be seen.

"They call him the Fat-Taker. They say his legend stems from stories of werewolves and ghouls." El Cucuy's eyes lit up. "You could be called a hairy man, like Talasam. One of many."

"That is so," Sacauntos said in his deep, hoarse voice. Talasam sputtered in fury, but was silenced by a warning crack of knuckles from his huge antagonist.

"Just another hairy monster, Talasam." El Cucuy was staring the outraged creature straight down. "Everywhere is the legend of the Hairy Man. Step out of line once more, and I will have Sacauntos replace you." He did not lean forward, but Talasam flinched nevertheless as the dead child's voice sank to a whisper. The assembled bogeymen had to strain to hear it. "You'll become a little spirit, Talasam. A voice on the wind. What worship you had will go to Sacauntos instead; you're so alike, there will be no difficulty in his filling your place. And when a hundred years have passed, and we assemble again for this meeting, you'll not be one of us. You will not be believed in."

El Cucuy did not breathe, nor did he condescend to make the gesture. Talasam was trembling in the shadows, and his yellow eyes gleamed wide. "So," the Cucuy said, "you will not mention Bavbav again. We will not contact him. He does not exist to us. Whatever problem we have with this belief and these children, we will solve it on our own. Bavbav is dead. Do I make myself clear?"

Talasam stared at the floor.

"Do I make myself clear?" The words were still steady, but they had a hint of a snap. In his corner next to L'uomo, Likho shook his head and fingered the brim of his hat uneasily. Talasam should have known better than to fight with El Cucuy, he thought.

The hairy man's voice was low. "...Yes, lord."

"Good." El Cucuy said in a brittle voice, stepping back. "Thank you, Sacauntos. Your service is well appreciated. Let us continue."

He clapped his hands, calling them to attention like a kindergarten teacher. His anger was apparently spent; the assembled bogeymen relaxed a little.

"The children are no longer afraid of us, and we are being picked off one by one. If we do not take action, it will not be long before we are *all* reduced to pages in the history books." El Cucuy's lip curled. "But I have been thinking a good deal, and there is much we can do.

"A campaign. A campaign of fear. And this is our first target."

There was a heavy thud as an atlas of the world landed on the ground. El Cucuy licked a finger, knelt down, and delicately turned the pages one by one. Likho watched the dead child closely—this certainly wasn't typical behavior, not even for the leader of the Family. Much too careful.

El Cucuy had found the page he wanted. "Here," he said, stabbing at the glossy picture with his forefinger. "North America."

The bogeymen gathered around it, staring down at the strange country outlined in orange. There was a moment of silence, eventually broken by the Mörkö. "WHY?" he rumbled. "WE HAVE NO HOLD THERE. WICKED COYOTE WAS THE LAST."

"I have Mexico, and it is close enough." El Cucuy glowered down at the picture. "But you all know what they are, brothers. Cynical and brutal, but intent on teaching their children that there is no such thing as evil in the world. There is no hairy man there, and no man with a bag. All they have are vague fears, and if their children continue to be lied to, there won't even be that.

"It's easy to see that you don't understand." He rounded on the rest of the Family, which flinched and stepped backward as one monster. "We rely on them. Their fear doesn't just feed us, it makes us who we are. America is an influence on the rest of the world, and the world will follow suit if they cease to believe in us. No more tribal fears, no more rural superstitions. Not even a bowl of milk on the doorstep to keep the elves away."

"What's the plan, El Cucuy?" Likho said quickly.

The child grinned. "I'm glad you asked, Likho. There are special assignments for each of you."

Almost two hours had passed when the meeting of the Family broke up. L'uomo Nero followed Likho, who walked out onto the pier and lit another cigarillo. He blew a huge plume of smoke and stared out at the water, thinking hard.

Oh, El Cucuy had always been mercurial. That was for certain. Occasionally, members of the Family would meet while they went about their business—he and L'uomo Nero traveled together constantly, and though this was a rarity, it wasn't unheard of for a pair of Family members to collaborate on a project. Likho was old, even by the Family's standards, and he had already been alive for hundreds of years when El Cucuy first came to be. Almost immediately, he had heard stories of the strange dead child who frightened the youth of Mexico within an inch of their lives. Nowadays, of course, bogeymen got much more attention from the academic crowd—humans could get diplomas in folklore, for crying out loud!—and El Cucuy had risen like a heat-seeking missile in that group. He'd been written about in books on cultural traditions, and in books on common fears and phobias. Even L'uomo Nero couldn't compare to that one, and that loony bastard had a *movie* named after him.

When Bavbav had been killed (Disappeared? Eliminated? Good idea not to ask, though there wasn't a one among them who hadn't had his suspicions) there was no question that El Cucuy would succeed him as the head and guide of the Family. Likho was human enough to know what he thought of that bit of convenient timing. And times *were* hard now, no question about that either. But this 'campaign of fear,' he didn't like the sound of that. And anybody who had been alive as long as Likho had, and who kept his eyes open, knew that when El Cucuy was so engrossed in an idea that he was petting a goddamn atlas—time to run.

Power corrupts, after all. And don't the humans say that absolute power corrupts absolutely?

"I don't like it," he said finally. In the distance, the faint strains of an opera played on, reaching them across the water. As Likho watched, the shape of El Nadaha unmoored her little reed boat and paddled off into the darkness; he knew for a fact that she would dissolve into the mist before she was fifty yards out, but it was appearances that mattered.

"Liking is hard to find," L'uomo Nero murmured.

"This is different," Likho said a little irritably. "Really, I don't. It doesn't smell right. Yeah, we threaten the kids all right, but it's a whatchamacallit—" He clicked his fingers vaguely, searching for the right term. "You know. That thing those guys always talk about. An end to a—no, a means to an end. Not the end itself."

L'uomo Nero's gaze was blank and lifeless. "You speak right, Likho. It is not an end. It should not be. Things should go on, not end."

"I think you've got hold of the wrong end of the stick there, but I appreciate the contribution." Likho shook his head a little helplessly at the blank look on the taller man's face. "And for the record," he added, jumping quickly to another irksome topic of conversation, "does anybody else think that Sacauntos was the worst possible choice for second in command? Anybody?"

The Italian did not respond, so Likho talked on. That was usually the way things worked. "The 'Fat-Taker,'" he scoffed, snorting smoke out of his nostrils. His right hand held the cigarillo loosely folded in his fingers, and supported the elbow of the right arm in the palm of the left. His stance was loose and restless.

"He's not even well-known," Likho griped through the last shreds of smoke. "I've got Russia and the Ukraine. That sick bastard's *Galician,* for crying out loud! Not that I've got anything against Spain, mind you, but he's not precisely a majority opinion. And what kind of a psychopath kills kids and sells their fat? That's some weird shit, even for us. No wonder our legends aren't told much any more; I know I wouldn't wish my rugrat sweet dreams with that bastard hanging over their heads."

"Hangs like an unripe fruit, withery to the walking mountains. The lady of kay will break down the wall of the sea, Likho."

Likho groaned. "I swear, pal, someday I'll figure out what happened to you," he muttered, glancing out across the bay again. His roving gaze found an object: the brilliant glow of the opera house.

"Someday I'll figure out what happened to that brain of yours," he amended after a moment's thought. "In the meantime, be a friend and tell me what the people across the water are saying."

The larger bogeyman concentrated on the distant shape of Sydney, Australia's most famous postcard model. "They say a lot of things," he said after a moment's thought. His brow wrinkled as he listened. "Right now, there is a woman saying 'I am dying, I am dying, oh how I am dying, and now I am dead.'" L'uomo Nero blinked confusedly, glancing down at his friend. "Who is dying, Likho?"

"Probably someone who stabbed her lover and suddenly suffered an attack of conscience or something. Dying of grief." Likho breathed out another fog of smoke through his nostrils. "That's how opera works, after all. People screaming at each other in Italian or German—sometimes French, but for the real heavy stuff, you need a language that's got some kind of national throat infection—about how they're in love and going to die because of it or in spite of it or what have you. Did you know that there's an opera that goes on for almost a week? In the end, it comes full circle and you wind up right back where you started, in a river with a whole bushel of naked swimming lady spirits. You can't tell me that's great art. A good time at the local casbah, maybe, but not art." He tsked in an irritated fashion, but his heart wasn't in it. "Isn't art supposed to tell you something?"

L'uomo Nero shrugged blankly. "She is still dying, Likho."

"Give her another fifteen minutes," Likho predicted.

"I can't. I have to see Giovanna."

There was a moment of silence before Likho carefully removed the cigarillo from his mouth. "Sorry, I didn't catch that. What did you say?"

"I'll be back soon, Likho." Already, L'uomo Nero's form was fading into the air. The black edges of his shape were as clear as glass, and his face was nearly gone. "I have to see her. The head is fogged, but she will explain."

Likho made a grab at the collar of the coat, but it slipped through his fingers as if it were nothing more than mist or marsh gas. Very few people, not even a fellow bogey, can catch up to a bag man when he wants to be going someplace.

"Hey!" Likho yelped. "Get back here, you—"

Too late. There was a final flicker, and L'uomo Nero had vanished. One crazy bogeyman, run off God-knows-where, with the mind of a little kid and the power of a god. *Not* good. Cursing, Likho threw his cigarillo off the dock and turned once on the spot, disappearing into the air.

Chapter Three

The police station had a small waiting room, and Abby was currently the only person in it. She closed her eyes and leaned against the wall, trying to arrange her thoughts as best she could. It was hard; her ears still ached a little from the echo of the gunshots in the store, and her fingers were stiff and numb after a long wait for the bus in the cold November wind. But in some way, she was glad for the distraction of her aches and pains. It provided another little sanity check, like the stab of guilt at the woman's death. If she felt she was being punished, even just a bit, then she felt that she could face the situation a little more calmly.

D.U.I. Great. She'd already gotten her car out of the impound, but she didn't know if she'd be able to get Jimmy out. He was a kid with problems, everybody agreed on that. John always tried to get her to send him to juvenile prison, but she hoped that if she stayed with him, he'd turn out better than he was.

It was a nasty situation. His therapy was already putting a bigger hole in her paycheck than she could afford. Luckily for her, there had been plenty of activity that month, and the doppelganger had been disposed with (though she hated the phrase) "minimal casualties." A bonus could well be in the cards. Even if her son did think she was crazy, her monster-hunting check would pay for his bail.

Not that she could say as much to him. How do you explain to your teenage son that the thing that had attacked you six years ago—breaking up your marriage and family in the process—wasn't a crazed mugger, but a ghoul on the hunt for fresh meat? She had tried, soon after joining the SSR, but he wasn't listening, and she couldn't blame him. Abby could hardly believe it herself, even after such a long time.

She had been doing the grocery shopping. Every week, like she always did, back when she was still Abigail. Terry had offered to pick them up, but as much as she loved him, she knew he had no idea of the difference between a chop, a roast, or a steak, and what could and couldn't be done with them. So she carried the bags herself and hurried, because the wind was getting cold and the light was failing. An early spring rain pattered down.

As she passed the mouth of an alley, something had fluttered in the corner of her eye. Abigail dismissed it as paranoid fantasy (in their early Chicago days, she had imagined seeing muggers and drug fiends everywhere—her peace of mind one more victim of the rising crime statistics), but then she had heard it: a mewling cry, one which turned into a fretful squalling. A small child was crying somewhere down the alley.

She'd stopped and listened, trying to decide whether to go back; her protective instincts warred with the many news reports on rapes and robberies that the television had run. But the crying had gone on and on, unabated, interspersed with the gulps and sobs of the truly lonely, so she had hitched the bags up in her arms and turned into the mouth of the alley.

It had hit her quickly, as soon as she reached the deepest patch of shadow. Something as heavy as a mallet struck her on the back of the head and she had fallen forward, the groceries scattering as they fell from her grip. The eggs collapsed into a sticky mess beneath her body. She had thrashed wildly, her own scream erupting from her throat, as a second blow came— against the shoulderblades, where an awful pressure was being dragged down her body. There was a tearing of cloth as something howled in response to her shrill scream, and oh God, it wasn't human. As she glanced wildly and twisted under its grip, she saw hands the size of meat platters. Curved claws snagged in the lumpy knit of her two sweaters—

It had keened again and tried to tear, but the elasticized threads of the sweaters had snagged its claws and kept the cut from being clean. Aggravated, it had stabbed down; Abby knew now that it had wanted to pierce her heart. She kicked frantically, and its hand had glanced off the pavement. With the other hand, or paw, still caught in her sweater, it had shoved her hard and slammed her head against the broken concrete, dazing her and leaving her helpless. The claws bunched, her sweaters tore, and the ghoul had screeched in triumph as blood spattered across the nearest wall. Abigail had prayed wildly, randomly, in a chant of "Oh God in Heaven, no, please, no," while it carved strips of skin from her back.

A gunshot, then another, and the world had gone mercifully black.

She had regained consciousness two days later, in a bed at Rush Presbyterian, hooked up to what felt like every machine in the place. She was propped on her side, and her back had felt stiff and hot, as if burned. A single, plaintive groan, and Terry had been by her side.

Mugged, the hospital staff had told her. Some kind of insane slasher had gone after her with what looked like a railroad spike; her wallet had been stolen. Two cops had heard her screaming and come running. The perp had made a fast exit, and they hadn't caught him, choosing instead to make sure she was alive.

"Did they shoot at him?" she'd mumbled, as Terry held the cup of water to her lips. "I heard shots...."

No shots, the nurse said. Auditory and visual hallucinations were not unheard of during such a traumatic incident. Abigail had digested that, and thought about what she'd seen in the alley—and decided to say nothing for the time being. It must have been an illusion. After all, she had been attacked.

Later, as part of the 'healing process,' they'd shown her a picture of her wounds, and she had become suspicious. There were five slashes, deep and dragging, with four running diagonally from her right shoulder blade to her left hip, and the fifth a twisted curve down to her right buttock. Four fingers and a thumb, clenched in rage or, more ominously, hunger. It was then that she'd mentioned her vision to the doctors.

The command went forth: therapy, therapy, therapy, hours and hours of it, physical and mental, until she didn't care what kind of tree she was and probably would have fallen in the forest as soon as there was nobody around to hear it. Terry coddled her, her son was unfailingly attentive, and that frustrated Abigail: she didn't want a sympathetic ear or another blanket, she wanted to know why she saw—and felt—a clawed hand as big as a turkey *before* the injury and blood loss. Jimmy had been worried, but after a few weeks, Terry's own frustration had matched hers, and the battle was on.

They couldn't afford plastic surgery, certainly not for an injury that never showed (Abigail was not a beachgoer, and wouldn't be caught dead in a halter top, even then; both her figure and self-esteem shoved her towards comfort rather than sensuality, although she did pride herself on her nice bottom), but Terry, as good as he was to her, hated the sight of the scars. Her whole back had little to no sensation. Once, Jimmy's pet tarantula had gotten out of its terrarium and crawled right across her back while she was lying down, and Terry had panicked while Abigail had never noticed. The keloid tissue made thick and ugly ridges on her skin, and Terry said he could always feel them, no matter how many layers she wore.

"Watch your diet," her physician had said. "If you ever get a serious vitamin C deficiency, those scars will break open and you'll bleed to death."

As time passed and the matter remained unresolved, Abigail had begun researching things on her own. Maybe there was a sick killer who liked to dress in costume: that would explain her situation, prove that she hadn't been hallucinating, show Terry that he was wrong. She hadn't found a killer. She'd found ghouls, and the SSR.

The latter had been first. By then, the divorce was being finalized—she citing irreconcilable differences, he complaining of a continued lack of intimacy and trust in the marriage. Nobody was sure whose fault it was. She supposed she could have had it much worse. But she had finally let Jimmy in on what was going wrong, and he had been incredulous. "Mom," he had said, "why are you doing this? Do you really think you got hurt by some kind of *vampire* or something?"

"I don't know, honey. It's all so strange."

"Look, Mom, maybe you should see Dr. Joey again."

She had found a post on a forum for vampires, in fact. Not real vampires, she knew, but people who were in love with the idea of being a creature of the night and wanted to inject some romance into their lives. The post was advertising for an "open-minded individual," with some self-defense experience, to do filing and clerical work for a research association. She needed work, and she applied.

It had been a strange interview. The bearded man who read her resume had seemed nice enough, but the rest of the people in the office had taken one look at her and suddenly become very busy. Then the bearded man had asked her how she felt about magic. Eventually, she'd met the genie in the bottle.

The two cops who brought her to the hospital hadn't been real. They had been imaginary, shadows conjured by the genie to explain the appearance of a badly injured woman in the emergency room. The little group had been tracking the creature that attacked her, and the bearded man—Oliver Kendrick—had fired the shots that killed the ghoul. He had stolen her wallet for verisimilitude; "to make it look like a mugging," he had explained.

She had thought they were crazy, until Kendrick rummaged in a filing cabinet and produced the wallet, with everything still inside. Abigail snatched it and made ready to leave outright, not at all ready to believe what she was hearing. Then one of the men in the office, a lanky Englishman with reddish brown hair sticking up over his ears, had put down what looked like a science fair project gone wrong and said: "Why don't you show her the salt pans?"

They had. "Here's yours," Kendrick had said, going to a tub halfway down the wall. He had shifts through the mound of salt and produced the most horrible looking thing Abigail had ever seen: a withered, half dried hand and forearm, with excruciatingly familiar hooked claws.

After that... well, there really wasn't any going back, was there? As John had later said, "We're not here because we're the best for the job. We're here because we're the only tossers who even know about it."

Occasionally, she wondered what the other groups were like. Abby knew from the intermittent records that the SSR had been founded in 1982, after an outbreak of lycanthropy had resulted in seventeen deaths in northern Illinois. It didn't get much press; the Tylenol Killer was on the rampage, and the newspapers were mostly concerned with product liability and cyanide. So Evan Jackson Willis, a defrocked Baptist preacher who had witnessed two of the deaths, formed the SSR as a way to combat supernatural threats. (Rumor had it that Willis had been expelled from the

Church for telling his bishop about the werewolves. This was untrue. Willis had discovered science fiction in the early 1970s, and chosen to leave the church after being reprimanded for preaching a sermon about the Messianic qualities of Arthur Dent.)

Abby had never met the former Reverend, since he'd died long before she joined the group. But she knew from table talk, and the occasional field report, that there were other crews like the SSR.

Were they more professional? They had to be. The SSR's beat was a significant portion of the Midwest, and they could barely keep a lid on everything as it was. Nowhere else had their kind of trouble. Abby would pick through the morning newspaper and find headlines like "Mysterious Disembowelings of Farm Animals in Des Moines," groan, and pour yet another cup of coffee. Maine, New York, Florida, or California never seemed to have outbreaks of vengeful undead. Their newspapers were depressingly normal. Whereas the Midwest had the whole pantheon of evil, plus Mad Cow, bird flu, and mercury in cans of tuna fish.

If she didn't know better, she'd say that Chicago was a supernatural bus station. It seemed to be a perfect place for people of all types to display their bad-tempered and antisocial sides. Of course, it hadn't always been like that—before the werewolf outbreak, there hadn't been a magical crime in the Windy City for one hundred and ten years. Now you couldn't throw a rock without violating some spirit's personal space, and then all hell would break loose.

Obviously, not all the creatures that flocked to America's breadbasket were malicious. Some of Abby's fondest memories had come from encounters such as those: a group of ghosts playing poker for eternity, a were-snake who had prevented a mugging, and a tree with the power of human speech. That tree had had the most beautiful speaking voice she ever heard, too—a deep velvety sound that filled you up inside like a warm cup of cocoa on a cold day. They had arranged his transplantation to a national forest in Vermont, and everyone in the office had chipped in to buy him a bag of high-grade vitaminized fertilizer.

But SSR or not, she was still Jimmy's mother, even if that fell by the wayside sometimes. It was her job to look after him, not let him steal the car keys from her jewelry box and get D.U.I.s. Terry was still doing his best to be involved in their son's life, but most times, she was all Jimmy had. Family came first.

Right.

Family.

There was a rustle of footsteps, and the door swung open. A surly green-haired teenager emerged, escorted by a tired police officer with one firm grip on his shoulder. "Mrs. Marquise?" the officer said. Abby nodded.

"We'll need you to sign the release form," he continued, handing a paper on a clipboard to her.

"Sure." Abby took the clipboard and, after glancing perfunctorily at the paper, signed at the bottom. The terms and conditions hadn't changed from the last time.

Her son followed her sulkily out of the station. Abby could feel his accusing glare boring a hole in her back, and she shifted uncomfortably as they walked down the steps. The family Toyota had been parked some distance from the building, and the walk back to it was heavy with silence.

"Jimmy—" she began as she opened the driver's side door. He responded by slamming the passenger door hard behind him, flopping into his seat and crossing his arms. He refused to meet her eyes. Abby sighed a little and turned her attention to the dashboard, sending up a silent prayer for calm.

"Jimmy, why did you take the car?" she said. Her son remained hunched in his seat, the green-dyed tips of his hair obscuring his eyes. He looked like a classical statue: The Sulker. "Jimmy," she repeated, a little more sharply. He stayed still, glaring straight at the glove compartment in front of him.

"Jimmy!"

"What?" he shouted, drawing his shoulders in closer. "Let me guess: I screwed up, right? I shouldn't have taken the car, I shouldn't have made *friends* with those guys, I shouldn't have even *thought* about stepping outside. Right?"

Abby breathed an exasperated sigh as she pressed the gas pedal. The car slowly eased into traffic. "Jimmy, I'm not trying to say you can't have friends. But taking the car and then going drinking with those boys—! Do you want to get yourself killed?"

"By what? The wolfman?" Jimmy's voice was tinged with bitterness. "They're cool guys, Mom. They're normal friends. I *need* normal friends, since I can't have a normal family."

"Oh, for crying out loud! Jimmy, we are not going to have this talk again." Abby bit her lip, watching the traffic stream by. Her gaze was on the road now, but she could see out of the corner of her eye that her son was still slumped over, glaring at nothing. "I love you, your dad loves you. It just didn't work out between us. It doesn't mean you're not our son—"

Jimmy kicked the underside of the glove compartment fiercely. "Mom, it didn't work out because you want to hang out with guys who think they're hunting Bigfoot!"

She could feel tears beading in the corner of her eyes, but she forced herself to pay attention to the street. There would be no point in arguing if she wasn't going to live to resolve it. "What do you want me to do, Jimmy? Say I'm sorry that I got attacked?"

"Fine, you think it's real," he muttered. "Whatever. But you couldn't have *lied* about it?"

And she didn't have an answer. They drove the rest of the way in silence, and the bitterness hung thick between them.

The office was quiet by the time she returned. The heating system was working overtime, and the air was thick and musty, like the worst kind of summer day. Abby groaned as she closed the door behind her, and pulled at her jacket with fingers that were already sweaty: the layers that were so practical outside made the office feel even more close and stifling. The jacket was dumped unceremoniously onto her chair, followed quickly by the two sweaters. The sunshine-yellow pashmina, which had seemed so cheerful when she picked it up that morning, now looked tiresome and shrill. She opened her desk drawer and stuffed it in before banging the drawer shut again with a firm shove of her palm.

She waited for the expected smartass comment from John, but to her surprise, there was none. He was there all right, hunched over his desk like a troll on a heath, but his eyes were fixed firmly on the computer screen.

Any annoyance drained away as Abby saw his face. His expression was pinched and worried—not psychotically angry or pale as a sheet, but good old-fashioned human worry. It was such an unusual thing to see on him that for a moment, she wanted to laugh at the incongruity of it all. "What's going on?" she said instead, hurrying over to his desk. "Is everything all right?"

"Oi, look at this," he said. Shaking his head, he leaned back in his chair. "Newsflash off CNN: kidnappings in West Virginia. Family with five kids—all of 'em gone."

"Suspicious?" she asked quietly. John shook his head again.

"Just came over the wire, so no details. Don't think so."

Abby pulled out the chair at the nearest desk and sat down, running a hand through her sweaty hair. "That's something, anyway."

Her words seem to remind him of something: he came alive for the first time since she had walked in, and fixed her with an interrogative stare. "And how's the sprog?" he asked, his tone blunt. "You two been having it out again?"

She groaned and covered her face with her hands. "John, please. Not now."

"How bad was the fine?" John said.

"John—"

"I'm not badgering, Abby, I'm worried. People get worried, y'know." She knew by his tone that he was trying for casual amusement, but John had never been very good at sympathy and it fell flat. But at the moment, she was just too emotionally wrung out to have another argument with another hard-headed man in her life, and she dropped her hands in defeat. "It wasn't a fine, John. There was bail. He was D.U.I. They'll contact me to set a court date for his hearing."

John whistled, long and low. "Runt's really done it this time, huh? Shite." He shook his head again. "You all right, Abby?"

She wasn't, but she didn't want to talk about it. "I'm fine," she said, forcing a quick smile. "It's just... on top of everything, that's all. And it wasn't that bad. He's still a minor, so he'll probably just get community service. And his license is still good."

"Could've been a lot worse," John agreed noncommittally. Abby had the impression that he wanted to say something, but whatever it was, he kept it to himself. *Good,* she thought bitterly to herself.

Instead, he raised his left hand and showed off the faded tattoos there. "Just you be sure to keep him on a tight leash. Youthful shenanigans an' all don't always go away once they hit majority."

Oh, God, she wanted to smack him. Did he think she didn't know that? Did he think she didn't know that she had *screwed up,* she was failing her son, and him piling on *even more* wasn't going to make things any easier, that crazy bastard—

But John had turned back to the computer, clearly uncomfortable with the situation, and Abby's temper had lost its moment of white heat. Rubbing her eyes with the back of her hand, she settled back in her chair, trying to organize her thoughts.

Chapter Four

Since the days of Nothing and that first legend, the ranks of the mythical creatures have increased. Gods, demons, ghosts, household spirits, legendary birds of the air and beasts of the field—all of them grew out on their own upon their invention by the humans. Some were so real that nobody really knows if they were there before the humans themselves, perhaps leaking through a thin place in the fabric of reality and planting their ideas in the developing consciousness of the human race.

As ever, the spirits that grew up in a place were shaped by the minds of the people who invented them. Many creatures of African legends are the clever beasts of the savannah, while the Native Americans told tales about the buffalo and the coyote. Chinese dragons, German hairy monsters, Irish banshees, old English elves and fairies.

Likho was a ghoul of Russia, a land with a harsh climate and a tumultuous history. He was one of the oldest of the Family, and had watched the human race grow up with a certain amount of embarrassed pride, like a distant father figure whose child has finally learned that dirt doesn't taste very good. He had perched on a hillside and watched Napoleon's army struggle through the deep snow, and done the same with that German fellow who had the mustache and the incredibly depressing tendency to kill everybody. Further back, there had been Ivan the Terrible, whose only lasting contribution to the nation had been the ugliest cathedral that Likho had ever had the pleasure to stay out of. And even before then there had been the Mongols; all of Europe had been laid out for them to take, and Russia had been their pit stop, a place to knock the mud off their boots and leave behind a large contribution to the gene pool.

Likho had watched all of that, but he had remained ambivalent until the twentieth century. That had brought worldwide communications, the spread of democracy, and—oh yes—communism. Likho been present during the October Revolution, although that had been a bit of an odd time for him. The Communists couldn't quite decide if he was a remnant of a credulous, myth-driven past or a proud element of their unique history, so they'd mostly left him on his own. The execution of Anastasia had been a benchmark for him, the moment when he decided that all humans were batshit crazy. Something to do with all that breathing, maybe.

But there were other spirits out there, whose particular existence defied even the Communist cultural white-washing. Whenever he couldn't find L'uomo Nero, he went to see one of them instead.

It was a forest, and this forest had that special quiet which was hard to ignore. The woods were tangled and thick, a dense nest of pines, oaks, and fir trees with their branches knotted in with one another and their tough ropelike roots coiling across the hilly ground. Bushes and the winding vines of bracken formed a near-impenetrable barrier between the gnarled trunks, and what little sunlight there was on this cold winter day reached the ground only in weak, grainy speckles. Here and there was a swish of movement as a squirrel whisked its tail out of sight, but no birds sang and no animals chattered in the underbrush. It was far too silent; the only noise was the rustle of the leaves and needles in the chilly breeze which touched only the top branches. There in the thicket, the air was still and stifling.

Likho turned out of the air, and his foot caught in a curl of root, sending him stumbling. Clearly exasperated, he aimed a poisonous glare at the bracken bushes, which immediately withdrew their vines and parted as if in apology for daring to block his way.

The old bogeyman straightened the battered hat atop his head. "Lead on," he said to the bracken, which twitched in acknowledgment. One long tendril unraveled from the bush and snaked along the ground, purposefully leading him deeper into the thicket. The trees shifted about and lifted their branches away to keep from snagging on his long coat, and the drifts of leaves rose up around his feet in wakes.

There was a narrow track through the forest, barely distinguishable to the naked eye but easy to spot for a man who knew what to look for. The roots of the trees usually obscured it whenever a human traveler came close. For Likho, they lifted themselves away and bowed to him as he passed.

After only a few minutes, the leading bracken vine stopped dead at what looked like a solid wall of ivy. Likho nodded to it and stepped towards the wall, which parted by itself. The trees and the vines shrank back as he put first one foot forward, then the other. With a rush, the ivy closed behind him, and Likho found himself alone in a wide clearing.

Here, too, there was almost no sunlight. The branches of the trees had grown together and interlocked far above a man's height, creating a natural dome under which no grass could grow. The ground was bare and hard, studded with patches of dead leaves and pressed down where huge feet had passed. The feet of a bird, by the looks of it.

He didn't have to look far to see what had made those footprints. Standing at the very edge of the clearing was a ramshackle old cottage on two huge chicken feet. There was a door on each wall of the cottage and the feet were forever pacing, turning it around and around. The door posts were set with human finger bones, the skull of a rat served for a knob, and a rickety fence of rib cages surrounded the patch of dirt on which the cottage stood.

Likho didn't hesitate at this strange spectacle. It wasn't as if he hadn't seen it before.

"Little house, little house!" he called out, using the old greeting. "Turn your back to the trees, and your door towards me. I'm hungry, and I want to come in."

The chicken-footed house stopped dead and bent at the knees, lowering the nearest door to ground level. Likho stepped briskly through the gate, barely even noticing as the fingers of the lock folded themselves together behind him. There was a click as the yellowy-white knuckles met. The bogeyman stepped up to the door and knocked briskly, fighting the urge to run away.

Every boy has a grandmother he's frightened of.

An old, old voice, with a cackle and a rasp so ancient that it might have been Mesozoic, shouted back: "Foo, foo, foo! I smell the blood of Russians. Who's there?"

"It is I, Likho!" the bogeyman said loudly. "I come to ask advice of the wise Baba Yaga!"

"Enter, then!"

Likho lifted the latch and stepped over the threshold into the one-room cottage. The wooden floor trembled under his feet slightly as the hut raised itself up on its legs again, and began to turn around and around.

Inside, the little house was crude and bare. There was a chair, a table, and a rickety bed that was little more than a sack on a box; lying on the table were a painted basin and a cracked porcelain jug. The basin was stained yellow with age. An open cupboard held a crust of bread, a scrap of cheese, and a bundle of dried herbs. A huge mortar, nearly as tall as a man, was leaning in the corner, and a pestle of equal size lay near it. There was a barrel of beer, already tapped, and broken crockery was piled on top of it. A crude broom was propped against the stove, which was made of roughly fitted square blocks of stone. Its labyrinthine chimney wound its way all around the hut.

On that stove lay Baba Yaga, a sight not for the fainthearted. She was a gnarled, raspy, wicked old woman, with wild and dirty gray locks and the beginnings of a beard on her hairy face. Her chin stuck out from her face like the jaw of a wooden nutcracker, and when she spoke, it was unhampered by the few crooked brown teeth she had left. The voice was a nasty grating sound with a croak in it.

"The prodigal son!" she chuckled, kicking her heels wildly against the hot bricks of the stove. "What do you want, hider-under-beds? Cat got your tongue again?" And off she went into a wild gulping cackle, making Likho cringe.

"I've come to ask a favor, grandmother," he said as humbly as he could manage. "A friend of mine has vanished, and I can't track him down. And yes, again."

"He's gone once more, has he?" the old crone whooped. "Oh, he's a tricky one, he is. The man with the bag, gone to see his sweetie! Mad as a hatter, he is. Well, that's easy as can be!" She leapt off the stove and stuck her nut-cracker face into Likho's, causing him to flinch backwards. "But first," she said, "you must eat with me. That's the rule. You uses the old greeting, and I gives you a meal like a wise baba should."

"Grandmother, that's really nice, but I really don't have the time...."

"You should always have a bit of time for your granny, Likho. That's how the world works." And before Likho could do anything, a rickety wooden chair came sweeping forward and knocked him off his feet. He cursed as he landed hard on the unforgiving seat; he'd rather taken to his human form, but a bruised behind was difficult to get used to. The chair drew itself up to the table, neatly sandwiching Likho between it and the table's edge.

Baba Yaga took no notice of him. She swept around the small house like a hurricane, throwing a raggedy gray cloak around her shoulders and whirling the ashes out of the stove's fire pit with one sweep of her twig broom. Soon, she had set the table with mismatched crockery and had drawn a fresh jug of beer. "Bring us a meal, servants!" she called out in her hoarse rasp.

This part was something that Likho could never get used to. Three pairs of hands appeared out of thin air. These were Baba Yaga's servants, and they catered to her every need with a kind of folkloric magic that even the bogeyman couldn't get his head around. Their names were Pale Dawn, Burning Sun, and Deep of Night. During the day, they were hands, but at the proper times of day they took on their true forms and went riding in the forest. Now, they wore armor-clad gloves; one in white, one in scarlet, and one in black. Right then the hands carried a jug of hot potato soup, a loaf of black bread, and a pot of salt. They set everything on the table and whisked themselves out of sight.

"Traditional food, huh?" Likho grunted. That was always a hazard when you visited Baba Yaga. Likho had been Westernized along with the rest of the country, but the old witch still stubbornly clung to the way she had always been. Sure, it was pretty good traditional food, but pizza had a charm that transcended time itself.

"That's the way it goes, little bed-hider. Eat, and I'll be telling you what you must do."

As ever, the baba never ate, but instead perched on the stove and drank steadily from the jug of beer. The hands of Pale Dawn reappeared with red wine in a pewter tankard for Likho, which he gratefully accepted: legend had always dictated that, though she sometimes ate her visitors, Baba Yaga served them nothing but the best beer and wine. Putting your skull on the fence could come later, depending on what kind of mood you put her in. Some wandering princes had even been given the hands of her beautiful granddaughters in marriage.

"There's something afoot, I'm thinking," Baba Yaga croaked after a long silence between them. Likho nodded through a mouthful of hot soup and bread and the old woman rubbed her fingers together, watching him intently as he ate. "Something terrible," she continued, and once again got a nod from the bogeyman. "And you're needing to find your friend, then. So why's you coming to me?"

Likho knew the form for this one, too. "I saved a mother bird from a ravenous lion," he began, putting down the sharp knife he had used to slice the loaf of black bread, "and in payment for her life, she told me that I should always seek out the wise Baba Yaga if I should be in need of advice. I come to you to ask your advice now, grandmother."

"A good answer. Comes straight from the collected edition, that one." Baba Yaga peered through her mat of filthy hair, fixing her 'grandson' with a look that saw right through him. The bogeyman flinched and shifted uneasily in his chair. Suddenly, the lumpy tan surface of soup became the most interesting thing in the hut. This only made the old baba screech with laughter as she watched him; her voice was like a steel file on a cheese grater.

"There's more to this than sticks and stones," she said slyly. "I smell it in your salt, hider-under-beds. Come now, tell your old granny—what's troubling you?" Baba Yaga's own gaze never wavered, and the smile was worse than a glare or a dramatic threat. "If you won't be telling, grandson," she added through her toothy grin, "I'll eat it from your eyes."

Baba Yaga never indulged in idle threats. The bogeyman knew that, and immediately decided that it was better to spill his guts than have the ghastly grandmother spill them for him. Generations of Russian men had lived their lives in fear of their babas; Likho's blood would have run cold, if he'd had any.

"There's trouble in the Family," he muttered into his cup of wine. Baba Yaga merely grinned her crooked grin and ordered him to continue with a flick of her hand. "Big trouble," he amended reluctantly. "El Cucuy's decided that the best way to deal with the crisis of belief is to launch some kind of war against the humans. We're going to step up the child-snatching. Even the—" he grimaced "—*good* kids. There may be some deaths."

"And you're thinking of holding back?" the monstrous granny said.

"Well, no, obviously, I'd be asking for a swift one-way trip to the history books if I did that. I'll do what I'm told. But..." Likho paused uncomfortably, the spoon tapping against the edge of the earthenware bowl. "...Maybe they don't have shrines to us any more, but humans are humans. There's always someone frightened enough for us to get by. This isn't the way things should go."

Clearly uncomfortable, he rattled the spoon loudly against the side of the earthenware bowl and took a loud slurp of the thick liquid. Anything to make her stop *looking* at him. But when Baba Yaga did nothing, and Likho got more and more nervous, he deliberately overturned the salt pot. The crash as it fell to the floor broke the silence.

"Oops," Likho said to no one in particular as the three pairs of hands swept up the mess. "My bad."

Baba Yaga leaned forward until the whiskers of her beard almost touched Likho's forehead. The bogeyman cringed backwards in his chair a little.

"You shouldn't be letting that happen, grandson," she said, and they both knew she wasn't talking about the salt pot. Her breath stank of the pipe she always smoked in the long, dark winter evenings. "Your friend, the boy of Italy, you can't let him go on his own. Gone to see the girl, he has, and it'll bring him to grief. You go and find him.

"Take this ring," she continued, and there was a flash of dull gold between her fingertips. "Follow it whithersoever it goes, grandson. It will lead you to your friend, it will."

Warily, Likho took the ring. It was heavy, old, and dirtied, with a dark opal in its setting. "Thank you, grandmother," he said formally. "What will I do for this?"

Likho knew the score as well as anybody else did, and Baba Yaga's eyes glittered. "Only this," she whispered hoarsely. "You puts it in your friend's bag when you see him again, and you leave it there. Say nothing of what it is." Grinning, she tugged on the bogeyman's pallid cheek. "Old Baba Yaga knows what this is about, grandson. The Cucuy's not as good as you thought he would be, and you're thinkin' treacherous thoughts."

"What—" Likho began, but Baba Yaga twitched a finger and his mouth glued itself shut. The bogeyman clawed at his lips, nearly dropping the ring as he pried at them, but to no avail. Baba Yaga let loose another grating laugh as she watched him silently struggle with himself, and was still grinning as she leapt back onto the stove.

"Oh, your secret's safe with me, grandson." The brown teeth smiled at him, but there was not a trace of amusement in the deep-set eyes amidst their mass of wrinkles. "I knows more than you think, for all the Cucuy daren't deal with spirits and ghouls. But you've lessons to learn, and learn them you will before this year is through." Likho's mouth unglued itself, and the bogeyman clutched at it, gasping. Baba Yaga watched him dispassionately. "Now get out," she said. "And do as I say!"

Breathing hard, Likho legged it out the nearest door. He didn't bother to latch the gate as he tore out, back into the forest. When he had made it a safe distance from the cottage, he stopped to catch his breath. Now he remembered why he never had any truck with the other spirits of Russia; that old baba, she was the worst of the bunch, and he supposed he had gotten off lightly with merely the threat of annihilation.

But at least he had something. Likho weighed the heavy ring in his hand and threw it onto the ground, where it immediately began rolling. A moment later, both bogeyman and ring faded, vanishing into the shadows that filled the dark forest.

Hunched a little, Likho hurried down the sidewalk, unnoticed by the people who jostled to the left and right of him. Nobody saw him, but then, nobody walked into him either. An empty space formed around him where he walked. Animal instinct, wired directly into the hindbrain, made the pedestrians veer away from where he stood.

He glanced up, running his gaze over the tall red-brick building that loomed before him. St. Luke's Hospital appeared to be in the midst of renovations: clear sheets of plastic fluttered at a few windows, and some of the red-orange bricks were flecked with white dust where walls had been broken down and then replaced. For a moment, the building turned transparent in his gaze as he concentrated, scanning left and right for his missing friend.

There were two main buildings. One was clearly a children's ward, an L-shaped structure that struck north and east, and it was mirrored by the center for geriatric medicine which faced south and west. There was a courtyard in the center, occupied by a clump of shedding maple trees and a small dry fountain. A few children were running around under the watchful eye of a nurse, and one old woman in a wheelchair was letting her head nod on her chest as she slept.

And there he was. L'uomo Nero stood motionless in the shade of a dying elm, invisible to those around him, watching. Not the children—Likho might have understood if the dozy bag man was looking at a future target. No, it was the old lady he was watching.

Likho was about to step through the wall and grab L'uomo by the arm, but his attention was distracted. A little girl was walking down the gravel path, carrying a small Dora the Explorer doll under her arm. She had a shrunken look to her, with a head that seemed a little too large and limbs a little too spindly. There were dark circles under her eyes, and a drag to her step that Likho recognized as lack of sleep. She looked confused, and a little uncertain, but she was heading straight towards the old woman.

Slowly, Likho turned himself intangible and slipped through the walls of the hospital into the courtyard. The little girl had stepped up to the wheelchair and was tugging on the old woman's sleeve, looking vaguely nervous.

"Hey," the little girl said. The old woman's eyes shot open, and she fumbled for her glasses, grappling at them with stiff fingers.

"Who's there?" she demanded sharply. "Hello?"

Finally, she got the glasses onto her nose, and regarded the girl with surprise. "Oh, hello."

"'Scuse me," the girl said. "Are you Mrs. Shepherd?"

"I am," the old woman said, sitting back again. "And who are you, young lady? Isn't someone watching out for you?"

"They're over there." The girl pointed her right hand towards a group of children, all in a mixture of hospital clothes and everyday garments, who were playing hopscotch under the careful eye of the nurse. "And my name's Mikayla Reese-Heathers."

"Mi-kay-la good grief, what kind of a name is that?" the old woman said, shaking her head. "Sounds Russian, I think. It's a silly name for an American girl. Though I have to say, there's a lot more silly names around than there used to be," she added, clearly warming to her theme. "Knew a young girl in the children's ward not long ago; her name was Bailee Kendra Kaszandrya O'Toole. Name tag as long as your arm. Quite silly to see the new arrivals trying to pronounce it."

Mikayla looked slightly offended, pouting as she hugged her doll. "Well, what's your name?" she demanded.

"Giovanna Shepherd," the old woman said gravely. Likho nodded to himself, watching from his little spot of shadow. L'uomo was definitely here for the old woman. "Neé DiFrancesca."

"Well, that's stupid. Who named you nay?"

"No, no, 'neé.' It's got a little accent mark over it. Means 'used to be,'" Giovanna explained. "When I were a little one like you, my name was Giovanna DiFrancesca. Changed it when I was married."

"My mom didn't change her name," Mikayla informed the old woman. "Mom said she didn't want to give in to the pastry achy of America."

"Pastry achy?"

"That's what Mom said. Pastry achy."

Giovanna shook her head. "Not that," she said. "That word is 'patriarchy,' and your mamma needs to get off her high horse. Taking a man's name doesn't mean you're becoming his slave. So which was she, Reese or Heathers?"

"Reese. She made Dad put her name first."

"It must be a lovely marriage. Now tell me, Mikayla who is also Heathers and Reese, what do you want to talk to me about? I've heard of you—you're the little girl who's always being given all the expensive medications."

The girl looked distinctly uncomfortable. "I've been seeing things, Mrs. Shepherd—"

"Giovanna will be fine. What sort of things?"

"Big blue shadows that talk to me."

"Well, that's not right," the old woman mused. "Is that why you're here, little Mickey?"

"Yeah. I told Mom and she said I was imagining things, so I told Dad and he brought me here. They give me medicine to make the stupid thing go away, but it doesn't. I even told him he was stupid and he wouldn't listen to me." Mikayla looked angry, even from the distance that Likho was observing. "And I asked the other kids if they saw him, and they didn't. So I listened all around the hospital and I heard one of those nurse people asking you about the man you saw."

"You're a sharp one," Giovanna said. She shifted a little in her wheelchair, settling back and crossing her legs at the ankle. "Keep on going, Mickey. What do you see?"

The girl squirmed a little. "A big blue shadow on the wall. It talks to me, but I can't really get what it's saying. It's like the words don't actually go through my ears—they just like turn up in my head."

"How often does he appear?"

"Every night."

"And he's never tried to hurt you?"

"I really don't know, I guess. I see him, and I don't remember what happens afterwards. I just wake up. Mom says its like a bad dream or something."

"They're not dreams." Giovanna folded her hands in her lap. "I've been seeing one like that for seventy-five years now, and it's never a dream. Bogeymen are like that."

Mikayla snorted. "I don't believe in the bogeyman. That's just like a bunch of stuff that old people make up to scare us."

"Children come in two breeds, Mickey—those who believe and those who don't. And you don't believe, so nothing I can say will convince you. But because I'm a nice old woman, I'll give you two rules to prove myself." Giovanna held up one thin finger. "First, when he next appears, don't be scared. Ask him his name. If he's got one, he's a bogeyman. If he hasn't, he's something out of your imagination. Bogeys have to have names."

The girl was still looking skeptical, but nodded nevertheless. "And what's the second rule?" she asked.

Giovanna raised a second finger. "If he's not talking to you, put your head under the blanket, quick as you can. They go away when you do that. I'll never know why, but they do."

"Put my head under my blanket?" Mikayla scoffed. "That's not going to work!"

"Well, if you don't want to talk about it, then I'm not going to be laughed at," Giovanna said crisply. "I go and gives you some valuable advice, and you repay me by being nasty?"

"Boy, they're right," Mikayla sniped. "You're like some kind of crazy old cat lady or something, right? I bet you've never seen a real monster in your life, not like the kind I have to see all the time."

"Why don't you go on and show me, then?" Giovanna said calmly.

"What?" The girl look surprised.

"Show me. I'll come down to see that bogey myself."

"But," Mikayla began, looking uncertain, "the doctor says other people can't see it, 'cuz—"

Giovanna shook her head. "Little miss Mickey, I've seen Egypt and Rome, and I can see bogeymen. One talk with your bogeyman, and he won't bother you any more."

The girl bit her lip. "You can make it go away?"

"I've got bogeyman friends," Giovanna said. Still invisible, Likho scoffed. He had no idea what she was talking about, but he had an idea it had to do with his friend who still stood under the elms. When would an old baggage like her have gotten the opportunity to see Egypt and Rome, anyway?

Mikayla shifted on the gravel, clutching her doll. "I... um... I'm spending tonight with my parents."

"I'll come by tomorrow."

"Are you sure you can make it go away?" Mikayla demanded.

"Cross my heart, Mickey."

"Well... all right then." And without another word, she turned on her heel and raced back up the garden path. Giovanna leaned back and closed her eyes.

Likho was about to dart forward, but he saw L'uomo Nero move instead and paused. The bag man was still invisible, but as he detached himself from his little pool of shadow, a slight gust of wind rippled the edge of the old woman's robe. A second breeze tugged at her scarf and nearly pulled it off her head. She looked vaguely put out, but as a third breath of wind set a small set of chimes dancing in the trees over her head, she straightened up and closed her eyes. L'uomo slowly detached himself from the pool of darkness under the elm and drifted over the paving towards her. In the distance, the children played on, seeing nothing.

"You're out there, aren't you." By no means was it a question. Giovanna leaned forward in her wheelchair, delicate hands clasping each other in her lap. "You've been turning up much more often these days. Something's gone wrong?"

L'uomo's voice was soft and sad. "They don't believe in us."

He began to fade into sight. Giovanna nodded her head as he solidified, smiling a little.

"It's a fine line, the kind you people walk," she said to him. "Can't expect children to be afraid of a man with a bag any more."

"But you believe, don't you?" L'uomo Nero knelt down by the wheelchair and sat back on his haunches like a little boy. "You walked with me, years ago."

The old woman shook her head. Her heavy-lidded brown eyes were still closed.

"There's a difference between knowing something and believing it, black man. When you came after me, I was just a little girl, and I believed. Now I'm an old lady, and I know. Believing is knowing without seeing. I knew you were out there. These days, I don't have to believe."

"But I still hear them calling," L'uomo murmured. He leaned forward, letting his head flop against the armrest bar of the wheelchair. The old woman sighed and laid a hand on his hair, patting a few dirty strands back into place. "The Family gathered for their meeting. And there was calling. There is always calling, even now, when the mammas and papas like to be so silent about us. Come take my boy away, I hear L'uomo Nero coming for you!" He shuffled a little on his knees, closing his eyes and thinking. After a moment, he raised his head again and looked up at the old woman. "But the bag doesn't want them—does it?"

The old woman coughed a little, a dry, coarse sound that left a few flecks of spit on her lips. Slowly and carefully, she patted her mouth with a handkerchief held in a trembling hand. "It's not my business to say what the bag wants."

"But it wanted you."

"'Cause I was a bad girl, black man. I was bad, and my mamma believed in things that most people don't. It's not the people who don't believe, it's the world."

L'uomo's voice was sorrowful. "El Cucuy says we must work harder to remind the children what we are."

"Children aren't the problem. If this cuckoo boy's not getting the results he likes, then that's not their fault. Trying harder to scare them won't change anything." The woman leaned back against the headrest and closed her own eyes, resting a little. "I can't have this... not at my time of life," she murmured.

That was enough—more than enough. Likho could hardly believe what he was seeing. Bogeymen didn't associate with humans; it was as taboo as anything could be for creatures that normally lacked bodies. Humans had created them, but the human influence was malicious, encouraging bogeymen to become concerned with physical things rather than the job they were required to do to keep the belief coming. Likho himself was aware of his own failings there—he smoked, and enjoyed food and liquor when he could get it. But socializing with humans was far beyond the pale.

"L'uomo!" he shouted, charging through the last wall into the courtyard. "Get over here!"

Both the old woman and the bogeyman straightened up at the sound of the voice. The woman's eyes snapped open, and her free hand clutched the opening of her bed jacket, closing it against the sudden chilly wind. "Who's there?" she murmured.

Likho was checked sharply. "She can hear us?" he hissed. He slipped halfway into reality and snatched at L'uomo's coat, unceremoniously hauling him to his feet. L'uomo glanced sorrowfully at the woman, who was staring around as if... as if she had seen a ghost, really.

"Likho? Are you in need?" L'uomo said dazedly. "What is wanting?"

"What's wanting? I've been looking everywhere for you, you loon!" Likho snapped. "You scared the hell out of me, wandering off like that! What if your mind had gone while I wasn't there? You could have killed someone, or worse, been seen! And now I find you hanging out with some wrinkled old... what? A psychic?"

"Who's there?" the woman repeated, much more sharply. "What do you want?"

"She can't see you, Likho," L'uomo continued. "She walked with me once."

Now there was disbelief mixed with the anger in Likho's voice. "You gotta be kidding me. You go traipsing off when there's work to be done, just so you can... can..." he spluttered, but was having trouble voicing his thoughts. "So you can visit some kid you scared back in, what, 1775?"

"I heard that," the old woman said firmly. Likho was beginning to hate her. "Now, whoever you are, that's a bad attitude. There's no reason to bad-mouth the black man for giving me some company. He's got manners, anyway. Now introduce yourself like a human being, and we'll see how things go from there."

Likho glanced at L'uomo Nero. This old woman was too Baba to be believed. "Is she for real?" he asked cautiously.

"You can touch her," was the reply.

"For the love of—I mean, was she serious?"

There was confusion on the tall man's face. "No... I think she was a little girl."

The woman curled her lip. "Don't worry, black man. Yes, Mister Rude, I am serious. What's your name? Where do you come from? You can't tell me you're a Yankee spirit, no matter how flat you make those a's of yours."

"Well, you're not one either." Likho stopped for a moment and considered the withered profile. "Italian?"

"Naples, born and bred."

"Russia for me. Pleasantries over now, L'uomo. Let's go."

Reluctantly, the taller spirit turned to his companion. "Giovanna says the plan will not work, Likho. World, not children, is wrong."

"Yeah, well, El Cucuy says different. And he's the leader of the Family, last time I checked." Likho shot a glance at Giovanna, who was clearly trying to find out where he was standing so she could aim her glare at him. If looks could kill, the Dutch elm would have been firewood. "El Cucuy says we work on the kids, we work on the kids."

"The cuckoo's not very bright, then," Giovanna said. "Children get their ideas from their parents, and if their parents aren't going to tell them about it—because it's not nice to scare them, they think—then you won't get any belief. Change has to come from the top of the stack, not the bottom. And don't forget to visit," she added, watching L'uomo Nero. "Nobody around here tells me the truth. They think I'm some kind of idiot, just because I'm an old woman."

To Likho's great surprise, L'uomo Nero knelt down again and laid his head in the old woman's lap. Giovanna sighed and patted the lank, greasy hair. "Don't be a stranger, black man," she murmured in such a low voice that Likho was barely sure he even heard it. "You can't take me to the pyramids any more. But don't let yourself down just 'cause of that, hmm? You get your work done."

L'uomo Nero nodded sadly and rose to his feet again. He turned his back on the old woman and took a step forward, fading away. Likho followed suit.

Chapter Five

"The apparent simultaneous kidnapping of literally hundreds of children has left a nation shocked and grieved. Last night, at approximately midnight Eastern Standard Time, a truly staggering crime was committed in homes all across America. Reports are still pouring in—"
"Devastating scenes all over the city today—"
"—eighty-seven children, all missing under similar circumstances—"
"—slight traces of blood found at the scenes—"
"—and mourning the ones not yet found. So far, of the thirty-two reported abductions in San Francisco, bloodstains found at the scene indicate that at least three of the children are likely to not have survived—"
"—a dark day for parents everywhere—"
"—Manson-style cult murders—"
"—police investigations—"
"—horror—"
"—shock—"
"—grief—"
"God."

Abby, still wrapped in her bathrobe, stood motionless in the doorway of her living room. She didn't normally turn the television on so early, but today, she had thought the morning news would be a distraction from a long night of bad dreams and dark thoughts. Abby flicked through the news channels, feeling unsteady. Anchor after anchor, breaking news after breaking news, the story was the same.

Mass child abductions. She felt a cold hand clutch her heart, and instinctively turned to glance towards the staircase, but she already knew that her boy was safe: she had heard him shuffling back and forth to the bathroom, and the clacking of keys as he played one of his shooting games. But when something like this happened, suddenly her son was a tiny child again, and she ached to protect him.

"Jimmy!" she called. Her white-knuckled fingers clenched the remote as she waited for the reply. After thirty heart-pounding seconds, a door slammed, and she heard him yell "What?"

Abby breathed out. "Time for school," she called, flicking the channel button again. Another news report. All the channels were carrying it.

"Mom, it's Saturday!" he shouted. "Leave me alone, I'm busy!"

"Sorry, hon." She thought fast. Mass abductions... she already knew what was going to happen. "Listen, Jimmy," she called. "Come down here for a minute, will you?"

Another door slam, and with heavy footsteps, her son came loping down the stairs. He was still wearing yesterday's clothes, and there were dark circles under his eyes. Abby thought she smelled the odd, molten-gummy smell of those energy drinks he liked.

"Hon, I have to get going." She put down the remote and hurried across to the banister, where her purse was hanging from a wooden knob. Avoiding his interrogative look, she dug in her purse for her wallet. She always kept an emergency twenty-dollar bill tucked into the lining, and with care, she extracted it before turning back to her son. "I'm going to be working late. Here—" and she handed him the twenty, making him stare suspiciously first at the money, and then at her. "When you're finished sleeping, I need you to go to the store and get a gallon of milk and some plant food. If I'm not back for dinner, you can order a pizza; there's a coupon on the fridge." Jimmy hadn't moved yet, but his heavy-lidded look was starting to unnerve her.

"Where are you going?" he said, crumpling the twenty and shoving it into his pants pocket.

"Work." She wished she didn't have to say the word. "Something's come up."

Before he could object, she hurried back past him and began to move up the staircase. "Have a good day, hon," she added quickly. "I'll call you if I'm going to be back too late, all right?"

"Mom, what the heck—"

"There've been some news reports. I think they'll need me at the office." Unwilling to talk further, Abby leapt up to the landing and quickly turned down the upper hallway, ignoring the shout of "Hey, wait a minute!" Her bedroom was at the end of the hall, and she shut the door and latched it behind her, just in case. She knew she was being cowardly, but right then, she thought that cowardice existed for a reason—to keep people from getting into sticky situations. She could make it up to Jimmy later (*that's what you said last time*, her conscience taunted her, before she firmly quashed it). She knew she couldn't win a fight with Jimmy, but she was certain she could help the other agents.

Dressing was a quick and easy business: comfortable pants, long-sleeved shirt, broken-in running shoes. There were no clean socks left in her drawer, but she stole two fairly inoffensive ones out of her laundry pile and yanked them onto her feet. More important was the book. *Tarwell's Guide to the Supernatural*, volume fourteen—abductions. It was a valuable resource, and as the SSR's bookkeeper, she preferred to keep the rare volume at her home rather than in danger of explosions or chemical spills at the office.

By the time she came downstairs, Jimmy had vanished. It was with mingled feelings of regret and relief that she let herself out of the house.

Officially, the SSR was run by the Director, who preferred to remain anonymous. The de facto leader, however, was John Sawyer. Like most of the members, he was the sort of man whose great worth was balanced against an equally great list of personal defects; in an ideal world, Abby sometimes thought, John would not be anywhere near a command position. That didn't mean he was a bad leader; it did mean that he was a good leader for a group that did an unfortunate and dirty job.

In the winter, when the small office's heating system would sometimes be the fritz, the SSR members tended to gather in the kitchenette. It was a hexagon-shaped room that had been left over accidentally when the building's original owners had failed to measure their drywall properly, and had been tiled in white linoleum that was now stained a dirty butter color. When the oven was on—as it usually was—it could be stiflingly hot. Abby automatically headed for it, and was not at all surprised to find John already seated there.

He was slumped at the table, watching the eight o'clock news on a small tabletop television set. A familiar green glass jar sat next to him, and from inside it, a pair of malevolent yellow eyes watched the scene without blinking.

"Morning," John said, eyes never leaving the TV. "Picked up Harvey 'round dawn. He's got nothing."

"Good morning to you, too," Abby replied. She pulled off her stocking cap and quickly dropped her dog-eared copy of *Tarwell's Guide to the Supernatural* onto the table. Its lurid green cover was warped, and it had several brown circles from erratically-placed coffee cups. "Came as quick as I could," she said, shucking off her wool gloves. "Have you got anything?"

"Not a thing," John said as he poured her a cup of coffee. Abby took it gratefully, breathing in the steam and not even batting an eye as John added a generous portion of whiskey to the mug. "The police band's gone off like nothing, but there's no word as to what's been up to what."

Abby took a gulp of the steaming coffee. "What's that, then?" she asked, her eyes watering a little as the hot liquid burned her throat. She pointed with her free hand at the counter, where a map of the United States had been spread across the linoleum and anchored down with the cookie jar and a broken alarm clock. States and major cities had been checked off in red Sharpie, and several lines of John's scribbly writing were graffitied across the Midwest.

"Been marking down the reports as they come in." John's fingertips were stained with red ink, and he had left pinkish smears on the ceramic mug that had bled onto Abby's own fingers. Putting down the whiskey bottle, he moved across the kitchen and picked up the red laundry marker, tapping the state of Illinois with the marker's much-chewed end. "Most of the major population centers—five hundred thousand people or more—seem to have been hit right off; none of their coppers saw a damn thing, and their losses add up to an average of—let's say— four to six thousand all told. That's a load of screaming brats. The only such city in the north not reporting abductions so far is our very own Chicago, Illinois." He uncapped the marker and circled the small dot next to Lake Michigan. "The only one in the south is Raleigh, North Carolina." This, too, was circled.

"So?" Abby ventured, cradling her mug in both hands. "What do you think that means?"

John groaned and scratched the side of his nose, leaving a faint pink streak behind. "So far? Means shite-all, far as I'm concerned. Haven't got one thing to go on. Crime syndicate? Rabid grannies not getting enough visits from their kids?" He shot a glance at the copy of *Tarwell's* and flashed a dispirited grin, showing red-stained teeth. "Turn up anything yet?"

Abby shook her head a little dispiritedly. "I just woke up. When I saw it was on the news, I came here as fast as I could."

"Tell me you've got something, Abby. I'm lost." John picked a crumb of bread off the table and flung it at the television.

"Theories," Abby conceded reluctantly, looking down at the book. She took another sip of spiked coffee, gripping the mug with her left hand while she flipped open the cover of the thick volume with the other. "Fairies and elves are the number one suspects right now. Remember that fairy ring out in Fond du Lac two summers ago? Fairies are sadists, and they love kids."

"But that was only about a dozen fairies, at most," John pointed out. "You'd need fifty, sixty rings all working at once to get this kind of phenomena."

"I thought maybe they were collaborating, plotting together—?"

"Doesn't happen," a gloomy voice put in from the pickle bottle. The cap slowly unscrewed itself, and Harvey emerged in a cloud of gray smoke. The doleful yellow eyes regarded them with weary cynicism. "They're not bright enough to do this kind of thing," he continued in a dour tone. "Fairy rings implode after thirty years at most. You get a bunch of supernatural oiks together, what do you expect? There's no way they'd coordinate, not when they'd rather be curb-stomping each other's heads."

"I can see that," Abby conceded. "But what about elves? You know their reputation for child-snatching."

John had grabbed someone's discarded drawing pad and was making a list in red marker. "Again, so many?" he pointed out, but added "elves" to the list anyway. "And yah, tradition says they nick kids. But they always replace them with changelings. If the pointy-eared bastards were making trouble, we'd never know it was them. Making a public outcry's far off their mark. They like to be quiet."

"I can see that, too." Abby was paging through the index of her book, looking for ideas. "Unfortunately, those two are usually my biggest suspects for child abduction. How about mages and malevolent wizardry?"

"That one might work. There's some high-powered disappearing spells that could produce a similar effect. Always be prepared to back an outside chance." John scribbled at his list. "Poltergeists?"

"Nothing like that. Poltergeists aren't listed as kidnappers," Abby said. She ran her finger down the list of ghosts. "And it's probably not anything from the flesh-eating family. If the people were eaten, there'd be more bloodstains, probably at every site. Ghouls especially tend to go for adults, anyway."

It was easier to say people than *children;* that was a thought that none of them really wanted to deal with. Abby's fingers danced over the angular columns of strange beasties as she tried to think. Some of the news reports had mentioned something about a cold wind. "What about vampires?" she said cautiously.

John snorted. "They eat and run, they don't do carry-out."

"But a lot of them?" Abby pressed. "I mean, they're smart, they work in sync when it benefits them—and some of the news reports mentioned, um, winds and mysterious voices."

"Theatricality and lots of ominous grandstanding. Sounds like a vampire to me," the voice of Harvey put in darkly. John looked skeptical, but he put them down on the list as well.

"Hope to God it's not vampires," he commented as he dotted the i. "If it is, we're down to breeds and behavior patterns. All the bloody supernatural monsters out there, and the most troublesome has to be the one with ten thousand breeds."

Abby flipped towards the back of the book, looking for the V section. "Here we go: vampires known for the abduction of children include... good grief, that's a lot. Where do you want me to start?"

"Begin at the beginning, go on until you come to the end, then stop," John said. As a rule, Marotte was the one who quoted things around the office, but John had a special affinity for the Mad Hatter. It didn't surprise Abby in the slightest.

"All right... the bruxsa, of Portugal, is a female vampire created by witchcraft. She is known for her shape-shifting abilities, her notoriously bright green hair, her habit of devouring children and her complete immunity to all usual methods of vampire slaying."

There was a groan from John, and he gulped his cup of coffee as if it were about to be outlawed. "The defense rests, your honor," he said.

A pall of gloom settled over the office, aided by the distant groans of the laboring heater. With a long list of possibilities, no clues, and the distant thought that it was far too early to be spiking the coffee, the SSR agents sat slumped at the table.

Their dark thoughts were soon disrupted by brisk, businesslike footsteps. The door to the cellar opened, and Marotte emerged, wiping his hands on a towel. As ever, he was dressed in white and gray, but the sleeves of his shirt were pushed up to his elbows and his clothes were protected by a long green rubber apron. Several gruesome stains showed that he'd been busy in the basement—dissecting their latest kills and processing the data.

Marotte was yet another member of the SSR who had washed up there for lack of any other option. Nobody knew much about him, but then, members didn't always volunteer information about themselves. Abby pegged his age at between forty-five and fifty, but his general demeanor was much older than that—sixteenth-century, she'd thought more than once. They did know that he was a classically trained actor, and that before his own encounter with the supernatural, he had studied medicine. He was given to reciting the works of classical authors and playwrights, which made extended conversations with him a sometimes painful process... but he was good at his job, and it wasn't as if there weren't other personality quirks around the place. And on a grimmer note, he sometimes served as the SSR's headsman. A lifelong fencer, he could be relied upon to behead creatures that might not be killed any other way.

Abby thought that was unnerving, and didn't particularly like the idea. It made her think too much of executioners. John, on the other hand, seemed rather taken by the concept of having an official headsman. Marotte himself had never said a word about it.

"I've examined your doppelganger, Abigail," he said. Oily gray fluid still stained his hands, and he scrubbed at it with his usual fastidiousness. "The results are printing now."

"Anything worth talking about?" John asked.

Marotte finished drying his hands and folded the towel corner-to-corner. "A few strange items. Its autonomic nervous system was in full fight-or-flight response, and every cell was at complete extension, as if it were panicked. Doppelgangers rely on camouflage for their survival; they rarely suffer such an extreme reaction. Given the confrontation you describe, I doubt it would have been so unusually upset at the moment of its death." There was a laundry basket in the corner, and he moved over and carefully dropped the towel into it. Even Abby would have just tossed it, she knew. That was Marotte for you.

"Starving, scared—same thing," John said dismissively, leaning back in his chair. "Don't s'pose it kidnapped six thousand kids?"

"Highly unlikely," Marotte deadpanned. "But it wasn't starving. Its stomach contents indicated that it had eaten far more than just one person." He poured himself a cup of coffee, ignoring John's offer of the whiskey bottle. "It may have been preparing itself for hibernation."

John whistled. "Doppelgangers hibernate?"

"In times of extreme danger, it is theorized." Marotte sipped his coffee slowly, with the air of a judge considering important papers. "It was never noted in the Anthology, but the Reverend once told me about it. It is a form of Darwinism. The less intelligent and less vicious do not sense an impending period of trouble, and are thus wiped out."

Abby glanced down at the smeary list on the table, and picked up the red marker. "What kinds of trouble?"

He shrugged his broad shoulders. "I cannot guess. Our files are unfortunately incomplete. A few specimens were captured in the early nineties, but they were not intelligent enough to answer questions."

"But the doppelganger definitely sensed something." John, too, was eyeing the list. "And it was all stretched out. Doppleys stretch when they transform." His eyes narrowed.

"I've never heard of a doppelganger changing in public," Abby said. Her curiosity was piqued, and she could feel her breath coming just a little faster. Twelve hours before thousands of children disappear across the nation (and her heart squeezed at the thought—focus, Marquise, focus), a supernatural predator senses an unusual danger and starts getting ready to hide. A danger sufficient enough to warrant not just hiding, but a period of hibernation. "Maybe whatever took the children is the doppelganger's natural predator!" she said excitedly. "We should go through the archives and see if they have any specific enemies. They're Black Forest creatures—maybe a goblin? Goblins sometimes take children."

"Clever," John said with a grin. "It's a place to start, anyway." He swallowed the last of his spiked coffee in one huge gulp and wiped his mouth on the back of his hand. "Abby, hit the books. I'll watch the news and police bands. Mal, go through J-STOR and see what you can dig up on the mythology of the bloody thing."

By ten o'clock in the morning, the SSR members had compiled a stack of data. As more reports came pouring in from all across the country, the agents sifted and searched, ferreting out the pertinent details that connected the abductions. The tragedy had taken place in state after state, to seemingly randomly-chosen victims, but there were a few connecting factors: time after time, parents reported hearing whispers and feeling a cold wind.

The news stations were keeping a running tally of victims, and Abby felt her throat tighten as the numbers climbed. Soon, she moved out of the kitchenette and back into the main office, where it was more crowded but there was no television to distract her with its images of crying families. By the time she poured her sixth cup of coffee, the other members of the SSR had come streaming in.

More coffee was made, and more papers piled up on every available surface. Soon, the office was packed. Marotte and Dummy had taken over listening to the police band and the news reports, thankfully via headphones. They were seated in the corner of the office, with Marotte perched on a bar stool dictating information to Dummy, who hastily transcribed it with both hands working on different notebooks.

Mary, the psychic, had joined Abby at the older woman's overflowing desk to go through the heaps of reports from the past few months. Doppelganger research had run dry quickly, and now they were looking for any sign of a conspiracy or disturbances leading up to the day's cataclysm. Given how many different types of malevolent magic there were, it was often impossible to spot the warning signs until after the event had occurred.

"Rain of frogs on Buenos Aires?" The teenager offered, holding up a smudged printout. Abby took the paper, frowned at it, and put it back down.

"Could be... we should check the Anthology. I think rains of frogs usually fall under biblical-type disasters, not perversion of the natural order."

Mary clambered to her feet and stretched, pulling the kinks out of her muscles. "I think we're looking at a biblical type, Abby."

"Whispers and cold wind are classic signs of perversion of the natural order. That's the way it usually works." Abby moved a cold mug of coffee and peered at a sheaf of newspaper clippings. The cup had left a brown ring behind it, and the cheap paper was wrinkled. "Oh, heck. Who left this cup here?" she demanded of the office at large, but nobody answered.

"I'm telling you, Abby, it's biblical!" Mary insisted. "First-born sons and all that stuff."

"Just check the book, would you?" Abby snapped irritably. "And put the cup in the dishwasher next time you're in the kitchen."

She regretted her words immediately, but not enough to apologize. Mary needed pushing sometime.

The teenage psychic rolled her eyes heavenward, but pushed her chair away and loped across the room towards the overflowing bookcase. The office collection was eclectic and devoid of any filing system known to man, and Mary muttered to herself as she rummaged through the tottering stacks of books. As usual, the thing being searched for was right at the back—in this case, hidden under the battered 1952 DA-DE volume of the *Encyclopedia Britannica* and somebody's edition of the complete works of Marabel Morgan.

The Anthology was not a printed book, and it would be very difficult to find in anybody's reference works. It was a series of six or seven cheap notebooks, cut apart and pasted together between faux-reptile leatherette covers in some semblance of alphabetical order, written in the shaky scripts of people who had just been through a life-threatening experience and had to get everything down quickly before the details faded from their minds.

It was the record of several things—including of the omens and supernatural signs, usually of a prophetic nature that the SSR and its associates had encountered over the years. Many of the entries had been written by the Rev. Evan Jackson Willis, the SSR's founder and a man who had no truck with paragraphs or punctuation. Alphabetizing the entries had only been dealing with the tip of the iceberg.

Mary plunked the Anthology down on the desk. "Here. Are we ever going to clean this thing up?"

"The book or the desk?"

"Both."

"If I want a dirty desk, I can have one. Besides," Abby pointed out, "if you're complaining about the mess, then you should do something about that guinea pig's cage. I'm not the one who brought Stinker in here. Rains of frogs, right?"

The psychic nodded as she flopped down in her chair again. "Rain of frogs, singular. Buenos Aires. Do they even *have* frogs in Buenos Aires?"

"I guess they do now." Abby paged carefully through the yellowing, blue-lined pages, trying not to crack the fragile paper. "Frogs, frogs, frogs... here we go. 'The presence of a frog or multiple frogs may suggest use of malevolent black magic. Frog skins, eyes, and legs are all critical components in spells cast with the aid of the infernal authorities.'" She closed the book slowly and pulled a handwritten list towards her. "So frogs turn up in black magic spells. That could be a hint."

"But that's just frogs," Mary objected. "Lemme see it." Quickly, she filched the Anthology and flipped it open; Abby winced at the crackling of its spine. "*Rains* of frogs," she read aloud, "tend to accompany... perversions of the natural order of reality. Crap. You win." Mary slapped the book's covers together and dropped it back onto the nearest pile of paper.

"Don't worry," Abby said. "If it's any consolation, that narrows down our search." She set aside her notes and flipped open the Anthology again. "Perversions of the natural order involve belief-based creatures... Schroedinger's Cat writ large. And there's not many of those. Poltergeists, ghouls, mythic and folkloric creatures, that sort of thing." Chewing a little on the end of her pencil, Abby made a quick note in the margins and closed the book. "Leave that with John, would you?"

"Will do," Mary said, taking it with exaggerated care. "Where is he, anyway?"

"I think he's in the workshop with Adam. If we get any leads, we'll be heading out right away, and he wants to make sure the Desert Eagle is working right."

"Why does he use that thing, anyway?" Mary said curiously, running her fingers along the edges of the anthology. The leatherette had its own rings from carelessly-placed coffee cups. "Is it a man thing? Like the guys on those books who always have those gigantic spears and stuff?"

"What?" Abby's felt her face warm, and knew it was turning red: luckily, she was turned away from Mary. The thought of John possibly compensating for something was embarrassing; it wasn't the sort of thought she usually entertained, and she felt slightly scandalized that Mary had. "I don't know. I think he just wants to be able to defend himself," she said quickly.

Mary paused for a moment, eyes half-shut and focusing on nothing, then laughed out loud. Heads turned and the buzz of conversation rose all across the room as she doubled up, clutching her stomach. Dummy looked up from his work, shifted slightly in his chair, and cracked a broad grin at a shared thought.

"Sixty-six Eighty West Milwaukee Avenue," Marotte said tersely, focused on the police reports. "Reported... no, just a burglary."

"'Just' a burglary?" Mary repeated, clearly amused. "What were you hoping for? Grand theft auto?"

"There are still no kidnappings reported within the Chicago area," Marotte replied, picking up a pencil and making a note of his own. "The nearest is Springfield. Odd, all things considered." He drummed the pencil on the desk. "It could be a clue. What separates Chicago from all these other cities? Abby?"

"I'm on it." Abby scooted her chair over to the bookshelf and tugged an atlas out of the morass. "Mary, if you're just going to think at Dummy all day, could you take that Anthology down with you?"

"Yes. Please." Marotte again, sounding long-suffering. Beside him, Dummy was still grinning silently, and Mary squinted as she transmitted another thought to him. Abby picked up the book and gently but firmly wedged it into Mary's grasp.

"Go deliver the book, Mary. No taunting the other staff, remember?"

"You guys are no fun," the psychic muttered, but did as she was told.

Downstairs, things were much quieter. The basement of the SSR was a vault of concrete, lit by flickering fluorescent tubes and possessing an atmosphere eerily reminiscent of high school shop class. Battered wooden tables were littered with power tools, pieces of metal and glass, tangles of wire that looked like hair pulled out of the sink, broken batteries, and apparently random pieces of machinery.

At the moment, Adam Starczynski was examining a large, heavy pistol, while John leaned against the nearest wall and scuffed his shoes against the concrete floor. He had discarded his polyester suit jacket, and was absentmindedly tapping his fingers against the wall while he scuffed. It was obvious that he hated waiting.

Adam turned the gun over, examining it carefully. "You know what they say about men who carry big guns, John?"

"Yah, they kill big things. Trying to make a point or what?"

"Just checking." Adam hefted the pistol experimentally. "It's pretty front-heavy when unloaded; I never understood why you wanted to carry this piece of junk. The accuracy's crap."

Mary and Dummy had their own particular abilities, and Harvey was quite useful, but most of the SSR's present members had no real powers that could help them in a scrap with a demon or a vampire. Therefore, they did in fact indulge in a sort of compensation—by carrying the most powerful legal or illegal weaponry they could get their hands on. Abby's Beretta was only the tip of the iceberg; Adam's workbenches were cluttered with everything from a World War II-era carbine to a Mossberg pump-action shotgun, and a few other, more specialized pieces were stored in the cabinets. This was Adam Starczynski's territory. He was rarely seen anywhere else.

Adam was unique in their experience: he was admittedly schizophrenic, but most of the time, the monsters he saw actually were there. It often fell to him to clean and maintain the equipment that the rest of the team tended to abandon on sofas or use to poke mysterious jars full of ectoplasm, and he wasn't too happy about that.

His biggest problem, aside from trying to maintain a vegetarian diet in a paramilitary group that lived on takeout, was John Sawyer's Desert Eagle. The handgun had been left behind by Oliver Kendrick, a former member of the SSR who had decided to retire to the peace and sanity of Detroit. John had promptly appropriated it, and spent at least an hour of Adam's time every other day getting some piece or other fixed.

"If it's such a piece of shite, then give me the FN P-90," John challenged from his spot by the wall. Adam's eyes widened.

"Are you crazy?" There was a slightly shrill edge to his voice. "Hand you a delicate piece of equipment—the only Fabrique Nationale piece we've got—and let you drop it on bathroom floors and bang it into walls and leave it in the kitchen sink? Dream on!"

"Didn't think so," John said. "So if you're not going to give me the P-90, then make sure the pistol works properly, would you? And stop your moaning."

Adam glared at his friend, who groaned theatrically. "Just fix it, would you?" John carped, changing from scuffing the floor to kicking the cabinets with his heels. "I'm not hunting down some undead spook and then finding your gadget's decided to cop out on me."

"Have a little patience." The technician pulled a Q-tip out of his pocket and gently swabbed the inside of the muzzle opening. "Some carbon buildup... not surprising, really. After all, the Desert Eagle's unreliability is legendary. How often does it stovepipe on you, John?"

"Pardon?"

"Stovepipe," Adam repeated a little testily. "When the empty cartridge doesn't eject from the firing chamber. How often does it do that?"

"Occasionally."

"I figured." Adam hefted the gun again, chewing the inside of his cheek as he thought. "I won't lie to you, John—this thing is a piece of junk. I just replaced the gas mechanism in June, and it's already starting to choke up again. I've run over this thing God only knows how many times. I think it's cursed. Not to mention the fact that you tend to just leave the extra assemblies lying around, and do you *ever* clean it properly?"

"I. Don't. Care. Can you make it work?"

"Oh, it'll work." Adam set down the gun with a clunk. "For a while. Here." He reached into the pocket of his bathrobe and produced a magazine of nine rounds. ".357, just as you requested. High-velocity, and expensive, so no spray-and-pray bullshit."

"I need some kind'a tracking rounds," John said. "We need to tag this thing and track it."

Adam grimaced. "John, I've told you a hundred times. *There are no such things as tracking rounds!* Hollywood made it up! What d'you want next? Blasters? Pulse rifles?"

"Right, right, your majesty. No need to get sarky about it." John picked up the magazine and examined it. "But how am I supposed to keep an eye on it? You know they don't take tranquilizers; we can't tag the bloody thing like it's a lab rat."

Adam's momentary hysteria faded away again as they got back to business. John made a mental note not to watch any action films with him in the future. "Just shoot once. It runs away, you follow the trail of blood."

"And it won't kill it?"

"When you find out what the it is, then ask me," Adam responded. "No, the real question is if it attacks and kills you instead of deciding to go on."

"Because, yes, that's going to put my faith in your equipment," John said.

His friend ignored him. "I don't know why you're so pissed off about getting this thing working, anyway. We're just going back to basics. Shoot it, follow it, trap it. Simple and straightforward." He paused. "That *was* the plan, right?"

"Supposedly. Things have been known to change." John looked up, hearing the creak of the basement stairs. "Who is it?" he called out.

"It's me," Mary's voice came back. "I've got the Anthology for you. Oh, and can I stay down here? Abby and Marotte kicked me out of the room again."

"Sending dodgy comments into their brains?"

"Just a little bit, yeah."

"Grab a table. And chuck us that book, would you?"

The psychic hefted the book and tossed it. As John neatly caught it between his hands, Mary scrambled down the rest of the stairs and took up a perch on one of the work tables, making Adam wince a little as she carelessly shoved the wires and equipment aside to make room for herself.

"How're things going upstairs?" he asked.

"There's still lots and lots of reports to go through," Mary said. "I should probably get back up there soon." Nevertheless, she made no attempt to move from her perch. Her expression was mostly lighthearted, but she watched Adam work on the handgun with wide eyes. "John—hey—what do you think did it?"

"Something that made a blood-sucking, shapeshifting, ugly-as-sin German horror-story monster scared shitless."

Mary pulled a face. "Do you think it'll come back?"

"I don't know. How long does it take to eat six thousand sprogs?"

"John!"

"Just trying to be realistic," he said bluntly. He took the Desert Eagle from Adam's outstretched hand and tested its slide. "And we don't know what sorts they're after, either. You stick close by us, Mary, you got that?"

"Roger, captain."

Chapter Six

The fear was almost tangible, and it was already beginning to feed them. Fear roiled off the streets of the cities and swept through town and country alike, permeating every house and tainting every spoken word. The news reports flashed from coast to coast, from country to country, proclaiming one of the direst crimes in modern history. Theories ran wild.

The night before, thousands of children had been abducted from their beds by some unknown force. Some of them might have died. Shell-shocked and horrified, the nation ground to a halt: as bereaved parents waited by their phones in hopes of reports, and law enforcement agencies were forced onto double overtime, the effects of the disappearances spread like ripples in a pond.

Even the weather seemed changed. A series of vicious snowstorms spread across the Midwestern United States. Kansas was snowed in, Iowa was snowed in. Cabin fever skyrocketed, and the reports of the resulting misdemeanors and assault charges followed shortly. A few paranoiacs told police about invisible figures driving the storm on, but nobody listened to them. Chicago, protected by the radiating warmth of the lake, weathered the storm—much as it had weathered the nationwide bereavement.

Nevertheless, the Navy Pier entertainment complex was at least half empty that afternoon. Only the tourists, who were not in a position to simply choose to visit another time, filled its shopping district and wandered through the botanical garden. In a fast-food restaurant almost at the water's edge, two figures sat alone in an almost empty dining room, invisible to those around them.

The restaurant had paid a contractor a good deal of money to make the place look upscale and modern. The contractor had done this by installing crackling purple glass tubes with flashing energy conductors inside, and ordering new plastic chairs of the type that were so upscale and modern that the average human behind could not fit into them comfortably. Likho and L'uomo Nero were the only people in the place who weren't visibly squirming. The air had the usual fast food smell of grease and salt, but it was battling for dominance with a citrus air freshener and several liters of Pine-Sol.

Every surface was squeaky-clean and shining, and it was making Likho edgy. L'uomo Nero didn't seem to mind, or even notice; he had taken off his hat, a rarity in itself, and was staring blankly at the wall through a curtain of stringy dark hair.

"Shouldn't there be more trash?" Likho wondered aloud through a mouthful of cheeseburger. "More hobos sleeping in the corners and questionable meats in the food? More posted warnings from the health department? This place is less real than the counter-jockey's tits. How am I supposed to trust food that comes from a plastic factory?"

"We should talk to Giovanna again," L'uomo Nero said firmly, ignoring his friend's complaints. Perhaps he didn't even hear them. "The bag will not take them. No walking this time. We should talk to Giovanna. No walking."

"Talk to Giovanna all you like, it won't get us out of hot water," his friend growled, putting down his sandwich. "It was that old battleaxe's nattering that got you to disobey El Cucuy in the first place, and me being the damn idiot I am, I went running after you."

"Giovanna is wise. She knows how things ought to go."

"Maybe she is, maybe she isn't." Likho finished the last bite of burger and scrunched up the discarded pieces of lettuce and tomato in the paper wrapper. "But she's human, and that's good enough for me. Humans are always looking out for their own interests. She probably has grandkids that she doesn't want anybody snatching."

L'uomo Nero continued staring blankly at the beige wall, as if it was a script he had to follow. "She... does not. She was married, but has no issue."

"Then she's got a nephew or something. *Look,* if we don't do as El Cucuy says, it'll be our heads on a platter—not hers. Ergo, it's none of her beeswax what we do." Likho twisted the paper lump into a screw and lobbed it cleanly over his friend's head. It bounced off the back of an oblivious woman's head and landed in the trash can. "Hah! Two points. Besides, El Cucuy said we're not killing them, so why do you care?"

"They haven't been bad, Likho."

"All kids are bad. Fact of life."

His friend shook his head vehemently. "No. They have not been bad enough, and their mammas and papas haven't called us for them."

Likho quirked one gray brow, smirking a little, just a little, at that. "Being coherent again, are we?"

"This is important, Likho." L'uomo Nero leaned forward. The deep-set eyes were clear and unclouded, and he stared unblinkingly at the Russian bogey. His voice was suddenly harsh. "We live to help humans, not hurt them. We are the motivation for children to be good. If they are not good, we teach them to be good. The truly bad ones are removed, and they make way for the better—"

"Natural selection," Likho cut in. "I know, pal, I know. What's your point?"

"The dead child is power-mad. He wants everybody to fear us, regardless of whether they deserve to be so used or no. He wants the era of gods and demons to return, and he wants us to be the gods." L'uomo Nero's eyes narrowed. "We are *not* gods. His actions will only upset the order of the world."

For a moment, everything was silent in the small restaurant. Even the other patrons, who couldn't see the bogeymen unless they tried to actively focus on them, felt that something was wrong. The chatter of conversation ceased, and the humans glanced at each other uneasily. The only sound in the place was the radio, which played on regardless. *"The only boy who could ever teach me was the son of a preacher man...."*

Barely daring to move in the unnatural pause, Likho reached across the table for the salt shaker. His twitchy fingers fumbled the slick glass, and the salt shaker dropped to the table with a *thunk* that echoed in the sudden silence. At the sound, L'uomo Nero twitched, and the light began to fade from his eyes. The black man's head fell, his features seemed to blur as the awareness leached out of them. He blinked muzzily, looking around at the restaurant as if he had never seen it before.

Reality snapped back into place with a lurch. People shook their heads or rubbed their eyes and returned to their discontinued conversations. The sound system was once more drowned out by the babble of talk, the clatter of trays, and the constant ringing of the cash registers at the counter.

Likho groaned as he picked up the salt shaker and set it upright again. "Again with the salt. Is that going to keep happening? Because if it is, I'm putting in a request for a new partner. And believe me, when I start sounding like a cop show, it's that bad."

"Sorry?" L'uomo Nero blinked again, trying to clear his vision. "Is what?"

"Never mind." The Russian bogeyman gathered up the rest of his trash and put it on the plastic tray. As usual, L'uomo Nero didn't eat. Likho could never understand that: it wasn't as if they had to worry about cholesterol or heart disease. Even if you were pretty far into a body, you could focus your will and wish away the inconvenient problems, or the organs entirely if you wanted to go insubstantial. "You still want to see that old bat of yours?"

"She's not a bat, Likho." For a moment, the look was back, and Likho twitched involuntarily. Then the black man's customary expression of vaguely friendly concussion replaced it. "Yes... I want to see her. Even if tonight, we do as the child asks, we could speak to her. She is old."

"So are we," Likho pointed out as he stood up with the tray. L'uomo Nero rose as well, unfolding the thin black-clad limbs like a massive spider clambering out of its web. He put a hand on his hat, slowly raising it to his head as if performing a ceremony; which, when you thought about it, wasn't far from the truth.

"It is not the same," he said calmly. "We do not see the things she sees."

"What... colostomy bags and ugly nurses?"

"Do not make fun, Likho."

"Wouldn't dream of it." Likho tucked his hands into his pockets, and stopped for a moment. "Wait a minute.... L'uomo, give me your bag."

L'uomo Nero did as he was told, and Likho took it. A sharp lance of pain shot through his hand as he lifted it, but he shook it off and opened it. Inside was all grayish-brown burlap. Reaching into his pocket again, he withdrew a heavy golden ring with an opal in its setting and dropped it into the bag. "Don't say I didn't do it, grandma," he muttered, knotting it closed and handing it back.

The other bogeyman looked confused, but he took back his bag as if nothing had happened. "Likho," he said, and his voice was thin and high, like a whining child. "I want to see Giovanna."

"Don't you dare vanish on me again," Likho warned. He watched L'uomo darkly from under the brim of his squashed felt hat. "We'll see her later, all right? But L'uomo, we can't afford to sneak out on the Duty again. I'll bet you anything that El Cucuy's already wondering why two cities didn't report any losses." Glancing quickly up at the air, he groaned. "And we're already late. L'uomo—"

"I want to—"

"*L'uomo,*" he interrupted. L'uomo Nero winced, chastised. "Look, L'uomo. I know you hate him, and frankly, he's a little douchebag. But we can't really afford to get on El Cucuy's nerves. Not when he's the leader of the Family."

"Bavbav is the leader of the Family," L'uomo muttered.

"Not right now, he isn't. Things change."

"Things change, bogeymen change, stories change. But Bavbav is leader of the Family."

"Not now, L'uomo. We have to go."

In Chicago, the afternoon sun still glinted off the buildings, but night was wearing on over the waterfronts of Sydney. The warehouse was the same as it had been before, deep in shadows, lit only by El Cucuy's oil lamp. But though he was surrounded by the gathered members of the Family, El Cucuy seemed quite alone in the circle of light. His hands were raised and his eyes closed as he listened to the wind, and he smiled as he drank in the fear.

—Benjy, where did they take you?

—locking all my doors tonight—

—a reward is offered for information leading to the apprehension of anyone connected with—

—a national time of mourning for those we have lost—
—not gonna get me, that's for sure—

El Cucuy opened his eyes and the voices fell silent. Currently, the leading theory was that it was another secret terrorist attack, similar to 9/11. But of all the assembled bogeymen, El Cucuy knew best that as the abductions continued, and locks and weapons failed to halt the invisible intruders, the panic would only increase. People would begin to wonder, and then to whisper, and finally to worship in hopes of stopping the attacks.

The Family watched him, eyes glinting in the light of the lamp. El Cucuy grinned.

"Brothers, we're proceeding well." He indicated the map. Behind him, his first lieutenant—the Sacauntos, silent as usual—grinned as well. The flensing knife was in his hand, and it gleamed as if it was alive. He always kept it well polished.

"I have a fresh plan," the dead child continued. "Tonight, you all receive new assignments. Target the homes of young parents with one or two children; if there is an animal in the house, kill it. Bring me the children unharmed. If one resists—and they will, there will always be would-be heroes—hurt as few as possible."

"You still wants them alive, eh then, you does?" said the seven o'clock man. Then he added in a lower voice: "So I's not to eat today, is I? I was so hungry, and you has to says 'don't kills'... and there was kills, but I's not part of it, and that is hurt the poor *bonhomme*."

"Those young ones are our greatest asset, brother," El Cucuy said.. "I know it's dull, but eating is not necessary. Their parents know we can kill, and that makes them fear us. Now let them know that the children are still alive, and they'll wonder what we can do with them. Keep those children long, keep them frightened, and their belief will be as strong as that of their parents."

In the back ranks, Likho shifted restlessly. "Good plan," he murmured to L'uomo Nero. "Let's see if it goes through. I know for a fact that at least one New Jerseyan is going to be carrying a silver cross tonight."

"Likho!" El Cucuy snapped.

The elder bogeyman cringed backwards. "I'm sorry, Lord, I didn't mean to be disrespectful."

El Cucuy's expression softened a bit. "No concern, Likho. I know," he said, addressing the whole group, "that we have never done something like this before. It's in the nature of the Family to lurk at the edges, feeding on their normal fears—not to cause them."

There was some muttering from the group, especially from the men with the bags. One or two of them, grizzled specimens with wild hair and brushy beards, nodded violently.

"But if we don't," El Cucuy continued, "we won't last long enough to see the old ways return. Like it or not, the world is continuing into a new era of human existence. For ten thousand years we've been tribal ghosts, nature spirits, *gods*—but the humans do not have those any more. We have to find a new place for ourselves, and for our beliefs, or we'll die out like any other useless remnant."

The oldest and frailest of the bag men spoke up. He carried a wicker cage instead of a bag, and wore only a loincloth to protect his skinny frame. His skin was tanned almost black, and his eyes were bloodshot. When he spoke, it was in a strange clicking dialect that no human had spoken for thousands of years; El Cucuy nodded at every word.

"The Man-who-hides-in-the-ground raises a question. Is it our time to die?"

There was a definite ripple in the crowd this time. Several hairy men shook their heads, while the bag men nudged each other and muttered in low tones. Someone called out: "No fear!"

"Maybe it is our time," El Cucuy amended. The outburst was more direct this time; even the Talasam was growling and scuffing the floor in anger at the suggestion. "But we would not be alive if we succumbed without a fight." He smiled in fond recollection. "During the time of the Conquistadors, a young Aztec child was thrown into a well. He drowned. That night, his identical twin brother stabbed the offending soldier as he lay asleep. Nobody ever discovered who did it—only that the wounds on the body were too shallow and too low to have been made by a full-grown man. Some whispered that they had seen the dead child walking about with a knife."

He spread his arms, gesturing to the frail, shadowy body. "And thus was I born—from a boy's revenge and some idiot's desire to keep a crying child quiet. But even though I was created from these petty beginnings, I have life. And—" the thin, high voice grew harsh. "And I refuse to throw away that life simply because the humans refuse to fear *what exists.*"

"I agree with our Lord the Cucuy," La Llorona added. She was another Mexican spirit, a tall woman wrapped in gauzy white rags, her long blonde hair streaming down her slender back. She might have been beautiful until you looked at her face: an eyeless peeled skull, yellowed with age, turned its blind gaze on the assembled Family. The jaws clicked with every word she spoke. "No matter how we began, we're all here and we're all alive. Humans kill animals and eat them. I say we do the same. Let's bring back the old ways!"

There was an answering roar. The hairy men stamped on the floor with their huge paws, and the bag men shouted and laughed in their cracking, hoarse voices.

L'uomo Nero and Likho had arrived late to the meeting. L'uomo seemed entirely back to normal; his eyes were glazed and unfocused, and his words were semi-coherent, at best. Likho watched him carefully for any signs of sudden intelligence, but none seemed to be forthcoming.

It was no secret that Likho didn't like the atmosphere in the meeting: he had seen humans do this same thing, usually in Red Square. As the other bogeymen clustered around El Cucuy, clamoring for more assignments and cheering their fool heads off, the Russian plucked at his taller companion's arm. "The crazy in here is killing me," he muttered. "Come on out with me. I need a smoke."

Outside on the pier, dawn was coming on quickly. "Seems like we see a lot of wharves these days," Likho commented in a falsely bright tone as he patted his pockets for matches. "Not half so nice as the one at the 1807 meeting, though. The seagulls are less friendly."

"The child is an idiot."

Likho's head shot up. L'uomo Nero was staring out across the water, but his normal expression of blank amiability was gone. The deep-set eyes were narrowed in anger, and the cracked lips curled in thought as the tall bogeyman watched the waves lapping against the dock. He clutched his bag in his right hand, almost throttling it, and the cords stood out in his neck like folds in a heavy quilt.

"Well, spit it out," Likho finally said, snapping off the end of a cigarillo with a tiny pair of clippers. "What's eating at you?"

"Idiot. Blind, blind idiot, him and his plans and schemings," L'uomo Nero growled. His glare was almost boring a hole in the wall of the distant warehouse. "He wants to be more than just a household god. If he has his way...."

"You got any matches?"

"No."

"Suit yourself." The Russian bogeyman finally turned up a silver Zippo in an odd pocket, tucked in amidst a nest of bits of string and what looked like a tarnished hip flask. "You're being oddly coherent again. Who am I talking to?"

"More than household gods. More than shrines and altars."

"Ah. Hello, L'uomo."

The tall creature slapped angrily at the railing, sending a reverberating thrum through the rickety metal. He seemed not to hear Likho, and maybe that was for the best; the legends of the old L'uomo Nero had made it clear that he wasn't the sort of person sarcasm could be used against. "That's the difference. We change, we protect, we make better. We don't cause the problem, we fix it. Cause the problem, and you become the one you pray to us for protection against... he wants to take us back into the Dark Ages."

Likho was watching his friend intently. "Well, you have to admit that the Dark Ages were a pretty good time for us," he said as casually as he could, while the tip of the cigarillo flared to life. "Some of the old songs are still around, you know. Good tunes. You could whistle 'em, even if they're all about death and destruction. Especially the English ones. I tell you, Nanny Rudd was wasted on England, but the tunes were good. 'I went down to Satan's kitchen, for to get me food one morning—and there I got souls piping hot, all on the spit a-turning.' That would be *Boys of Bedlam*, if I remember my crazy English bards well enough." He sighed a little. "Good times, good times. Bedlam. You remember Bedlam? Amazing place, once you got used to the smell. Tuppence for a stick to poke the madmen with."

There was a growl of frustration. L'uomo Nero ground his teeth and clenched his fists, almost kneading at the air, as if he was trying to catch his thoughts and mold them into words. From his expression, it was clear that he was losing the battle. "It... there was all the belief, but not... not right," he finally managed. "There was the Inquisition. Wrong kind of belief. Didn't taste right. Fear of things, not of us...."

"Hey!" The cigarillo dropped to the ground as Likho jumped forward. L'uomo Nero's legs gave way under him and he collapsed to the ground, hands still pawing uselessly at the air. Likho knelt down beside him, tugging ineffectually at his coat. "Hey, buddy, hey, pal, come on, wake up! You okay? Buddy? Black man?"

"...Likho?" The voice was wispy and vague again. L'uomo Nero blinked confusedly in the dim lights, looking somewhat lost. "The head is fogged...."

"No wonder." Groaning, Likho clambered to his feet and gave his friend a hand up. "You had a bit of a sociopathic moment and started talking about flavors and Dark Ages. Everything all right now?"

The black man swayed a little bit as a gust of wind whipped up from the river. It snatched ineffectually at his hat, which stayed firmly anchored to his head. Some parts of reality had no truck with the members of the Family, and vice versa. "It seems as if all is well," he murmured, still blinking. "Something went into the bag again, Likho."

"Did you, now? Well, maybe the bag can get me another smoke, because that was my last one." Likho kicked the smoldering butt off the quay, where it hissed as it hit the river. "Too much is going on here, and right now, I don't feel like figuring it out. Come on, we'd better get back inside before we're missed. You know how El Lorde and Grande Mochaccino El Cucuy hates having people not pay attention. Dammit, Bavbav never made us call him 'lord'...."

It was apparent that they hadn't been missed. El Cucuy was standing over the map, surrounded by a cluster of some of the oldest bogeymen;

Man-who-hides-in-the-ground was chattering and clicking maniacally as he gestured to the map, while El Ogro and Hombre del Saco (both of them frightening enough in their own special way, especially given that El Ogro might have been mistaken for a wall with a fur pelt and fangs. And who could forget that Hombre del Saco was the only bogeyman to go on duty with a pint of rum in each hand? Anybody that did that earned a wide berth from Likho) looked on. A gaggle of hairy men and bag men had their heads together, apparently deep in conversation, and the Llorona was by the window—obviously issuing final orders to a group of creatures in female form. She flashed a skeletal grin at L'uomo Nero before joining the rest of her crew in their flight from the open window.

Likho slipped into the crowd, trailing L'uomo Nero behind him. El Cucuy looked up as the pair approached, and nodded cordially to them.

"L'uomo Nero, Likho—excellent. I've been meaning to speak to you. Sacauntos, please take the map and the list; I want everybody on the move within forty-five minutes. As for you two, please follow me."

The dead child led them away from the table and over to an isolated corner of the room. He crossed his arms and turned to face them, a serious expression on his small features. Likho stared back at him uncertainly.

"Tell me," El Cucuy said in a low voice. "Tell me exactly why you failed to carry out my explicit orders."

Likho gaped in astonishment at him. "What do you mean, lord?"

"I mean," El Cucuy noted icily, "that I assigned the two of you to Chicago and Raleigh. Neither of those cities reported any abductions. Would you care to explain yourselves?" His bright tone had completely vanished, and the claret-colored eyes were narrowed ever so slightly as he looked at them. Likho gulped just a little.

"Allow me to guess," the dead child continued. "You had a better idea? Or were you simply unwilling to go through with it?"

L'uomo Nero shifted slightly. "We had a better idea," the raspy voice said. Likho winced and closed his eyes. Bad choice, black man. Bad thing to say. Not to *El Cucuy*.

For a moment, there was silence in that little corner of the room. By the table, El Ogro rumbled on, rustling the map and shuffling his huge feet. There were murmurs of conversation among the Family members gathered there, and occasionally a little choke or scream of hoarse laughter. Sickly yellow light filtered into the warehouse from little windows set high above them, admitting the illumination but providing no view of the outside world.

"So tell me," El Cucuy finally said. "What was this better plan, then?"

Hastily, Likho stomped down on L'uomo Nero's foot as subtly as he could. "It wasn't better, it was just different!" he explained before his colleague could butt in. "We were trying an experiment. Since there was so much crime in Chicago already, we thought we could try approaching as specifically supernatural so nobody would waste time talking about whether the kids were abducted, but there wasn't enough belief around to sustain us—"

El Cucuy made an impatient noise in his throat, and Likho fell silent. "So you made an idiotic decision and wound up being unable to complete your assigned task because of it," the child summarized. Likho nodded frantically.

Finally, after one agonizing moment, El Cucuy nodded curtly. "It was a mistake," he finally pronounced. "Don't do it again. Can I trust you to carry out tonight's mission?"

"Yes, lord, absolutely," the Russian ghost said eagerly. "We're both strong and capable, things will be done—"

"Fine." El Cucuy cut off Likho's protests with a twitch of an eyebrow. "Night will fall in North America in six hours. By then, I want both of you in place. Likho, you're to be sent to Iowa. Take any town with more than fifty thousand people. L'uomo Nero, you'll have the southern half of Florida. Thieve, steal, take the children but do not injure or kill them. Be as silent as possible. Every pet in the house must be put down as quickly and cleanly as possible. Frighten them to death, if possible."

"Medium-sized cities," L'uomo Nero murmured, swaying slightly in place. Likho shot him a quick look—it was certainly a bad time for the man to become coherent, if he was planning to do so—but L'uomo Nero just shook his head vaguely. "Medium cities for medium people."

"Can you control him?" El Cucuy said sharply.

Likho shrugged. "To be honest, lord, he's been more than a bit crazy lately.... I don't know if he can do the job by himself."

"Lo, how the conquering hero fails," the dead child commented. He stared straight up at the Italian bogeyman, whose eyes were unfocused and blank. "And we still don't know what's gone wrong with him."

"I can accompany him, lord, if you're uncertain about his abilities—"

El Cucuy nodded to him. "That would be wise. If we can manage to bring him back... ah, he was vicious. In the meantime, keep a close watch on him. You may work both areas as a pair, if you wish. Just bring me the young ones and don't cause a fuss. Is this clear?"

"Yes, lord." Likho hauled hard on L'uomo Nero's arm, guiding the dazed bogeyman like a mother steering her tired toddler. "We'd better be going, then. Excuse us, lord." With L'uomo Nero trailing behind him, he hurried towards the door. He was certain he had another cigarillo around somewhere. Bogeyman or not, he wanted a smoke.

He knew he had better go back outside to do it, though. El Cucuy wasn't a fan of "human behavior," and tended to frown on smoking and eating. Of course, that wasn't the only thing. Likho's proper name was Babay, but he had decided around 1900 that it sounded too ridiculous and adopted the other title of Likho for general use. And that was what was now worrying Likho.

When he had decided on a nickname, El Cucuy had made a stink about it. The dead boy had insisted that "human titles" were demeaning to "the stated and unyielding purpose" of the bogeymen, and roundly damned Likho for his transgressive behavior. So what Likho wanted to know was: why was El Cucuy suddenly using his name?

"Act natural," he whispered to L'uomo Nero, who paid absolutely no attention. Once they had reached the door, Likho fumbled his cigarillos and "accidentally" spilled them all over the floor. He scrambled around on his hands and knees, collecting them and hamfistedly jamming them back into their paper packet. While he did so, he focused on the conversation now taking place across the warehouse.

El Cucuy was standing in a small huddle with El Ogro and La Llorona. They seemed to be conferring about something. A moment later, El Cucuy made a gesture, and the glowing blue shape of the Mörkö glided across the floor to join the group. More suspicious huddling and whispering.

El Ogro's voice was the loudest. "You know, Lord, he unknown, he bag unknown, just like old scratch Bavbav."

That made El Cucuy flinch, and he snapped something angrily that Likho couldn't hear. Then, as one, the four bogeymen turned to look at L'uomo Nero.

Oh-oh. Time to go. Likho hurriedly grabbed the last of his cigarillos and stuffed them into his pocket.

"C'mon," he mumbled, and L'uomo perked up a little. Taking his friend's arm, he turned on the spot, and the world dissolved around them.

Chapter Seven

The insistent ringing of the phone dragged Abby out of her dreamless sleep. Blearily opening one eye, she squinted at the bedside table. She vaguely remembered dropping her phone next to her before falling into bed a scant three hours before hand, but now it was nowhere to be found. Yet still the ringing continued.

Groaning a little, Abby propped herself up on her forearms and crawled to the edge of the mattress. Finally, after a moment of painful rooting around, she found the phone lying right near the edge of the bed. She flipped it open and tumbled onto her back, holding it to her ear as her eyes closed again. "Yes?" she mumbled.

"Abby?" John's voice sounded strained. "What's going on? Are you all right?"

"I'm exhausted, John."

"That's not what I mean. Is your son still there?"

"John, what—"

"Just look!"

Abby sat up and reached for her shoes, but she didn't need to; she could hear the clatter of keys and the faint thud of Jimmy's compulsive pounding on the keyboard. "He's fine," she said wearily. "I think he's playing Counterstrike again. What is it?"

"More news reports coming through. Chicago's not immune anymore."

She felt a freezing hand clutch at her heart. "Oh, no," she whispered raggedly. "It happened again?"

"Stats are hitting twelve thousand and rising. You're needed."

"Oh, God." She tumbled out of bed, the sheets wrapped around her legs. She was still dressed in yesterday's clothes, and the fabric was crumpled and damp with sweat. There were red lines impressed in her skin where the wrinkled clothes had marked them.

There was certainly no time for anything fancy. She tore off the dirty clothes and clambered into new ones, making a claw out of her fingers and pulling them quickly through her hair. John was talking rapidly, reciting statistics, reading information, a constant blur of data that he was pulling from god-knows-where. Abby lost the stream for a moment as she pulled a sweater over her head.

"Sorry, say that again?"

"One of them lives near us," he repeated quickly. "The news interviewed her. Tasteless, shovin' microphones in her face. Single mum, works at Jeri's

Grill, down by Montrose. We're going to talk to her."

"Not at work—"

"She'd be mad to be at work on a day like this. We'll see her at home."

Abby pulled her hair back into a ponytail and nodded, then remembered that he couldn't see her. "All right, if you think we should. I'll be there in ten minutes."

Jimmy caught her in the entrance hall, as she was putting her coat on. "Where are you going?" he asked suspiciously. "Mom, what's going on?"

"I'm going to work." Abby zipped up her jacket and hastily stuffed her cell phone into her pocket. "We've just got some interviews to do. Stay in, all right?"

"Interviews? You're not going to be—Mom, seriously, what's going on? Are you gonna be out all night again?" The boy's eyes were narrowed, and he was standing between Abby and the door.

For just a moment, Abby's thoughts instinctively flicked to the Beretta under her arm. It was only a second, and it was followed hard on its heels by a wave of surprise and guilt, but it was hard to remember at that second that he was her son. He was radiating hostility.

He was almost as tall as she was now, but she could still slip past him. His arm moved, and he seemed almost ready to try and block her path; Abby got her hand on the doorknob and quickly pulled it open.

"Goodbye, Jimmy," she said, and slipped out into the street.

New York was supposed to be the city that never slept, but Abby had always disagreed; no matter what the hour, Chicago was always a madhouse of activity. Until now, that is. It was pushing seven AM—rush hour, when all the urban dwellers jumped into their cars and took off for another day, clogging the streets and sending a steady stream of garbage into the gutters. But now, the city seemed paralyzed.

As Abby drove, she watched the sidewalks. It was too early on a cold, vicious morning, and nobody was out who didn't have to be except the ones who were so well-off that they never had to do anything. A man in a lemon-lime track suit had jammed white earbuds into his ears, securing them in place with a pair of earmuffs; he jogged steadily, ignoring the homeless man who shook a paper cup in his face in the universal language of begging. It made Abby think of her hometown, where the city government didn't care if cups were made of hardier Styrofoam and there were so few panhandlers that they were known by name. Breath clouded in the air, mixing with the steam from the grates and the updrafts of warmth from hot dog and coffee carts.

By the time Abby pulled into the little concrete lot behind the SSR office, the sun was beginning to rise. The sky grew lighter under the urban haze, fading from dirty indigo to pale gray. The few stars that could be seen over the light pollution had gone, absorbed into the general fog. As she got out of the car, the streetlight overhead flickered out.

She walked the path to the door at least twice every day, weekend or weekday. This time, though, she was met at the door. Mary came hurrying out, arms wrapped around herself, wearing a stocking cap over her jumbled mess of red-blonde braids. "Abby!" she shouted, clutching the bizarre paisley shawl draped over her shoulders. "Abby, Sawyer says I can't dress up for the interrogation! C'mon!"

"Mary, what are you—" Abby began. The teenager cut her off with a high-speed stream of complaining. It was unfair, she should get to do it the way she wanted to, it was her talent, she'd been working on her routine for weeks—

Mary didn't seem to want a reply, just a willing ear for her grievances. She followed Abby, who headed straight for the kitchenette. The smell of coffee drew her as strongly as a rope.

John was in the main office, still wearing the clothes he had had on when they had said goodnight the evening before. He had apparently passed the stage where coffee would do any good. There were half a dozen bottles on his desk, all various concoctions promising quick energy and calm focus. Stinker, the guinea pig, was rooting around in a plastic tray that contained the remnants of a Lean Cuisine now several hours old.

"Abby," John said wearily, pouring two yellow liquids into a glass, "tell her she can't play Madame Cleo in front of our fucking witness."

"What do you mean?" Abby asked carefully.

"We're using Mary to do a quick scan of our witness's thoughts, but she—" the man jabbed a finger at Mary, who made a face and straightened her stocking cap "—wants to get herself up in scarves and shite, and tell people she's a fucking professional psychic."

"I am a pro psychic, jerk!"

"*We* are the professionals. *You* are a junior partner on retainer. Whether or not you're psychic, you're still a kid, and you're still our responsibility." John cracked open a pill bottle, tipped two or three into his hand, and swallowed them with a chaser of yellow energy drink. "Abby?"

For a moment, his voice was almost pleading. Mary flopped down on the edge of the desk and pointedly ignored him, clearly out of sorts.

Why are you asking me? Abby wanted to say. She had no idea what John expected her to do. It wasn't as if they had another psychic who could substitute if Mary didn't want to do the job. But however he was going about it, it was the wrong way. She did remember enough about her own teenage willfulness (Jimmy had come from someplace, after all) to know that getting angry wouldn't be the way to go about it.

"Mary, this woman has just lost her kid," she said as reasonably as she could. "I don't think a gypsy fortune-teller is the kind of person she wants to see right now."

Mary looked down. "It's a good disguise."

"It's cruel," Abby said quietly. "Mary, hon, I know you want to help. But I can't imagine this poor woman is going to want to be harassed by some-one calling themselves a psychic. Not today. Can't we be more subtle about it?"

That seemed to do it. The group remained in silence for a while, as John handed Abby a scribbled handful of notes.

Sarah Linds. Age forty-two. One son, Patrick, aged twelve. Her report had come in over the police band at about five-fifteen AM; she had felt a cold wind, as if the door was open, and had gotten up to check. It was then that she had found her son's bed empty. She was badly upset and had already been harassed by the television people, so Mary had bullied her way into being part of the interrogation, insisting that her mind-reading skills might be necessary to get a clear answer. John—never very good at dealing with unhappy witnesses—had agreed. However, they were dis-agreeing on method.

Abby couldn't blame them. The SSR had thought hard before recruiting a psychic; it opened up whole new avenues of questionable ethics.

Sarah Linds lived on a second-floor walkup over a bakery on Gunnison Street. It was a small, pungent building, the sort where you didn't leave a pot of water uncovered overnight because you'd find a drowned cockroach the next morning. Abby had lived in a few of those, during the early days of her marriage.

Abby had swapped her health department badge for a detective's. Dummy had aged it realistically, and her photograph on the badge showed her with a horrible late-90s hairstyle of the kind that most would wish to forget. John had a similar one, but there was no way that they could pass Mary off as anything other than a sketch artist.

There was no way to go up through the bakery. Access to the Linds apartment was via a set of wooden stairs around the side of the building. The stairs creaked ominously as the agents climbed upwards, the wood sagging slightly in the middle of each step where years of passing feet had worn them down. Damp-smelling steam from the dryer leaked out into the cold November air.

John rang the doorbell and then stepped aside. A few hesitant footsteps approached the door. A moment later, it creaked open, and Sarah Linds appeared. She had been pretty in her youth, Abby thought, and was now fading to dignified handsomeness; her dark hair was turning salt-and-pepper, but there were deep bags under her eyes and reddened tear tracks on her face.

"Ms. Linds?" Abby said. She opened her wallet and showed the other woman her ID. "I'm Detective Chambers. We realize this has been hard for you, but we need to ask you just a few more questions."

"Have you found him?" Sarah burst out. Abby cautiously shook her head, and the woman's face crumpled.

"I'm sorry," she said as gently as she could. "We just need a few more details. May we come in?"

Sarah nodded slowly and stood aside, opening the door all the way to admit them. The three agents trooped in.

The apartment was small and old, with close walls painted a dull tan and dark gray carpets designed not to show stains. The door opened into the kitchenette, which was even smaller than what the SSR agents were used to, and could barely hold two people, let alone four. Sarah Linds beckoned them inside, and they followed her single-file down a claustrophobic hallway to the front room.

She sat down on a love seat and blinked hurriedly. Abby felt a lump in her throat at the familiar expression of distress, and for a moment, she had an irrational urge to throw her coworkers out of the tiny apartment.

"Please, sit down," Sarah said in a low voice. Mary, looking uncomfortable, found a perch on a small stool next to the television, and Abby sat down on a folding chair. John remained standing, his hands tucked into his pockets. "What can I do for you?"

John leaned forward. "Ms. Linds, how many people have actually talked to you about what's happening?"

That was a standard opening question. It sounded official, with just a hint of interdepartmental communication issues, and it helped the agents spy out the lay of the land without making any obvious mistakes right away. From Sarah Linds' expression, and the way she was sitting with her shoulders hunched, Abby guessed that she'd been treated like just one more abduction victim in the crowd. The woman's words bore her out.

"Just the 911 people, and those television reporters." She ran a hand through her graying hair, fiddling uselessly with the strands. Her eyes were anywhere but on the agents. "When... when I found the bed empty, I called 911, and they sent a policeman... he took a statement, and he said they'd phone me if they got any information... then the TV people showed up, and while they were talking, the policeman said they'd phone me if they got any information." She glanced up worriedly. "Is that why you're here?"

"Please, Ms. Linds, don't worry," Abby jumped in hurriedly. "We're doing everything we can to find your son." The knife edge of guilt twisted a little harder. She told herself that it was true, after all. "But we're going to need to take a statement. I know it's difficult for you, but if you could please just begin at the beginning...."

Sarah mopped her eyes with the back of her hand, quickly and clumsily. "It was about five AM. I was sleeping, and there was a cold wind in the bedroom—it woke me up. I thought—Pat—Pat had left the window open, like he does sometimes. He always gets too hot in the middle of the night." Her voice cracked a little, but Abby nodded and looked down, giving her a moment to compose herself. After a moment, she picked up the thread of the story again.

"I was checking the windows in the kitchen when I heard whispering. It sounded like someone was in the living room."

"Was it one voice, or more?" John broke in. Sarah Linds gave him a surprised look, but her brow furrowed as she thought.

"Two voices, I think. It sounded like a woman and a man. The man had a sort of gravelly voice; he must have been older. And I think the woman's voice was accented. She sounded like she was Mexican."

The three agents exchanged glances. An accent was a place to start. Unfortunately, there were dozens of monsters that could take the form of, or sound like, old men; it was a popular disguise in the supernatural world. Mary made a note on her pad.

"I checked the living room, but there wasn't anybody there. And it was still so cold. So I thought maybe...." Her voice cracked again. "I went into Pat's room. The window was open. He wasn't there."

Reiterating the story must have been too much for her: she broke down and buried her face in her hands. Her shoulders shook as she cried, the enraged and broken sobbing of a parent whose child had been taken away. Abby stood up quickly, ready to comfort her, but John put a hand on her arm and held her back. She was about to shake loose from him when Mary leapt into the gap, dropped her pad and hurried across to the love seat. The psychic put an arm around Sarah's shoulders and began to rock, crooning wordlessly, one hand resting on the distressed woman's head. Abby saw Mary's eyes flutter closed.

"Take a moment, Ms. Linds," John said abruptly. "We'd like to have a look at the bedroom."

Sarah wordlessly flapped a hand, nodding through her tears. The two adults hurriedly excused themselves from the room, leaving Sarah and Mary sitting together. Sarah's face was slowly sliding into a blank as Mary's eyes drifted close. The psychic was going to work.

"That wasn't fair to her," Abby said in a low voice as the two of them stood in the hallway. "She's lost her son, and Mary's in there reading her mind."

Hands still in his pockets, John refused to meet her eyes. "Her subconscious might've picked up something that her surface brain didn't. It's worth a shot, at any rate."

Abby knew that intellectually, but a visceral part of her still refused to admit it. Losing a child, being harassed by television reporters, and then having her brain picked by a psychic.... Sarah Linds was due a long vacation and a lot of positive karma after today.

The boy's bedroom was the smallest of the five rooms in the apartment. Its door jammed against the end of the bed, forcing the agents to slide through sideways. Here, the claustrophobic atmosphere was even worse: the boy had wallpapered his room with posters and magazine cutouts, leaving wide-eyed anime characters staring down at Abby and John in a thousand different versions of defiance, confusion, and amusement. A Playstation console was wedged between the television and the bed, and a stack of secondhand games had overflowed from the top of the TV and were piling up around the sides of the stand. The footing was uneven; at least a week's worth of dirty jeans and socks were scattered around.

There was no indication that the bedroom was a crime scene. It didn't surprise either of the agents: Chicago had reported dozens of these same abductions, and other cities in the nation were even worse. The real police hadn't had the time for more than a few photographs and some quick witness statements.

The window was still open, and the cold November air swept through the room, making the loose papers rattle and the carelessly draped bedclothes flutter. Abby's eye was drawn to the movement, and a moment later, to the bed itself. The sheets were drawn up.

"John, look at this," she whispered to him, stepping over a discarded backpack. "If he was grabbed, wouldn't the sheets be pulled back?"

"Good point." John fished in his pocket for his cell phone, and took a quick picture of the bed. The sheets were still mostly on the mattress, half covering the skewed pillows, and tightly packed into ridges. John crept over to the edge of the bed, shooting a glance at the window before lying down on the floor next to the mattress. "You like the window open...." He turned over on his side. "You get cold...." He mimed pulling sheets up around his shoulders. "And back to sleep. But you get snatched in the middle of the night. And the abductor stops to put the sheets back, but leaves the window open?"

"You never know what a sick mind obsesses over," Abby pointed out. "Like *Lolita*." The thought was disgusting, and she looked away from the bed, her eyes searching for something else to occupy her mind. The stares of the animated characters locked with hers.

John shook his head and pointed to the bedclothes. "No stains. And if there was some sick piece of shite drooling over this kid, I'd put money on him puttin' the blankets back perfectly neat." He stood up, tucking away the cell phone and putting his hands back in his pockets. "Leaves us with two options: kid knows his attacker and puts the blankets back before going with him, or kid is forcibly abducted and the sick fuck puts the blankets back himself.

"Or...." His eyes went to the center of the bed. The wrinkles were packed tightly around a long, loose pocket, now collapsed, where the boy himself would have lain. "Kid's teleported out, never even wakes up."

That was a distraction, all right. It was easier to think of monsters and teleportation; the idea of someone human committing the kidnapping was somehow even worse than the idea of a supernatural creature doing it. "That, or they were turned intangible," Abby pointed out quickly.

"Loads of possibilities there. Bodysnatchers."

"Poltergeists."

"Any sort of house spirit, really."

"I'll cross-reference Mexican legends with teleportation and intangibility. It's a place to start, anyway."

"Start with the ghosts. Ghosts are classic." John shot a look at the door. "Shall we check in on the mind-reader?"

The living room was empty. They found Mary in the kitchen with Sarah Linds; Mary was boiling water, and the distraught witness had been seated on another folding chair next to the refrigerator. One glance revealed that Mary's face was shockingly white, and she swayed slightly as she poured the water into a mug.

"Reilly? Everything all right in here?" John said briskly. Mary nodded. "Yes, sir."

Sarah glanced up from her spot by the fridge, searching John's and Abby's faces with a cautiously hopeful expression. "Did you find anything?" she asked, almost plaintively.

"I'm afraid we can't discuss evidence collection, ma'am," Abby interjected quickly before John could decide to be "tactful" again. "But there were some useful clues in your son's room. We'll keep you informed." She stepped back, giving Mary room to hand the mug of tea to Sarah. "In the meantime, we'd like to thank you for your statements."

She saw the look rising in the older woman's eyes: thankfulness, she thought. Anybody who was thinking clearly, or had seen any kind of cop show, would know that "useful clues" could be anything and nothing. But Ms. Linds was tired, unhappy, and had lost her son, and it wasn't even ten o'clock in the morning yet. Useful clues sounded hopeful. Abby turned away.

They took a few more token notes and left the house shortly afterwards.

In the car, Abby gripped the steering wheel hard enough to leave ridges on her palms. Some useful information had come out of the interview, as short as it had been, but it was striking uncomfortably close to home. She had the dark feeling that Sarah Linds knew something she didn't.

Chapter Eight

L'uomo Nero had insisted. Likho could prevaricate as much as he liked, but the night's work had left a bad taste in his mouth: they hadn't been able to avoid doing the Duty, this time around. So when L'uomo had refused to take another step unless he went to visit his friend first, Likho hadn't been entirely against it.

Taking physical form was easy, just a matter of putting the right molecules together in the right order—not outside the powers of creatures who sometimes needed to touch their victims. Of course, they wouldn't take on full solidity (walls were just too damn much of a problem, as far as Likho was concerned) but sometimes it wasn't so bad to let themselves have nearly-human bodies. For one thing, the cigars always tasted better.

The sun was just rising when they appeared in a clump of oak trees about thirty yards from the hospital. L'uomo patted his chest vaguely, running the tips of his fingers over the newly solid weave of his coat with a confused look on his face; he didn't manifest as much, these days. Likho smacked his hand away and straightened both of their hats.

"Is strange," L'uomo Nero said, pushing his friend's hand away. "Feel odd. Since plan... since all began...." He wavered a little. His long pale fingers clutched the burlap of his magic bag as if he was afraid it would vanish. "So strange."

Not that Likho would ever say so out loud, but that worried him. His people were Russian and Ukrainian, good solid peasant folk whose imaginations were as down-to-earth and practical as they themselves. When they had created his legend, they had put together just enough embellishments to keep the kids good and terrified, and left it at that. But the Italians... well, they used to be Romans, and that said more than enough to a mind like Likho's. And when they had created his buddy L'uomo Nero, they'd conveniently forgotten to explain *why* it was that his magic bag was just so important. L'uomo didn't hurt kids or eat them—he just took them away in his bag, and when they came back, they were good. And that was bad.

Oh, sure, good kids were great. The whole point of their existence was to smack the brats into order. But nobody knew what that bag was. People *believed* that nobody knew what it was. That made it unknown, and if you don't know what it is, it could be anything.

Now, when trouble was crowding thick around them and the whole Family was choosing up sides, Baba Yaga had made him put a powerful traveling ring into L'uomo's bag. And suddenly L'uomo was clutching and cradling it like it was a... Likho's imagination failed him. Puppy, or something. This didn't bode well, in Likho's opinion. Better let the crazy bastard visit his damn friend, and avoid God only knew what.

Nevertheless, it was strange for them to be walking in the front door, as if they were completely normal. (Or as normal as people who looked like them could be.) There was no point in pushing it, though, and Likho preferred to do things as quietly as possible. Going in through the front door would subject them to the attention of front desk attendants, watching nurses, identity checks, and the restrictions of visiting hours. Likho had seen enough hospitals to know that the easy way in was through the emergency department: even in the early hours, the nurses would be busy and harassed, and it wasn't so hard to slip past.

Once through, a minor reconfiguration of molecules gave both bogeymen the long white coats of doctors. It was a good disguise for hospitals: two distinct and unfamiliar medicos in the emergency bay would attract attention, but those same two in the halls of the hospital would simply be members of another department. It took a while, but he convinced L'uomo Nero to remove his hat. Without it, the taller bogeyman looked somewhat reduced.

The old woman had a room in the long-time resident area of the geriatric ward. L'uomo picked up the pace as he got closer, his black eyes looking bright under the fall of greasy hair. As they drew level with the door, though, Likho shot out a hand and stopped his friend sharply, listening hard as he did so. There were voices in the old woman's room.

It was Mikayla, the little girl. Likho remembered listening to her—*blue shadow,* wasn't it? So she'd been seen by the Mörkö. This time, though, her voice made Likho twitch a little: she was worse this time. Almost ready for the bag.

Giovanna was berating her. For the first time, Likho agreed with the old woman: her tone would brook no disagreement, and the girl was getting more and more ashamed as she talked.

"'Cause how am I supposed to know where you've been? For all I know, you've got germs all over you. I'm not touching anybody until I know they're clean all over."

"That's not true! I'm cleaner than anybody around here!" Mikayla insisted.

"Oh, and how's I supposed to know that?" Giovanna countered. "When I see a girl who goes around shoving other girls down and running off again, I see a girl who's as dirty as they can get. And that's the kind of dirt I don't want anywhere near me."

The two bogeymen peered through the wall, not willing to interrupt just yet. Mikayla was pouting with her lower lip stuck out. "You're just some crazy old woman. What do you know, anyway?"

"I know plenty." Giovanna leaned forward a little. She had an excellently intimidating glare, and it fixed Mikayla fiercely. The girl squirmed a little and stepped back. "I know why that big blue shadow comes to see you, after all."

"Dunno what you're talking about," the girl snapped angrily. "Why don't you leave me alone?"

"Well, you're the one who came over to me. Don't you go telling me to leave you alone when you're the one who started it all, Mickey."

"Don't call me Mickey! And I didn't start anything!"

Giovanna took a slow breath, never letting her eyes leave Mikayla's face. "Oh, I know plenty about you now, little Mickey. I think your mamma knew you were rude to other girls, and knew you like to blame other little girls for what you did. And I think she told you the big blue man was gonna get you for being such a rude and disobedient child, didn't she?"

A look of shock spread across Mikayla's face, but she tried almost instantly to replace it with an expression of princessly disdain. "You're making it up," she said airily. "And I don't have to listen to some crazy lady who sees stuff that isn't there."

"It'll come back, you know."

Now there was no disguising the child's surprise. "What?" she said. "What do you mean?"

"Pushing down that girl today? Running off and insulting an old lady?" Giovanna said pointedly. "Just 'cause I told it off, doesn't mean it won't come back. You've been just as bad, and it'll come right back and get you soon enough."

"I don't want it to come back!" the girl whispered. Her voice was low, and her eyes were wide and panicky. "It's really weird! Can't you get rid of it?"

"Now why would I do that? The way I see it, that spirit's just doing what it was told to do."

"But if you see it" Mikayla said hurriedly, "tell it to leave me alone!"

Giovanna shook her head. "I won't. Not unless you show me some backbone and stop shoving those kids all over the place."

The girl bit her lip, thinking hard. She glanced around and looked worried; footsteps were approaching. Likho hurriedly looked to L'uomo and started spouting random medical jargon in a low voice. The nurse looked at the two of them, but didn't seem concerned. Instead, she stuck her head through the doorway.

"Mikayla, what are you doing in here? Mrs. Shepherd needs to rest. Come on, let's go."

"I'm sorry," the girl said. It was not directed at the nurse. Giovanna nodded, accepting the girl's apology.

"That's not good enough. You go and be nice, and I'll come and see you sometime," Giovanna replied gravely. "Maybe tonight. Is it a bargain? You going to be good?"

"Okay, okay!" Mikayla nodded fiercely as the nurse took her by the hand. Moments later, the girl was gone, and Giovanna sank back onto her pillows and closed her eyes.

It only took a few moments for the nurse and the girl to disappear around the corner. Instantly, L'uomo Nero's coat turned black again, and he rushed into the room. Giovanna jumped a little as L'uomo tumbled onto his knees next to her. His face was buried in a fold of the bedclothes.

"Well, look at you," she said, patting the stringy hair with one thin hand. "It's so good to see you, black man. And you've brought a friend."

Now the woman glanced up, eyeing Likho. He stayed in the doorway, hands in his pockets, feeling uncomfortable as her gaze raked over him.

"Yep, I'm here too," he commented a little weakly. Giovanna shrugged.

"Black man always comes. You, though, I don't figure you'd visit just to be friendly. Why'd you come, then? Something gone wrong?"

Likho was about to reply, but to his surprise, L'uomo Nero cut him off. "Too much is happening," the bogeyman said as he raised his head and blinked. Giovanna smiled a little at him, and he smiled back, looking more alive than Likho had seen him in years. "El Cucuy has moved his plans forward. He will make the mountains walk, even if they are tired. Too much ambition, not enough time. He makes wounds in the world."

"Then it is the bogeymen that's been stealing those children?" Giovanna asked. L'uomo Nero nodded, and the woman shook her head regretfully. "I'd thought so. That's bad, black man. I'd hoped you'd been staying out of it."

"The whole thing's rotten through and through," Likho interjected. There was a plastic-covered chair next to the nightstand, and he pulled it forward, settling into it with a sigh and undoing his ragged scarf. "If you want my opinion, El Cucuy's as crazy as a rat in a tin can. Paranoia can't even begin to describe it."

"Is that so?" Giovanna leaned forward and rested her chin in her hand. A quick breeze flicked through the open inch of the window, making her gray hair dance and tangle. "That's no good. I don't suppose there's any way to get rid of him? You people hold elections?"

Likho laughed sardonically. "Are you kidding? El Cucuy's in power now, and he's not going to give it up."

"Well, how'd he get in power?"

"Long story."

Giovanna's eyes narrowed almost imperceptibly. "Well, go on and tell it then. It's daylight, isn't it?"

"I don't know," Likho mused. "You could be a little more polite to me...."

There was a rustle of cloth as L'uomo Nero raised his head. "Go, tell it, Likho," he said. "She has not heard, and it will mean much in the hearing. She is not in the sky, now."

Likho glanced at Giovanna, who shrugged just a little. In the sky? he mouthed to her, but only got another shrug.

"Fine," he said shortly. "El Cucuy—he's our second leader. The first of us, the one who started the Family, was the embodiment of the unknown. His current name was Bavbav. Something happened to him; nobody knows what, but you can bet your ass that it was El Cucuy's fault." Giovanna began a question, but Likho carried on regardless. "Just vanished, in a puff of smoke. Literally. And oh, by the way, yes, it was a dark and stormy night. How about that?"

"And then the cuckoo-boy took power? How?" Giovanna asked.

Now Likho was the one who shrugged. "The usual way. He curried favor with all of Bavbav's lieutenants for years before anything happened; I guess they thought he would be a good puppet leader. Then, when he had power, he demoted or destroyed all of them and put his own thugs in the lead. Now his second-in-command is a freak named Sacauntos, who kills kids for their fat. Nice fella."

"Disgusting," Giovanna said flatly. "I never liked the rest of you bogeys; none of them had any kind of heart." She sat up a little straighter and rearranged the collar of her bathrobe. "But I would have thought they'd do things a little differently, being immortal—"

"Never going to happen. We're made of imagination and superstition, but the ingredients are all human." Likho dug in his pocket for a cigarillo, but changed his mind after a moment's search. He might look fairly innocuous, and humans had to concentrate a little to see him in any case, but the smell of smoke would definitely attract untoward attention. "Didn't affect me much, but it played havoc with old L'uomo. He always got along well with Bavbav."

"Likho says I went mad, but I know that madmen think they are sane. I know I am not sane, so I must be mad." L'uomo Nero's head was still raised, but he hadn't yet climbed to his feet. Instead, he remained kneeling, like an acolyte of some withered old priestess. "But madmen think they are sane, and I know I am not."

"He'll run in circles with that one all day, if you let him." Likho shot a glance at his friend. As he watched, L'uomo's attention began to drift vaguely, his eyes tracking to the open window and the sun far above them. If you stared at it long enough, you could see it move with the Earth's rotation. Likho had done that once, but he found it got boring pretty fast unless you spent time counting solar flares. "Mad as a March Hatter."

Giovanna shot him a stern look. "Watch your mouth. It's none of your business."

"Maybe it's not, but have you ever seen my business? Utter disaster. Floating hands and batty grandmothers everywhere you look." Likho shuddered. "I'll take this one, thanks."

"Now's not the time. You keep on talking."

"What? I told you everything."

"There has to be more."

"More for what?"

"More that we can use to stop the cuckoo-boy, of course."

Likho sat back, surprised, and automatically reached for a cigarillo— smoke be damned. "Say that again, would you?"

"You heard me." Giovanna put her hands on her knees and straightened her shoulders, the very picture of determined alertness. The image was counteracted by the fleece bathrobe. "We can't let this happen, can we?"

"You want to stop El Cucuy, huh?" Likho chuckled to himself as he lit the cigarillo with a slightly shaking hand. "Why am I not surprised? I told L'uomo Nero that you'd put strange ideas into his head. Didn't I tell you, L'uomo? L'uomo?"

"There is a cloud, and it looks like it wants to eat."

"Ah, he gets what I mean."

Giovanna tsked. "Just carry on talking. Even if we haven't got a prayer of doing something, I can't usually get two sensible words together out of the black man about what you people do. I want to know everything, mind you."

"Hey. Turnabout is fair play." Likho carefully fanned the smoke towards the window, past the ears of an oblivious L'uomo Nero. He'd answered the old woman's questions long enough, and now he wanted to satiate his own curiosity. "Tell us about the 'blue man.'"

He had the satisfaction of seeing Giovanna look surprised. She mouthed silently for a moment before she gathered her wits, and a knowing expression appeared on her face. "Shouldn't be put out, I suppose," she said, straightening herself a little. "It's simple enough. That girl's been seeing a big blue thing—Mörkö, its name is."

"And you went to see it too?" The cigar wasn't calming him, and Likho carefully stubbed it out on the knee of his trousers. The burn flickered and faded away seconds later. "Adding it to your collection?"

"Hardly. That girl's no great prize, I think, and I reckoned the blue man's been called up to frighten her. Not take her away, but scare her into being good." Giovanna snorted. "Doesn't seem to be working, either."

That explained a lot. Why had El Cucuy wanted to talk to the Mörkö? Maybe he knew that Big Blue had a believer—rare enough, these days, now that the Mörkö had become a children's book character.

So why had they been talking about L'uomo Nero's bag?

There was too much going on, and it was beginning to annoy the Likho. The country that had birthed him was a stark and practical one, and much as he hated it, there were more immediate concerns than trying to wrap his head around whatever crazy schemes El Cucuy was hatching next.

"Now go on," Giovanna said sharply. "What about Bavbav?"

"Well, on your own head be it." Likho inhaled, then blew out a stream of smoke rings. "What do you want to know, then?"

"Start at the beginning. Who was loyal to the one that was gotten rid of?"

Likho took a moment to puzzle out this sentence. "Loyal to Bavbav? Well, most of the less powerful bag men, for a start; the hairy men could push us around whenever they wanted if Bavbav wasn't there to stop them." Another few smoke rings followed their predecessors as he thought. "Then there's the undefined—the ones that don't really fit into any category. The Böögg—piece of work, he is—and that blue-light special Mörkö... and Hastrman, of course."

The woman opened her mouth to say something, but at that moment, they were surprised by a sharp beeping noise. Giovanna groaned a little and pulled back the sleeve of her bathrobe with trembling fingers, squinting at her wristwatch. The little digital display was beeping loudly.

"Best be going, black men. Almost my medicine time, and I don't want you two being found here. Plenty of awkward questions." She rearranged her sleeve and gently patted L'uomo Nero on the head again. "You be on your way."

Likho didn't need to be told twice. L'uomo Nero clutched the bedclothes and seemed reluctant to budge, but Likho gave him a sharp swat on the head and the taller bogeyman finally stood up. As the sharp tapping of the oncoming nurse's footsteps grew louder, the pair of them turned on the spot and faded away.

As they moved, Likho felt something brush against the edge of his senses. Something was coming. It felt strange—intrusive—and it set his teeth on edge. Angrily, Likho pushed it to the back of his mind and forced himself onward. Work to do.

Chapter Nine

As the day wore on, the sky clouded over. Gusts of freezing wind lashed the city, sending garbage flying and pedestrians scuttling for cover. Newspapers were pulled out of careless hands, and baseball caps went bowling down the streets, chased by their irritated owners. A few flakes of snow drifted down, only to evaporate when they touched the pavement.

In the SSR office, the mood was as gray as the sky outside. The agents had ordered Chinese food around noon and buried themselves in piles of paper, hunting for the elusive connection between a Mexican accent and possible child abduction. But as time passed and they failed to find anything, they were forced to widen the net. By three o'clock, Abby was halfway down the list of "accents that might sound Mexican to an American," and still hadn't turned up anything. Her moo goo gai pan still sat on her desk, half-finished and cold.

A doppelganger is frightened by something, and prepares to go into hibernation. Granted, doppelgangers are creatures of extraordinary psychic sensitivity, and only react in such a panicky manner to what they consider inhospitable changes in the environment. (At least, that's what Marotte theorized.) The only possible thing that could have scared it so much was the next clue—the vanishing children. Thousands of children disappear all across the nation, accompanied by cold winds and whispering voices. But what had done the stealing, that a psychic creature could sense?

And then there were the other clues. An accent which may or may not have been heard correctly. The possibility that teleportation may have been involved. There was nothing to connect all, or even any, of the clues to each other, and it was giving Abby a headache.

In her time with the SSR, Abby had seen a lot. Besides the wardrobe in Seattle, there had been doppelganger problems in downstate Illinois and Texas that she'd witnessed personally, and there were files full of information from the previous members of the group. Doppelgangers are secretive by nature. Doppelgangers play possum when threatened, pretending to be inanimate objects or dead bodies and relying on their next feeding cycle to restore any injured mass. Doppelgangers never, ever transform back in front of sentient beings.

So what had happened? If they didn't find out what was going on, even more people could be in danger—and God only knew what had happened to the ones that had already been taken. Beneath her oversized sweater, the old silver crucifix was warm against her skin.

Thank heavens that coffee was the one item they never skimped on. Who could expect them to deal with their typical workday on generic brand?

Her desk was slippery under her fingers. Intermittent culinary accidents in the tiny kitchenette, not to mention a couple of invading vampires that had once forced them to make a Molotov cocktail with the cooking oil— a Gorbachev wine cooler, John had christened it—meant that nothing in the so-called headquarters looked third or even fourth-hand. The place was a dump.

Yes, there were definite perks to the job. But sometimes... sometimes you saw things like the news in the paper, and you wondered why God made humans so easy to kill.

Her cell phone vibrated again, but she didn't bother checking it. Jimmy had been texting her all morning, demanding to know what was going on; as time passed and the texts became increasingly more angry, Abby had stopped answering. She thought of Sarah Linds, and caught herself wondering if she would cry like that if her son disappeared. It was followed a second later by a stab of guilt, and Abby groaned and put her head down on the desk. Things were going nowhere fast.

Their only solid clue was sitting on the desk in front of her. A scrap of pinstriped fabric, now reduced to blurred mush, swirled in formaldehyde; the rest of the creature was downstairs in the salt tubs.

"Surprise, surprise," said a voice above her. Dark gray mist swirled down from where it had collected near the ceiling, and yellow eyes blinked at her. "The dead doppelganger has nothing to say. I'm shocked. Will you get rid of that thing now?"

Abby shook her head. "No, Harvey. I think we're missing something." She turned the jar this way and that, watching the scrap twist slightly in the clear fluid. "It's been eating at me, ever since we got the data back. This creature knew *something,* Harvey. Something scared it badly enough for it to spike a living person, right in the middle of a crowded store. That's... that's just out of character. Doppelgangers hate people. They wouldn't even go into public places if they didn't need to eat."

Harvey's smoky form flowed upwards, hitting the ceiling and dispersing into a hovering cloud. "Consider my amusement expressed," it said in a bored tone. "You know, you guys really have it easy. Do you know what it's like, trying to do expressions without a face?"

"No changing the subject." The scrap moved again as John picked up the jar and squinted at it. He winced a little, turning his head from side to side as if he couldn't see very well. Abby recognized the symptoms of a bad headache, and wondered why he didn't just take an aspirin. Maybe he was trying to be stoic again.

"Right, replay time," John said briskly. "We get to the store. Abby spots the jacket being brought to the counter, engages the lady. Lady's clearly under the influence of the doppelganger, refuses to give it up. Doppel starts feeding right in front of her. Abby, you grab and throw it. I shoot, doppelganger falls apart." He scratched his scalp with dark, blunted fingernails. "It started to eat, in a public place."

"Building up enough energy for its hibernation was more important than staying hidden," Abby said. She shook her head at the thought. "That should never happen."

John set the jar back on the table with a heavy clunk. "Don't suppose anybody did anything that might've alarmed it?"

"Don't look at me. You know what I was doing."

"Harvey?"

"Because yes, I have time to take from erasing all those onlookers' memories to mess with the doppelganger and increase my own workload. Brilliant, Holmes."

"Right." John dug his knuckles into his forehead. His headache must be increasing, Abby thought. She knew that she wasn't feeling so well herself.

That was no surprise, though. Kidnapped children, long hours—none of them felt very good right then.

"What else was going on right then?" John continued. "Doppels are psychic; it could've sensed something. Abby, can you pull the files?"

Abby nodded and moved towards the filing cabinet. She pulled open the drawer labeled T-S and rifled through a stack of disorderly papers. "All right," she said aloud, "what has Keith been doing with the filing? 'Tarantulas, cannibalistic'—that ought to be in the *Unnatural Natural* file, people. T, T, here we go—timekeeping." She carefully extracted a smeared sheaf of photocopies. "On Friday, we had five check-ins besides us. Marotte and Dummy worked the radios for a while, but Mal signed out around four PM and went out to Western Springs. His pen went through the paper, so it must be zombies or something."

Hearing his name, Marotte put his head around the lintel. "It was," he said flatly. "Forgive my lack of accuracy on the time sheet; I was exhausted."

"Yeah, leaning against walls and selling people bridges really takes it out of you."

"Harvey, shut it." John flicked the edge of the jar, producing a pinging noise that made the cloud of genie roil and pull back. "Thanks, Mal." Marotte nodded and retreated, back to whatever mysterious business he had. "Who else?"

"Dummy and Mary were in, and they don't seem to have gone anywhere.

Mary's not doing fieldwork anyway. Adam was in, of course." Abby shuffled the papers again. "He's been signing in at seven A.M. every day for... eight days. Including this morning. Has anybody seen him yet today?"

Everybody paused at that, listening hard. After a moment, John moved over to the sink, knelt down, opened the cabinet and pressed his ear to the pipe. His brow wrinkled.

"He's downstairs," he reported, standing up. "Probably having nightmares again. I can hear his equipment at work."

"Did you hide the alcohol?"

"Done and done."

Abby nodded and returned to the sheet. "Okay... our last Friday check-in was Keith. At least, it's Keith's handwriting. He signed himself in as The Shadow." Sighing, she put down the papers and ran a hand through her matted hair. "Nothing. Nothing alarming. Undead in Western Springs wouldn't scare a doppelganger in Chicago, that's for sure. If somebody spooked that thing, it wasn't one of us."

"Another mystery to solve, then." John reached around Abby and snagged a cold egg roll from the plastic box at her elbow. "Hope you don't mind me saying this, Abby, but you look like the walking dead. How much sleep did you get last night?"

"Enough," Abby said, a little more sharply than she felt.

"Translation: barely any," Harvey chimed in. Abby groaned and half-heartedly tossed a rubber can cozy at the hovering mist, forcing it to disperse.

John shook his head. *"Don't talk any more, Harv. Until you start needing to sleep, you're not allowed to yap at the rest of us about it."* He put down the egg roll and took Abby by the arm. "Look here. I can't tell you to go home, because that would put you off the clock and none of us can afford it. But how about we adjourn to the pub for a while? Nobody's gonna be helpful if we're all out of sorts. We all need forty CCs of caffeine and a sandwich, *stat.*"

In spite of herself, Abby grinned wearily. "Have you been watching *Grey's Anatomy*, John?"

"Well, we don't get *Casualty* on this side of the pond, so I'll take what I can get." John turned around in his chair and raised his voice. "Oi! Everybody already having a bad day?"

The SSR offices didn't need an intercom; sound carried across the cheap linoleum like nobody's business. There was a chorus of assent from the nearby rooms.

"Right! Phones off the hook. We're out of here."

At MacLeod's Irish Pub, there were three slot machines, a couple of pinball shooters, and a wobbly old pool table with half the felt worn off. Someone had stuck a telephone directory under the broken leg of the table, but because it was the Chicago metropolitan listings, the other three legs were now too short. Nobody really cared; pool was not as important as booze. The long bar was meticulously polished, and each tap gleamed.

On that gray, blustery November afternoon, MacLeod's was about half full. Several regulars were lining the bar, glasses in hand, each with one eye on the football game and the other on nothing in particular. A few college-age kids were playing pinball, leaning over the machine, jostling and shoving each other, and whooping at each point scored. Alcohol had obviously been consumed in copious amounts. Three more of their number were seated at a corner booth, talking collegiate sports over the head of one bored dark-haired girl who was trying to study.

The SSR personnel descended on the small bar like a swarm of depressed locusts. John and Abby immediately monopolized the pool table, while Marotte (accompanied by Harvey, who was doing an excellent job of blending into the haze of cigarette smoke, city regulations be damned) caught the attention of the bartender and issued a very specific and complicated drinks order. Adam had been forcibly pulled out of the cellar and was, with effort, sitting quietly at a table and watching the other SSR agents through watering eyes. Mary ordered for both her and Dummy, and moved the albino man over to a table in the corner where they could talk without people realizing that Dummy's lips didn't move.

At the pool table, Abby carefully lifted away the black plastic rack, leaving a perfect triangle of colored spheres in the exact center of the table. "Call it," she said as she set the rack down on the edge of the table.

"Stripes," John replied instantly.

"You sure?" Abby asked. Solids were John's lucky side.

"Decided it was time for a change, that's all." John switched his cue back from left to right, flexing his fingers on the smudged wood as he did so. "'S your turn to break."

Abby nodded and splayed her fingers on the edge of the table, tucking the cue between them with practiced ease. There was a rattle and a click as the cue ball raced across the balding green felt, sending the other colored balls sliding.

Forty minutes passed in companionable peace. John, believing firmly in the hair of the dog that had bit him, took a whiskey sour and drank with every appearance of enjoyment. Abby had ordered a sandwich and some lemonade—she had to drive home that evening, and one drink could easily turn into five if she wasn't careful. Both of them had retired from the pool table after two games in quick succession. Marotte had some sort of complicated cocktail in one hand, and was now deep in conversation with the dark-haired studying girl, who apparently liked older men a good deal and was impressed by his verbose conversation. Adam had surrendered to the power of gin miniatures.

Harvey drifted in a cloud over to John and Abby, who were deep in conversation about different types of fouls. He hovered above their heads, looking innocuous. "I don't mean to interrupt the petting party," he whispered sardonically, "but it's about time for the news. Do we want to hang around for this, or are we going to waste the whole day?"

John reluctantly nodded. "'Spose we should at least pretend to get some work done," he admitted. Abby took a sip of her drink and gave a look of agreement. "Hey, Paul! Change to CNN, would you?"

The bartender had seen too much of the SSR personnel in his six months at MacLeod's, and the whole SSR knew that. It didn't help that Abby and John had a mysterious gray cloud over their heads. Hurriedly, Abby waved away a tendril of Harvey's mist and pretended to cough. Apparently satisfied, the bartender reached up to the television and changed the channel.

A familiar flood of colorful graphics filled the screen as the CNN logo zoomed in on itself. Two reporters appeared; one the requisite male in a dark blue suit, the other the requisite female in a bright red suit.

"Today in Washington DC," the woman began, "thousands gathered on the Mall to mourn the loss of the nation's future. More than twelve thousand children ages four to twelve have been recorded missing. All fifty states have reported abductions, with no end yet in sight."

"I changed my mind," Abby said quickly to John. "Go back to the college football."

John shook his head silently, eyes fixed on the screen. Graphs appeared onscreen, numbering the abductions from each state. The camera switched to footage from the gathering on the Mall.

The camera panned over a group of protesters, who were apparently demanding that the government do something about the missing children. Some carried signs linking the kidnappings to Israel, Palestine, Korea, or Karl Rove. Further on in the crowd, several prayer circles had been formed; people stood in groups, shielding lit candles from the wind and bowing their heads to the words of their rabbi, priest, or imam. Some milled dispiritedly between the groups, heading nowhere, lost looks on their faces.

The facts and figures piled up. None of the football-watchers asked to change the channel back; silence fell in MacLeod's as everybody watched the bad news unfold. When the station broke for a weather report, several people let out breaths they had been holding.

"Christ fuck-all," said a schnapps-swilling heavyset man to the room at large. "What the hell is going on?"

"Who knows?" one of the college students commented gloomily. He took a swig of Guinness, winced a little as some of it went up his nose, coughed, and slouched over the bar. "I think it's the next step in warfare. Atomic warfare, chemical warfare, psychological warfare."

"Oh, fuck, I hope not," another of the students muttered. "Mom keeps calling five times a day to make sure I haven't disappeared."

"Who the hell steals *kids?*" the heavyset man demanded. "It's gotta be terrorists or something. Al-Qaeda. Recruiting them to be suicide bombers."

A bearded man in a suit accepted another beer from the bartender. "I pulled my kids out of school," he said darkly. "Whatever's going on, it's not going to happen to them."

"That's no guarantee," Heavyset insisted. "These people on the news— their kids were taken right outta their beds."

"Got 'em under lock and key," said Beard. "We moved their beds into the basement and installed deadbolts and burglar alarms. It's helped us sleep better at night, that's for sure."

Above their heads, Harvey chuckled darkly. "Let's see if that stops 'em," he whispered in Abby's ear. Her heart sank a little at the thought.

Chapter Ten

As night came on once more, the bogeymen fanned out across the country. There was work to do. Sacauntos, La Llorona, and the rest made tracks for the places their leader had designated. They could as good as taste the fear that was building, and already it was making them stronger. And somewhere, L'uomo Nero trod along behind the Likho, head hanging low. Even he was working.

They followed the winding pathways that weren't marked on any human map, and soon found themselves standing in yet another town on yet another street. There was a burning sensation in the air, and the yellowy taste of *bad child*.

Things were done quietly, and with little fuss. There were two children in the house. One was quarrelsome, and the other—a little older—had been stealing money from his mother's purse for well over a month. L'uomo Nero stepped through the wall and confronted the quarrelsome one, who had only one moment to scream for her mother before into the bag she went. Likho whispered horrors in the ear of the little thief, and when the boy leapt from bed like the hounds of Hell were after him, he saw only the darkness as the bag went over his head.

Any bogeyman's bag could hold as much as belief dictated, and people were always ready to believe anything extraordinary enough. In the special places between the seconds where all the myths walked, the Family fanned out like an army, stealing through walls and locks that were to them as insubstantial as shadows. Dogs barked at their passing, cats hissed and rats hid beneath the sewer grates.

Animals could sense the passage of the bogeymen; because they held no beliefs, they saw only a hole in the world where none should be, and reacted with fear and aggression. Many households had a pet of some sort, and a hundred such died that night. Likho breathed on them, and dogs lay down to die in their kennels. The cats yowled as their hearts burst.

That part of the task was never enjoyable. Animals couldn't harm bogeymen, and Likho considered them inoffensively pointless. Killing them was just a waste of valuable effort. But after what Likho thought of as *the royal fuck-all of the last time*, he knew they couldn't very well afford to disobey El Cucuy's orders again. The pets had to go.

L'uomo Nero worked in silence. As the time flowed by, passing the bogeymen without harming them, he seemed to grow more and more distant. Through the wall, boy in bag, back through the wall. The dogs and cats simply collapsed when he walked past them. He said nothing, and made no sound when he moved.

Nobody needed to tell Likho that this wasn't good.

Sometimes, there was a person who could see them as well. One, a four-teen-year-old boy, would tell his parents that two men with bags stole his brothers and sisters. He'd be telling the truth, and no one would believe him. Perhaps he'd grow up embittered and fearful, starting at shadows and believing that anything might be lurking in the corners to come for him as well. And maybe, he would believe so fervently that a new bogeyman would be born.

The only thing they had to fear was fear itself.

Likho was having a hard time concentrating. There was still that same edge to the world—the feeling that something wasn't right. That something was *watching* them. It was getting harder to ignore, and it was pissing Likho off.

Scarcely a tick of the clock had passed when L'uomo Nero and Likho finished their alloted areas. Outside of time, the world around them took on an unreal hue: blackness was deeper, paleness was paler, as if it was a scene painted by an artist with nothing but a bottle of India ink. Every physical object was thin and slightly transparent, every living creature had a faint blue glow that drew the eye, and the people drifted like spectres through the unreal world.

Likho could hop from one reality to the other as easily as a human could change a pair of socks. But as he shouldered his bag and moved out through the wall of the latest house, he thought he could feel a strange tang in the currents around him.

He shook it off. Spending too much time out of time. When this was over, he was going to find the dirtiest, scruffiest, cheapest bar in Texas, order everything on the menu, pour it all into a big jug and challenge the local bikers to a drinking contest. Then he would step just far enough into reality to get an alcohol buzz, maybe fight the bikers when they lost, and end the evening with a 3 AM stopoff in Cuba for more cigarillos. Or whatever time it was in Cuba when it was 3 AM in Texas. He really hated time zones.

Perhaps, then, a sympathetic onlooker would forgive Likho for not paying more attention to that tinge that he had sensed.

There was a whirl of motion, and a cold wind sent both of the bogeymen stumbling backwards. L'uomo Nero's hat was ripped from his head, and the long dusty coat flapped open, exposing the clawed feet that were clutching the floorboards. Likho's scarf slapped him in the face as the bag caught the wind and pulled itself out of his grasp.

"What the—" Likho began, but was cut off by a mouthful of scarf. Cursing, he ripped the fabric out of his mouth and flung it away. "L'uomo, did you—"

"Is not good, angriness!" L'uomo Nero shouted. Likho chanced a look over his shoulder as he pulled his own coat closer against the cold wind. The Italian bogey was flattened against the wall, arms on the boards instead of going through them. His eyes were rolled up in his head, only the whites showing. His fingers dug into the wood of the wall, and the wall began to bleed.

"This is evil shit!" Likho shouted. "Run, L'uomo!"

A fresh blast of wind struck him, tearing through his clothing as if it weren't even there. A few strands of his hair waved stiffly in the corner of his vision, and he could see that they were coated with shimmering crystals of frost. His own hands had turned white, and a crack broke the surface of the skin.

"You have got to be kidding," he muttered.

Like a bad dream, the row of figures emerged from nothingness. A wraith was at their head, a wavering figure of mist that looked almost comical next to the looming, hairy wall that was El Ogro. There was La Llorona, skull grinning, eponymous white shroud trailing behind her as she stepped into reality and let the wind touch her. There was Dunganga, yet another looming rag-draped figure, eight feet tall if he was an inch and carrying a woven straw basket instead of a bag. Behind them was a dim horned shape that might have been the German Nachtkrabb, and the drooling monstrosity that was Lulu-khorkhore, "the one who eats everything up." On either side, still hidden in the shadows, the watchful eyes of Le Croque-Mitaine and Le Pére Fouettard stared at the paralyzed two. One was a bed-hider, and the other a bag man. Neither were friendly.

Likho gulped. All the heavy hitters of the Family were there, and their combined power far outweighed that of Likho and L'uomo Nero. His friend hadn't even moved; he remained slumped against the wall.

"Llorona," Likho called out. His voice was weak, and cracked on the first syllables. "What's going on?"

Her face was not capable of doing anything other than grinning, but the tone of her voice made it clear she meant it now. "You are under arrest," she said coolly, not trying to disguise the glee. "For crimes of humanity, and for conspiring against the Family. You will be taken to the Home to await trial and sentencing."

"*Conspiring?*" Likho yelped. "What do you mean?"

La Llorona made a pretense of examining her fingernails. "Smoking, breathing, eating, and taking the advice of a rotten old human woman over that of our leader." Sparks of cold blue light burned in the empty sockets. "For our plan to succeed, Likho, the humans must fear us as almost gods. Taking a body and playing about with the mortals is counterproductive, and therefore treason."

"Yeah," El Ogro clarified. He turned his head ever so slightly, keeping one eye on Likho. Dunganga and Le Pére Fouettard were binding L'uomo, who was barely making any kind of struggle as the hairy giant held his arms and the spiderlike human wrapped them with cord. His eyes were blank and lifeless. Then El Ogro snorted and barked a command in his guttural voice, and one of the hairy men snatched away L'uomo Nero's bag, tearing it in half in his great greasy paws.

That seemed to do it. L'uomo Nero came to life with a roar, and the two captors were shaken off as if they were rag dolls. He caught up the fluttering shreds of burlap, his thin fingers knitting them together with an instantaneous flash of light. Two more bogeymen dived for him and managed to tackle him to the ground, but the newly restored bag leapt on them with a life of its own. Likho blinked; when he opened his eyes again, the feet of the second enforcer was disappearing into the mouth of the bag.

La Llorona rounded on L'uomo Nero, letting out a long hiss of malice. She swiped at him with one clawlike hand, and a gap opened in the air. A clumsy shape tumbled out of nothingness and struck L'uomo Nero in the chest. He gasped and toppled backwards.

Likho forced his eyes back into the unreal dimension, and the darkness was stripped away. L'uomo was on the ground, clutching at the floorboards with his hands and writhing in pain. Laying on his chest was an old, battered stuffed cat, wearing a childish blue-and-pink ribbon.

Hairy men are traditionally lurkers: they're the ones who hide under children's beds and grab at their ankles, or wait in their closet as an ominous shadow that may or may not simply be a pile of clothes. Bag men are different, relying on stealth and cunning to snatch their prey at any opportunity. The child hiding in bed will not stop the bag men from snatching him. Therefore, when children fear hairy men, they will huddle under their blankets to keep them out. When they fear bag men, they set their favorite toys to guard them.

And because those children believe strongly in those measures, the bogeyman—a creature defined by human belief—finds himself at the mercy of two very unusual weapons. Simple childish objects are anathema to them, eating away at their existence like acid.

Likho gaped. "You—" he began, flabbergasted, even as Le Croque-Mitaine seized his arms. L'uomo Nero uttered a rasping cough and slashed at the thing, sending it flying; there was a sudden hiss and his hand recoiled, burned to the bone and charred black. Half his abdomen was eaten away, only a roiling mass of scorched ectoplasm remaining.

"You—you—" Likho mouthed. His sheer outraged horror choked his own words. "You fuckers!? He finally burst out. "You complete, utter... what the fuck is wrong with you?"

Use of children's belongings against bogeymen was the pinnacle of dirty, underhanded fighting. It was like burning down a house with the family still inside, selling your mother to pay your bill at the crackhouse, murdering a blind cripple—anything that was so low-down cowardly and disgusting that you could hardly bear to stomach thinking about it. Every member of the Family knew about the tactic, but none of them had ever disgraced themselves by actually *using* it.

"Less of the potty-mouth, human," La Llorona said mockingly. "I'm sure I have a teddy bear for you somewhere."

Likho's mouth opened and closed, but no sound came out. Horror warred with disgust in his expression. Le Croque-Mitaine kept a firm hold on his arms, but Likho didn't seem to be trying to escape; his eyes were fixed on the groaning form of L'uomo Nero, who was being hauled to his feet by two more shadowy bogeymen. His bag was clutched between the burned fingers like a lifeline, no bulge betraying the presence of the pair it had swallowed up.

"Get the bag," La Llorona ordered. El Ogro bobbed his head and strode forward, reaching out a pair of greasy paws for the rough burlap.

Then L'uomo's arm seemed to spasm. He flung the bag upwards; El Ogro snatched at it, but it twisted in midair and evaded the hairy grip. There was a ripple in the air, and the bag imploded on itself, sucking into some hidden drain of reality.

El Ogro cursed in a guttural tone and sank his paw into the ripple, but withdrew it an instant later with a roar. The tips of his claws were sheared off.

For a moment, there was no movement in the bare room. Then La Llorona clicked her bony jaws, and Likho felt his arms jerked roughly by Le Croque-Mitaine. L'uomo Nero, now unconscious, was hoisted into the air in Dunganga's grip; Likho was dragged after, guarded before and behind by the shadows.

Chapter Eleven

"We got something!" John shouted, bursting into the office. Abby, who had been leaning back in her chair, jumped in surprise and nearly tipped backwards onto the floor, only steadying herself with a grab at the edge of the desk.

"Good grief, John. Have a little mercy on those of us who aren't psychic." She leaned forward and massaged her forehead. "What have we got?"

John's hand was trembling as he shoved the piece of paper in front of her. Abby recognized Dummy's neat, spiky handwriting, but the paper was moving too quickly for her to read it. "Slow down," she griped.

"Sorry." John yanked the paper back. "Dummy was monitoring the police bands while Marotte's out. There's been some sort of a ruckus at St. Luke's—someone or something crashed through the wall of a little girl's room. On the fourth floor."

"What?" Abby said, snatching the paper back. She scanned it quickly, biting her dry lip as she absorbed the information. When she looked up, her brown eyes were gleaming. "This is it, John. This could be the break we've been looking for!"

"Why do you think I was so bleedin' excited?" Her friend grinned, ruffling her hair. Abby yelped and swatted his hand away, but she was in too good a mood to start a fight now.

"How should we go in?" she asked. "Dummy just cut some federal IDs. We can be FBI, CIA. Heck, we can be the Department of Alcohol, Tobacco, and Firearms if we want...."

John laughed. "You did theatre in university, didn't you?"

"Not with a seven-year-old son, I didn't," she said. "Wrangling him was probably more trouble than any theatre could be."

"Don't let Marotte hear you saying that, he might feel the need to defend his honor." John shot a look at the list over Abby's shoulder. "I think straight coppers would be wise here. No point in overdoing it and tipping our hand."

Lurching a little, the Toyota Camry pulled up in front of the hospital. Abby was driving; she didn't trust anybody else with her car, especially on the way to an investigation, when more than a few SSR members were likely to have a few shots of Dutch courage aboard. John and Harvey were riding shotgun, the Englishman transporting the pickle bottle in a duffel bag which he slung over his shoulder. Occasional muffled curses could be heard from within the bag, which John responded to by whacking the whole bundle against the dashboard.

The last member of the group was technically not a field agent, given that he hadn't finished high school yet. His name was Keith, and he was an experienced photographer whose eerily enthusiastic interest in the supernatural made him the perfect person to work after school at the SSR. Like the others, he was dressed in an anonymous dark suit and a heavy coat (the lip and eyebrow piercings had been removed for the occasion), but he had refused to pack his Nikon with the rest of the equipment in the trunk, so the heavy camera case was busily wrinkling his suit pants from its place in his lap.

The SSR agents liked Keith, to a degree. Unfortunately, he tended to look on the SSR's work almost as a gigantic performance arranged for his benefit, and he had an undue fascination with the "thrills" of monster hunting which left bad blood between him and the older, more sour members. Abby thought he could be a nuisance, but she knew John considered the boy only one degree short of an obstacle in their way.

The car stopped, rocking. John fished in the glove compartment and produced a box of latex surgical gloves. Every team member with hands donned a pair: there was no point in leaving extraneous fingerprints at a crime scene. At least one of them was already in the police database.

As soon as they were ready, the three of them clambered out. Abby, in her role as the officious police detective, briskly tucked the keys into her pocket and flipped open the leatherette wallet to check that her fake badge was secure. "John, give Keith the bottle," she said in a low voice. "You're supposed to be a Detective-Inspector, remember? He's Forensics."

"Catch, Gothika," John said casually, chucking him the bottle with Harvey in it. The genie muttered something indignantly as Keith fielded him clumsily. Abby felt a prickle of disapproval at the sulky look on the younger man's face. John had many lovely qualities—or a few of them anyway, on a good day—but tolerance was not one of them. Keith seemed to see SSR life as an adventure, and John thought he was a pretentious idiot. There was more to it (there always was, with this crew) but John didn't want to hear it. His way of thinking was hard to change.

She wondered if he really thought he had kept those little pills secret from the rest of them.

Getting into the hospital was a lot simpler than any of them had anticipated. John simply flashed his ID card in his best CSI manner, and the hassled-looking nurse at reception pointed the way to the childrens' ward. She didn't even glance at the dull golden badge, one of Dummy's best pieces. It had obviously been a long day already, and it was barely ten AM.

They certainly weren't the only official types hanging about. Yellow crime scene tape was stretched across the hallway outside Room 202, and a pair of forensics personnel were just emerging with their arms full of trays—hair and fiber samples, it seemed. A heavyset man in a plasticized windbreaker, who wore his department ID like a commendation from the Inquisition, was interrogating a harassed-looking young intern in green scrubs. Half a dozen policemen were scattered up and down the corridor, keeping watch.

As a rule, the group had more difficulty getting around the genuine law enforcement personnel. No matter how much they cleaned up, there was always something that a real policeman could spot a mile away. The best way through those situations was a straight bluff: badges in hand, they walked briskly down the hall, clearly on an errand of one form or another. The badges and IDs were good enough to pass a casual inspection.

Only once did they get stopped. One of the men from the nearest precinct wouldn't take no for an answer, and informed the agents that he had never heard of any of them. John, totally blasé under his annoyed expression, stopped and gave the suspicious cop hell for getting in their way. Two sentences into the reaming-out, a wisp of Harvey had flitted into the cop's ear. The djinn gave his brain a quick treatment of what he had once christened "the scrub," and the small party was free to move on.

Room 202 itself was a disaster area. Something huge, eight feet or more, had struck the interior wall with serious force. It had gone crashing right through and left half a shattered windowpane behind. The off-white walls were pocked with pinpoint holes where flying bits of glass had lodged, and a thin layer of reddish brick dust covered everything in the room, including the investigators. A stiff, cold wind was blowing in through the gaping hole, and they could see the bustling street far below. It reminded them just how high up they really were: not a comfortable feeling. The wind whipped their hair, dragged at their clothes with icy fingers, and hurried the dust up into clouds that made them cough. Broken glass was littered across the floor, and the bed had been stripped bare of sheets.

The genuine forensic personnel had already finished taking their photographs and samples, and a janitor was sweeping up the shards of glass. Abby bent down and retrieved one that a sweep of the push broom had sent skittering past her shoe.

"Well?" John murmured, tucking away his badge and eyeing the shard in Abby's hand. Instead of granules, the glass appeared to be made up of tiny cubes.

"Safety glass," the blonde confirmed as she turned the glass this way and that, examining it in the light. "This is the stuff they put in gorilla exhibits. No human smashed it. No human *could.*"

"Gorilla glass in a hospital?"

"You did hire me for office work," Abby reminded him a little resentful-
ly. She pointed to the remains of the window; the frame of the casement
was solid metal, now warped and broken. One edge had been twisted
backwards and out, a half-screw of steel stretched like taffy. "This used to
be an adult psych ward," she continued, tapping the shard with one gloved
fingertip "There would be metal mesh screens, to separate the casement
from the actual patients, but when it came to glass tougher was better. Violent patients sometimes cause damage."

"Good to know," John said. Abby shrugged a shoulder noncommittally.

The group fanned out around the room, and Keith unshipped his camera and took three quick shots of the room. The janitor barely blinked at
this latest intrusion. He did furrow his brows a little as a few strange wisps
of smoke drifted past his line of sight, but he shook his head and they
seemed to vanish. John watched as Harvey gave the man's brain a quick
examination.

"I think the mon—uh, perpetrator—came from the inside," Keith said as
he fiddled with the camera lens. "There's all kinds of cracks and stuff on
the inside of the wall, nothing on the outside. Plus, I think this-" he pointed "—is a claw mark."

The mark in question was an inch wide and seven inches long, according to John's tape measure. There were two more just like it, all sliced into
the brick.

"Something smashed out, but didn't smash in." John moistened his lips,
staring at the three tracks. "Harvey, do a bit of asking about. Who saw
what, where, and when? And find a nurse who can give us this girl's medical chart."

"Jawöhl, mein Führer," the genie said. It soared in a cloud past the now-
oblivious janitor and out into the hall, ignoring Abby's murmur of "attitude readjustment."

She stared at the ground, nudging the shards of glass with the toe of her
tennis shoe. She tried to think back to all the crime-scene TV shows. There
wasn't much glass on the floor, because most of it had gone out the window when it shattered. That supported the idea that the whatever-it-was
had come from inside the hospital.

She joined Keith, taking photographs and looking over the edge of the
hole for evidence. There didn't seem to be very much in the way of hair
and fiber evidence, and there were no droplets of mysterious liquids or
strange marks on the ground. Likewise, burn marks—something that
tended to crop up a lot with grandstanding supernatural creatures—were
nowhere in evidence.

Harvey streamed back into the room a few moments later, and settled over the three investigators in a cloud. Information (and complaining) poured into their heads, taken from the thoughts of all the police and authorities on the scene. Facts, figures, and testimony were all there.

"Harvey," John said during the pause, "have we ever told you how much we love you?"

"I'd snort sarcastically if I could," the reply came back. "Anything else I can do for Your Lordship, or should I just go back into my bottle until you need another deus ex machina?"

"He's so cute when he's angry," John whispered to Abby, who laughed a little. Harvey added something very rude to the new information and soared up towards the ceiling, where he collected in the vaporous clouds of a first-degree sulk.

John, meanwhile, had pulled out his notepad and was rapidly scribbling. Having a great deal of data channeled directly into your head was a useful option, but it needed to be quickly transcribed or a lot of it would be lost.

"We need to talk to the old lady," he said as he underlined a couple of items.

"And the girl," Abby reminded him.

"What? Why?"

"'Out of the mouths of babes and infants....'"

"What, there's a baby now?"

Giovanna DiFrancesca was staying in another part of the hospital, under long-term observation. It only took a few questions for the SSR to be pointed in her direction. They had found her sitting up in bed, apparently having an argument with a nurse. When they knocked on her door, she had her arms crossed, and was vocally refusing to take part in a therapeutic scrapbooking session. The nurse seemed almost relieved to let them question her.

It didn't take long for the conversation to take a very odd turn.

John carefully took down the old woman's information. *Giovanna DiFrancesca. Age: 87. Resident of the geriatric ward.* He clicked the end of the mechanical pencil and focused on the next sentence.

Apparently convinced that she is friends with the bogeyman.

"Yes, he's a good boy. Comes to see me regularly. It was one of the other ones, a big blue one, that broke that wall." Giovanna eyed John owlishly through her heavy glasses. "You going to do something about that? That Mörkö's no good to have around. He's not the sort of bogey you can look south of, since he's nowhere near as civilized as the others. Are you going to do something?"

"Sorry, ma'am," John said. "We can't put out an APB on a nightmare. You saw nobody else? No suspicious figures or activity?"

"I told you what did it, haven't I?" Giovanna said sharply. "Now what are you going to do? I'm sure you think I'm just some crazy old woman, but believe me, mister, I wouldn't be telling you this unless I didn't have a choice! That blue man was thinking of killing—not just scaring."

"Thank you, ma'am," John said briskly. "That seems to be all." He turned away from her and closed his notebook, shaking his head a little. Giovanna squawked indignantly.

"Watch it, you! You can't be treating me like this—"

"*Thank you,* ma'am. Marquise, take care of her, would you?"

"What?" The old lady shifted, trying to nail Abby with an intimidating gaze. "Am I in the twentieth century? Are you taking orders from the limey? Are we back in the British Occupation now?"

"We're in the twenty-first century, ma'am. Please excuse us. We have work to do." Abby suppressed a grimace. Long-time residents of the hospital, especially the elderly, didn't get much excitement. Mrs. Shepherd might not have had a visitor in days, maybe even weeks or months. If they'd been legitimate investigators, she would have had no trouble telling the inquisitive old woman that they couldn't listen to her any longer, but now she felt that she was satisfying her own curiosity at the expense of someone else.

"Listen to me!" Giovanna protested, flapping at Abby with one spidery hand. "You sit a minute and listen to me! I saw him, and nothin' you say is going to make it different. And if don't do something about it there'll be more holes in that there wall, and in your heads too! It was a big blue creature, made of light, and he was under orders!"

Abby turned to the nurse. "We're finished here," she said firmly. "I don't think we'll be needing to question Mrs. Shepherd any more." The nurse flushed pink at her charge's behavior.

"I'm sorry, officer. She's an old woman."

"We understand. Please keep an eye on her."

"You're not real!" the old woman shouted. "You're not real, and neither is that man of yours!"

Abby froze. "What?"

"I've seen too many black men to get written off like that!" Giovanna insisted. "I saw him, and I know what he is! Just like the one that broke that wall of yours! Just like all the ones you've seen too!"

"Mrs. Shepherd, please!" the nurse scolded. "The investigators are busy. Why don't you give another try at that scrapbook?"

"They're not real investigators," Giovanna snapped irritably. "And scrapbooks are for boring people who've got nothing to say and too many damn stickers to say it with."

"You know the rules, Mrs. Shepherd. Use of confrontational language isn't allowed in the ward."

Fifteen minutes of searching interrogation and a few scrubs by Harvey later, Abby had a copy of Giovanna Shepherd's medical records and life history in hand. Another twenty after that, as the SSR people piled into the Toyota and headed back to the office, the blonde was paging through the illicitly-acquired biography and getting more and more unnerved with every paragraph.

"What's so engrossing, Abby?" John asked, braking hard. The car skidded a little, making Keith drop the pickle bottle and curse as it landed on his foot, but Abby didn't even look up from her pages. "Still reading about the local madwoman?"

"It's just...." Abby tried to put her thoughts into words but stopped, frustrated. "She... well, she seemed pretty lucid for an insane person. And her history's pretty unusual. Says here that she was kidnapped when she was nine years old, and gone for a month. Her younger sister's children were the ones who had her put in the hospital in the first place; she broke both her hips falling down stairs, 'following the bogeyman.'"

"Well, maybe she got Stockholm Syndrome or something," Keith volunteered from the backseat. "If they never caught the guy, she could really believe that the monster in her closet did it."

John pulled the car left, narrowly missing a minivan, whose driver honked angrily. "You think she knows something, Abby?"

"I have a hunch, yes."

"Well, it's a start. Let's get back to the office and have a look at that 'Mörkö' thing."

"She was right."

John looked up from his computer, which was displaying a long list of abduction statistics. All of the agents had changed out of their official disguises as soon as they had returned from the hospital, and John's oversized white t-shirt and jeans were already rumpled and sweat-stained in the hot, airless office. When he glanced up, Abby was standing there, holding a copy of *Legendary Creatures from Around the World*—looking worn and red-eyed, but a little triumphant.

"Was she now?" John asked, taking the book. "And what was that one thing?"

"There's a Mörkö, all right," Abby said. Stretching a little, she settled onto the edge of his desk, and pointed to the book. She had it open at "Mischief and Guardian Spirits."

"Let me guess. A bogeyman?"

She nodded. "Finnish legend. Used by parents to frighten their children into being good."

"A bogeyman, then."

"That's the shape of it."

"Which means we may have a real lead." John paged quickly through the book. "Says here that the Mörkö was originally a dark, fearsome monster, but appeared in a series of childrens' books and television specials as a creature made of light, usually round and blue." There was an illustration, and he snorted. "Looks like that Grimace thing. Not very fearsome."

"I think I owe her an apology," Abby said. "Maybe. She could still be insane."

John looked up over the edge of the huge volume. "If she is, it'd be a bloody good break for us."

"Maybe," Abby repeated. She edged sideways and leaned cautiously against the desk, settling her rump on the edge next to the computer. Biting her lip, she glanced over at John, who was concentrating on a description of the creature in question. The leaky red marker was lying on the desk, staining a patch of wood, and his left elbow was propped almost on top of it; the smooth, ghostly pale skin was turning a lurid pink. Engrossed in the text, he didn't seem to notice.

"What do you think?" she asked after a moment of silence.

"I think we have a real lead," John repeated.

"But...."

"Yah?"

"It's nothing."

"Go on, say it...."

"The bogeyman?"

John's brow furrowed. "It's as good a start as any, innit?"

"Yes, but—it's the bogeyman." Abby ran her knuckles over the edge of the desk, trying to focus her thoughts. "I accept the existence of all the other things—creatures outside our realm of experience, vampires and so on. But isn't the bogeyman an abstract concept? It's not a person, it's an idea."

"Weren't you the one looking up those perversions of the natural order? The good Rev. Ev. always said," and John's voice took on a nasal quality, "'The line between real life and fiction is only as thin as you draw it.'"

"I always wondered about that. Does it actually mean anything?"

"Haven't got the foggiest," her friend said, leaning back and crossing his arms. A faint stain of pink appeared on the hem of his t-shirt. "But something's certainly not kosher in the state of Denmark, that's for certain. Reality disruptions, kids going missing, a giant hole in a wall and a creature made of blue light; bogeymen certainly fit the profile."

Abby bit down hard on her lip, and winced a little as a piece of dry skin tore away. She wiped her mouth quickly to cover it up, faking nonchalance. "Bogeymen or bogeyman? One blue creature doesn't make a massive conspiracy...."

"But even if the old bird's completely 'round the twist, it's a place to start looking," John reminded her. "Mad people are fantastic for sensing the supernatural, 'cause their minds aren't all there to begin with. And of course, they're willing to entertain ideas most people won't. Why do you think Adam works here?"

"Because we needed somebody who could fix your pistol, that's why." Abby stretched again and yawned. "But no offense to him, he's terrible in the field. You'll be leading the team, right?"

John shrugged. "I thought Dummy or Marotte."

"You just said—" she began. "What about the... what you said?"

The man's back stiffened. "What about it?"

"You said insane... could... well, you're always clutching things when you think no one's looking, and there's those little bottles of pills when you get...." Abby trailed off when she saw John's expression. It was cold and drawn, and his knuckles were white where he gripped the covers of the book. Abby knew she had just walked straight into forbidden conversational territory, and it was marked Here There Be Dragons.

"Never mind," she said hastily. "I mean, I didn't find out about this group until I got attacked by a ghoul, right? I think being entirely sane isn't even a good idea around here. Right?"

The joke fell flat with a nearly audible thump. There was a sharp, frozen moment of silence, Abby perched awkwardly on the edge of the desk, John slid so far forward in his chair that he was almost sitting on his shoulders, her gaze deliberately aimed at the floor and his at something nobody else could see. They stayed that way for a few eternal ticks of clock—posed like a Renaissance sculpture by an artist with a love of dysfunction. But then John let out a slow breath, and his grip on the book eased. Whatever went through him had passed now.

"We'd best talk to her, at any rate," he said calmly. Abby glanced up, sensing that the discussion was closed.

John closed the oversized book and set it down next to the keyboard, knocking a few errant soda cans out of the way with a quick sweep of a hand. "First thing tomorrow," he continued, "I'll call her up and see if we can bring her over here. I don't fancy talking ghosts and goblins with all those doctors and nurses around; we might get sectioned ourselves."

"That's a lovely thought," Abby commented. "Is that it for today, then?"

"That's it. You can go home if you like."

Abby nodded and stood up, dusting off the seat of her trousers. "Sounds nice. I haven't had a full eight hours in God knows how long. Good night, John."

"Night, Abby."

The office had fallen back into silence as she left. Abby closed the front door behind her and leaned back against the concrete wall of the building. Her breath clouded in the chilly air.

He'd wanted to attack her. He'd known it, she knew it, and he knew she knew it.

By all rights, they shouldn't have been in this situation. John, Abby, Marotte—none of them were the ideal. For the millionth time, Abby wondered what her life would have been like if none of this had happened. She might still be married, although that was hardly certain. But surely, there was somebody out there who could do the job better than they could.

Nobody actively chose to join the SSR. They were just the ones who found out about what was really going on: Abby had been attacked, John recruited after his workplace had been raided by a vampire, Marotte... well, he didn't like to talk about what had happened to him. But they'd been in the wrong place at the wrong time, and before they knew it, they'd learned that there were more things in the world than just humans.

Not all of them had chosen to join the SSR, though. There were a few out there. It didn't happen often, but sometimes there would be a witness, or someone who helped them out on one job and then didn't want any part of it. Most would just go back to their lives. Some went a little crazy, and tried to spread the word on the Internet or on the street corner; nobody paid attention to them. And on rare occasions, Harvey would have to clean someone's memory.

Abby had read fantasy novels, a few years ago. She liked them. Vampires had seemed like such a romantic concept, and she had loved the story of a dark and handsome creature of the night finding love with a human girl. In her adolescent dreams, she had deemed the material world mundane, and fervently hoped that the kind of creatures she'd read about really existed. Then she'd been attacked on her way home from the grocery store, and it turned out that there *was* more to the world. Unfortunately, it wanted to kill her. That part wasn't so romantic. Abby didn't read much any more.

John was levelheaded, and she knew he realized that his urges and twitches were a bad thing. Instead of a moral compass, he had a moral yo-yo, swinging violently between senseless anger and silent guilt. And she liked him, despite his problems. He might not have been an entirely sane man, but this muckup was only putting his already bad nerves on edge, and she hated to see him suffer.

Unfortunately, it didn't look like this would be a very easy operation for him. What was a bogeyman, anyway? The books had some information on creatures of belief, but not much. They were manifestations of thoughts, primal fears and frenzied dreams made real by the massed power of human thought. The theory was simple: if enough people believed in something hard enough, the world would readjust itself to suit that perception. Belief creatures were strictly conceptual. They'd never met one in real life.

If this old woman really was on to something, Abby knew that they would be facing something virtually unkillable: a wild imagination.

Chapter Twelve

As creatures separate from the demands of reality, the members of the Family had no fixed abodes. Each century's meeting was simply held in a place that was dark and fairly private. But nevertheless, each continent had its place where the bogeymen liked to gather, for one reason or another. This place was called the continent's Home, but Likho liked to call it the closet.

When L'uomo Nero returned to consciousness, some time after dusk, he could sense the presence of dozens of Family—close by, quite close by, but neither cloaking their presence nor slipping in between the layers of the world to keep themselves hidden. He was in a Home, it seemed. Someone, somewhere in the distance, was playing a Turkish pop song.

He rolled over but didn't groan. There was pain and the sensation of unraveling, splaying across his body like the veins in a human's skin, all different colors and intensities. Some of the pain, where he had been struck, was hot and icy blue and shimmering. He thought vaguely that it might smell like spearmint and cinnamon. Two flavors that humans never put together; why was that? They had tongues that were capable of tasting so much, but they never did anything adventurous with their sensations.

Except for spices. He *liked* spices. Odd that he'd never thought of that before.

As he lay, he looked around, reaching out for the sensations that would come. He was in a Home, that was for certain, and a deep one: the air around him was cold and stale. A basement. High above him, through stone and concrete, he could hear the air whispering through a huge hall, but he and Likho were lying in a ten-foot square of light that came from a single fluorescent tube set into the ceiling. Out in the darkness were— he recoiled. There was something he couldn't see, and it hurt.

He could sense the presence of many other members of the Family, all in various states of physical reality. El Cucuy was there, not far away. The traitor.

Curious, L'uomo Nero touched his own face and tugged at his hair. His whole form felt strange, as if he had just awoken from a very long, heavy sleep. Everything seemed sharper and warmer.

Likho was there as well, sprawled next to him on the floor. L'uomo Nero gently prodded him with one finger, and the Russian awoke with a snort and a muffled curse. His lank hair was matted with dirt and sweat, and his shapeless felt hat was long gone.

"Likho?" L'uomo Nero whispered. "Is bad?"

"Is bad," the other hissed back. "Is so very god-damned bad that it is a shame I lost my smokes, because a tobacco fix is something you get to rely on when you're a blasphemous body-taking humanized bogeyman!"

L'uomo Nero blinked. "What?"

"Oh, never mind," Likho said disgustedly. He pulled himself into a sitting position and glared at the wall as if he could bore through the cement with the force of his eyeballs. "Your brain is so scrambled that I couldn't get through to you with both hands and a jackhammer."

"You're insulting me, Likho." The other bogeyman's snarl had flared in the air, red and yellow and green, and left a coppery tinge that L'uomo Nero could finally understand. Insult. Likho was always insulting him, even though he meant it well. Telling the Family that he was out of his mind.

Well, he always had been, hadn't he? Talking about walking mountains and all the rest. So what had changed now?

Likho's sloping brow furrowed as he stared. "L'uomo, are you all right?"

"Never having been better," the taller bogeyman said. "The brain is fixing."

"L'uomo—"

"Is silent, Likho. All silent." L'uomo Nero's face was dark. "No bag, no mind breaking another. The child won't have it. It ran away, all by itself."

"What the—"

"The bag the child wants." He rose to his feet, unfolding himself. The square of light was bordered by a rim of thin shadow, and there was the glimmer of something white beyond that border. L'uomo held out a hand, but recoiled as his fingers passed out of the light. Whatever it was out there was holding them in place. "Is... all old. Very old. We cannot break through."

"We're in the North American Home," Likho said finally. He was looking sideways at his friend, clearly worried and uncomfortable. "You took a pretty nasty knock, L'uomo. Llorona and her cronies had kids' toys."

The Black Man curled his lip disgustedly. "The history and the belief makes us weak," he murmured. "There are children's things here, and above, age all around. Likho, we are well trapped."

"That's pretty much the understatement of the millennium... I can't get any particulars, but I think there's thousands of years of solid reality all around us. We're not going anywhere."

"We can't visit Giovanna today," L'uomo said quietly. Likho threw up his hands in exasperation and looked ready to spit out something nasty, but thought better of it when he saw the look on L'uomo's face. The other bogeyman was clearly unhappy—anger and sadness were both etched on his features, and more clearly expressed than Likho had seen in two hundred years.

L'uomo Nero moved to the center of the square of light and stood still, looking up at the skylight far above them. His thoughts were whirling cleanly and quickly, with more ease than he could remembering feeling before.

They were trapped, that was for certain. Everything that had protected him and defined his form was gone: the hat and coat had been taken, and his gloves were shredded. His bag had escaped without him. Those were the things the legend talked about, and without them, there was little to define him. His form wavered in the beam of light..

The Family had wanted the bag for something. The dead child's men had tried to tear it, but simply touching it had repaired it. The bag didn't want to be taken by El Cucuy, and the bag didn't want to be torn, so it wouldn't be. It was that simple.

The black apparition felt lost. What was he under the coat or without the bag? He didn't know. For the first time in ages, nobody was giving him orders. His bag was still out there, he knew he had mended it, but it wasn't coming back to him. It was as if something was pulling on it, dragging back. Clear thought felt slick and alien. Where was the bag? Why wasn't it telling him what to do?

He tried hard to focus his thoughts, remembering rusty old habits. Who else would tell him what to do? Likho. Likho always knew. But Likho was angry with him, and it would be the child El Cucuy's fault. Would El Cucuy tell him what to do? Yes, he would, but El Cucuy told him the bad things to do. Very bad. Kidnap the children, kill them don't teach them. The black man could hear the prayers in his mind: *oh god, please don't let it get me, please make it go away.* He always listened to them when they said that, but El Cucuy didn't. To do that would make him no better than the dead child.

But what was the black man without orders? It had been a long time, and L'uomo Nero struggled with the question. He felt lost. Would someone tell him what to do? Everything was suddenly far more complicated than before; it was as if he had spent years staring at everything through a pair of binoculars, and was only seeing the whole picture for the first time.

The girl. The girl the woman the married woman the old woman. She told him what to do. There was good there. She would help him. Egypt, pyramids, Egypt, walking on the sand. Hold on to Egypt, L'uomo Nero, black man. Now ask her what to do.

They've taken most of your powers, true. But you left your face in her little room in Naples seventy years ago, and your face is your power, L'uomo Nero, black man. She has it, not them.

Likho watched his friend with concern. L'uomo's face was distant, and without the coat and the hat, his form seemed insubstantial. Nothing like this had ever happened before, to Likho's knowledge; the Family did not turn against each other. They had only discovered the power of children's toys and blankets after several painful episodes, back when their legends had first taken shape. Bavbav's disappearance had been attributed to simple forgetfulness on the part of the humans. After all, a story which had begun in the Neolithic era could hardly be expected to last forever, or so El Cucuy had said. And Likho, with his stoically practical mindset, had overlooked the obvious and gotten on with his work as he always had.

He supposed he should have kept a closer eye on El Cucuy. True, the boy's plan was working, but it was Likho's experience that a number of positive qualities would always be balanced by an equal or greater number of negative ones.

After all, history was full of monsters. He'd met a lot of them. Many were considered geniuses, great intellects of the day who seemed to have a pocketful of answers for all the ills that were plaguing this sorry world. Often, they were highly principled men, living a life of stringent asceticism or holding themselves to a moral code intended to let them pursue higher things.

Unfortunately, there really was a fine line between genius and insanity. And as soon as they put one toe over the line, they got the urge to dance. Back and forth, back and forth; it became a game, like kids playing Capture the Flag and daring the other team to catch them in the enemy territory. Raising yourself high above all vices, Likho thought, simply made you more susceptible when you found the one you really liked.

His musings were interrupted by a crash. L'uomo Nero straightened up, and for a moment, his form solidified as his attention was concentrated. "What is?" he whispered to Likho.

"Dunno for sure," Likho murmured, "but I think we're bein' summoned to court."

Figures emerged out of the shadows. Every one was a hairy man, and they carried the tiny plastic objects with great ceremony. Each toy dragon or floppy doll was borne like a religious artifact. As the first of them stepped into the square of light, L'uomo Nero recoiled violently. Likho shuddered as he felt his form begin to waver.

"The Lord Cucuy calls for you," rumbled Sacauntos. When he moved, the smell of lard rippled from his greasy hair, and Likho twitched.

"Nice of him," Likho said as calmly as he could. He couldn't stand Sacauntos even at the best of times: the hairy man with the long knife was one of those legends that never should have been told. Now, with the toys uncomfortably close, he thought he was going to be sick. "What's he want with us?"

"Summoned to answer charges of treason and human sympathizing."
Sacauntos moved towards them, and both bogeymen stepped back quickly. "Move."

Likho glanced around. In the glowing light of the hairy men's eyes, he
could see a little further into the dimness beyond. There was a set of white
stairs, painted to look like marble, about fifteen yards beyond their square
of light.

"Lead on?" he suggested. Sacauntos took another step forward, and
Likho's eyes burned as the toy dragon moved closer.

"You go. We follow."

As the bogeymen climbed upwards, the air flow increased. The floor
beneath turned from concrete to pressed granite, and then to marble. They
felt, rather than saw, long corridors and vast rooms. The passing light of
the eyes gleamed off glass cases and polished brass plates. A museum.
Inwardly, Likho groaned.

Bogeymen had an ambiguous relationship with reality. Some things
lived longer than others, and some things weren't alive at all. Creatures
like the Family only existed only thanks to a cosmic error—the result of
human perception influencing quantum mechanics, if he wanted to be
technical. But the bogeymen were thin and insubstantial next to the solid
reality of an ancient cathedral or a Neolithic cave drawing. He had to
admire the genius of it: this was a Home established as a prison, not a place
of rest. Even a bogeyman at full power would have to leave the building in
order to vanish. Dually restrained by the children's toys and the age all
around, L'uomo and Likho weren't going anywhere.

And age wasn't the only thing surrounding them. The Home was alive
with rage—an almost solid sheen of fury, utterly implacable and streaming outwards from a single mind. It was like being punched in the face,
and the whole group of bogeymen flinched as they drew closer to its
source.

At last, they came to the largest hall of all. The dim light flickered over
the roots of marble pillars and shone on the faces of cracked statues, who
stood frozen in attitudes of prayer or penitence. Figures were on every
side, and here and there could be seen the gleam of the carved folds in a
flower girl's cloak, or the supplicant forms of Adam and Eve. The hairy
men trembled; Likho fell to his knees, groaning in pain despite himself,
and L'uomo Nero wavered like a reed caught in a storm.

El Cucuy had become the new leader for a reason: he was the most powerful of the Family. With the fervent belief of his country's children, the
dead boy flourished. In the dark and age-choked hall, he stood out as solid
and real, while the lesser bogeymen shuddered. But it was his rage made

him almost incandescent. The red eyes gleamed.

"You—" he began. A second later, he was interrupted by El Ogro, who came shuffling nervously up to him, paws folded.

"What?" he snapped irritably. "What is it?"

El Ogro looked nervous. "News," he said. "Three hundred fifty-seven taken. Three brothers not return."

"Put the children in storage. Which three?" El Cucuy's voice virtually demanded good news. El Ogro's expression grew more and more uncomfortable with every word.

"Le Croque-Mitaine, Chownki-Daar, and Mörkö." The hairy man hesitated. "No... Mörkö back. Trouble."

"Wasn't the Mörkö supposed to snatch one of his believers?"

"Yes, lord."

"What happened?" The dead child frowned. His rage, but for the moment, simmered quietly beneath the surface as his attention was directed elsewhere. "If he wants to rebuild his belief base, a solitary appearance won't do him any good. I want everybody available at this stage."

Likho knew that El Ogro was only one step upwards from a dumb beast, but to his credit, the hairy man did his best. "Old woman," El Ogro said hesitantly. "She repel. She say, tell about Bavbav."

Oh, hell. The old bitch must've questioned them after she couldn't get the answers from the Mörkö. The thought just had time to occur to Likho when El Cucuy shrieked—the high shrill yell of an utterly infuriated little boy.

"Bavbav! Bavbav! Bavbav!" he snarled, and the name was like an obscene mantra. "Whining over dead leaders! Worshipping grandmothers! Eating, drinking, swearing, smoking, *taking human names!* That's enough!"

It might have been a child throwing a tantrum. But he was the strongest among them, and when he howled, the bogeymen wavered and drew back.

With effort, El Cucuy restrained himself. Likho didn't have to guess why. Fury was an emotion, after all, and emotions were supposed to be a human trait.

"Don't you understand?" he said, a little more quietly. "That isn't what we are. Those are petty things. Useless. We have a purpose, a duty, an ultimate reason for being." The red eyes turned to Likho, but they were inexorably drawn to L'uomo Nero. Likho's eyes narrowed. He was targeting L'uomo Nero, on a charge of *humanity?* That didn't wash.

El Cucuy was quickly getting himself under control. He folded his arms and gently rose upwards, settling himself in the air five feet above the ground. No human chair for the leader of the Family.

"Brothers," he said clearly, staring down at the upturned faces. "Skull, bear-face, horse-face, ritual mask, toothless old man, ogre, beautiful woman, hairy monster—all of their gazes were fixed on him. "We come together tonight to deal with a very unfortunate problem. Two of our number—two bag men, old and powerful and respected by us all—have been guilty of betrayal. I bring them here before you, to stand trial for their offenses."

A murmur ran through the hall. Even Talasam, who Likho had thought could be counted on as an ally, gave the Mörkö a tap on the arm and muttered darkly into the blue creature's ear. The bag men's expressions ranged from fear to horror and disgust; the hairy men stood stoic and silent.

"What have they done?" a bag man finally said from the back of the crowd.

"They have become human," El Cucuy said shortly. "They have conspired with a human grandmother to make difficulties for us, and as a result, have nearly compromised our plan. Chicago and Raleigh were theirs, but apparently they knew better than I." The last few words were cold and angry, and the bogeymen looked at one another uneasily.

Sacauntos growled low in his throat. El Cucuy stepped forward. The ranks of gathered bogeymen parted, letting the childlike figure move towards the captives in hand. Likho glared up at the floating figure, but El Cucuy gazed right back at him, clearly unperturbed.

"Everybody knows," he said softly. "Everybody knows that the Family will only survive if we work together. Apart from his brothers, what does a bogeyman become? Rumor, then rural superstition. Before long, his name is forgotten, and he's nothing but a starving shadow. But what comes after that?"

El Cucuy let out a venomous snarl. Likho felt himself flinch while L'uomo Nero stared at the ground, still unmoving. "Death," El Cucuy said. The gathered bogeyman hunched their shoulders and muttered darkly to each other. "Do you think we're unable to die? We can! And death is far worse for one who could live forever, brothers. We're not like the living creatures who can't help but be swept up by time.

"But you—but these two, these who called themselves monsters like us—have done the unthinkable. They have put us all in jeopardy by choosing to act like humans. If humans do not believe us to be more than human...."

"Oh, come on," Likho said mock-cheerfully. "Cut the monologuing, El Cucuy, you're not a damn supervillain. Shouldn't you be saying 'they didn't listen to me, and got their asses handed to them for it—'"

El Cucuy snatched a stuffed bear from one of the guards and hurled it at Likho. There was a hiss and a smell of burning flesh, and the toy dropped to the floor, leaving behind a face half burned off. Likho growled, both in pain and in exasperation, shaking his head and sending bits of crisped skin and hair flying. The other bogeymen leapt back.

"Violenhh never hholveh hanything," Likho muttered. His lips were already growing back, but most of his nose had been eaten away by contact with the soft fabric. "Dirhty trick, bohh."

"You've gone native too!" El Cucuy would have been bright red in anger, if he had had blood beneath his skin or a face human enough to show recognizable emotions. "Listen to you, Likho. Even Hombre del Saco speaks no English. Man-who-hides-in-the-ground has not changed since the dawn of time, and the Llorona makes no concessions to what the humans call beauty. But you? You smoke, you scowl, you speak like an old west American cowboy with a grudge—do you call that kind of thing being true to the roots of the Family? You and L'uomo Nero both, you've become too *human*." He glowered, grinding his teeth a little. "And if you allow one of us to be thought of as human, then that puts every single one of us in danger. Even if you had not decided to disobey me, we could never have allowed you back into the shadows."

The burned and tattered skin on Likho's face was quickly regenerating as the bogeyman refocused his concentration on his form. "You're full of shit, El Cucuy," he mumbled through reforming lips. "Paranoia's a human thing."

"As are insults. Brothers!" El Cucuy shouted, rounding on the crowd. "What is a suitable punishment for those who have put our entire existence in grave danger?"

"And how do they do so, pray tell?" Another voice drifted out of the crowd. The bag men shuffled and murmured as a tall, skeletal figure with a shock of white hair moved to the front. "Would they be simply failing orders?"

Hastrman, of Czechoslovakia: not a threat, but then, not much of a bag man either.

"I'd expect no less of a question from the scarecrow-man," El Cucuy said calmly. "There has been an old woman, a user of the grandmother-power, whom L'uomo Nero has consorted with," he pronounced. The former disbelief of the bogeymen was nothing compared to the shock that now ran through them. Heads turned and mouths opened in disbelief. "He told her everything about us, about our plan, about the nature of our legends and belief. He and Likho both took her orders, and that is why they did not at first participate in our plan." El Cucuy shot a glance at the two captive bag men. "They speak, think, and act like she does. Their humanity is endangering the rest of us and poisoning our legends."

Hastrman nodded his great head like a wise bird. "So it would seem, lord, so it would seem. But where would this old one be?"

"I—what?" El Cucuy said.

"Where would this old one be?" Hastrman repeated. "If this a trial is, then bring here the old one too. Punish all."

"A plan is already in motion," El Cucuy replied. Likho knew it was a lie, and he was willing to bet that El Cucuy knew he knew. This whole thing stunk. The Family leader could bitch about humanity until the kids came home, but L'uomo Nero's bag had been the thing their captors grabbed for first. The humanity might piss him off—not to Likho's surprise—but it was a convenient excuse to get his hands on them. And Likho was pretty sure he knew what El Cucuy was looking for.

The unknown.

"Yes. Tomorrow, she will be brought here. Then the proper trial will be held."

He had to drag this out as long as possible. Give the bag time to get wherever it was headed.

"Don't you even think about it!" Likho shouted. "That old woman's a nightmare! If you're dying to stop the crisis of belief, you're looking in the—mmph!" His words were stifled as another toy bear hit him in the mouth. He convulsed, pain wracking his body, and the bogeymen laughed.

"Thank you, Sacauntos," the dead child said placidly. "Don't let him bite you. He might be contagious." A bout of nervous laughter spread though the hall. "Go do your work," he continued. "Capture the children alive, mind you, but seek to inspire fear and distrust. Snatch them from behind locked doors, atop skyscrapers, in airplanes. Do whatever the humans will be unable to explain. Remember, brothers: it's our future we're ensuring."

Chapter Thirteen

Another night, another sleepless night, getting up every twenty minutes to look into her son's room and wonder what would happen if she found it empty. She tried not to think about it, but it was hard to do otherwise. A dull headache throbbed in the base of her skull, making her bury her head in the pillow and try to wish it away. It didn't work.

The next day dawned no better than the last. A brisk, cold wind was skimming off Lake Michigan, and the first flecks of snow were beginning to fall. The sky above was leaden and dull, with no hint of the sun to be seen. The scurrying citizens wrapped themselves well in heavy coats and long scarves, seemingly afraid to look one another in the eye.

Abby parked her Toyota at the corner and clambered out, wrestling with three overstuffed grocery bags. On the way up the street, she stopped and glanced at a newspaper box: the *Chicago Tribune*'s headline was blaring the latest abduction statistics, and the pages were lined with black.

"This is getting ridiculous," she murmured, tucking one of the bags under her arm and getting a grip on the other two. She deliberately avoided looking at the totals; it wouldn't do any good if she got too upset to handle her work properly.

The office was warm and unusually crowded when Abby made her way through the front door. Mary was everywhere at once, rushing back and forth with armfuls of papers and garbage bags. The guinea pig's cage was being cleaned by Dummy's left hand, which neatly scooped the used peat litter into a plastic tray, which was snatched up by Mary on her next pass around the room. The owner of the hand was nowhere to be seen, but he was presumably close by.

Keith was rattling around in the kitchenette—Abby saw him hurry past with a fresh pot of coffee. She could hear the voices of Marotte and Adam echoing up from the basement, apparently arguing about something, and a dim mist hovering near the ceiling was most likely Harvey. (At least, if the boiler hadn't broken again.)

A door slammed, and John came hurrying into the main office, dressed in a cheap gray suit. He didn't seem to realize his jacket was on inside out.

"Morning, Abby. Got the groceries?" he asked, snagging one of the bags and digging into it. "More snacks, great. What about the coffee creamer?"

"You hired me to do office work, not run errands," Abby carped. She unceremoniously dumped the other two bags into his arms and pulled off her coat. "Powdered creamer should be good enough for you. Whew, it's roasting in here. And why's everybody in such a rush?"

"I mobilized the divisions. This place is a heap, and I'm not bringing some old lady into it." John struggled with the two extra bags, and wound up almost toppling onto the nearest desk. "Called up the hospital as soon as I could. We'll be picking her up in half an hour."

Abby shook her head. "You never cease to amaze me, John," she said dryly. "Just don't drop the crumpled one, it's got the milk in it. You, house-cleaning?"

"Office-cleaning, technically." The bags were deposited on the desk, and John straightened up again. "Besides, she's old. We don't want her choking on dust bunnies before we get our information."

"You big softy."

"Don't make me—"

True to their word, John and Abby were at St. Luke's visitor entrance half an hour later. A nurse escorted Giovanna, in a wheelchair and thoroughly wrapped up against the cold, down to the car. "Outpatient hours end at five o'clock," she warned them. John assumed an expression of near-constipated alertness and nodded officiously, but once she was back in the building he stamped down on the gas and fishtailed out of the lot at high speed. Two new strips of black rubber were laid on the pavement as he peeled out. Giovanna, sitting in the back seat with Abby, squawked and flapped at the back of his seat.

"That's enough!" she said hoarsely. John shrugged and slowed down, catching a demonic glare from Abby in the rearview mirror.

The rest of the ride passed in uneasy silence. When the Toyota pulled up in front of the office, Mary and Marotte hurried out to help the old woman out of the car, but Giovanna waved them off and insisted on clambering out herself. Leaning on her cane, she tottered towards the building, the four SSR people trailing behind.

A moment later, she paused on the threshhold. "Well, it's no secret," she said firmly. "I saw what I saw. And I'm not walking into this building until you give me your word that you're not going to patronize me rotten. I knew the minute I saw you all that you've been seeing things too. You understand me?"

Abby gently took her arm. "You have our word, Mrs. Shepherd," she replied. "We just want to know what you know."

"And no mocking?" The old woman's deep-set eyes were sharp and keen behind their bifocals. "There's too much going on to waste those children's time."

"Then let's get down to business," John interjected. "Every minute we take out here is one more that we could be warming up and learning something."

Giovanna bowed her head slightly and allowed herself to be helped into the office.

Inside, the group gathered around. There was a palpable sense of hope in the air; even Mary and Keith, barely out of the cradle, were praying for a break in the case, and everyone wanted to hear what this weird old woman had to say.

Dummy receded into the background, but not before carefully detaching an ear and laying it on the desktop out of Giovanna's sight. Marotte moved to pull up a chair for her, and Giovanna gratefully lowered herself into it, laying her cane across her lap. The psychic and the photographer crowded together onto one desk, and John and Abby moved their own chairs into place. Adam had scurried back to the basement, but Abby knew he could hear everything through the pipes, and it was no guess that he would be paying as keen attention as everyone else.

"First things first," Abby said. "Mrs. Shepherd—if you wouldn't mind, we'd like a sample of your DNA."

"What for?" Giovanna said. She folded her hands over the cane, as if somebody was getting ready to take it away from her. Her eyes were sharp behind the chunky glasses. "I thought we agreed no monkey business."

"There's no monkey business at all," Abby said quickly. "It's just for the archive. We've been trying to assemble a DNA database of all the people we've dealt with, so we have them on file."

"Any needles?"

"Not at all. Just a strand of hair and a quick swab."

When these had been collected, and Abby was putting them away, Giovanna leaned back and fixed them with an owlish stare.

"I knew you weren't real policemen, but I'm not blaming you for that," she began bluntly. "You're some sort of monster hunters, I suppose. You good at what you do?"

It wasn't a question they had been asked much. John cocked an eyebrow, and the teenagers shifted a bit.

"We catch what must be caught," Marotte said finally.

"And you kill what must be killed?"

"When necessary."

"Then you're just the people I need," the old woman acknowledged. "I'm no great lover of violence, but sometimes, it's all that works. And since I was young, I've seen a lot of people do awful things, but this beats most."

Abby leaned forward. "Tell us. Please."

There in the center of the circle, the old woman lowered her head a bit, thinking hard. A pause for breath and gathering thought, then she raised her chin again and began.

"I've been seeing the bogeys again," Giovanna said. "Been seeing them getting worse and worse. And three days ago, I heard my friend the black man and a rude friend of his screaming and cursing a blue streak. Now—nothing. Not a whisper." She leaned forward, grasping the cane in both hands. "If you're monster hunters, and you know the difference between what needs catching and what needs killing, then you're the people I want to see. I need to know things."

"Your friend," John repeated. Abby thought he looked unsettled at the words. "You're friends with the bogeymen."

"A bogeyman." Giovanna crossed her hands on the grip of her cane. "We've been friends since I was a little girl."

"You have to understand," John said, as diplomatically as possible for him, "this is all very new to us. There's no legend—and I mean *none*—of a so-called bogeyman making friends with anyone. Bogeyman legends are about torturing kids, not playing nice. What makes you so special?" Abby shot him a look. "If you don't mind telling," he hastily added.

The old woman shook her head, slowly and deliberately. "Then you're looking in the wrong books. Bogeyman legends, no. But what's a bogey? A creature out of myths. And myths never bothered about the details. Do a little more reading, mister, and you'll find stories all over the place. Helper spirits. Guardian angels."

John opened his mouth, then closed it. "Oh," he said. Then, after a moment: "But that still doesn't explain why he chose *you*."

"Damned if I know." Giovanna shook her head again. "But you know, I don't think anyone ever talked to him before." She looked upwards, her eyes fastening onto the opposite wall, where somebody long gone had taped up a Socialist Action poster. The heroic workers now showed years of graffiti, but the looming shape representing Corporate America was as dark and threatening as ever.

"I was a bad girl," she said frankly, after a moment's thought. "Fought, got in trouble, caused messes. My mamma, God rest her soul, had a bitter time of it. Papa worked in Naples, and couldn't be home often. Sent money when he could, of course, but times were hard, and I wasn't making it any simpler for her. Can't hardly blame her for calling the bogeyman for me.

"I remember. I was playing outside, getting into an awful mess as usual. Mamma came out into the yard and shouted 'If you don't behave yourself, the black man will take you away!' That's *L'uomo Nero*," she added sharply. "His name. I didn't believe her, of course; shouted to the whole world that I hoped he would, because I'd rather go anywhere else with him than be trapped with my family. Didn't mean a word of it, but I reckon he thought I did. The instant Mamma went inside, the bag went over my head."

Marotte leaned forward and voiced what Abby was already thinking. "And you are certain it was not a normal abduction?"

That earned him a scorching look from the old woman. "Yes, I am. I vanished for a month, and didn't have a single memory left of it. Only that it felt safe, see? Safe and friendly. But the next thing I knew, I was standing on the doorstep on a dry autumn morning, and Mamma was crying and pushing me into the house. Still wore my same dress... still just as dirty, and not a mite more. The mud on my shoes was still wet.

"And it weren't the last time, neither. Oh, I had such a childhood as you people would never imagine... traveled all over, I did. All over."

For a moment, her gaze was soft and distant. Then she seemed to pull herself back to reality, and her expression grew wary once more.

"An' that's why I agreed to talk to you people. You've got information, I think, and I reckon I can use it."

"What do you need to know?" Abby began cautiously. "There are some things we have to keep confidential, Mrs. Shepherd—"

"Giovanna will be fine. I want to know how you kill a bogeyman."

For a few interminable seconds, things were silent in the stuffy office. Then John cleared his throat rather theatrically and blinked, seemingly examining the old woman's impassive face for clues. "That's what we're trying to figure out ourselves."

She shook her head impatiently. "Don't play stupid with me. I want to know how a bogeyman kills a bogeyman. You can't shoot, stab, or poison that sort of thing." Deep in the mass of wrinkles, the watery eyes glared back at John. "How do bogeys murder their own kind?"

"Depends on the occasion..." John stalled.

"I think he's been killed, or someone's trying to kill him," Giovanna said flatly. "Black man or not, he's my friend, and I'm sure you know how important that is."

Behind the old woman, Mary flinched a bit. Abby knew that the girl had been raised with very liberal parents, who were quite clear about what was rude and what wasn't.

"Can we leave race out of this?" the psychic said. "I mean, I don't know when you were born or whatever, but... you know...."

"She doesn't mean African," John called across the circle. "Black as in black as night. All right, Gio," he added, "I think I know what you want. But are you certain your friends are bogeymen? We've been assembling a dossier, and there are some mythic elements, but it could still be a poltergeist situation."

The old woman made an impatient clicking noise. "He's no ghost, and neither is that friend of his."

"'The black man,'" John repeated. His eyes lit up as he turned the words over on his tongue. "You really mean that, don't you."

Marotte seemed to be thinking along the same lines, and he had half-risen from his chair when Giovanna uttered the words. "A man with a bag," he murmured.

"That's it. The black man." John seemed to be torn between grinning and staring in open-mouthed shock. Abby couldn't blame him; the whole group felt thunderstruck. "The black man with a bag, who takes bad children for a time... blimey, it fits...."

"You think so, do you?" Giovanna said sharply. "Took you long enough."

John's face split in a huge grin. He seemed not to have heard her last comment. "Absolutely!" he beamed. "Who hasn't heard of the bogeyman? When I was little, my mum used to tell me that there was a sodding great—" he stopped, seeing the look on the old woman's face. "It's not a bad word."

"I watch those English shows like everyone else, you know," she said. "I'm not stupid. And swearing's trashy." Giovanna settled heavily back into the chair, having laid down the law to her own satisfaction.

"Fine. A great monster who would chomp my feet off if I put one toe out of bed. Slept with socks on every night 'til I was thirteen. Everybody's got the bogeyman—every place in the fuckin' world has it!" Giovanna shot him a look, but John didn't even pretend to be sorry this time.

"Yes, but it doesn't always go according to the legend," Abby cautioned. She tapped at the edge of the table, a little frustrated and more than a little worried. This wasn't really a situation she wanted to think about. "Just because it walks like a duck and quacks like a duck, doesn't mean it's a quasi-mythical creature."

"I'm with her," Keith piped up. Even his seemingly unshakable faith in the essential drama of the situation seemed to be taking a beating. "Ghosts I can buy. And I saw that werewolf, and that thing in the sewer, and it was me who found the watchamajiggy with the big wooden thing. But... you know... the *bogeyman*?"

"And why not?" John shot back. "Hah, they're almost like gods, aren't they? The rituals of putting your head under the covers, the ceremonial turning-on of the night light, the prayers that it doesn't swallow you whole—I wouldn't be surprised if some enterprising creature of the night decided to become a bogey, just to get that kind of attention! This is it! The big one!"

"John, calm down—" Abby began.

Her coworker just laughed. "Fuck no, we've got work to do! Abby, don't you get that this is the break we've been waiting for? The *bogeyman* needs to be killed! It's as good as the World Cup!"

"You," Abby said as sharply as she dared, "need to calm down now. If it is the bogeyman—a bogeyman—then this isn't going to be some kind of trophy hunt!"

"Abby, it's our Moby Dick. Why shouldn't I be excited?"

"Because when Captain Ahab went to hunt the white whale, it brought him and his entire crew to the bottom of the ocean," Marotte interrupted. "These are highly powerful creatures that could kill us in an instant."

His words were a bucket of cold water over John's enthusiasm, and the Englishman sagged slightly.

"Mrs. Shepherd," Marotte continued in a slightly less icy tone, "do you have any pictures of your friend?"

"You could say that," the old woman said cautiously. She seemed a bit shell-shocked by John's sudden exuberance. One frail hand dipped into her purse and pulled out a yellow envelope, much worn. There was crackling noise and a hint of a musty smell as she eased it open, slipping out a photograph that was beginning to curl at the edges.

John took the print and examined it, and Abby leaned over to get a look as well. There, rendered in sepia tones, was a young Giovanna DiFrancesca—perhaps twenty years old, hair in braids, wide eyes peering out from behind a pair of steel-rimmed spectacles. She wore a long wool skirt and a much-distressed coat in a faded plaid print, and her right hand clutched the violin case tucked under her arm. The left hand was extended out from her body, and its fingers were loosely clenched.

"It's a nice picture," Abby said after a moment, "But what does it have to do with—"

John shushed her with a shake of his head. "Look at the sidewalk."

Abby did. And there, clear as day, in the shadows on the sidewalk where the young Giovanna stood, was the shape of a couple holding hands. The girl held something under one arm, and the man was pulling on her other hand slightly, raising it up a bit. The masculine shape wore a wide-brimmed hat.

"Who took this?" John asked gently, addressing Giovanna again. Abby took it and passed it to Marotte, who studied it carefully. The old woman tugged at her flowered scarf before answering, and when she did, her voice seemed to come from a long way away.

"My uncle Enrico—before they took him away."

"The bogeymen?" John asked.

"The Nazis," Marotte said from his chair. He handed the photograph on to Keith and leaned forward, putting his hands on his hips. "You lived in Italy during the second world war. Did the Nazis arrest him?"

Giovanna shook her head. "No. It was the police. They found out what he did, and I can't say I blame them. Of course, I knew already. The black man told me to be careful."

Now the other two looked very surprised. John leaned forward in his chair. "Sorry to butt in... did you say that the black man, the bogeyman, warned you?"

"He did."

Abby glanced at John, and they both nodded. "I think you'd better tell us the whole story," Abby said carefully.

The old woman took a deep breath and shuffled her feet, trying to get into a more comfortable position. "It was the summer of 1949," she began. "My uncle Enrico had just returned from an American P.O.W. camp in the States. The Yanks let him work for American dollars, and he bought a new camera with some of his savings; he said he had hopes of becoming a photographer, and that America had all the best ideas and there wasn't anything for us in in Italy any more. He said he'd make me his first subject, Girl with Violin, and took me out front to photograph." She raised herself up a little straighter. "As he was reaching for the shutter, the black man grabbed me by the hand. I thought he was just being nice, and let him stay that way 'til the photograph was done. Then, when my uncle had gone, the black man told me that Enrico wasn't trustworthy, and that I should be careful."

Mary shot a nervous glance at Abby, who shook her head and put a finger to her lips. The psychic subsided a little.

"Two days later, the military police came to our house. They said my uncle had been working for the Nazis and helping them cause trouble in Naples. That was why he'd been away so long. The Americans didn't know, and our men had only just found out. When they came to get him, he threw petrol on all his books and papers. The only thing that survived was the film in the camera."

"And that still leaves us with a problem," John added, tapping his chin thoughtfully. "Look, Gio, you can say 'legendary creatures act mad' as much as you like, but it still doesn't explain it. Maybe you really were the first one to talk to him, and that might have something to do with it. But didn't you ever think that this is, as Mal so kindly reminded me, a *bogeyman?*" He looked around the circle, watching the agents' reactions. "Bogeymen are supposed to frighten, kill, pull your skin off your bones and all that. So why's this one hanging about to play nursemaid?"

Giovanna snorted. "I always knew he was a gentler sort than the bag. There's no call to be leaping to conclusions all over the place."

"Wouldn't dream of it, Gio."

"Nevertheless." She hesitated for just a moment. "Mind you, he did once say that he... felt like it was the right thing do to." Her face fell. "He was always about that bag of his. It was giving him orders, he said. Maybe it told him to come back for me."

Now it was Abby who was surprised. The pile of folders from the hospital had been left on her desk; she stood up and edged over to it, shooing Mary aside. She picked up one of the folders and began to page through it furiously. A nasty thought was tugging at her. John carried on, but not without a sideways glance at his fellow agent.

"Did he follow you everywhere, Gio?" he asked gently.

"Not everywhere." Her thin lips were pursed. "When I met my husband and moved out to the middle of Iowa, we lost touch. It was my fault—I told him I didn't want my childhood nightmares following me across the sea. I thought being married meant I was all grown up and older than having invisible friends. And like he would, he took me at my word. I didn't see him again until after I was divorced. Mr. Shepherd knew about him, but he always laughed about it. For a long time, I thought it was the laughter that kept the black man away."

Now, Abby couldn't resist. She glanced down at the file one last time and then looked Giovanna straight in the eye. There it was, in black and white, and her heart sank a little. She didn't want to challenge this strange old woman. "This Mr. Shepherd—your husband, correct? William Kenneth Shepherd, stationed in Naples during the postwar occupation?" she began.

"Yes." Now it was Giovanna's turn to give the fish-eye. "Why?"

"According to this, you were divorced in February 1961. One month later, your ex-husband William Shepherd was found beaten and unconscious by the roadside in Sarasota, California, correct?"

"Yes, that's correct." The old woman's thin lips twitched. "Nasty accident."

"And it's possible that it was your 'childhood friend' that inflicted severe head trauma and left him in a coma for six days." Abby's voice was sharper than she felt. "And during those six days, you neither visited him nor sent any money to pay for his care."

"I didn't know it had happened," Giovanna snapped. "I was having enough trouble, and didn't need more!"

"So you admit that the creature known as L'uomo Nero was responsible for the beating?" Abby continued relentlessly.

Giovanna glowered at Abby. "The black man wasn't coming to me about it," she said stiffly. "And whenever he comes around, he doesn't need me asking questions about what he's up to. It's none of my business. What's it of yours?"

"Protective spirits and ghouls can be incredibly dangerous creatures." Abby put down the folder. She hated dealing with this kind of thing, but she couldn't understand how the old woman could be so... so... *unconcerned* about it. Abby had encountered too many unfriendly monsters to be able to shrug the idea of the bogeyman off so casually. "*Mainly*," she continued, leaning forward for emphasis, "because they don't attack randomly.

They've got their own completely strange code of conduct, and they don't think about the consequences to a normal, powerless human. Perfectly innocent people have been frightened, injured, maimed, and killed when protective spirits have felt motivated to act." She reached down and closed the folder with a flap. "If your L'uomo Nero falls under the heading of a protective spirit, then he'll have to be contained. From the looks of things, he's nearly killed once."

There was a warning glance from Marotte. "If the creature really is protecting her," he said sharply, "then perhaps we shouldn't make it angry. Are you wearing any silver?"

"You don't need to be nasty." The old woman's tone was crisp, cutting into the impending argument. "The black man's been gone for days—as I said. I think something's got hold of him and his friend, and I want to know what we should do about it."

Abby wanted to say something, but John cut her off with a casual jab of a pen. "Maybe he's on holiday?" he suggested, dropping the implement and settling into place at the table. "If he's got enough personality to care about a human, let alone come see her for eighty-some years, then the man's got to take a break occasionally."

"Yeah, we once met a guy with—" Keith began. John shut him up with a look.

"He doesn't take vacations." Giovanna gazed at the far wall while her wrinkled fingers smoothed the edges of her dress. "It's not a job that you can have time off from. It was a stretch for him to come and see me as often as he did... his friend was complaining, the last they came, about the time and trouble. He said there was work to do. Now—nothing. Not a peep."

"And what's the work?" Mary asked cautiously, drawing up her legs onto the edge of the desk and tucking them under her.

"Stealing the children, of course. Stealing kids'll help them out somehow, though I don't know how. The black men are all belief creatures-"

Abby leaned forward. "Would you call them a perversion of the natural order of reality?"

"Would you stop interruptin' me?" Giovanna demanded. "You brought me here asking for information, now would you care to be hearing it or do I have to wait for you to quiet down?"

"Sorry."

Abashed, the blonde woman settled back, and John moved into the breach. "So it's definitely the bogeymen doing all this," he said, shaking his head slightly. "And we don't know why. Abby, write this down, would you? We'll need it. Better yet, use the tape recorder, I can't read anybody's handwriting when I'm pissed. Right. So he's gone. How long does he usually take off?"

Giovanna closed her eyes for a moment. "Four days to a week or so, depends on what time of year it is. Around the holiday season, he doesn't come for weeks at a time. And of course, at Halloween, the spirits are out in force and the parents use the black man to make sure the young ones are home before dark."

"Interesting." John was watching the old woman's face carefully. Abby had found the tape recorder and plugged it into the wall, and was fiddling with the volume settings. After a moment, she signaled John and pressed play.

"So he comes to visit you?" John continued.

"That's right," the old woman said firmly.

"How does he come?"

"Sometimes, he takes a human body. I asked him to do that; my eyes aren't what they used to be, and glasses don't do any good if you want to see into another world. Makes those nasty gossiping bitches—" John pulled a face in surprise, and Giovanna wrinkled her nose at him. "Don't look like that, I can say what I want. I'm too old to mind my language."

"Sure are," John agreed.

"Anyway, him turning up makes the knitting circle take notice." Giovanna lifted her chin a little. "And a few times, he comes to me in my dreams."

John raised an eyebrow. "In your dreams?"

"Are you going to keep on interrupting?" Giovanna said warningly. "Yes, in my dreams. He's a good boy."

"Settle down, Gio. I think you'd better tell us the whole thing. Start to finish."

As the wall clock wearily ticked off the minutes, the old woman cradled a cup of strong tea (lemon, two sugars—she refused to touch milk) and told them everything. She began at the beginning, with a nasty little girl who was taken away by a spirit. That had been only the beginning.

"And what happened then?" Keith asked. His eyes were practically glowing, and he had long ago abandoned his perch on the desk to sit cross-legged on the floor. It was an odd picture, a heavily pierced teenager all in black staring rapturously at a hunched old woman, but he was soaking up the story eagerly. Marotte was all ears too, although he was being much less obtrusive.

"I spent years with him," she replied. The tea, barely touched, had long cooled. "Every few nights, I'd wake up, and there he'd be at the foot of my bed. And don't you go reading nothing into it, neither; he was kind as anything. Mind like a child, sometimes." She shook her head. "Someone was always givin' him orders. If it wasn't that bag, it was me. He had all sorts of power, and when he weren't called to do his duty and snatch other children, he'd let me walk with him. Egypt, I remember. I wanted to see the pyramids."

Abby shook her head at the thought. "What about your mother?" she said. "Didn't she ever find you gone?" It was a frightening image. She knew that the thought of her son vanishing in the middle of the night filled her with a quavery horror. Even if he did get angry sometimes, she couldn't imagine feeling otherwise. Finding your child gone was a mother's greatest terror.

"Never a time," Giovanna said firmly. "First time, I was gone for a month, after she called the black man for me. Then, she saw it. Thought I were abducted. Gave a shriek and clutched me, screaming about monsters and kidnappers and the Nazi German spies that people were still afraid of. Weren't 'til later I found out I'd been gone a month, and didn't remember it at all." Her deep-set eyes were pensive. "Afterwards, when I'd go for the night, she'd never know it. Even in the early days, when she slept in my bed, she'd never see me go. Slept harder and better, those nights." She smiled a little at the memory. "I was glad to see it."

She set down the cup and looked around at the assembled SSR agents. "I know you're still thinking I'm a mad old woman. But I was a different child when I came back. My supper seemed to taste so much better. And the mud... I still liked playing in the mud, but I always washed my feet clean before I was called for anything else. I wasn't nasty anymore, because I knew it wasn't a nice thing to do. He made me nice."

"Certainly beats out years of seeing a psychiatrist. So that was the first time you met L'uomo Nero, was it?" John crossed his legs and leaned forward. "When did he start coming to see you?"

"Two years later. He turned up in my room one night, asking me if I knew him. I didn't then, but I soon found out he was the one that brought me away."

"And the idea of the bogeyman turning up in the middle of the night didn't bother you?" John put in.

Giovanna shook her head. "He never laid a hand on me. There wasn't any leaping from closets, screaming or lurking under the bed like people expect the bogeys to do. He was like a child. Once, me being an inquisitive girl, I asked him what he wanted. That was when he said he didn't like the bag ordering him about." She took a sip of the cold tea. "First I heard of that bag giving him orders. He said it was the way to the 'other place,' and he only took away what it told him to. I never knew if it was true, or if it was just some idea of his."

"And he kept on coming back?"

"Like clockwork. Mamma, God rest her soul, was so frighted of me disappearing again that she slept in my room with one wrist tied to mine. Didn't stop the black man, though—he'd step in twice a week, and take me for walks all around the country." She smiled, shaking her head slightly at the memories. "And more than just the country. I saw the whole world, when I got older."

The ticking of the clock seemed very loud now. On the other side of the office, Stinker was awake and snuffling around his food dish, and the scraping of his paws could be clearly heard in the office. Silently, Abby rose and retrieved the battered tea kettle from the desk. It had long grown cold, so she moved into the kitchenette to refill it. She could hear the other agents shuffling, and couldn't blame them. It was one of the strangest things they'd ever heard of, in their long years working there.

The bogeyman. It was hard to believe. She snapped on the stovetop burner and set the kettle down on it. As she watched the flame flicker, she wondered what that kind of freedom would be like. To be able to go anywhere in the world, anywhere at all, with no consequences, guided by a supernatural ghost of fear...

"What sorts of places?" John finally asked as Abby came back into the room. She settled herself back into her chair, watching Giovanna carefully.

"Oh, all kinds," Giovanna said, giving her tea an impatient stir. Clouds of undissolved sweetener billowed up from the bottom of the cup, and when she extracted the spoon, it was coated with a tarry layer of sugar. "He was the type of man who didn't know what he wanted half the time. And me, I was a precocious child, always eager to show off what I knew. So when he came I'd ask him to take me to all sorts of different places. The pyramids of Egypt. And when all my friends grew out of their imaginary playmates, mine didn't go anywhere."

"What about the dreams? And the hole in the wall?" Keith interjected. "What about all that? At the hospital, you said it was caused by a giant made of blue light, the—mook—Mörkö. *Mörkö*, that's it. Was that true?"

"God's truth, every word of it." The old woman took a sip of her tea, grimaced, and leaned over to the table to set it down. "And that dead cuckoo-boy, him that my black man calls *El Cucuy*, is behind all those disappearances. It's some sort of 'campaign of fear,' I hear."

"Tell us about the dreams."

And she did. Marotte shifted the tape recorder closer to her and sat watchfully, scribbling notes with one hand. Abby started the coffee maker. Mary stood up and stretched out her cramped limbs, Keith chewed on a stick of beef jerky. John stood and paced. The words flew past them: the bogeymen and their campaign, the fears that the children were losing belief. The mystery of Bavbav. The boy-leader, El Cucuy. Facing the Mörkö.

"And now L'uomo Nero is missing. Bloody hard to believe that a bogey who can just whisk you off to Egypt with no trouble whatsoever is just going to vanish into thin air." John tapped his front teeth with one forefinger. "Simply not happening. Mary, would you check the records on bogeymen? Me and Marotte, we'll see what we can turn up."

"Then you'll help?" Giovanna said quickly.

"Bogeymen kidnapping kids left and right's a bit of a tall order," John said. "But us, we're no kids. We'll take care of it."

And then the wall exploded.

A gust of wind swept through the office, sending books and papers scattering like leaves. Abby had a vague glimpse of a riot of figures, all dark and somehow two-dimensional, before she was knocked head over heels by a blow from a surprisingly solid fist.

The leader went straight for Giovanna. It was a huge thing, taller and broader than anyone in the room, draped in rags and wielding a long curved blade that was shiny with grease. It snatched up the old woman with one massive hand, nearly enveloping her as the long rags snaked out around her like tentacles. Harvey's bottle went rolling past, its cap still firmly on, faint cursing echoing from within the green glass.

Abby landed hard, crashing into a desk that toppled onto its side. She crouched down behind it and scrabbled around for a weapon, but it seemed like the impromptu office-cleaning had removed everything that she could have possibly used to attack the... the *bogeymen*. Mary was on one side of her, whimpering a little and cradling a heavily bruised jaw. Keith was unconscious on the floor. Somewhere off to her left, she could hear John's ragged breathing, and the clunk of an empty magazine being dropped. At least somebody had something. She risked a quick look over the top of the desk.

Giovanna's wrinkled face was pale, the veins standing out in her neck like worms. One hand was tangled in the gray rags that the bogeyman was wrapped in. The other flapped wildly at his face, trying to scratch or slap or at least do something. "Put me down!" she shrilled. "Put me down right now!"

Abby leapt over the turned-up desk and scrambled towards the commotion, reaching out for Giovanna's hand. Marotte fumbled in his own desk, reaching for the long knife that everybody knew he kept in his bottom drawer. John had both the pistol and the magazine, nearly dropping them both, but nevertheless had a round chambered and the gun raised by the time Harvey's bottle had rolled to a stop.

"Drop her!" he shouted. The creature just showed his rotting brown teeth in a grin and threw Giovanna into the air. Someone screamed—

nobody knew who—as the old woman's outstretched fingers slipped through Abby's. Then a wrinkled creature flourished his bag, and Giovanna fell straight into its gaping mouth, her shriek abruptly cut off as the rough wool closed over her.

John squeezed the trigger twice. The rag-man didn't even flinch as the bullets passed right through him, though something made of blue light ducked to avoid getting hit and another hairy thing hissed between his tombstone-shaped teeth.

"Go ahead, John Sawyer," a voice said placidly. "But then, I don't suppose your sister ever spoke to you again."

The ranks of the bogeymen parted. Out stepped a small human figure— perhaps nine or ten years old, were it not for the pallid color of his thin face. His clothes were loose and nondescript—a pair of gray trousers and a worn shirt so baggy it might have been a poncho. He rolled his r's very slightly, and his eyes were red. Abby shivered as the world gave a heave around them, and she knew that they were all afraid for a reason.

"I like this," the young boy said, staring at the crouching John. "I like this a *lot*. You have more unresolved conflicts than any healthy human being should. But then, you're not healthy, are you?" The boy tilted his head sideways, fixing John with an unblinking stare. "She said so, right?"

John grunted in surprise even as he reflexively pulled the trigger a third time, sending a wild shot ricocheting off the wall. All the humans and two Family members reflexively ducked at the sound of the shot, and El Cucuy frowned.

"She didn't, I suppose. Yes, it was her fault; she shouldn't have pushed you around. A bit of a social climber, wasn't she? A bad trait in a teenaged girl. And, of course, a habit of blaming you for her mistakes. Humans— slack-jawed morons with grudges against anything they don't understand." He shot a glance at Hombre del Saco, who raised the hand that still held the bag.

There was no movement from inside it, and the woolen fabric hung limp. There was no way it could contain a person, even one as thin and frail as Giovanna. Abby's mind flew back to the old woman's account of her own first encounter with the bogeymen. Wherever the bag led to, Giovanna was already gone.

"Bring her back!" she shouted, pulling herself clumsily to her feet. Her hands trembled, and she squeezed them into white-knuckled fists in an effort to control herself. Her blunted nails made deep crescents in the flesh of her palm. "That's not fair!"

El Cucuy paused theatrically for a moment and considered. "No," he said with a grin, cocking his head. "She's caused us a lot of trouble. You would rather release a rabid dog into the children's ward. And you, John Sawyer," he continued, addressing the white-faced man, "you won't hurt any of us by waving that pistol around, so I suggest you lower it before you injure somebody you *do* care about."

John was rattled. His eyes were widened, his teeth showing in a ghastly grimace, both hands grasping the gun like a lifeline—but the muzzle of the Desert Eagle never wavered.

"You don't get to talk any more," he said in a flat, dead voice. "That's it. No more talking."

The dead child just grinned. "You're too easy, John Sawyer. I can see all the open spaces in your head, and you couldn't quiet me if you had the whole world at your command.

"And it's not just you, is it?" The heat had leached out of the office, and chill crept into everyone's bones as the dead boy turned. His eyes found Marotte, who was staring a hole in him, knife in hand. "Everybody here. You—oh, I like this. I *adore* this. The Duchess? You called her 'the Duchess'?" He laughed a little as the actor turned white.

"I said, you don't get to talk any more," John repeated from behind him. The gun still had not wavered. El Cucuy turned again, calm and collected with just a hint of humor, the master of all he surveyed. It was some ghastly inversion of the schoolroom, with a teacher that had no qualms about corporal punishment.

The crucifix was warm against Abby's skin.

"Wait a minute!" she said loudly, voice wavering only a little. Heads turned, and El Cucuy transfixed her with a stare like a shark's. She flinched, but forced herself to stand upright.

"Wait a minute," she repeated shakily. "You're creatures of belief, right? Giovanna said so—you're made by people who believe in you. And you're El Cucuy, the cuckoo boy, right?"

"El Cucuy will do. And if you intend to use my name against me, I'd advise against it." The boy shook his head. "We're not demons, Abigail Marquise. You will find that I am indifferent to it."

"Listen—I don't believe in you."

There was a heartbeat of silence. John kept his eyes on the bogeymen; most of them appeared blank or unconcerned, but one or two looked uncomfortable and the big blue thing (the Mörkö?) flinched visibly. El Cucuy turned his head and hissed at the blue giant, who shrunk backwards at the motion. Calm again, he looked back to Abby.

"Belief is not everything, human. And whether you believe or not means very little to us."

El Cucuy shook his head. Outside, the wind whipped up, and the air grew colder. The overhead lights in the office died with a flicker, leaving them in a gray gloom. In the basement, the furnace choked, spewed out clouds of oily black smoke that flooded the room through the vents in the wall. John shouted something that was lost in the commotion and dived at the dead boy, but landed hard on the bare floor instead. They had gone.

Chapter Fourteen

Things had gone well, but it was no secret that El Cucuy was displeased. He had returned to the Home in triumph, dragging an unconscious old woman and looking to enjoy his victory over his rebellious brethren. Likho would bet that he had been hoping for an angry or a horrified reaction. Blank stares, followed by insults, were all he'd responded with.

So El Cucuy had fallen back on an old reliable tactic: violence. Likho's regrown face was suffering some heavy battering.

"Hold it!" He interrupted desperately, as Sacauntos drew back his huge fist. "Maybe I don't *like* being true to my roots. Never could stand borscht and sour—"

The fist shot through the air and struck Likho again. He turned his head just in time, still dripping blood, and the blow impacted his temple. A blue and black bruise flowered across the left side of his face, making him wince.

"You *bleed!*" El Cucuy shouted. He was pacing, circling the scene like a hungry rat spying out a possible meal. His hands were clenched, the fingers flexing as he tried to put his thoughts into words. "Is this really so hard to understand?" he said finally, exasperated. "We have no blood! We never need to bleed! It is not something we do! Take a human form, yes. Take a human *body?* Unacceptable! No wonder you decided to listen to that old woman!"

Behind him, Talasam growled. "Even I never went that far," he muttered to Hombre del Saco, who nodded sagely. Likho shot him a glare.

By his side, L'uomo Nero was staring at the ground. His normally pale face was chalk-white, and the lanky locks of greasy hair had fallen into his eyes. The hat had been dropped in their struggle for freedom; without it, he looked smaller than his seven feet and entirely lost. The huge feet hung limply, dangling as they were above the floor. The hairy men who had him by the arms were taking no chances. Even without his bag, the cruelty and power of the Black Man of Italy were legendary. So what if he had been without malice for more than two hundred years? Nobody wanted to be the first one to fall if he should decide not to be so peaceful.

"No good, no good," he murmured to himself, shaking his ponderous head and making the long dark hair swing dispiritedly. "It is all wrong. It so should not be. I hear much, like the groaning of the mountains, and there is damage. Will they listen? What voice is there in hemp walls? You fight as they fight in the storm."

Even through the blood and crack of bone, Likho's mind was elsewhere, focused instead on the low voice at his side. Pain he could take in stride—you don't sustain existence in harsh countries like Russia and Siberia without learning a bit about it—but L'uomo Nero's newfound coherence was frightening him. His mind was working again, albeit in a roundabout way. Worse still, none of the other bogeymen seemed to even notice or care that things had changed, and Likho suspected that they were setting themselves up for a very nasty fall.

"He's making no sense," El Cucuy ground out. "Someone quiet him!"

For a moment, the other bogeymen shifted uneasily. Then El Ogro, shooting a sideways glance at the limp L'uomo Nero, shrugged his huge shoulders. "Maybe I bein' stupid," he rumbled, "but maybe he doin' unknowing thing again."

"Oh, keep silent!" The dead child put a hand to his pale forehead, as if a headache were brewing there. "I think we have established that both L'uomo Nero and Likho are *no longer with us*. They've chosen a human existence, and should be treated as such. Now quiet that thing, and let's get on with our work!"

The members of the Family glanced at each other. A few of the hairy men made tentative moves towards the hanging L'uomo Nero, but desisted when he raised his head and looked around at them. The deep-set eyes were dull and glassy, and the lack of anything—fear, dread, amusement—in them made each ancient nightmare think twice. Humans often used their eyes to communicate, but the Italian black man's stare made them think of nothing human.

"HE DOES NOT SEEM TO BE A THREAT," the Mörkö volunteered after a long and painful silence. El Cucuy rounded on the huge blue shadow, letting out a long wordless hiss like a cat turning to attack the boy who pulled its tail.

"You too, Mörkö?"

"I DID NOT—"

"Out!" El Cucuy snapped. The Family hesitated, but the small ghost stamped its foot and glared around at the assembly. "As soon as it's dark, bring Likho and the idiot to the sculptures, and put guards on them at all times. Sacauntos, stay by my side. The rest of you—out! I have too much to think about, and your whimpering is making my bones ache. Out!"

It was La Llorona who spoke up next. "So be it, lord," she said coolly. The skull betrayed no sign of emotion, and her stance was calm and relaxed. "But what shall we do? Capture more of the children?"

"Make your presence felt," El Cucuy ordered curtly. "Hide under staircases, burst out of closets, snatch at the single toe put out of bed. Do as we always should. Now go!"

Nobody needed to be told twice. The room swirled as dozens of huge creatures burst into shadows and mist, or simply vanished into the texture of the air. Talasam slid into the shadows, a shaken Mörkö simply faded away. And La Llorona grinned a skeletal grin as she sank into the floor and vanished, for a moment leaving nothing behind but the glint of half-light on polished bony jaws.

Plotting and scheming was one thing, and so were reigns of silent terror. But like many of the Family, the Llorona had been born for one thing: to snatch the bad children and make them feel fear. El Cucuy could plot all he liked; she preferred to work.

The basement, again. Likho groaned a little in spite of himself. Bodies were a hard habit to get out of, and since his form was still recoiling from its abuse at the hands of his fellow bogeymen, he was feeling distinctly battered. The old woman was lying on the concrete only a few yards away, but with the tight barrier of plastic figurines holding L'uomo and Likho in their small space, there wasn't much they could do with it.

Dunganga and El Nadaha were standing in the corners. Their eyes were fixed on the old woman, but outside the physical spectrum, Likho could see that the edges of their auras were tense and shuddering. They hated her.

Time passed, slowly. Giovanna raised her head. Likho watched as, clearly determined to master her nerves, the old woman stared boldly at the bogeyman guards. He could see her examining them, memorizing them, showing them she wasn't afraid as best she could. She was, of course. Even in his reduced state, Likho could sense it—but her face betrayed nothing. That amused him, somehow. Humans were so used to keeping things locked up in their little flesh prisons; they never really would be able to deal with beings who could see their thoughts written inside their skulls.

He couldn't blame her for feeling unhappy. Dunganga and El Nadaha were no picnic to stare at. Dunganga was a hairy man, a huge, stooped creature dressed in rags, with long locks of matted hair and the edge of a crooked tooth protruding from between his fleshy lips. A child-sized straw basket was propped against the wall by his feet. El Nadaha was a slender Egyptian woman draped in rushes and dead reeds. Both stared back, unblinking, never breathing or scratching or shifting their feet, until Giovanna was forced to drop her eyes.

Dunganga stared at her. *No wonder you cannot look,* he said. *We are not all as solid as L'uomo Nero. We are unique.*

"Not nice, putting your thoughts into my brain," Giovanna murmured, laying her head back. "I never give you permission."

We are not as humans are. We go where we like, do as we like. Your mind is our territory, should we choose.

"Enough of this 'we' stuff," Giovanna said testily. "Maybe I'm not some gigantic god-monster thing, but my mind is still mine." Groaning, she shuffled her limbs and managed to raise herself up on her elbows. Slowly, she rolled over and sat up, scuffing her now sadly bedraggled clothes on the floor. "You've got names, don't you?"

There was still no motion from either of the staring figures, but the thought appeared in her head nevertheless. *We do.*

"Well, what are they?"

For the first time, the two stern guards showed some reaction. The heads turned to stare at each other, and each leaned forward slightly. After a few seconds of glaring, the Egyptian woman flinched backwards slightly, and her lips parted to show just a glimpse of pointed teeth. She moved forward again, perhaps no more than an inch or so, but the huge man reacted as if he had been hit in the face with a fifty-pound hammer.

Even trapped inside the circle, Likho grinned a little. The argument was taking place in a way that the old woman could never sense, but it was nasty nonetheless. Oh, El Nadaha... the ladies were always the ones to watch out for.

Giovanna's intention was clear. There was no way she was going to live through this, but Likho knew that she wasn't going to make it easy on the Family, either. He approved. He didn't like her, but he approved.

After a few moments of this deliberation, both of the sentries turned back to Giovanna. *We are well known,* she was told. *We are Dunganga and El Nadaha.*

"Oh, nice, very nice," Giovanna said distractedly. "So you tell me, which is which?"

We are Dunganga and El Nadaha.

"Still isn't an answer. Who exactly are Dunga and Elnada?"

We are Dunganga and El Nadaha.

"Sorry, I'm not getting that. Maybe you're used to talking to the kids you steal, but I'm hard of hearing. Which is which, and speak up!"

We are Dunganga and El Nadaha.

"Dung-something, that I get," Giovanna replied. "Stupid name, but I suppose you can't go choosing the name you want. You're made by the humans, aren't you? Don't they choose your names for you?" She had pulled herself upright, and was doing her best to direct an intimidating fish-eye stare at the larger of the guards. "I would have thought they'd name their fears after things they fear, but who knows? I can see giving your fears a stupid name. Who's afraid of a pile of shit?"

Likho couldn't stop himself this time. He barked out a laugh, and Dunganga whirled on him, forcing him to subside reluctantly. It was good to see the old woman show some fangs, he thought: it spoke to the old country in every bogeyman's soul, where the grandmothers weren't afraid to slap the hell out of anybody who dared to get in their way.

The guards felt it too. *We are Dunganga and El Nadaha,* Dunganga repeated stolidly.

Giovanna looked up at him, and smiled a friendly little-old-lady smile. "So you'd be Dungy, then?"

Dunganga. Use your ears, woman!

"That's anger. I thought you bogeys didn't like emotions?" Giovanna asked a little nastily. "Bit human, isn't it?"

The Dunganga displayed his tombstone teeth in a sneer. Giovanna leaned back as far as her back would allow. Likho would bet his last cigarillo that she was getting a whiff of the Dunganga's legendary halitosis. "Well, aren't you charming," she said in a muffled voice. "So anger's allowed, is it?"

We do not feel in the way that humans do. The Dunganga returned to his former position next to El Nadaha. She was smiling—just a little—but it wasn't a nice smile, and it wasn't aimed at Giovanna.

"Now, that don't make sense." Giovanna drew her knees up and shielded her mouth and nose with the sleeve of her robe. "Aren't you made of human thoughts and fears? Brought into life by all that stuff?"

We are.

"And you steal children?"

Correct.

"Well, why's that?" Giovanna asked. "What did they ever do to you?"

It is our purpose. We must punish them for being disobedient.

"You don't like that?"

No!

"Makes you angry?"

We have said, old one, that we do not feel as humans do. Dunganga's voice was smug. *If you want to trap us with our own words, you are going to fail. We are wiser than you ever will be.*

"Maybe I'm just trying to learn how you work," Giovanna insisted. "I'm not gonna live forever. I'd like to learn as much as I can, with the time I've got left. That's the way we humans work. Is there harm in that?"

The Dunganga made to step forward again, his arms already rising, but El Nadaha clamped a hand on his shoulder. Her head tilted slightly as she stared at him, and the Dunganga shot back a stern glower at her. El Nadaha responded with an even firmer grip, to which Dunganga relented. Likho giggled a little.

We have decided, Dunganga said after a moment. *You cannot hurt us, and there is no fear in us. You will be silent.*

"But that's not—" Giovanna wheedled.

We are not friendly either. Silence.

She grinned. "That's humor. Getting more human all the time—didn't know bogeys liked cracking jokes."

It is not a joke. It is a law.

"And that's all I'll be getting, is it?"

El Nadaha craned her head slightly, fixing Giovanna with an unblinking stare. *When the sun goes down, we may go to work,* she said. Her voice was softer and sweeter than the Dunganga's, but that didn't make it more friendly. *And we will make our next attack. At that time, our lord El Cucuy will tear you apart and eat your flesh unless you tell us where the bag of Italy is. That is all you will be getting.*

The old woman shuddered a little, settling back against the cold wall. "I'll pass it by, thanks."

Tick tock, old one. Six hours to sunset.

"And that—that one's cruelty."

Call it what you will.

Likho's attention was suddenly drawn by a rustle of cloth. Turning, he saw L'uomo Nero raising his head slightly, blinking the onyx eyes.

"You all right, buddy?" he whispered.

"I... think so." L'uomo Nero brushed his hair out of his eyes and looked upward, fixing his eyes on the ceiling. Kneeling in the circle of toys, with eyes raised and shoulders set back, he looked like a penitent saint. But watching, Likho knew that it wasn't regret that was making him stare at the stained concrete ceiling. His eyes closed again, almost meditating.

He was calling for the bag. It was another part of him, and maybe more. Likho wondered what had happened to it.

Chapter Fifteen

The SSR's office was now nearly deserted. In the first few minutes after the nightmare fight, most of the people had sat slumped on the floor, trying to put their thoughts back together. Mary had cried softly, being rocked by a mortified but still-silent Dummy. Keith, knocked on the head by his impact with the wall, had been sent home, and Abby had insisted that the psychic do the same. Adam had never emerged from the basement, but when they had gone to check on him, they had found him hiding under the workbench in a catatonic state. Marotte, tight-lipped, had picked up his cell phone and left the office.

Now Dummy, Abby and John were the only ones left. Abby checked her watch for what felt like the fifteenth time. Ten-thirty AM. They had put most of the desks right and gathered up the papers to be refiled, but the magnitude of the task ahead was weighing down on all of them. Even Stinker had escaped to the basement, and was probably hiding in a vent somewhere.

There was an eight-foot hole in the wall, and the main office was littered with remnants of furniture and broken concrete. Shards of glass stuck out amidst the drifts of junk, or lurked treacherously in the worn carpet like a house cat waiting for a bare foot to attack. A fine layer of plaster dust covered everything, including the three of them, making them cough and sneeze. They had nailed a sheet of plywood over the hole, but gaps of chilly blue sky showed through the cracks around the edges of the square, and cold air followed it.

They had no hope of fixing the wall themselves; a contractor would be needed. In the meantime, the jagged cracks in the surrounding walls were getting some attention.

"Abby, go home," John said, dropping the half-filled can of plaster. "You're not getting anything done. Everyone else has already gone. Except Dummy, and he sleeps here." The white giant nodded slowly as he wiped the dust off the wall with a wet rag.

"Things need to get done," Abby responded as she haphazardly slapped Spackle onto the cracks in the wall. John muttered something and picked the spatula out of her hands, prying the stuff off. "Hey!"

John shook his head. "Not like that. You don't fill in the cracks yet, not without cleaning out the broken bits first. It'll get all manky if you do."

"Sorry." Abby grabbed the instrument back and scraped at the plaster. Sweat was beading on her forehead, and her hair was slipping down out of her bun and falling in choppy strands into her face. She was less work-ing on the wall than hitting it. Gusts of heat from the choking furnace fil-tered out through the vents in the walls, and condensed into clouds as they flowed through the hole and into the cold, blustery world outside.

"Abby. Go *home*. You're doing no good here."

"I don't want to," she said in a low voice. "Give back the Spackle."

"Spackle. Sounds like a bird with a cough," John commented to the air. "Spack-le. Spack-le. Isn't there a bird called a spackle?"

"I think that's the grackle. Just give it to me, would you please?"

"See what I get for trying to cheer you up."

Sighing, Abby leaned against the wall. The warmth of the office was being cut by gusts of chilly wind from the outside, and her sweat was freezing on her forehead. Dummy's bone-colored hair was sticking to his round face, and even his childish cheerfulness was suffering: his lips were pressed tightly together, and the huge shoulders hunched.

It had been a long few days. John was singing something, some rock-pop ditty, and trying to put a good face on things as he worked at the wall, but Abby could see the strain. His fingers were trembling ever so slightly, and he gripped the can of plaster like he wanted to throttle it. The joints of his knuckles were white and bloodless. Was he having another attack?

John was... unusual, to say the least. In a few unguarded moments, he had talked with her about all sorts of things; Abby had plenty of memo-ries of time spent in the little kitchenette, chatting over a cup of coffee. But there was something nasty in the mix, and whenever she accompanied him on hazardous missions—when killing was needed—she would see his teeth grind and his pupils contract just before he pulled the trigger. After such a mission he would be physically and emotionally drained, and he would gulp one or two of his little yellow pills.

And, of course, the anger: you never knew when the anger would jump out at you.

She thought that he played his own role too hard, whenever he deliber-ately used the European names for things or amped up his more out-landish behavior when he felt threatened. And there were always the anger and the pills, constants in his strange routines; she'd gotten burned a few times, asking about those. But he helped her out, so she wasn't going to pry too much. They all had their own issues; if they hadn't they would have gotten better-paying jobs.

Trying not to be obvious, she glanced at her watch again. 10:34. When she looked up again, John was staring at her with a bemused expression.

"Fine," Abby said shortly. "I'll leave. But only if you leave too."

"Sorry, I can't." John picked her discarded jacket up off her desk and tossed it to her. "You take the day off. I'll see you tomorrow, bright and early; we've got a lot to cover if we're going to get this place fixed."

"So it's housecleaning again? What about the insurance?"

"No point in spending more money when we can have ourselves a nice little office-warming party right here."

This wasn't making sense. There was anger there, but it wasn't the right kind. Normally, John would have been champing at the bit for mayhem. Abby tried a careful experiment.

"John, why are we hanging around here?" she asked, shrugging into her jacket. "Shouldn't we be out—following up clues, asking people—getting the word out?"

"Nah. We've got better things to do."

"Cleaning the office is better?"

"Cleanliness is next to godliness, innit? No sense in alienating any more powerful sorts."

His back was turned to her, but he could hear her draw in a deep breath.

"Well, I suppose," Abby said cautiously. She put a hand on the edge of the nearest desk and stepped towards him, swaying a little on her bruised knee. "But Mrs. Shepherd gave us a lot of good information we can use. Start checking the papers, see if we can find out where the bogeymen are hiding...."

There was a dull scraping sound as John dug a chunk of plaster out of the brickwork and flipped it aside. "'S out of our jurisdiction, I should think," he said over his shoulder. "Isn't this city the only place that they *haven't* attacked? We should be enjoying our vacation, by my reckoning."

"Well... yes, it is, but there's been losses reported downstate—Peoria and Springfield."

"Abby, the coppers are on it." Another scrape, another chunk. "D'you honestly think we could add anything to the investigation? They've got... cameras, and crime labs, and computers and things working on it."

Abby brushed a few papers aside, and held up the Anthology. "Yes, and we've got years of experience dealing with supernatural threats. Fine, we're not Buffy or a SWAT team, but I think we've done a pretty good job so far. We're all still alive."

"Which is more than you can say for some of the people those buggers kidnapped." John put down the pick and turned to face her. His face was flushed from the heat, and the coat of dust on his face was streaky where droplets of sweat had washed it away. "Abby, go home. We can talk about this tomorrow."

"I hate to sound dumb, John, but we can talk about it now." Abby dropped the Anthology back onto the table, punctuating her statement with the heavy thud of two hundred pages of hardbound experience. "Why aren't we following up on the information she gave us?"

At those words, the voiceless Dummy put down his chisel and, careful-ly, moved away from the wall. Neither Abby nor John paid any attention to him.

"And what exactly are we supposed to do with that information?" John said in a brittle tone. "I didn't see her handing anybody a treasure map."

She floundered for a moment. "Well—we can look up the bogeymen, see if they have any weaknesses, like vampires and garlic..."

"They're bogeymen, Abby. Creatures of the imagination, specifically cre-ated to embody our worst fears." He crossed his arms and stared at her unblinkingly. His voice was flat. "These aren't offshoots of biology, some sort of mad idea of Mother Nature's that got a rep as a supernatural crea-ture like banshees or vampires. Bogeymen are belief-eaters. People believed in these things so much that *reality itself* changed to accommodate them. What exactly are we going to do about that?"

Abby gaped.

"But Mrs. Shepherd... she's an old woman, John! She can't defend herself! We have to do something!"

"Such as?" John snapped angrily. His hair, now whitened with plaster dust, stuck up over his ears like a porcupine's quills brandished in self-defense. "Abby, let me make it plain. We don't know where they are, what they do, if they're connected with the abductions, or how to confirm any-thing about them. And even if we did—d'you think we could just walk into their home without so much as a by-your-leave?"

A white hand planted itself on John's shoulder, and the huge figure of Dummy interposed itself between the two of them. John angrily shook it off and pushed past him. When Dummy tried to stop him, John reached up, snatched the giant's head off his shoulders, dropped it into a desk drawer, and slammed the drawer closed with his foot. Blind, Dummy's body blundered backwards and thumped into the wall.

"How could you—" Abby began, flabbergasted. There was a thud as John kicked the desk, and the dummy's flailing body fell to pieces, scattering limbs across the floor. Abby's shoulders bowed in instinctive preparation for an onslaught. She couldn't believe it. John was getting so angry... over his desire to *surrender?* It was like the world had turned upside-down. "Look, I don't know how we're going to do it," she muttered. "I just think we should."

"No. Forget it. Not happening."

"Why not?"

"'Suicide, that's why!" John shouted, bringing a hand down on the table and making the cups rattle. Weariness and frustration made a potent com-bination, and his widened eyes were bloodshot, his lips drawn back in a grimace, his teeth bared like a dog making a show of dominance. His height gave him the advantage, and Abby flinched a little. He had clearly flipped from manic to depressive, and she took a step backwards.

"Think about it, Abby," he said. He leaned forward a little, and the knuckles on the clenched hands whitened. "*Bogeymen.* Everything you were ever afraid of, every nasty little fear that hid in your closet or grabbed at your toes when you were in bed. If we fight that, all of us are going to die. No crawling away with minor injuries, no chucking a Molotov in the mail room and calling it a day. Die. Dead. All gone, no more, end of the road!"

"The Cucuy wouldn't be scared if we couldn't do anything to him," she pointed out, trying to keep her voice steady. "And anyway, if he could kill us, I think he would have."

"Oh, stop it!" John spat. "He probably left us alive because he couldn't be bothered to deal with us!"

"You're worried," Abby said flatly.

"Don't you—"

"You are." Her own lip curled ever so slightly. "That kid played you like a violin. A lot of stuff that I don't understand and you don't want to talk about, but whatever it is, it's got you spooked. Your sister?"

If she hadn't been looking for it, she wouldn't have seen the tips of his ears grow red. But Abby had known John for a long while, and she knew the signs of when he was lying. And right now, his ears were reddening and his accent was growing purposely thicker. The man was getting ready to lie like a possum on the highway.

"Abby, I'm just being cautious," John said in a low voice. He slowly released his grip on the table and sat down on the edge, trying to relax. The little pills had been left in the kitchenette, hidden as always behind the salt. "Bogeymen are amazing creatures—never thought I'd hear myself say that—but I don't want to have to tussle with one. I know what I'm doing, Abby. Trust me."

"No!" Abby snarled. Now she was the one looming over him. "John," she said, and the name was like a slap in the face. "Don't you *dare* tell me what to do! Fine, you've got a gun and, and you can hit people. But weren't you the one going 'oh! Brilliant! Bogeymen!' and all that? And didn't you tell me how amazingly evil and destructive the bogeymen were? You can't just leave an old woman to certain death because you don't think it's a good idea to help her!"

She raised a shaking fist. Her arms trembled as the muscles clenched, and the stubs of her nails left white crescents in the pad of the palm. She was tired, headachy, a little drunk, and angry, as angry as she could ever remember being; it was with extreme effort that she controlled herself.

"You're afraid that somebody in here is going to get hurt," she continued in a more level tone of voice. "Don't think I haven't noticed. And I think whatever brought you to this group made you like that. That's fine. We all have problems. But when yours start keeping us from rescuing an old woman and a herd of children—some of whom probably did *not* deserve to be taken—from whatever that sick little bastard is doing, then that is *not acceptable!*"

"Acceptable, my arse!" John shouted. The redness in the tips of the ears had spread as he grew angrier. He leapt to his feet again, and his fists were balled. "D'you think your son would be better off if your body was all over the boardwalk?"

"Don't you talk that way to me!" she shrieked. Anger was now mixed with hysteria, and she felt like lashing out. She wanted to slap his face off. Didn't he *think?* God, it would be good to hit him. He *deserved* it.

John growled deep in his throat. "Team leader, Abby! When a subordinate is acting out of line—"

Abby's mouth was already open to respond when she heard a soft noise, as gentle as a leaf fluttering to the ground. Then came the glare of white light, and the much louder noise: it began as a pure wave of sound that battered the eardrums to pieces, then tapered off into the audible realm of a great gulping roar like the descent of a tornado.

And after that, came the shockwave. An invisible force struck Abby and John hard, knocking them off their feet. Abby's baggy clothes caught the surge in the air like a kite, sending her dragging backwards and ripping half the rubber off her sneakers. John, lighter and easier to throw, was tumbled head over heels and hit the wall hard. For the second time in an hour, they were tossed like dolls. Curses were muffled by the roar of the wind, and the pieces of Dummy scattered across the floor.

John scooped up an arm as it rolled past. When he managed to raise his head, he saw the rip in the world.

"I am fucking *sick* of this!" was the first thing out of his mouth.

The air bubbled and heaved, a patch shining like liquid diamond in a brilliant white glow tinged with blue. Reality warped along near-invisible lines as the air itself seemed to congeal. Within the distortion, the background of the office rippled like the bottom of a pond, and in the center the picture was completely blotted out by the burning light. The wind stopped, cut off as if a switch had been thrown, and Abby and John tumbled forward onto the floor as the force they had been fighting abruptly disappeared.

John was the first on his feet, clambering to his feet with Dummy's flailing arm held in one hand. He moved stiffly, and it was no doubt that he would have a fine set of black-and-blue marks all over his back, but his attention was clearly not on his bruises. Across the room, Abby was disentangling herself from a chair, but her eyes were fixed on the hole in the air.

Slowly, the two moved across the room. As they drew closer to the distortion, their steps fell into rhythm with each other. Now they could see things a little more clearly; there was a sheen to the air. It was as if the edges of the rip were made of gelatin, making the scene seem wavy and depthless through them. It shimmered, refracting the light that bled through it and off of it. As it pulsed, a gentle breeze puffed from it.

"Air displacement, I think," John said, tilting his head and watching the thing. It hung in the air, pulsing like a glowing heart. "There's always cold winds—in the paper, when the bogeymen broke in. They appear, displace the air. Instant scary breeze."

"So the laws of physics still apply to them... at least a bit, anyway." Abby put out a hand to touch it, very pointedly ignoring John's motion to stop her. Her heart pounded, but she put out one finger and gently brushed the softness. The world breathed again as her hand came away unscathed, making the patch shimmer and shudder in reaction to her touch.

That seemed to be the catalyst. The gleaming surface bulged again, and before either of the humans could think about leaping to safety, something slid through the quivering surface and fell gently to the ground. Abby recoiled as the pool of reality sank in on itself, slurping into the air and fading away. Ripples spread through the air, and the gleam died away with the light. In seconds, it was gone. The only remnants of its presence were the overturned furniture and the scattered Dummy, whose loose left hand now clutched a plain burlap bag.

It took fifteen minutes' hunting behind the desks to piece Dummy back together. Now John and Abby were crammed together in the little storage closet that housed their laboratory equipment, trying not to look at one another. The explosion had been like a reboot and started things again from zero. Neither of them wanted to bring up the fight.

"It's burlap, John," Abby sighed, prodding it with a pencil. "Plain old burlap. I've turned it inside out ten times now, and there's no 'place.' No amazing bogeyman power source thingy. Nothing. Just some cheap burlap."

"Try it again." The Englishman was leaning over her shoulder, staring at the crumpled piece of fabric lying on the table. Abby was currently examining a corner of it under a microscope, looking for something—anything—which might give them some information. So far, absolutely nothing had turned up. "It didn't come from nowhere, Abby. It has to be a bogeyman's bag. And a bogeyman's bag's got to have more powers than you can see with a spectro-what-have-you."

"Spectrophotometer."

"When'd we get that?"

"September."

"Necessary?"

"Yes."

"Expensive?"

"Oh, very."

"Stolen?"

"From American Science and Surplus. Can you please focus?"

John quirked an eyebrow. "Tall order, but I reckon I'll manage."

"Oh, suddenly you're calm again?" Abby said. "No more 'trust me?'" Had he taken another pill?

"The day anyone's fate rests on trusting me, you can look out for the Horsemen of the Apocalypse." John shrugged. "Besides—I've got a feeling that someone sent us this thing. Hate to disappoint 'em." He grinned humorlessly at Abby, who smiled back despite her misgivings. For a moment, their shoulders brushed against each other, and Abby felt her face turn warm. Trying to ignore her sudden discomfort, she returned to the microscope. *Just go with it,* she recited silently. *Worry later. Now's not the time.*

"Nothing?" John asked.

"I've said it before, and I'll say it again. *Nothing.* Burlap, jute, a few brown hairs stuck in the weave but nothing extraordinary. No residual smells. No dirt or gravel that we could trace for a convenient chemical sample. Nothing!" In frustration, she picked up the bag and shook it.

For a moment, the world flickered. Then the bag shuddered; Abby dropped it in shock, and the burlap made a small **thud** as it hit the floor. A plain gold ring with a dark opal in its setting bounced out of the mouth and landed on the floor.

"Well," John said. "That's not usual."

"John, this is a bag. A bogeyman's bag."

"You think I don't know?"

"For the love of God, tell me you have Mal's cell phone number," Abby whispered as she picked up the ring.

John called Marotte immediately, and he asked them to be careful until he got back to the office. "There are more things in heaven and on earth, Horatio, than are dreamt of in your philosophy," he said. "Don't get yourselves killed."

The ring and the bag were left in the tiny room that served for their laboratory. Seeking a distraction, they walked in silence into the kitchenette, each determinedly staring in a direction that did not contain the other.

Abby fiddled with the lid of the cookie jar, turning it over and over in her hands as she sat at the table as her mind churned uncomfortably. John had polished off three cookies in quick succession, and was reaching for a fourth, when Abby spoke up.

It had taken some soul-searching. She wasn't at all certain what was going on, but she knew she didn't want it to happen again. It had been a long time since she'd openly fought with John. And now that they had some sort of temporary peace, she was willing to say anything to ensure that it was kept.

"John—um—I'm sorry."

Her partner glanced up, surprised. "What for?"

"I shouldn't have gotten mad at you. I guess you have your reasons for doing what you do, and, um, it wasn't nice of me to bring them up." Abby ran a fingernail along the edge of the lid, unable to meet his eyes. She wasn't sure how much of it was a lie. Was she sorry? For starting the argument, certainly. She hated arguing. "And you're right about the mission, too. It's extraordinarily dangerous. I need to control my temper, I know, I get angry too easily. And I hope you're not going to... well... I hope I haven't affected our working relationship by acting out of line."

John sat silent for a moment, and then to Abby's surprise, he laughed. It was humorless, though not malicious. Her head shot up as he slapped at the table, grinning through a mouthful of crumbs. "Christ!" he said, laughing almost despite himself. The surface of the table vibrated as he slapped it again. "Oh, Abby, you and your fucking *guilt*."

Abby bristled. "What do you—" she began, but checked herself and closed her mouth. John shook his head.

"No, no, let it out! Don't you keep it bottled up! Do you know," he said conversationally, gripping the fourth cookie and waving it about like a flag, "that I've been waiting for a year and a half to have a good row with you?"

"What?"

"Angry? Angry? Abby, God love you, you're a fucking doormat! Maybe you've got the anger, but you haven't got the nerve. You're so afraid of being wrong that you feel guilty whenever you do anything that someone might not like!" John was grinning from ear to ear, but it wasn't a mocking expression, or even a really amused one. He leaned across the table and tapped it with the edge of the cookie, right in front of her folded hands. "Anger problem, you? Not likely. What you've got is a nerve problem. You haven't got guts. If you got angry with certain people more often, I guarantee you wouldn't have so much bloody misery. And take it from me—I know what being a misery's like. I'm a misery to every fucking person I meet. Not a good thing to be. You should get angry more often, you."

Crumbs scattered across the table from the cookie. Abby made a decision and reached across. She neatly plucked it out of his hand, making John grin even more widely, and shot him a pointed look as she popped the cookie into her mouth, sweeping at the crumbs with the other hand. John rolled his eyes heavenward, apparently making a silent plea for mercy.

She knew it wouldn't last. Maybe he meant it now, but sooner or later, the temper would come back. For the meantime, though, there was a little oasis of calm in their lives.

Strange. They were waiting on the edge of something so much bigger than them: even now, her thoughts were dragged inexorably back to the drawer where the ring and the bag waited to be examined. It was a bogey-man's bag—and that made it a solid piece of legend, created wholesale out of nothingness simply because someone decided to make up a story. But even so, poised to topple over the precipice into God only knew what, they were stealing each others' food and enjoying an inexplicable, fleeting moment of peace.

She did her best to enjoy it. It would be gone soon enough.

Chapter Sixteen

Hours passed. Far above them, in the high arching halls of the Home, hundreds of people passed to and fro. If Likho strained, he could hear them—and no more. Surrounded by age, and hemmed in with the ridiculous little plastic toys, Likho's powers were at an all-time low. He hated it. Physical bodies were nice places to visit, but he didn't want to live there, and right now he didn't have a choice. Maintaining a solid form helped keep him together.

L'uomo Nero still hadn't moved. The old woman's head had slumped on her chest; she might have been sleeping. And the guards remained as still as ever, silent and implacable. Likho knew better than to hope for a sudden human intrusion to relieve his boredom—if the combined forces of El Nadaha and Dunganga didn't want to be interrupted, then they wouldn't. Granted, they were in what looked like a subbasement, and Likho bet that nobody would have looked in anyway. But his last cigar had been crushed by Dunganga hours ago, and Likho was bored.

But he knew that El Cucuy wouldn't leave them alone for long. The air rippled in his ears, and the threads of reality plucked and wavered. He straightened up: another bogeyman was coming. It was a strange presence, but one he recognized. The two jailers grimaced and faded away, stepping back through the walls. The newcomer's unique presence demanded privacy.

What was the shortass thinking, sending *him* in? Likho's lip curled as the door opened. It must have been El Cucuy's way of gloating.

The Czech bogeyman was one of the few Family members that was difficult to classify. He had as many as a dozen aspects, each stranger than the last, and he could not be strictly called a hairy man or a bag man. Instead, his legend put "lost souls" into his care, child or adult, man or woman. That made him unique, and unique could be dangerous. Nobody stepped on Hastrman's toes.

Even Giovanna seemed to sense him coming. She opened her eyes and straightened up, wincing only a little at the motion, and brushed one limp hank of white hair out of her face.

"Trouble, is it?" she said. The words echoed slightly in the dim basement.

"Depends on how you see it," Likho said.

The door ground unevenly over the slightly warped concrete as Hastrman made his entrance.

Hastrman was built like a stick insect, so tall and thin that it made Likho think he would snap in two any minute. He had two pale jaundiced eyes that sat uneasily, like two halves of a boiled egg, in oversized sockets, and the bones of his over-large face jutted out against the light. He seemed to be all sharp angles and patches of shadow, from his deadly thin arms and legs to the awful concertina of a rib cage that looked ready to burst out of the overstretched skin. Lines of shadow in every cranny made him a matchstick sculpture in sharp relief.

His sole concession to weather or modesty was a ragged piece of cloth, tied and looped around his hips to cover what a bogeyman had no need for. His hair was a flaxen yellowy-white, and stood out from his head in a wild tangle that even the patches of grease and dirt couldn't keep down. In his hands, he carried a folded piece of woolen cloth.

"What's going on up there?" Likho called out. Hastrman ignored him.

"Well, look at you," Giovanna commented, easing towards the wall a little. "Don't believe I've seen you before. Who are you, then—or aren't you allowed to say?"

The skeleton man shook his head. "I give my name as freely as I like, old one."

"Then give it, please. And mind what you call me; if you are what I think you are, you're older'n I'll ever be."

"Apologies, grandmother." Hastrman bowed his head a little, and moved a few steps closer with a rangy, loping stride like a huge cat. "I would be Hastrman, grandmother. They call me scarecrow or bugbear, who would talk about my doings."

Giovanna eyed him a little critically, but Likho was prepared to bet that she was feeling more friendly towards the newcomer. "Well, you're fairly civil for a bogey—that's not saying much but it's a nice enough change. What's this business of yours?"

"With your permission, grandmother, I come to measure you."

"Measure me?" Giovanna repeated, surprised. "Now, what on earth for?"

"It is a full moon tonight, grandmother," Hastrman said calmly. "Upon nights of the full moon, it would be my duty to weave clothes for the lost souls that have been gathered."

"And I'm a lost soul?"

"You were brought here," Hastrman replied. "The Cucuy has given orders, and I obey. By my reckoning, you will be lost soon enough. If you would be pleased to rise, grandmother, I would get on with my task."

The old lady shook her head. "No, you don't. I know how this goes. I've got no intention of going to the grave any sooner than I have to—and especially not of digging the pit myself."

Hastrman inclined the great head again. Poised so awkwardly, with the explosion of tangled hair standing out above his thin frame, he looked like a ritual mask which had been left hanging on a stand. "Grandmother, you will be proclaimed lost whether I would measure you or no. It is not a matter of worry to me. I would like to do so, however; it will make things very simple for me when I weave tonight."

"Oh, yes?" Giovanna said, eyeing him beadily. "Well, I'll stand for you and be measured if you answer me one question. Can bogeys do that?"

"Bargaining and questioning the spirits is as old as we ourselves," the Hastrman replied calmly. "Ask what you would."

Keeping her gaze fixed on the tall figure, Giovanna drew her legs up and wrapped her skirt more tightly around them. "All right, then. What's this lost soul business about? I'm not a child. What makes me lost?"

"You are a grown-up, grandmother," was the reply. The Hastrman unfolded the length of cloth and shook it out; although the wool thread itself was very coarse, it was of a fine, tight weave. That was Hastrman for you: he did his work, and he did it well. "Many of the Family are most unhappy. They say it is not within our power. Few of us take grown-ups—though I myself am numbered among the exceptions to the rule. The Cucuy, to quell the murmurings, declares you a lost soul and therefore within the boundaries of our power."

Giovanna rose to her feet, and the Hastrman shook the cloth once more. "Well, then," she said, as he moved forward, "that does answer my question. But I don't suppose you'll give me one more?"

"It's all one to me, grandmother." The Hastrman stretched out the length of wool and held it against the span of Giovanna's bony shoulders.

"What's the dead boy after, then?" she asked. "Why's he want me? I know he's behind the disappearance of L'uomo Nero, and that rude friend of his, too."

"Hey!" Likho called from his place across the cellar. Now Giovanna, too, was ignoring him.

"But why me? I never did him any wrong."

The Hastrman gently but firmly took one of her arms and measured the length of it with the end of the wool cloth. "He would see you as a corrupting influence, grandmother. It was on your advice that L'uomo Nero and Likho did against their orders, and the Cucuy does not like that. He fears that L'uomo Nero hides something from him."

"I own up to giving the black man some advice...." Her voice trailed off momentarily. The Hastrman used the silence to wrap the cloth around her neck, marking the width of it. "What's he hiding, then?" she insisted peevishly as the wool was taken away.

"You would not know, grandmother?"

"I don't know a thing of your affairs. I've never seen any of you but L'uomo Nero, and him only, for more than eighty years."

"He will not tell us," the bogeyman said calmly, but for a moment there might have been an edge to the low monotone voice. "He says he wants the bag of L'uomo Nero, but for what he says nothing. It is the unknown."

Giovanna tsked. "You bogeys are amazing. Never seem to get away from that stuff about the unknown. Wasn't your old leader made of I-know-not-what?"

Now there was no mistaking the sudden tension in the rangy frame of the Hastrman. "That would not be of any of my concern, grandmother," he said in a low voice. "And if you wish to live long enough to see the garment I would weave you, then you might do well not to say anything of that."

"I can't say I'm surprised. A death like that, there's got to be some mystery 'round... Bavbav, yes?" At the visible flinch from the Hastrman, she nodded. Likho silently applauded. "Bavbav it was, then. I never have any trouble remembering any of you people. Of course, at the hospital, it's a different story—all made-up names like a cat walked over a keyboard. But then, you bogeymen can't just make up your own mess of letters. Didn't think so. But then, it's none of your business, I suppose. My apologies, my good spirit."

The Hastrman had finished his measuring, and was standing with his head cocked, staring intently at her. After a long moment, he nodded and began to refold his cloth. "I thought so," he said.

"Hmm?"

He moved to go, walking much more stiffly than when he had entered the small room. He was at the door and reaching for the knob when a thought seemed to strike him. Perhaps he could feel Giovanna's eyes on his back, but at any rate, he turned around and faced her again.

"You are not a grandmother, but you are an old woman nonetheless," the Hastrman said. "Keep a hand on that, and you'll have more power than you'd think."

Giovanna's eyes were bright, but she watched him carefully. "You're insane," she said in a flat voice. "Crazy. I'm an old woman, not a witch."

"That is as may be. But children have grandmothers, old woman."

And with that, he opened the door and slipped through, cloth in hand. Giovanna's mouth only had time to open, for he was already gone.

A moment later, he was replaced by much less amiable company. Dunganga and El Nadaha faded back into existence. El Nadaha moved to Giovanna and seized her roughly by the arm, while Dunganga stepped across the line of toys and roughly kicked them away.

Get up, the hairy man ordered. *El Cucuy will see you all.*

"Well, isn't that generous of him," Giovanna said tartly. "You lead the way. I've got a few things to say to that boy."

"I'll bet you do," Likho muttered.

The room was hugely wide but not very high, a basement writ large. Everywhere were wooden crates and strange, gauze-wrapped bundles of something-or-other. The place was clean and swept, and at the far end, there was a wall with several doors and a wide glass window set into it. Likho had seen enough of the Home before to recognize it as a mixed preservation room and storage area. It was a place where people cleaned and cataloged pieces of the past.

In the center of the—for lack of a better word—hall, there was a stack of old wooden crates neatly pushed together to form a wide rectangular platform. El Nadaha, who still gripped Giovanna by the arm, gave her a shove that sent her sprawling to the ground in front of it. She gave a little gasp as she landed. Likho thought he heard something crack.

The air shimmered, and El Cucuy stepped into existence. He nodded to the darkness around them, and the world twisted a little as several more figures popped out into the scene. Likho glanced around, eyeing the newcomers carefully: mostly hairy men, with a few of the more bestial bag men thrown in for good measure. Even the Mörkö was there, though he seemed less comfortable than the rest.

The old woman didn't look at El Cucuy. Instead, she pulled herself up onto her knees, her muscles trembling under the wrinkled skin, and turned to look at L'uomo Nero.

"Black man," she said. "Black man, you're still alive?"

L'uomo Nero's face was drawn and paler than ever. "Still I exist. My belief... is sufficient."

At that, El Cucuy growled low in his throat, and Dunganga grabbed L'uomo Nero by the neck of his coat. Greasy claws slid out from the huge paw. Moving instinctively, Likho charged at the hairy man, but a shriek from the old woman made him halt in his tracks. Giovanna was on the floor again, with one of El Nadaha's feet planted on her head. Dunganga's eyes gleamed, daring the Russian bogeyman to move another inch.

His hands trembled with barely suppressed rage, but Likho stood still. El Cucuy nodded at him from his platform before turning to L'uomo Nero.

"Give me Bavbav," El Cucuy demanded bluntly. L'uomo Nero stared deadeyed down at him. "Give me Bavbav, and I'll let the old woman go. Recall the bag."

L'uomo shook his head. "No."

Likho knew it was over as soon as he turned his eyes to the face of his leader. El Cucuy was a smart little bastard, that he had to admit; he would have caught the slight tremor in L'uomo Nero's voice. And now he knew just what he was going to do.

"If that will not do, then let me say it differently." The red eyes were completely unblinking. Always, El Cucuy had rejected the lure of the physical form. For as long as Likho could remember, he had refused to let his human form influence him, as some of the other Family members had. "If you do not give me Bavbav," El Cucuy continued, enunciating each word carefully, "then I will have the Llorona pull her skin off, inch by inch. I will have the Chownki Daar take out her eyes. I will let the seven o'clock man break every bone in her body. And I will let it continue, until I have Bavbav." Even now, there was no blinking, no breathing, no tell-tale twitch in the face or the hand.

But there was one in L'uomo's face. Likho watched as his friend's head slowly raised. There was the slightest trembling of the lips, a quiver in the corners of the eyes. L'uomo had loved being physical. His emotions were written on the human face he wore; always had been, always would be. If he had currently had one, Likho's heart would have sunk. L'uomo slowly lifted a hand, uncurling his fingers as if he was holding a bag—

And there was a furious inrush of breath from across the room.

"Oh, *no you don't!*" the old woman shrieked. The assembled bogeymen flinched at the sudden sound of her voice. "I won't listen to that, you little twerp, not at my time of life!"

Apparently ignoring El Nadaha, who seemed unsure of what to do, Giovanna pushed herself into a sitting position. Likho felt like cheering. Good for you, you old bitch—put the fear of Granny into 'em!

"Black man, if you give him that bag you'll be more of an idiot than—"

El Cucuy was quick, that was for certain. He leapt down from the platform and struck her hard across the face. The old woman's head snapped backwards like a piece of laundry in the wind, skull slamming into the hard surface of the wall. Her skin burned red and raw where he had touched her. Tears were growing in her eyes, but she recoiled and glowered at El Cucuy despite her obvious pain.

"That all you can do?" she snapped. El Cucuy—his hand already raised to strike again—stopped dead.

Giovanna glared at him. "You think you can bully him into giving you that bag? For *my* life? I'm eighty-seven, for God's sake! Two or three more years, and it's a cheap casket and 'ashes to ashes' for me. You can't threaten me with death. But there's plenty enough out there who *would* be worse off, and I'll be damned if I'll see that dear dumb idiot being responsible for whatever scheme you've got!"

"It's a matter of survival!" El Cucuy shouted. His voice echoed throughout the vast whiteness of the strange, dim room, and his own red eyes were widened. "Your stupidity has interfered with my plan to keep us alive! *You* are meant to die. *We* are not."

"That hasn't got anything to do with that bag!" she snapped. "Whatever's in there, your eternal life hasn't got anything to do with it, and slapping me around isn't going to make you any easier to believe in!"

"How do you—" El Cucuy began, but stopped dead with a little laugh. His sudden rage had vanished as quickly as it had appeared. "Practically an almanac," he chortled. "L'uomo, if you had gotten any closer you would have married her." He clapped his hands and laughed again, the high, joyous giggle of a child at play. "Mummy, please, Mummy, may we keep it?"

L'uomo Nero's voice was low. "Say what is said, the bag will not come to you."

"I've a bit of an idea about that." El Cucuy turned to face him. "The rest of the Family will return with their catches at the night's end. I would like to have them here when we condemn you, after all; we all need belief, and their belief in my power is always enjoyable. As for the old woman... fear is also a form of belief. She'll doubtless feed some of the lesser brethren."

There was a rumble, and the Mörkö leaned forward a little. "LORD, PERHAPS I MAY—"

"*No.*" The Mörkö flinched backwards, and El Cucuy stared at him coldly. "Take her back to her holding cell," he said over his shoulder to a pair of hairy men. "You can lock her in and go about your rounds. I'll be finished with the two rogues soon enough."

Likho was careful to watch the old woman as she was dragged off. If he wasn't busy worrying about the next round of interrogation, he might have called the expression on her face triumphant.

He hoped, as El Cucuy advanced on him, that he would get to see many more generations of humans. They were even weirder, and more interesting, than he had previously thought.

"Babay," said the child. His voice was an odd little coo, as if he was trying to be ingratiating. The little punk was definitely trying a different tack. "Babay, you-who-call-yourself-Likho. What do you think of all this?"

Likho shook his head. "You should have tried Good Cop before Bad Cop, Cucuy. That's what I think."

"Survival isn't about being good or bad, Babay."

"What is it about, then?"

"Being the best."

"So is that why you tried to kill Bavbav?" Likho said loudly. He was aware of a subtle change in the air; at the words *kill Bavbav*, one or two of the hairy men had shifted on their feet, and a low murmuring filled the room. El Cucuy's stony facade never flinched.

"Likho, you like humans." El Cucuy folded his arms, regarding Likho critically, like a little boy who refuses to believe that people in Australia don't walk around upside-down. "They're capable of so much. They created us. But do you really think... Likho, did you ever honestly believe that they should dictate what we do?"

"That sounds like a trick question to me." Likho cocked his head, watching El Cucuy carefully. "I seem to remember that Aristotle dingus, back in the day, saying that the ultimate good is for everything to do what it was intended to do. And us, well, we can't exactly have identity crises, can we? We know what we're supposed to do. Make the kids good. That's our *raison d'etre*, if you wanna get technical."

It wasn't his imagination: he'd definitely got a twitch out of El Cucuy that time. The boy's air was still determinedly unaffected, but there was something in the red eyes that told Likho he'd touched a nerve. So to speak.

"But if we simply do so, *Babay*, they'll stop believing in us. It would be stupid to go about our ways, letting ourselves be annihilated by the march of civilization. The further they get from the animal, the less powerful the stories they tell, and so-" his voice rose "—so we are diminished!"

There was an answering roar from the bogeymen. El Cucuy's shout had them firmly back on his side. Likho paused for a moment, considering his next answer.

"Cucuy... you're a kid." Likho raised his head high and looked around the circle, fixing his gaze on one bogeyman after another. "Civilizations come and go. Some of us have been at this since Ur, and fuck it, *before*.

"And that's why you wanted Bavbav out. He wasn't just a bogeyman, he was Father Fear. He'd seen it all, he knew we would still manage to survive. But you, your legend makes you an ambitious little cunt—"

Down he went, his words choked by Sacauntos' fist. Funny, how even creatures of belief would resort to good old-fashioned violence. Even as his face crashed into the floor, and his form shuddered with pain, he heard the scream in El Cucuy's voice. Likho had broken him.

"How dare you?" the dead boy shrieked. He stamped wildly, his heels crashing down on the back of Likho's head. Surrounded as he was by age, Likho had no chance of discorporating, and his body had no choice but to take the blows. "Human! All of you!" El Cucuy howled wildly as he struck again and again. Bone cracked under his assault. "You pathetic piece of shit, you useless ass, you *human*, you're not fit to be called a member of this Family! When the old woman's dead, I'll jam a child's toy down your throat! The hairy men will kill every single damn brat who believes in you, and when they die, you'll be nothing but a screaming ghost! Do you hear me, you fucking human? I'll eradicate you!"

Still shrieking, he rounded on the assembled bogeymen. "We may be born from humans, but we are not on their level! *They make us weak!* Any Family member caught indulging in human behavior will have their believers executed! Do I make myself clear?" There was a despairing groan from the ranks of the Family.

Shuddering, Likho rolled over on the ground, trying to sit up. For a moment, blood leaked from between his lips, but then he focused himself and the injuries slowly began to knit themselves back together. As he looked, he saw El Cucuy stalking the line of bogeymen like a mad Patton, glaring wildly at the assembled ranks.

Then, he stopped. One white hand shot out, a gesture of *j'accuse* pointed straight at a huddled blue shape. "Him. Dunganga, Sacauntos, bring him here."

Likho squinted, trying to see through the red haze of pain. The Mörkö was shuddering, making pitiful groaning noises as the other two hairy men hauled him forward.

"You, Finland," El Cucuy said. The voice had dropped, and was once again icy calm. "You questioned my orders earlier. And you said to me yourself, the old woman frightened you away from your prey."

"PLEASE, LORD," the Mörkö said quickly. "NEVER HAVE I BEEN UNFAITHFUL—"

"Fear and doubt. Human traits, Mörkö."

"NEVER!" the blue giant retorted, but there was real fear there. "I HAVE ONLY BEEN A LITTLE WEAK. THE BELIEF GROWS STRONG, AND IT WILL SOON RESTORE ME—"

"You're not one of us," El Cucuy said coldly. Likho winced in sympathy as the Mörkö visibly quailed. The poor bastard was weak, and that made him El Cucuy's sacrificial lamb.

"You've become too human, Mörkö. You're not part of the Family."

"I AM ONLY DIMINSHED. I DO NOT DIE. I DO NOT GROW HUMAN. IT IS ONLY A CHANGE. ALL OF US HAVE BEEN THROUGH SUCH TIMES."

"Not like you. Be quiet."

The blue creature convulsed as if he'd been electrocuted. "BROTHER, I—"

"No more!" The dead child cut off the Mörkö's pleas with two sharp words. Some kind of anger burned in his youthful face, the anger of a king facing someone guilty of treason. "Brothers," he continued, turning to the rest of the assembled bogeymen—those who were, even now, watching him with still, searching eyes. "You see what the real danger is here.

"It is not just belief. We have survived on less belief than we have now. But when they see us as *human*—" he spat the word. "We become like the Mörkö. His strongest sources of belief came to see him as something like them. Weakling and flesh-bound. And so he has become like them!"

"BROTHER," the Mörkö pleaded desperately. It would have been almost comical, this ten-foot-tall behemoth of blue light begging a frail, pale child. But El Cucuy didn't even look at him.

"During our abduction of the grandmother, he flinched when shots were fired. Fear." The small, thin voice was bitter. "He could not capture a child, thanks to that old thing we have. Failure. And now, he questions my orders in a manner like that of the traitors... nervousness, insecurity, temperament, and uselessness."

"BROTHER! I DID NOT—"

"Leave us," El Cucuy ordered shortly. "Eat, drink, and hide in fear. But if you show yourself here among us again—" and the terrible voice began to rise in anger "—then by every whining little human saint, I'll break you so well that they'll dream new nightmares from your shredded remains! *Out!*"

His words ended in a shriek of rage. The Mörkö let out a single despairing wail, and began to fade away. By the time it had reached the wall, nothing was left but a pale corona of blue light, which dispersed like a morning mist and seeped into the brickwork.

"It's a plague," the dead child murmured to himself, resting his head in his hands. "All of us are in danger. Even us. Even me. The infection is getting to us all. A shameful thing, one which we can't escape or fight off. But we *have* to. They see us as human. This must not be. Forgotten or changed! The Mörkö is dead now."

Likho stared as El Cucuy babbled to himself. Was he losing it? The Mörkö was by no means one of their oldest or most powerful, but they had all thought that his new appearance was just a change of shape—the sort of thing that they were all used to, after thousands of years of existence. And now El Cucuy had thrown him out.

Their leader was going insane. And Likho was certain that he wasn't the only one thinking it.

Chapter Seventeen

Abby and John were in the small room that passed for the laboratory, poring over the strange items, when the office temperature dropped fifteen degrees. Both stiffened, but the open door only admitted a haggard-looking Marotte.

"I returned as quickly as I could," he said, dropping his gloves on the nearest desk and unwinding his checkered scarf as he came into the small room. "You said something about a magic ring?"

Abby gave him a quick summary of all that had happened since the interview with Giovanna had been disrupted. "And now we have a bag, a ring, and a few hairs, none of which are telling us anything."

"Tell me about the hairs," Marotte said. "Are they human?"

"We think. They're normal, at any rate—boring, even. No blood residue—"

"Nothing that *CSI* could use, in other words," John interrupted. He squeezed Abby's shoulder as he leaned over the table, making more room for Marotte. "But they had to come from somewhere, didn't they? Anything like that? 'Made in China'?"

Abby frowned at the microscope, looking as if she would dearly like to throttle it. She knew there were bags under her eyes, and her hair was dampened with sweat. Not that John would mind, she thought darkly; by now he had a forest of stubble on his chin, and a distinct whiff of Bailey's Irish Cream and stale cigarettes hovered around him.

"They're worked pretty deep into the fabric," she concluded after a moment's examination. "Like they were part of it, knitted right into the weave."

"Okay, now we're gettin' somewhere. Think. How could it get into that weave?"

"I don't know!" Abby snapped, a little wildly. "How many ways do you want me to say it?"

Marotte carefully slid past John, moving between the two tense agents. "Be calm, please," he said levelly. "We have work to do. Abigail, with your permission—the ring."

The ring was lying where she had left it, in the center of a square of waxed paper. Abby handed Marotte the box of latex gloves, and when he had pulled on a pair, she put the plain opal ring into his hands.

The ring lay in his palm, dirty and dark. Marotte turned it over with nimble gloved fingers and stared at it, murmuring to himself. A moment later, he looked up.

"Dummy?"

An arm scuttled through the open door and tapped on the ground, awaiting orders. "Fetch me the Anthology, please," Marotte said to the hand.

"It's a ring," John said skeptically as the hand scuttled off. "Going to chuck it in the fire, then?"

"Three for the elven-kings under the sky, seven for the dwarf-lords in their halls of stone," Abby recited as she peered at the small gold ring in Marotte's hand. "Nine for mortal men doomed to die, one for the SSR to throw them a bone...?"

"In the land of Chicago, where the voters lie," John finished.

"Hardly. Look." Marotte turned the ring over again, holding it up to the light bulb. "I'm rather surprised at you both; there are markings you never spotted."

John craned his neck to look at the small object. "Where?"

"On the inside of the band. The alphabet is Cyrillic, and they look very old. There may be something in the Anthology which has... thank you, Dummy." A headless body appeared in the doorway with the battered book. "Knowing our good friend the late Reverend," he continued, taking the book and leafing rapidly though it, "and taking into consideration his truly astounding range of interests, it would not surprise me in the slightest if he should have encountered or imagined something just like this."

"Yes, but you're in the section on fairy tales," John pointed out. He seemed needled that someone else had spotted something he overlooked, and his tone was peevish. "Reality distortions're in the back."

Marotte pulled a piece of paper towards him and began to sketch with his free hand. "This seems to be it... yes... that'll do. Here." And he pushed the paper towards them.

Ба́ба Яга́, it said.

"Those are the markings inside the ring?" Abby asked. Marotte nodded, and Abby gnawed on her lip as she stared at the paper. "They look familiar... the backwards R makes a -ya sound, I think. Babayaza?"

"A hard G, Abigail. Baba Yaga."

"Baba Yaga?" Abby's voice cracked a little, and she could feel her heart sink. It was a name from her childhood, and a nightmarish one at that. "*The* Baba Yaga? Grandmother of all ghosts? A house on chicken feet, skulls on the fence posts, riding through the woods on a mortar and pestle?"

"The one fairy tale that you never ever tell your kids?" John chimed in. "Bloody hell, of all the legends to come true!" He glanced around the office. "Did someone break a mirror a while back? Our luck's been pretty fucking rotten lately."

"The question is, what is a ring with Baba Yaga's sigil doing in a bogey-man's bag?" Marotte asked.

"Well, she does hand out magical objects," Abby pointed out. Her mind whirled as she thought frantically, trying to sift out information from the tangle of memories. A bearded man on a bar stool, rocking back and forth as he recited 'Little house, little house, turn your back to the trees,' in between gulps from a beer mug, rose to the fore. "Magical dolls, magical bones, magical balls of string... and magical rings, of course. Usually rings of invisibility, strength, flight—things like that."

John took the ring from Marotte and examined it closely. "It's nothing you wear, at any rate. My mum had a ring with her birthday carved inside, and the letters got all worn down. And the inside's clean, but the outside's dirty." He tossed it up in the air and caught it neatly. "So it's a ring which nobody wears... how about it?"

"Wait a minute!" Abby exclaimed. She darted out of the room, pushing past Marotte, and went straight to the half-collapsed bookshelf. A moment later, she was back in the small room with a worn brown book in her hands. "'Cast it before you,'" she quoted from memory, "'and follow it wheresoever it rolls.' Baba Yaga gave Ivan Tsarevitch a ring like that; Andre the Archer traveled to I Know Not Where with a ring like that; Mashka found Fenist the Bright Falcon with just that kind of thing!" She dropped the book on the table and hurriedly paged through it. "There's no description. But a ring that rolls on the ground and never got worn—"

"Would look just like that," John agreed. "The question is, what do we do with it?" He tossed the ring, caught it, and tossed it again. Abby felt a surge of annoyance as he caught it again. "I hate this kind."

"For God's sake, John, it's not a toy!" she snapped. As it soared up into the air again, she leaned over and snatched it before it could fall into his hands. "This is a serious—"

—and she fell into nothingness. Pressure crushed in on her like a vise in the blackness, her shriek of surprise dying stillborn in her throat. She tumbled voiceless through the nothingness, the ring burning in her hand.

Then, light. A stone floor rushed up to meet her, striking her hard against the back and sending pain shooting through her head. Even as her vision blurred, horny-nailed hands gripped her face, and Abby found herself staring into a pair of bloodshot eyes whose gaze shot through her like an arrow. A nose like a ship's prow was pressed against hers.

"Good girl, granddaughter," a hoarse voice laughed. The overpowering stench of beer filled her nostrils, making Abby cough and flail. It was useless; the hands held her in a grip like steel. "You found it. I'm no friend of yours, but I'll have no wretched spirit playing King of the Mountain. Now take the ring, or I'll take your skull, good girl though you are." The fingers tightened, and stars danced in front of Abby's eyes.

"Yes, you are a good girl, I say. Your grandfather did well, telling you my stories. But no questions, girl—there's no time. There's something else coming for you. He wants blind revenge, but what he needs is killing. Go."

And once again, the crushing darkness surrounded her.

Light blinded her. Then she felt hardness under her again, wood instead of stone, and the familiar bite of the desk's edge against the backs of her thighs. Somebody shouted. She lashed out blindly, trying to fend off whatever creatures were about to attack.

"Abby!" John's voice shouted. "For fuck's sake, what happened?"

Abby groaned and rolled over. Papers. Pencils. Her desk ornament shaped like a Labrador retriever. Her desk. She had landed on her desk. Good God, her computer must be destroyed. Something under her head felt like her keyboard, that was for certain. For a moment, she wondered vaguely why she was in pain, but then her brain gave a jolt and she rolled off the desk.

"Baba Yaga," she panted, pushing against the carpet in an effort to stand. For a moment, she flopped uselessly. Hands gripped her by the arms and pulled her to her feet. "Baba Yaga," she repeated. "I saw her. Oh, God, I saw her. It's a traveling ring. John, Mal, Baba Yaga—"

"Did she hurt you?" John said in a strained voice. His hands were still gripping Abby's arm uncomfortably hard, and his face was white.

"Just fell." Abby's head was swimming. Baba Yaga. She remembered the stories all too well. Grandpa George and his afternoons in the poolroom, bribing her with soda pop and fairy tales to keep her from telling Grandma where they'd been all afternoon. A house on chicken legs. Three servants, only disembodied pairs of hands. Magical gifts, for good or ill. A warning? "Oh, lord," she breathed. "John, she said something's coming. A monster. It's going to kill us."

Marotte instinctively reached for his knife. "Bogeyman?" he said quickly. "I think so."

"Shite," John muttered. But he let go of Abby's arm and ran to his desk, pulling open the drawer where Abby knew he kept his spare ammunition. "South wall's weak; it'll probably come through there again. Did she say how many?"

"Just one, I think." Abby mopped her face with one trembling hand. It came back wet. She hadn't even known she was crying.

John had chambered a new magazine while she was talking, and now he was fumbling with a box of shotgun shells. "Fuck, fuck, fuck," he said to himself, almost chanting. "We need weapons. For fuck's sake, where's the Mossberg?"

"In the basement. We need a barricade. Mal, help me!" Abby called out.

John turned around quickly. His desk had been tipped onto its side by the chaos of the day, but its drawers were facing the ceiling. Abby looked up as he tossed her her loaded Beretta: she caught it with one hand and, with a grunt, pushed her own desk over onto its side. Marotte pulled three chairs into a row and crouched behind them, holding a long-barreled revolver that had apparently been concealed in the file drawer. Within seconds, the room looked like an impromptu reenactment of the Alamo.

They were ready, and not a moment too soon. There was a wordless roar, and the floor trembled as heavy footsteps thundered through it. Blue light poured into the office as a huge hand burst through the plywood board, shattering their patch and scattering chips of wood across the floor. Its long curved digits ended in wicked blue claw. Every inch of it glowed, its radiance tinting the destroyed office in shades of bluish-purple and gray.

"Horrorshow!" John hissed to Abby. Against all odds, a manic grin was appearing on his face. Abby had no idea what he was saying. She gave one wild thought to the medicine cabinet and the little yellow pills. Too far away now.

Another roar, more enraged this time, and the flimsy patch was torn out of the wall. Ten feet of Mörkö, trailing bluish smoke, burst into the room with the wooden rectangle still hanging off one of his arms. Every time his feet touched the ground, a scorched foot print was left behind. The linoleum blistered under his huge paws, and the stench of rot came pouring over them.

The three weapons barked. One, two, three four five six seven eight as shots were emptied into the creature's glowing chest, the eruption of gunfire deafening in the tiny office. A textbook spread of holes appeared as if by magic, and the Mörkö uttered another roar, this one of pain, and clawed at its own torso. There was blood there, oozing from the tattered wounds.

Crouched behind the overturned furniture, the agents were ready. Abby saw John snatch another magazine out of his pocket, jettison the empty one, slide in the new load with the speed of a striking snake, and chamber the first round with a **click** that sounded like a coffin closing on a man who was not likely to be missed. "Thought he might," he hissed, trying to ignore the ringing in his ears. "Human enough to be hurt."

"YOU WILL PERISH IN FLAMES!" the Mörkö roared, still clutching its monstrous stomach. "MAY THE FIENDS OF HELL DEVOUR YOUR FLESH AND BONES!"

By the chairs, Marotte had discarded the now-empty revolver, and was unsheathing his Bowie knife. Abby rose to her feet, Beretta held loosely in her right hand. Her grip trembled only a little as she raised it, pointing the weapon directly between the huge blue creature's eyes. The Mörkö flinched and hissed in pain. The blood oozing between its clawed fingers was orange-red and a little watery.

"You're not in a position to make threats," Abby said as flatly as she could. "Where does El Cucuy like to hide?"

"A THOUSAND FIRES OF DAMNATION TO TEAR AT YOUR SKIN AND CRUNCH YOUR BONES!"

Abby gave John a shaky smile, but her gun never wavered. "Goodness, he's a lot shorter in person, isn't he?"

"MAY LIGHTNING TURN YOUR EYEBALLS TO GLASS AND BOIL YOUR BLOOD WITHIN YOUR FILTHY HUMAN VEINS!"

"Definitely," her partner responded. He, too had cracked a toothy grin, and also covered the bogeyman with his pistol as he rose. "You can start talking any time now, Mr. Mörkö. Incidentally, there's umlauts over that, right? On the O's? Or whatever those little dots on top are called. Is it umlauts? Don't remember. How do you pronounce that?"

"Umlauts," Marotte confirmed flatly.

The Mörkö snarled. "YOUR PAIN WILL BE ETERNAL AND UNEND-ING!"

"Ree-pe-ti-tion," John sang in a taunting voice. "Mörkö, kindly step up and receive your Certificate of Redundancy Certificate, certified by the London Redundancy Certification Board of Greater London."

"Besides, I don't think eyeballs can actually turn to glass," Abby added. She thought she understood a little of John's mania; the rush of adrenaline was making her feel bizarrely giddy, and for a moment, her fear complete-ly left her. "They can fry, I think, but you need sand to actually become glass. Highly unlikely at best. Who has sand in their eyes? Beachcombers, perhaps?"

"Surfers?" John offered. "Those scary middle-aged women who really shouldn't be wearing bikinis and always seem to turn up in the tiniest ones possible?"

Abby shook her head. "You're no treat to look at yourself, mister. Those who live in glass houses—"

"—had better spend a hell of a lot on blinds."

"TOUCH ME AGAIN, HUMANS," the Mörkö interrupted in a snarling voice, "AND YOU WILL NEVER TOUCH ANYTHING AGAIN. YOUR FINGERS WILL CRISP AT THE ROOTS AND BURN AWAY AS YOU SCREAM IN TORMENT!"

"Awfully stuck on burning, isn't he?" Abby pursed her lips, running one finger of her free hand over her chin. "Do you think he touched a hot pot when he was little?"

It was a stupid thing to say, and she knew it. But with adrenaline singing through her veins, she was flying high, and the spectacle of the Mörkö cowering in fear had gone to her head like a shot of heroin. Schadenfreude, dishes best served cold—call it whatever they liked. For a second, she thought she knew why John was always smiling.

"Don't know. I'd move more for 'abusive relative who lived under a heating pad,' myself. Like one of those frightening old nans who'll as soon chuck a ceramic poodle as look at you." John posed, making a play of considering thoughtfully. "Or maybe somebody poured a kettle on him. He's a bit twitchy, after all."

The Mörkö was visibly writhing. "Well, look at that," John observed. "Mockery does him no good, it seems."

"He lives on fear." Marotte eyed the creature coldly. "Fear is opposed by humor, not love. You can fear that which you love, but you cannot fear something you find amusing."

Abby shrugged. "Too *human*, I guess." She smiled when the Mörkö glared at them. "All right, Mörkö. Where does El Cucuy hide?"

"Say it now," John added, "or we'll bring out the light bulb jokes."

The Mörkö shuddered, conflicted. The door was still stuck on his arm, and there was blood beginning to drip from the places where the spears of shattered wood dug into his glowing surface. His bluish substance was more solid than it looked, apparently. The huge shoulders hunched, and the light around him flickered and flashed nervously. If one looked closely, it would have been easy to think the glow was fading a bit.

"I SHOULD NOT TELL," he rumbled at last. "IT IS NOT MY PLACE."

"Oh, come on!" John exclaimed, waving his pistol in an impassioned gesture. Abby ducked as it went flailing past her head. "You don't have any reason to protect the little sod any more, do you? You know it, you're a smart fellow, even if you do act a bit blue. Talk to us, and you'll get immunity. Who knows, maybe we can find you a job here."

"Please," Abby added. The rush was beginning to fade. For a moment, she wished it wasn't, but sanity made its cold return and she knew she had to focus. "Tell us what happened, and tell us where they are. We need you to help us."

The Mörkö squirmed visibly. "THERE IS A PLACE, A HALL. THE HOME OF NORTH AMERICA. PEOPLE DO NOT GO THERE AT NIGHT."

At those words, John grinned a grin with no humor in it whatsoever. "I thought so. Next question: why are the bogeymen panicking? Why now? What's making them act so mad?"

"I HAVE DONE MY DUTY—"

"No, you haven't!" Abby's voice was as sharp as a razor despite her fatigue, and the Mörkö flinched as if she had fired another shot. "You haven't done your duty until we're satisfied that you've told us everything you know. And we're not satisfied, and you haven't, so never mind the lying. Why did El Cucuy get rid of Bavbav?"

"CHANGES COME UPON US. WE MUST FIGHT TO SURVIVE."

"Changes? What sort of changes? And don't lie." In a frantic burst of aggression, she added, "Lying makes my trigger finger itch."

"KILL ME IF YOU MUST, I WILL SAY NO MORE."

"False Cressid," Marotte intoned in a low voice. "Let all untruths stand by thy stained name...."

The Mörkö looked confused and off-balance, and Abby couldn't exactly blame him. "John, watch him. I'm going to tie his arms," she said.

John lifted the Desert Eagle and aimed it very definitively at the Mörkö's forehead, right between the massive glowing eyes. If the Mörkö could have gulped, it would have; as it was, the creature settled for looking vaguely horrified. The oozing blood had slowed to a scarlet trickle, and it was beginning to dry in the air. Blue light scabbed over the wound.

Abby, meanwhile, was rooting around in the cabinets. With a triumphant "A ha!" she held up a tattered plastic packet containing a long coil of clothesline, relic of somebody's abortive attempt to bring organization to the chaos that was the office filing system. Pinning crime scene photographs up on long ropes hadn't been as much of a success as they'd thought, mostly because Adam had come in after only getting half an hour of sleep, wandered right into the thick of things, and practically cocooned himself before anyone else had gotten in.

It was the work of only a few short seconds to unravel the loose hanks of cotton. "Hands behind your back," she ordered the Mörkö, who—faced with the Desert Eagle—took the path of least resistance and did as he was ordered. Abby swiftly wrapped the rope around the thick wrists, once, twice, three times, securing it with a fiendishly difficult knot that she had accidentally invented while trying to put up curtains in her living room. The Mörkö grunted and tugged ineffectually at the clothesline, but something made to withstand the buffeting winds and vicious hazards which may befall the standard American washing line would not surrender to a bogeyman with a failing source of belief. The knots held.

"All right," John added, as Abby gave the knots a final yank and made sure that she had tightened them to her satisfaction. "Mal, we need to keep a guard on him. Take the first hour, would you? Abby and I have some research to get on."

"So I shall," the actor said. "Loan me your pistol, then. What will you be searching for?"

John ran a hand through his hair. "To be honest, I wish I knew. Any ideas?"

"Yes." Marotte's eyes met him, and the expression was sharp and clear.

"Those hairs in the bag, the ones we could not identify. They were woven right in. Someone put them there."

"We're on it." John saluted. "Keep an eye on Big Blue for us."

As Marotte prodded the bound Mörkö out of the room, Abby was already back on her feet and reaching for a spare piece of paper. Her hands shuddered a little in the aftermath of the adrenaline rush, but this was no time to be tired. She forced herself to keep her thoughts focused, even as the fear and exertion took its toll out on her trembling limbs.

"John, if someone put those hairs there—" she began.

"They became part of the bag," her friend finished. "And Gio told us that L'uomo Nero complained about being controlled by the bag."

"The bag is the defining part of a lot of old legends. That's how they're identified—hairy man, or man with a bag. It's part of himself, the fabric of his being." Abby bit her lip, thinking hard as she struggled to transcribe her thoughts on paper. There was a complete idea there, but it was as slippery as a fish and hard to grasp. Her hands still ached from the recoil of the Beretta. "So someone put those hairs in L'uomo's bag to... what? Control him? Make him fall from grace?"

"Grace?" John's laughter was mixed with a sarcastic snort. "Reform him, more like it. Bogeymen, especially the old ones—nasty pieces of work. Kill you as soon as look at you." He leaned over, putting his hands on the table, thinking hard. "Something or somebody who had access to the bag did this in a direct, conscious effort to change that Black Man's behavior. I'll lay ten to one odds that those hairs came from the head of one Giovanna DiFrancesca, aged seven."

"But who could have access to the bag?" Abby asked, shaking her head. "L'uomo Nero's legend says that nobody knows what it is. That bag is the direct definition of the unknown." Abby gnawed on her fingernails. "Who can get into the unknown?"

John's grin was back. "Perhaps a fellow unknown?"

"You mean—that thing she mentioned? Buh... buh... *Bavbav?*"

"Fact one." John shot up his left forefinger. "As far as we know, this Bavbav bloke disappeared two hundred years ago, give or take. El Cucuy takes over the Family after his disappearance." He put up a second finger. "Fact two: around that time, L'uomo Nero goes mad. Fact three: L'uomo Nero's bag is called the unknown. Bavbav is also the unknown. Conclusion: Bavbav, knowing he was about to get his number called up, faked his own death and hid in that bag you've got there. Having done so, he sets out to influence L'uomo Nero's behavior." He waggled his fingers meaningfully, making Abby grin in spite of her exhaustion. "Thoughts?"

"Why would Bavbav do that?" Abby wondered. A small piece of her thumb nail tore off between her teeth, and she spat it out impatiently. It landed in the saucer that she'd been using to keep her coffee spoon on; she didn't want the linoleum to stain even more than it already was, after all. Not that it seemed to matter with the brand-new hole in the wall. "Change his behavior, I mean. L'uomo Nero's. You'd think it would be to his advantage to leave him the way he was. Doesn't Bavbav stand for the old ways?"

"And that's the question," John said. "No doubt he had an agenda of his own. Being the 'unknown' covers quite a load of territory, after all."

"But L'uomo Nero... by Giovanna's description, he's gone completely insane. She said he babbled a lot. Why would Bavbav being in the bag make L'uomo act strange?"

"Easy. Bogeymen are defined by belief, yes? And the one thing you hear about the most, with any bag man, is the bag. It's the center of their existence." John made a revolving motion next to his temple, the universal symbol for 'crazy.' "Having a bigger, meaner chunk of the unknown in there... maybe it overloaded his mind. Severed a wire or something."

Abby was ready with another question. "But why? Why would he hide in the bag?"

"'Unknown' again. Probably a smart cove, too, running the bogeyman mafia for a few thousand years. He probably saw this whole thing coming."

"Saw what? El Cucuy's takeover?"

"Maybe. Or there could be something else in this. Why are they so desperate to get it right? It's not like they haven't been through changes before."

For a moment, all was silent as the two friends mulled it over. Abby tapped her fingers on the table, chewing on her lip, thinking hard.

"He talked about a change..." she said finally. "Something awful, so bad that even he couldn't tell us."

"Well, if the Rev. Ev's theories are correct—and that's quite an if, mind you—then the bogeymen are based on belief. Human belief defines them. Stands to reason that they would change as their legends evolved." John looked up, and there was a glint in one brown eye. "So what if they're changing into something they don't like?"

"Fairy tale characters. And if the tale is rewritten, the details change—then they change too!" Abby leapt up, suddenly energized despite her fatigue. The book of fairy tales was lying, covers spread, in a pile of discarded junk, and she seized it with a manic enthusiasm. "John, the stories they tell today aren't the same ones that were told years ago. It used to be the wicked mother, not step-mother. The Little Mermaid died in the end! She doesn't now! There's a generation of kids growing up hearing nice versions of their stories!"

John laughed out loud, head flung back, grin manic. "Hah! I like that! Change the stories, the kids grow up thinking of them differently... as something human! El Cucuy becomes My Pet Monster—

"And if I figure right, Abby, then that's their weakness." He pointed towards the door through which Marotte and their blue captive had departed. "When they invaded the first time, I saw some of 'em flinch at the bullets. Seems to be a handful who are turning human already—or something close to it. Something we can hurt."

"Which explains the bogeyman plan. They want to be feared, not liked."

"Going too far, though." John and Abby exchanged a glance, and Abby was certain that he was thinking the same thing she was. "They're just snagging kids whenever they can, never mind whether they've been bad or not. Bogeys got a right to exist, just like everyone else, but that's going far out of the way."

Abby turned a little, glancing around the ruined office. The gold-and-opal ring lay where it had fallen, its surface now lightly flecked with plaster dust from the rebroken wall. "Aren't we in the money, then—getting a magic traveling ring just when we need it?"

"Isn't that the way it always works in the stories? Maybe we're getting lucky for once."

"Actually, it isn't." Abby looked down at the ring. She remembered the bite of nails into her face, the reddened eyeballs and the beery breath— and they soured her enthusiasm. "That was Baba Yaga I saw, John. She doesn't give people things just because she likes them. It's always a bargain. Like in *Silence of the Lambs*— 'Quid pro quo, Clarice.'"

John was watching her carefully. "Strings attached?"

"I'd bet anything."

"So what d'you think?"

"You were telling me a while ago that you were the leader, John. What do you think we should do?"

Her voice was sharp, surprising even herself. Strange, that she could be petty even after the last hour she'd had. John didn't rise to the bait, though.

"Take the ring, owe the witch, possibly save a load of kids. Don't take the ring, continue searching for El Cucuy's hangout the old-fashioned way, watch more people get abducted. Clear choice, I'd say." He shifted his eyes to her. "What kind of strings?"

"I don't know. We may have to travel to the 'thrice-ninth land, in the thrice-tenth kingdom, where lives Koshchei the Deathless.'"

"Is that another mythical figure?"

Abby nodded. "Granddad told me his story."

"Then I reckon we can chance it." Before Abby could say anything, John bent down and picked up the ring. For a moment the world held its breath, but nothing happened—it lay there in his palm, old and slightly dirty, apparently benign.

Abby smiled a little, though whether it was relief or humor, she wasn't sure. "So what happens next?"

"Oh, the intrepid heroes make a raid on the evil villain's domain and rescue the damsel... golden-ager in distress and her two noble protectors-knight-bodyguard mates. You, me, Mal, Harvey, and Dummy."

"No Dummy. Dummy stays behind."

"Why's that?"

"To watch out for Mary and Keith. We promised Mary's parents that she wouldn't get involved in any fights, but if we mess up and some of the bogeymen come looking for them, the kids need protection. Anyway, Dummy's useless in the dark."

"Sharp thinking," John said. "Got any other bright ideas?"

She shrugged a little. "Well, we should probably wait for nightfall... reduce the chance of collateral damage. Fewer humans around."

John let out a short bark of laughter. "We're not official enough to leave collateral damage, Abby. Property damage, maybe. Personal injury, absolutely. Random and wanton destruction, sign us up. Collateral damage is for the military, or one of those organizations where the name spells something."

"Well, whatever it is, there's sure to be plenty of it." Abby turned away from the ring and began to rifle through the mess that had once been her desk, looking for a clean sheet of paper. "Sun sets early today... give or take, four hours to get ready."

"I'll talk to Mal," John said, stretching the kinks out of his muscles. "We're not leaving that blue thing here—he'd go on a rampage. We'll have to bring him with as a hostage."

"You do that, John."

As John moved out through the door, Abby stood still for a moment. Then she sighed and ran a hand through her tangled blonde hair, attempting to gather her thoughts and put them in some sort of order. It was one of those moments where she felt like the world was spinning too fast, and she was about to lose her footing and go rocketing off into space.

Trying to relax, she settled into her chair and leaned back, closing her eyes. Bogeymen. Nobody in the SSR had ever dealt with bogeymen before. Heck, nobody in the SSR had even thought bogeymen *existed* before. Their policies were lenient when it came to things like ghosts, vampires, werewolves, giant snakes, objects walking and talking that definitely shouldn't—but that was because they had hard evidence, usually in the form of a scar or a story that didn't get told unless everybody had had a few drinks.

On a whim, Abby straightened up. Her own computer was trashed, but Mal's was still working, and she quickly punched up Google. A search for "bogeyman" (and variant spellings) produced nothing in particular; Wikipedia had a good entry, but it covered information they already had. Refining the search by adding the keyword "kill" narrowed the parameters somewhat, pulling up quotes from several scholarly articles concerning the various myths of the bogeyman, El Cucuy among them. He seemed to have made quite a hit with the cultural anthropologists. Nothing on how you kill a bogeyman.

Source of belief....

Bullets had been effective against the Mörkö, but his legend had been altered by popular conception. There was no guarantee that any of the bogeymen still at large had the same problem. However, it was all they had to go on.

Abby slid out of her chair and scooped up her silver crucifix from its perch on her overloaded in-tray. Then she made her way across the room, towards the thinly-carpeted basement steps. Adam probably wouldn't appreciate her raiding his things, but he would know just as well as she did that physical force was the Old Reliable of supernatural disposal. If it could be hit, it could probably be hurt.

When Marotte came clattering down the basement steps a few minutes later, he found Abby standing over a workbench with a knife in one hand, a taser in the other, and an annoyed look on her face. To his credit, he did not immediately reach for his own knife or back up the steps at high speed.

Sweat was beading on Abby's forehead, her shirt was rumpled and stained with machine oil, and the chain of her silver cross was again tangled in a clump of her hair. She had filled three polyester tote bags with paraphernalia, including a glass-cutter and a roll of razor-sharp concertina wire. At least three short-range pistols were in various states of cleanliness on one side of the workbench, and the knife she held was actually the larger half of a broken machete that Adam had picked up cheap at a flea market and filed back to sharpness.

"Abigail?" Marotte called out carefully. Abby had heard him come down the stairs, and didn't look up from her work: the taser went into one tote bag, and she began wrapping the blade of the halfchete in tough cotton bandaging.

"Yeah?" she mumbled, pushing her sweaty hair out of her eyes with her left hand.

"John spoke to me," the older man said as he drew level with the bench. "A grand assault is planned, I hear."

Abby bit her lip as she shoved the halfchete into the corner of the most full tote bag. "That's the plan. Where is he?"

"Keeping watch over our blue captive. An intriguing creature."

"As long as he's not slacking off," Abby said shortly. "Ten to one he's playing video games and hasn't even uncapped Harvey yet." Her ears turned red as she realized what she'd said, and she looked down hurriedly at her work. Being too nice was a hard habit to break, even if the other members of the team were all right with her practicing.

Marotte just raised an eyebrow at this, and turned to the wall. A rack of his personal items—mostly over-decorated swords, relics of his stage career—was hanging there, and he carefully unhooked a long rapier from it. The weapon he laid on the table, next to the bags, and then pulled two of the totes over to him. Abby grunted, resenting the intrusion a little, but was too tired to get in a fight. The stress was definitely catching up to her.

"Just the three of us, against an army of bogeymen?"

She glanced up. "What?"

"Three of us," Marotte repeated. He had emptied out one of the bags and was carefully repacking it. "Racing into the dark, facing what could very well be our deaths. Have you thought about it? The implications?"

"I'm trying not to." Abby picked up her Beretta 9mm and tested the slide, wondering whether that small catch in the action was something to worry about, and whether it was worth finding Adam over. The small weapon was heavy and cold in her hand, and she hastily set it aside. "What are we going to do? There aren't authorities we can report this to. We *are* the authorities, as silly as that sounds."

"What of the others—Keith and the young ones?"

"John sent Dummy to look out for the kids. Mary—"

"Mary will not be involved," Marotte cut in. The two shared a quick look, and Abby knew that they were thinking the same thing: *over my dead body.* "I suppose John already mentioned the possibility of doing nothing?" he continued, quickly changing the subject.

"Yeah, we had that fight. Please don't bring it up."

"Hardly." Marotte finished packing the second bag and stood up, stretching his arms and shoulders to work the kinks out. "But what about your son?"

"He thinks I'm insane, anyway," she said bitterly. Maternal instinct warred with petty selfishness, and for a moment, the selfishness won. "If I die, his father gets custody, and they both get the insurance," she continued. "It's not as if I'll be missed."

"So you're running into the jaws of death to spite a petty teenager?"

"No. I'm 'running into the jaws of death,' thanks, because it needs doing. I don't want to, but nobody else knows enough to do it. Can't call the police. Hell, we probably can't, but..." Abby paused for a moment before turning to stare at Marotte. "Are you sure you're not going to start an argument?"

The tall man shook his head and smiled a little wryly. "I was merely making inquiries. As it is, I think we are indeed doing the right thing."

Abby wasn't sure at all. For the next few minutes, as they packed in silence, she thought about her college graduation. Four-year-old Jimmy and her husband Terry, waiting with her in the god-awful summer heat, just so she could get a piece of paper that said Bachelor of the Arts. They'd all gone out for pizza afterwards. Ten months later, a ghoul had leapt out of an alley and tried to tear the skin off her back.

Would Jimmy be better off without her? He certainly thought she was insane. He'd tried, not long ago, to convince his school counselor that she was hallucinating. Yet she couldn't promise herself that she'd be content to leave him with her ex-husband. Terry was a good man, true, but she had the sinking feeling that she would be remembered as a sadly disturbed woman who had finally gone too deep into her insanity. It was the kind of thought that could either drive someone to excel or encourage them to slit their wrists.

Tears beaded in the corner of her eyes as she checked the slide on her Beretta again.

"John," she called. "I left something at home. Give me half an hour."

She had, in fact. Abby kept an OTF knife—a vicious little variant on the switchblade with a spring-loaded blade that shot out from the front of the hilt. It was almost as good as a ballistic knife, and twice as sneaky. She kept it hidden in her nightstand, under a few pairs of pantyhose and a folded nightgown. Abby promised herself that she would retrieve the knife, and check on her son quickly.

The drawer was closed, but the clothes had been disturbed. Abby's heart sank as she lifted them up. The knife was gone.

She remembered putting it away. It was her insurance policy, the thing that made her feel safe after a long investigation had turned nasty or a house two doors down had been broken into. But someone had taken it. And the sad part was, Abby knew who.

Jimmy's door didn't have a lock; it was one of her few unshakable household rules. Still, he had the keen hearing that all teenagers seemed to have. When Abby opened the door, he was sitting stiffly on his bed, with one hand still half under the pillow.

"Where is it, Jimmy?" she said. Her son's eyes darted around the room.

"Where's what?" he demanded. "What are you doing in here?"

"My knife, Jimmy. You took my *knife* out of my nightstand." Abby marched over to his dresser and jerked open the top drawer, beginning to pull dirty clothes out. Jimmy leapt off his bed and tried to slam the drawer shut, but it was too late—Abby had found the magazines. There was a moment of silence, then she threw them aside. "Where is it?" she repeated. "Jimmy, where is it?"

"Mom, get out of my stuff!" he shouted. He grabbed the magazines off the floor and hurriedly jammed them down the back of his desk. "I didn't take anything!"

Abby shoved the drawer shut and pulled open another one. More wadded-up clothes, scattered papers, and three or four comic books. "You found the car keys in my makeup kit, so I know you go through my things. I check that drawer every night." Sweat was beading on her forehead, and not from exertion. She wanted to scream, shout, break things, but she had no energy for it. "No one else has been here, Jimmy. Or have they?"

Her son couldn't meet her eyes. He glared at the ground, face splotched red and white with frustration and embarrassed rage. "You're always screaming about monsters! And with the kidnappings and stuff, I thought I better have something to defend myself with—"

"You're not listening to me, Jimmy!" Abby's voice cracked slightly. There—at the bottom of the last drawer, hidden under a pair of balled-up socks. She snatched it up and tripped the switch. The knife blade flicked out cleanly and smoothly. "If you were, you'd know that the things doing the kidnapping aren't going to be scared off by you carrying a knife! Stay inside, lock the door, and if I don't come back, call your dad. There's a strongbox under my bed, and he has the key. Understand?" Quickly, she snapped the knife closed and shoved it into the pocket of her coat.

She couldn't read Jimmy's expression. The blood was draining from his face, leaving it deathly white. His eyes narrowed. "Mom, what are you doing?"

"No matter what I tell you, you won't believe me, will you?" Abby zipped up her jacket with trembling fingers. "Hon, I love you, but I have to go now. I was supposed to be back ten minutes ago." She vaguely thought that she should say something—something wise and maternal, something which would clear up all their misunderstandings and convince him that she was telling the truth. She couldn't think of anything. Time was ticking away. "Bye, honey," she said, leaning over and giving him a perfunctory peck on the head. Jimmy squirmed violently away.

The door of the house rattled closed behind her as she stepped out into the cold November afternoon.

A few hours later, the five figures were assembled in the wreckage of the main office. It was almost five o'clock, and outside, the sky was almost completely dark. The bags were packed, notes had been left, the door locked and the key hidden under the mat. Harvey, already out of his bottle, drifted in a cloud above their heads. Marotte and Abby were carrying the equipment, now packed into rucksacks, and John still had his gun trained on the sullenly silent Mörkö.

"Right," John said, his voice calm. "Abby, the ring's your responsibility. Pick it up as soon as we're through, and don't let it go. Mr. Mörkö, you're going to walk ahead of us at all times. Try anything and there'll be hollow-point bullets in whatever passes for the base of your spine. Do good, prove to us that we can trust you, and you won't need a source of belief. *We'll* believe in you. So in fact, it's in your best interests to play nice with us. Is that clear?"

"I OBEY," the huge monster rumbled. Then it realized what it had said, and the deep-set blue eyes twitched. John grinned.

"Marotte—tactical offense, as always. Harvey, distractions and sabotage." The genie began to say something, but John cut him off. "Not now, Harv. You'll do what we say, when we say, without any whining. End of story. Abby, are you ready with that thing?"

"Ready." Abby fished the ring out of her pocket. She folded her palm around the tiny gold ornament and raised it to her eyes, murmuring a quick prayer to herself. "Take us to where they're keeping L'uomo Nero, Likho, and Giovanna," she said to the ring.

Nothing happened. Abby could feel the gazes trained on her closed fist, and her face flush warm. "Please," she amended. "We need to find them. And, um, I think our intentions count as pure, if that's what you need. You can use the route that the Mörkö knows—" She stopped dead as the ring began to struggle, growing hot in her grasp. When she opened her fingers, the heavy gold circle leapt from her hand and tumbled to the ground. It immediately began to roll forward.

"I think it wants us to follow it," she said. The ring stopped and twitched knowingly, then set off again. Hastily, the group snatched up their gear and followed it. The Mörkö tugged at his bonds, but John shoved the muzzle of the gun into the small of the creature's back and forced it forward.

As the ring tumbled out into the open, it turned on the spot. A shimmering doorway opened on the scorched linoleum, its edges blending and twisting as if it were made of the same celestial gelatin. Keeping a keen eye on the Mörkö, John prodded him into the gateway. Abby held tightly to the halfchete, but her other hand slipped into her pocket and curled around the crucifix.

"Lord have mercy," she said in a low voice. Then she followed the blue monster and her friends into the swirling light of the door.

Chapter Eighteen

In fairy tales, people can travel miles in a single second. In real life, it's a little more complicated.

Abby thought she was going to die. Her body screamed in pain as it was warped impossibly, stretching and crushing all at once in perversion of the laws of physics. There was no light, no sound, only a hideous blackness that seemed to consume her, body and soul. She thought it was a moment; she thought it was a thousand years.

But then the world gave a lurch, and Abby gasped for fresh air as she tumbled forward. She heard her companions coughing and choking as they fell to their knees beside her. Color returned to the world, and time resumed its flow. Behind her was only a blank wall.

The Mörkö was still in pain, but for a moment it was the most steady of the group. If it had thought of making a run for it, though, the creature must have dismissed the idea: despite the horrible passage, John's pistol had still not moved from its place at the Mörkö's back. After a few agonizing moments, they regained their control, and began to take stock of their surroundings.

The scenery was like nothing Abby had expected. As a rule, the other-than-human figures which the SSR tracked hid in dark, out-of-the-way places where they could work in private, but not... this. They stood in a long cream-colored hallway, the walls cordoned off by red velvet ropes and hung with ancient-looking tapestries in faded colors. Tiny golden squares glinted alongside each tapestry, glowing unnaturally in the blue light of the Mörkö. Ahead, the hallway curved to the left, and a fine white statue of a kneeling woman sat in the corner. There was a vast darkness beyond, suggestive of some huge hall.

Marotte figured it out. "The Art Institute!" he breathed, flexing the hand that held the rapier as if he were itching to grab things. "We're in the upper gallery! I should recognize this collection anywhere... this place is legendary... as fine an assortment of French Impressionists as one could hope to find in this country." He shook his head in amazement. "And of course, 'American Gothic' is here as well, and 'Sunday on La Grande Jatte'...."

"Wait a minute," Abby said, still a bit unsteady from the journey. She loosened her grip on the crucifix, revealing a red cross-shaped indentation in her lined palm. "We're at the Art Institute? Why would it bring us to a museum?"

"It was a place the ring felt we ought to be, I suppose," John replied. He glanced left and right, eyeing the blue-tinged shadows. "If the bogeymen are all about the imagination, an art museum must be as close to a temple as they've got."

The scene was stark and stunning all at once under the high light of the day. Suffused with the bluish glow of the Mörkö, everything seemed to leer and skulk. As they moved down the corridor, following the turn, they felt a rush of air: the ceiling now soared far above, and the light of their captive barely touched the corners of the vast room.

Directly to their right were a set of glass doors, through which could be glimpsed dim galleries filled with dark shapes in opulent frames. To the left stood a massive statue of Samson wrestling a lion, set against a waist-high wall that kept visitors from toppling over the edge of the balcony. Before and behind were corridors lined with examples of wrought iron-work and architecture recovered from 1870s Chicago buildings. Far across the dim shape of the sweeping white stair was another glassed-in gallery, through which could be seen tantalizing slivers of brilliant color that stood out against the scuttling shadows of the place. The walls were hung with enormous canvases, some fifteen or twenty feet long, and splashed across them was a bloody history of the human race.

Saints and sinners raged back and forth across landscapes rendered in brilliant pigment now cracked with age. There was John the Baptist in four separate panels, the stump of his head fountaining a fine mist of red-orange blood and the discarded head a pale green, a parody of life. Crucifixions by the dozen lined the walls, with every Christ from suffering to benevolent to triumphant and back to suffering again. Angels were everywhere, Genesis to Revelations, aiding God in forming the world and announcing its destruction all in one white-walled room. Four horsemen came thundering out of the clouds; Death was a withered old man, Pestilence an oozing wreck, Famine a greedy fat merchant, War with the heads of the ungodly tied to his saddle.

The SSR people automatically drew closer to each other. Abby tightened her grip on the crucifix again.

"Oh, no, the medieval period," Harvey groaned from over their heads. Two pale smoky eyes blinked at the gory canvases. "I *hate* the medieval period. Nothing but God, God, God, and oh by the way, you're going to hell *right now.* It's not like their god ever did anything for them, even."

John shook his head, ignoring the paintings for the time being. "Shut it, Harvey. We asked the ring to bring us to where the bogeymen are. Mörkö, what are they doing here?"

"Mörkö?" Abby said sharply. "Well?"

The huge blue creature nodded its glowing head. "THERE IS MUCH AGE HERE. WHEN WE MUST IMPRISON, WE MUST DO IT WELL."

"Why not the Natural History Museum?" Marotte asked, rattling the rapier in its long sheath. "There are things here hundreds of years old, but any other museum would do just as well—even better, among the geological specimens."

"I think I know," said Abby. "There's no imagination in rocks, is there?"

"ART IS IMAGINATION. WE ARE AT HOME HERE."

"Old art..." she said. She turned and surveyed the deep-shadowed scene, her eye catching the blue glint of the Mörkö on the far-off gallery glass. "Very real, isn't it?"

The Mörkö shuddered a little. "VERY." The SSR members looked at each other, sharing the same thought.

How do you trap something that has almost no reality of its own? Surround it with the real, and watch it try to escape.

"All right, but it's a big museum," Abby interjected. Her eyes adjusted quickly in the dimness, and she was looking uneasily around her into the shadows "Maybe Marotte has this place memorized, but I know I don't. Not to mention the security alarms that must be everywhere—"

John shook his head. "Harvey?"

There was a nasty noise from the genie. "Do the speech."

"Harvey, do you have to do this now?" Abby asked, fatigue making her voice sharp. But the genie remained firm, forming the shape of a pair of crossed arms and a tilted head in midair. There was a simultaneous groan from the humans.

"Security enshrouds us, a trap set all too clear," Marotte quickly parsed out. "Cut out their web, that we walk without fear. Will that do?"

"Oh, all right. If you *insist.*" The thick smoke spread out over the heads as tendrils of the genie sought out the hidden cameras and wires. There was a brilliant flicker, a shower of sparks, and a momentary smell of burned metal. "Offline, thanks to the only worthwhile lifeform here. You're welcome, by the way."

"Noted," John whispered. He dug in his huge pockets and produced a small flashlight, flicked it on, and played the beam over the huge statue of Samson. "But you heard the lady, Marotte—where's a good place to keep a prisoner who's not too fond of straight reality?"

"The sculpture court," Marotte said instantly. In the glow of the flashlight, he looked almost as noble and inhuman as the Samson statue, and his knuckles were white where he clutched the hilt of the rapier. "Dozens of statues, marble and bronze by numerous American masters, all around as far as the eye could see. Not many walls, perhaps, but plenty of age and imagination to stifle your most persistent ghoul."

"Drama whore," Harvey muttered.

Meanwhile, Abby was poking around on the other side of Samson. There was nothing much of interest, besides a bench and a trash can. She put her head and shoulders through the plastic flap of the trash can to rummage around among the discarded newspapers and crumpled programs. "Found something!" she called out in a muffled voice, flapping and wriggling to extract herself from the tight-fitting box. One hand emerged triumphantly, waving a laminated map of the museum like a flag of victory.

"That'll do nicely," John said, plucking the map from the outstretched hand and unfolding it. "Sculpture court, sculpture court. Good as any place to start." He squinted at the map and looked around them, searching for landmarks, then applied himself to the map again.

"We're by the Samson statue," Abby pointed out helpfully as she brushed a few fragments of paper from her hair.

John shot her a frustrated look. "Fine, but the statue's not *marked* on the map."

"Well, it says 'Pritzker Gallery' on the glass over there."

"But all the galleries just have little numbers on here. There's no names!"

"Look for the map key... no, the other side. Look, right there—sculpture court, number 417."

"Easier said. Where are we, anyway?"

"Depends on what kind of art's in the Pritzker Gallery, I guess. I think it's laid out by period."

"Looks like a bunch of depressed dead cows to me."

"Great, that narrows it down to about... three thousand years. Harvey, could you get some light on that?"

There was another put-upon groan from the djinn, but he obediently flowed through the glass and began to glow softly. "Says here 'El Greco, Assumption of the Virgin,'" Harvey reported in a carrying whisper. "Told-ja. Medieval."

"Isn't it a bit too... cheerful... to be medieval?" John pointed out. "The fourteen-hundreds were big on spurting blood and sinners getting dragged into the Inferno. That looks practically *nice*. Renaissance, easy."

"Italian?" Abby asked.

"What, with a name like El Greco? Maybe, but I doubt it. The Renaissance happened in more places than Italy, y'know."

"Look, we're in the galleries, all right?" Harvey snapped as quietly as he could. "Let's head for the big staircase. Map says the sculpture court's that-a-way. We should be able to find our way from there, and would you *please* try to be a little smarter than usual and keep it down?"

"Seems that's the way it's to be." John prodded the silent Mörkö in the back with the Desert Eagle. "Best foot forward, you."

"THIS WILL NOT END WELL, HUMANS. I PREDICT THERE WILL BE DEATH."

"Isn't that a song?" Abby asked, looking up at the blue giant.

John shook his head. "No, that's 'I Predict a Riot.' Either way, though, it works." They rounded the corner and headed towards the vast white marble staircase, trying to step softly. "No telling what we're going to find, eh?"

Giovanna's face looked burned where El Cucuy had touched her. Likho couldn't help but feel sorry for her; she was an annoying old bag when she wanted to be, but she didn't have the option of fixing her physical form whenever she wanted to. Nevertheless, she seemed to be bearing up well. He watched as she ran one trembling hand over her stiff cheek.

Without his bag, L'uomo was growing steadily worse; he seemed almost catatonic, frozen in a kneeling position with his eyes fixed on the floor. Attempts to rouse him did nothing, and even when their bestial guards taunted him or threw things at his head, he remained motionless. Likho felt trapped. It had been easy to keep his spirits up when L'uomo was babbling vaguely, or the old woman was hauling off and giving El Cucuy a piece of her mind. But now, the silence in the cellar was wearing on him.

Both Giovanna and L'uomo Nero were, in their own way, figures of power. L'uomo had been created from the fear that surrounded the legendary Hannibal, back when Italy trembled at the mention of the name and the seemingly insurpassable Alps no longer offered real protection. And Giovanna—well, old women have always scared children. Likho's native land feared ancient crones, setting them up as wisewomen, witches, or even demons. Seeing one of them silenced and broken was disturbing to Likho on a primal level, and it made him shudder to look at her.

And the hours passed. The sun had reached its zenith long before, and Likho could sense it descending, high above him. Night, the bogeyman's time, was quickly approaching.

As he felt the sunlight die away, the shadows in the dimmest corner of the basement began to lengthen. The silent forms of El Nadaha and Dunganga straightened up as Sacauntos solidified into existence, knife in hand. The two guards bowed ceremonially at Sacauntos' appearance.

"Sundown," he said. "You are all called to court."

Giovanna stirred. "Care to give me a hand?" she sniped in a querulous voice. Likho's spirits rose momentarily as she came to life again, giving Sacauntos a beady-eyed stare from under thin brows. Her words were slightly slurred by her burned face. "What with you all being so kind to me, giving me a nice cold floor to sit on, I haven't got much left in these legs."

"Tonight is our triumph," Sacauntos pronounced. "We will no longer act as human. Now is not the time to walk."

He raised his arms, and the room melted away around them. Likho saw

Giovanna lurch as the stained concrete slid away, replaced by smooth marble. The walls dissolved. White pillars bloomed from nothingness, shooting upwards into the dimness. Plinths sprouted from the marble. The ceiling shot upwards, receding into the dimness that was now hundreds of feet away, while high above their heads a balcony knit itself into existence.

Likho was ready with a sardonic remark, but it died on his lips. Bogeymen were all around them, and each of them clutched a small figure between its hands.

They were in a great hall, ringed with poised statues. Some architect had chosen to replicate the great Greek temples in smooth marble and white plaster, creating a sculpture court that in daylight would seem calm, even beautiful. But the bogeymen ringed it, and they held their captives in unforgiving grips.

The children were alive: they were moving, squirming, trying to bite, or crying softly. The noise of their whimpers was like a gunshot to the head after the silence that had gone before.

"Sweet Mary," Giovanna whispered. Deep in the shadows, a girl's voice called out for her mother; there was a sharp thunk, and the voice was silenced.

Likho was struck dumb. Rows of faces stared back at him, the inhuman ones showing glee, the human streaked with tears or white in fear.

Giovanna, however, reacted with blind fury.

"The—how could you—" she began, seemingly trying and failing to find the words. For a moment, the scene before her left her unable to speak, and she choked on her own outrage. Her headscarf lost its fragile hold and slipped down around her shoulders.

"*How dare you?*" she finally hissed, every word laden with venom. "How *dare* you? What gives you the right? Snatching them, torturing and killing and kidnapping and wrecking lives? You're disgusting! You're all mean-spirited little bastards, and by all that's holy you'll regret it!"

Giovanna stopped, panting with the effort of her outburst. Silence thundered down on the scene, and the tension stretched like a rubber band. From his place by the frozen L'uomo, Likho felt the urge to close his eyes. It was going to be ugly.

"Maybe I'm no bogeyman," she said coldly. "But if you do things like this, you don't deserve to live any longer."

"Survival is an important matter," an all-too-familiar voice replied from behind her. The old lady braced herself against the floor and scooted around, her back held stiff as she tried not to show her pain.

"Even humans know some little about surviving," El Cucuy said calmly, unfazed by her outburst. There was a spark in the small red eyes as he spoke, his gaze fixed on her. "Think of us as a more sophisticated sort of vampire. After what these children have seen, there will be no reason not to believe. Even better, if only these few see..." he leaned in close, speaking in a whisper that echoed through the hall. "The few that live will tell their stories, and new brothers will grow from them."

The old woman recoiled, and glared down her nose at him. "No need to explain. You let them see an old lady get torn apart, and it feeds you their fear."

"Not quite. I have to bring L'uomo Nero and Likho up, first. And when—"

El Cucuy stopped short. His back stiffened, and he raised his head and stared around.

"Exiled," he said. "Here. Sacauntos!"

He shouldn't have bothered. Even Likho sensed it: the Mörkö's unique aura, somewhere close. What the hell was he doing here?

"At your service, lord," Sacauntos said, lumbering forward.

"The Mörkö is here. The Mörkö and... others." El Cucuy's eyes unfocused. "Their minds are... different, somehow, but they're here."

The dim shadows shifted and glanced at one another. Tightening claws made the children squirm and whimper. "How?" Talasam could be heard murmuring, and El Cucuy hissed.

"It seems the blue man has decided to throw in with the other side. Sacauntos, take La Llorona, Hombre del Saco, Nachtkrabb, Babaroga... choose a few others, too... and bring them here. This could be fine fodder for the legend."

Sacauntos bowed his head and loped towards the mass of shadows. At a glance from him, six bogeymen stepped forward; as the prisoners watched, the children they had been holding vanished into the darkness. The remaining children were clearly scared out of their wits.

Poor kids, Likho thought. *I wonder if any of them'll see the sunrise.*

In the dimness of the gallery, illuminated only by the blue glow of the towering figure, whispers could be heard.

"Check the map, would you? Where are we?"

"Eh... not sure. It's too dark in here." There was a rustle of waxed paper. "Here we go. Boniface Gallery, artifacts from the Church of the Hagia Sophia."

"Don't be silly. That's a kabuki mask in that case."

"And how do you know, Mademoiselle Clever Dick?"

"It has those strange exaggerated features, and the big eyebrows. It looks almost like something from a ritual, and I remember reading that kabuki was partly religious...."

"Ritual mask it may be, but that's never kabuki. Too stylized. I'm betting Noh theatre. And you know what they say about Noh theatre?"

"An awful pun, probably."

"Stop bickering. And that is a sacred tribal mask from Nigeria, used in fertility rituals circa 1780." Marotte pointed to the map gripped in John's hand. "The African gallery," he whispered. "The number on the wall matches the number on the map. That means the sculpture court should be not far ahead, after Arms and Armor."

"Say again?" John said. "Arms and Armor?"

"Part of the Harding Collection, yes, and very handsome."

There was a shifting of feet, and a rumble from the Mörkö. "AND WE MUST WALK THROUGH THIS?" he asked.

The three humans glanced at each other. "That was the plan," Abby said finally. "Is there a problem?"

The Mörkö shuddered and tried to step backwards, but ran into the gun at its back. "I WILL NOT," it said. "I WILL NOT. I WILL NOT. THERE ARE BETTER WAYS TO GO."

"This is the quickest route," John told the thing impatiently. "We're wasting time, Blue. Move."

"*I WILL NOT*. THERE IS AGE IN THERE."

Marotte glanced curiously towards the door of the Arms and Armor collection. "This museum is filled with age, Mörkö. Why is this gallery so different from all the others?"

"How is this night different from all other nights?" Abby heard John mutter in a low voice. She wondered what he was thinking, but shook it off: the Mörkö's sudden reticence made her curious, too.

Harvey, in a cloud overhead, gave a low groan. "Isn't it obvious, you lunkheads?" he said, gliding down like a miniature foghead around the mountain of the Mörkö, who growled low in his throat and batted at the mist of the genie. "Age has power over these guys. A ring of old sculptures traps 'em. What would old weapons do?"

Now the Mörkö was groaning. "I WILL BE KILLED," it said, wringing its massive hands. "THEY WILL HUNT ME TO THE ENDS OF THE WORLD. IT WILL BE THE END, AND MY LEGEND WILL DIE—"

Since John was not tall enough to pistol-whip the Mörkö, he did his best. He stamped on the creature's foot with one steel-toed boot, and when it rounded on him, he jammed the muzzle of the Desert Eagle under its luminescent chin. "I said," he repeated shortly, "that we're wasting time here. Get moving or get out."

That seemed to be the final straw for the Mörkö. With a roar, it rounded on its tormentors, and its fear for its life gave it more strength than it had ever shown before. One huge foot sent John sprawling, the Desert Eagle flying out of his hands and skittering across the marble floor. Abby raised her Beretta, aiming for the Mörkö's head, but indecision paralyzed her: a gunshot would almost certainly echo through the whole museum, bringing God only knew what down on their heads. Marotte's slash at the creature's arm missed.

The Mörkö wailed as it turned and fled, arms still bound behind it. "I WILL KILL YOU!" it sobbed to itself. "YOU HAVE DISGRACED ME, AND I WILL BRING YOUR BODIES TO EL CUCUY FOR MY PENANCE...."

They had no hope of catching it. In seconds, its voice died away, and the blue light faded from the gallery. Only the dim grayish glow of Harvey remained. With a grim look, John switched on his Maglite and played the beam over the glass cases.

"He'll bring the whole crew down on our heads," Abby whispered to the men. In the aftermath of the sudden struggle, their voices sounded louder than ever in the dark museum. "Shouldn't we get moving?"

"Just a minute," John said slowly. The beam of light stopped on the sign at the door to the next gallery. "If they know we're coming now... Mal, you said it was a good collection?"

The other three team members were quick on the uptake. "There will be alarms," Marotte said instantly.

"Not if we deal with them," John replied.

"How?"

"Correction," he said. "Not if Harvey deals with them."

Abby glanced up at the hovering cloud of genie, which was being as nonchalant as a gaseous being could be. "The gallery's laced with alarms," she began, speaking slowly as she thought. "If they go off, we've bought the farm. We know you can handle, computers to scramble, so... please do and lay off the smarm."

"Technically, it should be an a-b-a-b rhyme scheme in iambic pentameter," Harvey said dryly from overhead, "but you get bonus points for originality." He drifted over their heads and into the gallery. "Art theft, coming right up."

Chapter Nineteen

The Mörkö was easy to find. In mere minutes, Sacauntos and his pitiless brethren were dragging it into the sculpture court, its arms tied in... clothesline? Likho shook his head. The assembly watched as El Cucuy, full in the flush of his belief, thrashed the thing to a ragged shadow. The children whimpered and cringed around them.

It took only a few short minutes to make the Mörkö beg. "PLEASE!" it howled. "LET ME GO FREE. I WILL NOT ASK FOR BELIEF, ONLY FOR LIFE—"

"And what do you have to offer for life, human?" El Cucuy snapped. The Mörkö was bleeding freely now, and the small boy stepped back, a disgusted expression on his face.

"THERE ARE PEOPLE HERE."

"I know. Is that all?"

"THE ONES YOU STOLE THE OLD WOMAN FROM. TWO MEN AND A WOMAN. THEY HAVE A MAGIC RING, A RING FROM THE BABA—"

Likho felt his heart sink as El Cucuy cut the blue giant off sharply. "A ring from the baba? Baba *Yaga?*"

The Mörkö nodded, then looked chagrined at the human gesture. Fortunately for him, El Cucuy didn't seem to notice the slipup; he was staring at nothing, and insofar as his face showed any emotion at all, he did not appear to be happy.

"Baba Yaga," he repeated. "The worst grandmother of them all. So far gone that I don't believe she's even a bogeyman, or a ghost, or a goblin... this certainly complicates things. Advice from the baba is one thing. Artifacts are quite another." He rounded on Sacauntos. "They'll try to rescue the old woman, certainly. Go get them!"

There was a moment of hesitation among the bogeymen. "They captured the Mörkö..." one of the hairy men pointed out. El Cucuy stamped his feet.

"The Mörkö is half-dead and human already! These are meat bags, small things that live sixty or seventy years and die wailing in puddles of their own piss! Do I have to ask you to catch a child? Step on an ant? Go!"

The minute the search party was gone, El Cucuy rounded on Likho and L'uomo Nero. "Go on, then," he hissed. "Tell me what you know."

Likho put on an exaggerated expression of confusion, trying to ignore the cold sweat that was beading under his shirt. "About what?"

"About. The. Humans."

"Look, your majesty, the only one we ever paid attention to was the old lady. And, by the way, that was all L'uomo." Likho glanced at his friend, and felt his heart leap slightly as L'uomo stirred. "L'uomo. L'uomo! You awake, buddy?"

Heavy-lidded eyes blinked, and the Black Man of Italy raised his head slightly. "Is close," L'uomo whispered. "Is close. Come soon. Is come back to me...."

That got El Cucuy's attention. "The bag?" he said sharply. "Is the bag coming to me?"

L'uomo scowled. "To *me*, small one."

"Then we'd better finish this." El Cucuy waved a hand, and two hairy men came loping forwards, bowing to him. He turned to face them, clearly not caring that his prisoners could hear every word he said. "As soon as I have that bag in my hand, take our people to Italy. Kill every child that believes in that *thing* there. When you've finished, do the same in Russia."

Likho blinked.

"You've got to be kidding," he said in disbelief. El Cucuy looked over his shoulder and smiled a child's innocent smile at him.

Death. A bogeyman, dying. It wasn't something Likho had ever anticipated. He had always thought that he would fade away, slowly and peacefully, as his believers grew up and failed to pass on his legend to their children. It would be a long illness, but a natural end. Not something like this—a bloody and untimely murder.

Kill the believers. It was possible, he knew. There was no cosmic law that prevented them from using their powers any way they liked, as long as they took the children and did their duty. And any bogeyman could smell another bogeyman's believer a mile away. But to actively kill someone who believed... it was unthinkable. It was murder. The bogeyman would begin to fade, or just vanish....

"So that's how he did it," he murmured.

He could scream, and for a moment, he almost did. But could he say he was unfamiliar with death? Likho had watched his native country suffer for thousands of years, and followed its rise and fall under the leadership of more people than he could count. In some ways, Likho was Russia... and Russia was an old country, with a long memory. It was used to hard times, and so was he.

So even as his damaged physical form shuddered, Likho did his best to keep himself under control. Showing fear would give El Cucuy satisfaction, and Likho was as proud as he was old: it would be a hot day in Tobolsk before he gave the little bastard one more reason to smirk. So he did the only thing he could.

"You know, L'uomo," Likho said conversationally, turning to the kneeling bogeyman by his side. "This could be the end of a beautiful friendship."

L'uomo turned. "You quote again, Likho?"

But could he say he wasn't prepared for it? He'd watched his native country suffer for untold thousands of years, and followed its rise and fall under the leadership of more people than he could count. In some small way, Likho was Russia... and Russia was an old country, with a long memory. It was used to bitter hardships, and so was he.

He could scream, but that would give El Cucuy satisfaction. Some part of him wanted to. But there was more that he could do.

Graveyard humor. He'd seen enough graveyards, and he felt it was his time to laugh.

Show the little bastard he wasn't going to beg.

"You know, L'uomo," Likho said conversationally, turning to the kneeling bogeyman by his side. "This could be the end of a beautiful friendship."

L'uomo turned. "You quote again, Likho?"

"Yes, I quote again. Not much else to do around here." It was a weak attempt at a joke, but hell, you had to start somewhere. "By the way, do you think I could borrow your scarf before they kill us? I don't want the last thing I smell to be Sacauntos' BO."

"As you wish." L'uomo Nero rose to his feet. He had not bothered to heal the wounds suffered during their imprisonment, and they didn't seem to be affecting him at all. On the contrary, his back was straight and his voice was clearer and steadier than it had been in years. "I have finished my thinking. Be ready, my friend."

That was worrying. No, it wasn't. Likho had surpassed worry a long time ago, and was putting down stakes around Sheer Panic.

The gallery was crammed. Long glass cases lined the walls to the right and left, and upright displays were scattered around. These held suits of armor, most of them intricately detailed and designed. The right-hand wall showed a fine display of altar relics from a Byzantine church, but the left-hand...

...pure art.

As soon as the alarms were disabled, they went to work. John muffled his hands with strips of rag and dug out the glass-cutter, eyeing the long panes of glass in front of him with a professional air. Abby slipped on her pair of fleece-covered gloves and stood ready by him. They were well familiar with the theory of theft, if not the practice, and without the alarms they were fairly safe even if they made mistakes.

It was the work of only a few seconds to cut a wide square out of the glass. As soon as John had made the final incision, the pane began to tip forward; Abby stepped forward and gently caught it with both gloves, whose soft pads would protect her fingers and leave no prints. With

Marotte's help, they carefully lifted three of the lightweight broadswords out of their brackets. Marotte immediately appropriated two of them—a basket-hilted blade and a gilded monstrosity that looked like it had been designed for the Las Vegas Renaissance Fair. "Good weight," he murmured, testing the heft of it. The third was deemed too big for use and put aside.

They moved down the gallery as quickly as they could, cutting through the glass wherever they spotted something that would be useful. Everybody took a chain-mail shirt from the freestanding dummies, and Abby dragged a seven-foot halberd free off its stand. ("Pool?" John had asked her. "Street hockey," she replied.) When she rested it on her shoulder, her fingers tapped at the wood nervously, and she forced herself to steady them. And John, to nobody's surprise, lit upon the biggest crossbow to be found.

"Are you sure that thing's going to work?" Abby whispered as he wrestled the wooden-and-iron contraption out of the case. John ignored her; there was a gleam in his eyes as he tugged on the braided straw rope that served for a string. He fumbled with the iron pulley, using all the strength in his thin shoulders to nock the bow. It creaked with tension.

A moment later, there was a **crack** as the centuries-old catch failed and a deadly swish as the bolt went sailing across the hall. It ricocheted off a pillar, sailed through the cloud that was a very surprised Harvey and shattered a case of Byzantine altar artifacts. There was a clatter of glass and metal as gold-plated goblets tumbled to the ground, echoing hollowly and bouncing across the tile.

After thirty seconds of heart-pounding stillness as the group stood frozen, the last reverberations of the accident died away. As one, Marotte, Harvey, and Abby turned to glare at John, who mouthed an obscenity and kicked himself in the leg.

"Well, that wasn't suspicious at all," the smoky cloud of Harvey said in a voice so low they could barely hear it. "Well done, meat-boy. Where should they send your remains?"

"Harvey!" Abby hissed. "Quiet!"

Spineless, the genie put into her head. Abby ground her teeth and threw the balled-up museum map at him, making his smoke cloud disperse again. The tendrils of mist exuded a distinct pissiness as they tried to reform their body.

There were no approaching footsteps, as the team was used to expecting. Instead, the shadows grew deeper and blacker, and a chill began to creep into the room. John said nothing. He discarded his glass-cutter, undid the rags from his hands, and retrieved another bolt from the display case. His arms shuddered a little as he forced the old mechanism to work, and he bit his lip when the catch slid into place with a deadly little snap.

Now there were voices in the shadows. Something echoed, a long way off in the dim galleries. A door slammed in the darkness, and a cold wind whipped past them, making the dim shapes of the tapestries dance and sway. There was the click of polished bone, the drag of claws scraping against each other, and the heavy dampened coppery stench of blood and dirt.

The agents instinctively drew together. "Well, that's that," Abby murmured shakily. "Now what?"

"Run?" Harvey suggested.

Marotte shook his head. "No time," he said curtly, dispensing with the elaborate speech. "Stand and fight. Abby, are you ready?"

She gripped the spear and hefted it, feeling its weight. "I can hit people. Will that do?"

"Keep that chain-mail on," John ordered. He moved to the broken case and scooped up a handful of crossbow bolts, which he stuffed into his pack. "You've got the ring. If we die, run."

"You're being chivalrous, or trying to." She shook her head a little. "Blow it out your ear."

"You have a way with words," he said, giving her a wry grin. Overhead, Harvey said something very rude as he spread himself out, seeping into the corners and feeding tendrils into every part of the room.

The shadows deepened. Bodies began to take shape, molding themselves out of the air. The darkness textured itself, sinking in to form the near-invisible lines of a bending limb, flowing out and turning paler as heads moved forward to look, fleeing altogether where white and yellow and red eyes watched the humans. The three humans waited in the center of the room, back-to-back-to-back, at the ready.

"Remember," Marotte murmured in a low voice, raising the twin rapiers. "They're not practiced at physical combat. They fight children, not adults. Think outside their realm of experience."

John leaned back a little and braced himself. "Aimhay ighhay andhay uckday. Okay?"

"Ogerray," Abby said. The shadows swirled around them, lines of ink spreading through the fabric of the world. Her silver cross pricked her skin where the cloth of her jacket was lying heavy against it. For a moment, she saw again the claws reaching for her head, and thought of the wail that had led her down the alley. The beginning of something entirely new. Did it have any idea it would bring her here? She wondered, as she shifted her grip on the halberd.

Without a sound, the first rank attacked.

It was like a nightmare. Creatures with fangs and claws, no eyes or fifteen eyes, swept into them. Abby swung her weapon in a clumsy slap shot and tore through the midsection of a howling hairy man. Beside her, the hollow sound of the crossbow's string reverberated through the air as its single bolt went tearing through the eye of one of the huge creatures.

Marotte, the most experienced fighter, was pulled away from the other two by the duck and sway of combat. A rapier in each hand, he found himself facing off against a wild-haired figure with a wicker cage in its arms. He blocked a wild swing, ducked under the outstretched arms, and rammed one of the blades home under the ribcage. The thing screeched and fell apart, swirling in mist form away from the steel. Marotte turned the stab into a sideways slash, almost wrenching his shoulder, and landed his blade squarely in the center of the reforming bogeyman. Grayish ooze dripped from the wound as the creature dissolved again with a howl.

Above them, the genie cursed as he streamed in and out of the clashing figures, trying to blind or disorient them. A few fell, tripped by their reliance on the senses of the physical world, and Harvey laughed out loud as they flailed like overturned turtles. But the more the attackers were pushed back, the more of them dispersed their solid bodies and started pressing their advantage on the immaterial. A tide of cold fear swept through the gallery.

Beside Abby, John was fumbling a magazine into the Desert Eagle. Abby cut the axehead of the halberd towards a screeching shadow that was reaching for him, but the creature vanished before the old metal could even touch it. John nodded quickly and cocked the pistol. Abby winced in anticipation.

The sounds of gunfire echoed off the paneled walls and marble floors, making the humans' ears ring. A few of the more solid bogeymen howled as well, clutching at their heads as physical pain came from an unexpected quarter. But the bullets themselves were barely effective on the swirling nightmares, and John, slipping on the ooze now beginning to coat the floor, flailed his way to the case and snatched a broadsword from the rack. Marotte slid past him and thrust into the heart of a hairy man.

Abby had indeed played street hockey—only the single main street of her home town had been broad and firm enough for her roller skates, and she had spent long afternoons scrapping with the other kids between two goals made of garbage. She'd been a damn good goalie, too. Automatically, she settled into a practiced crouch and shifted her grip on the shaft of the halberd. A shrieking demon, with the body of a woman in white shrouds and a skeletal face, leapt for her; she cross-checked the creature, slamming the polearm into its midsection and sending it flying.

The solid reality of the weapons were holding the bogeymen at bay, for now. The horde was handicapped by their own experience: killing and kidnapping frightened children does not prepare you for armed adults fueled by pent-up rage and frustration. Yet for every bogey that disintegrated before a notched blade, two more changed their tactics. Now there were the voices.

Voices everywhere, shrieking, babbling, cursing, laughing wild gulping laughter and mocking every slip or misstep. Abby's fingers grew numb on the wood as they chuckled in her ear, whispering all the little things that nobody was supposed to know about. Secrets and shames slipped past into the darkness, leaving each of their lives laid open.

...you knew they were trapped inside...

...he's not your husband's son...

...a drunken fury, throw him down the stairs...

You can't lie to us.

John shifted the sword to his left hand and emptied four shots into the taunting face of a wizened spirit with bear teeth. The shape flashed and fell apart, dissolving into clayey mud. John's foot slipped again on the slick substance, and the bogeymen pounced, ready to be in at the kill.

"Foul!" Abby gasped as she swung. Weighted and ponderous, the axe-blade and long spike moved like Poe's pendulum, scything through the leaping figures and sending Abby reeling as she struggled to control it. But the few seconds was all John had needed; he caught hold of a bag man's trailing rags and hauled himself to his feet, using his momentum to crack the bogey on the back of the head with the heavy butt of the Desert Eagle.

And still, the more they dispelled or drove off, the more there were to attack. The humans were tiring fast. Voices of fear whispered in their ears, and half-crazed with terror and adrenaline, they were attacking more wildly and carelessly than ever before.

"No good!" Marotte shouted above the clash. "Run!"

The other two were back-to-back, being forced towards the wall of tapestries. As Marotte called, John flailed out with one arm, grabbing hold of the back of Abby's chain-mail shirt and pulling her sharply to the side. The claw of a masked apparition whizzed past her face by a tenth of an inch.

"How?" the Englishman screamed back. "We're fucking surrounded!"

Marotte lifted one of his rapiers, slipped his fingers out of the ornate guard, and flung it sideways. The throw was a thing of beauty; the long sword spun like a top, cutting a swathe through the ranks of bogeymen and clattering to a halt on the floor at the far end of the gallery.

They ran. Shoes skidding on the slick marble floor, clutching their weapons in white-knuckled hands, they ran for their lives. And behind them, the bogeymen sent up a howl.

"Left!" Marotte panted. "Downstairs—we can lose them—"

The white steps had small dips in their centers where decades of passing feet had worn them down. Burdened as she was with the weight of the halberd, Abby's heart stopped as her feet hopped out from under her, and she took the first staircase flat on her back. John and Marotte each caught one of her arms and pulled, hauling her to her feet, and the chase resumed.

There was a tinny noise, and Abby pulled to a halt. "The ring!" she gasped, turning and flailing as she slipped a little. The gold ring had fallen through her fingers, and was still sliding to a halt on the slick tile. Her companions took a moment to regain their footing and rounded back. Diving, Abby snatched the ring up and clutched it in her fist against the wooden shaft of the weapon. The shadows were closer.

"Take us someplace they can't follow!" she gasped, and once again they fell into crushing nothingness.

A soft green glow illuminated the scene as they stumbled out, panting, into another corridor. The walls were lined with benches, and a small recess held a kiosk. The light illuminated wooden shelves were lined with souvenirs—sticker books, rubber erasers, hand puppets, novelty pens, and refrigerator magnets, all new and wrapped in plastic. There was nothing that could be used as a weapon.

"Where are we?" Abby whispered as the light of the flashlights played over the scene. "And what's that glow?"

"I believe we're in the basement," was Marotte's cautious reply. He took a few cautious steps towards the left, where the hallway seemed to open up into a wide room. The green light was coming from within.

Cautiously, the three humans peered around the corner. Abby gasped and flinched backwards, Marotte uttered a vicious oath, and John stared ahead grim-faced.

It was the children's section. They found themselves in a low-ceilinged room with doors opening into galleries on either side; the walls were lined with pencil and paper-stocked desks and wall-mounted mirrors, allowing kids to sketch their own portraits. The doorway to the left was built on a ramp and lined with fluorescent green tubing, and a sign said "Gateway into Art." But there, in the middle of the dead and silent night, were piles of motionless children.

At first glance, they might not have been human. All stiff as corpses, frozen still as if they had been simply paused in time, and piled in heaps like discarded mannequins.

"Oh, Lord," Abby whispered.

A few were frozen in outrageous postures—running away or leaping in their attempts to escape from the bogeymen, but most were piled haphazardly here and there as if still asleep. The air was stifling cold; the three humans' breath clouded in front of them, and their fingers grew numb as the blood retreated from the appendages.

Tiny crystals of frost collected in the childrens' hair and stiffened their clothes into solid shapes, and every one of them was unnaturally pale. None breathed.

Abby bit her lip, trying to stop the tears from coming. The tiny crucifix felt hot against her skin, and her eyes burned behind their lids even as she blinked. Like an automaton, she stumbled stiff-legged towards the frozen forms. They still had a job to do.

Beside her, she heard John utter a creative profanity. Marotte had been forced into silence; when she turned her head to look at him, she could see that he was almost as white as the unmoving bodies. Behind them, Harvey was hovering motionless, apparently at a loss for words.

Carefully, trying not to look too hard into the eerie open eyes, Abby shuffled towards the nearest figure. It was a young boy—about nine years old, she would guess—with hair her own color and a severe cowlick. He had been leaned carelessly against the wall, and his eyes were open and surprised. Abby extended two fingers and carefully pressed them to the side of his neck, where the pulse point would be.

For a moment, she was silent. Then she let out a breath, her shoulders sagging in relief. "He's alive," she murmured just loudly enough for her teammates to hear. "No pulse and no breath, but he's definitely warm. I think they're just... in some kind of suspended animation."

John stepped up beside her and bent down to stare into the boy's face. He waved a hand back and forth, but the eyes didn't track. Cautiously, he tested the flexibility of the child's wrist; it moved, but when he let go, it snapped back into the exact same position.

"Not rigor mortis," he pronounced. Abby's shoulders sagged a little as the tension receded. There was a scuff of feet behind her, and she looked over her shoulder: Marotte's color was returning, the paleness of fright was replaced by the brilliant red tinge of anger, and he was moving along the heaped bodies towards the left-hand wall. Harvey collected himself into a vaguely human shape and floated past Abby and John, muttering to himself as he swept smoky tendrils over the heads of the immobile people.

John was tapping his foot nervously as he looked around the exhibit room. His right hand had snuck into his front pocket, and was clutching something.

Pills, no doubt.

"Why did the ring bring us here?" Abby wondered aloud.

"Probably the best it could do under the circumstances," John said. He carefully prodded the forehead of a girl who looked about twelve; she continued to stare blankly. "Mal? What do you think?"

Marotte stooped and peered through the green-lit doorway. "Toys, games, and costumes," he reported. "They doubtless feel uneasy here. Note that all the frozen young ones are simply left in a pile or tossed about; I would hazard a guess that none of the bogeymen wanted to spend enough time in here to order them properly."

"So what, they just dumped them in a pile?" Abby's voice cracked. "How could they do that?"

"Are you really asking that?" came John's harsh voice. He was walking around the main pile of children, eyeing them carefully. Sweat stood out on his forehead. "These are bogeymen, Abby. They could give a damn about human lives."

Abby tried to ignore him. Carefully, as respectfully as she could, she brushed a strand of hair off the forehead of a small dark girl. The child was wearing blue pajamas, and Abby's blood thundered behind her eyes. "Are all of them here?" she asked, trying to remain calm. Fear and anger warred with relief at finding the children alive.

"There are many more in the next hall," Marotte reported, gesturing towards the green-lined doorway. "There are numerous ramps and rooms, and there are many bodies piled out. Three hundred, I would say. Perhaps more. And there are other galleries through the other way... in a museum this size, I'm sure they could find room."

"But what? They just left them here, in the children's section, where they could be spotted by anybody passing by? By the security cameras?" John moved round behind the pile and peered through the green doorway. His brow furrowed, and he instinctively reached for the Desert Eagle. "Not bloody likely. And there's no way this could be all of them."

Marotte's lip curled. "The bogeymen doubtless have their own methods for keeping their prey hidden from the cameras. These are only tonight's catch."

"That's disgusting," Abby said bitterly. "They just freeze them in time and drop them anywhere. Like a..." words failed her.

"Tissue? Be glad they're still alive," John replied. "El Cuckoo-clock must want them for something; they'd be dead, else."

Abby wanted to make a sharp remark—anything, supposing she could come up with something really crushing—but now was not the time. Damn him, he did have a point. "We have to get them out of here," she said. "Can they be moved?"

John tried an experimental heft with a nearby toddler. "Like moving mannequins," he replied, setting the boy down carefully. "But they're just as heavy as they always were. We won't get more than a dozen or so out."

"Well, we can't go for the police. They'd think we were crazy and lock us up," Abby said. She shifted her grip on the spear and thought, gnawing on her lower lip again as she did so. The skin was dry, and she tasted blood when she bit a little too hard. "Ow! Dammit!"

"The cannibal's got a point," Harvey said from overhead. Abby glowered at him, fingers pressed to the cut in her lip. "Moving the kids won't do squat, and I, for one, don't have any arms to contribute. I suggest we start getting a plan together; those guys aren't going to wait for us to come back out in the open."

"You took something from the hag?"

Likho was not a happy camper. His sense of humor had apparently annoyed El Cucuy more than he planned. And it wasn't even as if he was the one suffering for it.

That was why L'uomo Nero was on the floor in front of him, pinned down by the burly Sacauntos. A toy dragon was pressed to L'uomo's throat. The skin had already burned away, but his friend was keeping silent. Likho hoped it wasn't because his vocal chords had been severed.

Now El Cucuy's gaze was fixed on Likho, and the red eyes seemed to bore a hole right through him.

"Yeah, I got the damn ring!" Likho snarled back. "Is that a crime now? Does there just so happen to be a rule that I wasn't informed about? Maybe you decided that the Family is better than the other spirits? Is that how it works? Christ fuck-all, get that thing off him!"

The dead boy nodded, and Sacauntos rose. Likho flinched as the tiny figurine swung past his head in the hairy man's grip.

"But why?" El Cucuy pressed. "You say you were worried about L'uomo Nero being on the loose. I find this unlikely. Why go to Baba Yaga about it?"

"You know as well as I do, kiddo—when the humans see you as the *unknown,* you can be pretty goddamned hard to find," Likho said. "Maybe he's no Bavbav, but he's got a bag of it. Baba Yaga is the one who knows things we can't even get near."

"And she told you to give him the ring. To put a magic *traveling ring* into his bag!"

El Cucuy was furious. The red flush of rage suffused his face, and his small fists were clenched as he faced down Likho. "Did you ever, in your ten thousand years of existence, think before you did anything?" he screamed. "You knew as well as I did that Bavbav was in that bag!"

Once again, the name evoked a rumble from the watching Family, but El Cucuy was beyond caring. "Who knows what this could do?" he shouted, aiming a wild blow at Likho's face. Likho fell back, blood streaming from his newly rebroken nose. "You blind, stupid bastard!"

"Calm down," Likho muttered from the floor. His face throbbed, but physical pain was hardly a surprise at this point. "Cucuy, you're losing it."

El Cucuy stopped. His face turned white as the full implication of Likho's words struck him—and Likho knew, by the murmurs from the assembled bogeymen, that they knew it too.

Just how human was their leader behaving?

Far off in the darkness of the empty galleries, a low, mournful howl echoed and re-echoed off the high ceilings. Once again, creatures began to coalesce out of the air, spinning themselves into existence from threads of shadow. Under the blank gaze of saints and sinners, they moved down the long halls, searching for the runaway humans.

This was the sort of hunt that none of the Family had ever really participated in before. Chasing down terrified children was one thing, while tracking armed adults was quite another. There had been a mass refusal to volunteer for the search; after watching the torture of Likho and L'uomo, none of them knew for certain that they couldn't be hurt. After the first confrontation in the armor gallery, even Sacauntos went gingerly. Galacia was not as big or as solid in belief as he would have liked.

La Llorona had barely dragged herself back together, and was throwing her energies into finding the humans' hiding place. Her legend was widespread, touching several continents and cultures; being attacked and worse, *hurt* by a pack of apes with old weapons was enough to make her corroded teeth grind. With her power base, she could just barely feel them out, and she was angry enough that she didn't even try to be stealthy.

The bogeymen were gathering all the power available to them. The shadows grew darker, and the walls around them began to shift ever so slightly as the Family warped reality. Where La Llorona moved, beads of moisture collected on the tiles beneath her; moss had already begun to grow on the frames and statues. There was a chittering sound, the noise of insects and small animals that hid in the night far away from human dwellings, and the stench of dry baked earth and dead livestock.

The charge paused a moment on the steps to the basement level, sensing with unease the presence of the children's exhibits below. But many of their members were driven by hatred, and where Sacauntos faltered, La Llorona stormed forward to take the lead. A tide of fear-born monsters surged down the staircases and into the green-lit gallery.

A flurry of motion met the enraged bogeymen, and roars of anger mingled with shrieks. Crouched behind an overturned desk, Abby and John were hurling things as fast as they could. The gallery and kiosk had been raided, and coloring books, art guides, heavy metal magnets, and any loose detritus lay piled at their feet. A child's suit of armor had been dismembered, and its helmet went sailing through the air to strike a bag man square in the face.

"Child!" one of them howled, clawing at its face. A Rubik's Cube hit it in the midsection and slid right through, cutting it in half. The SSR agents had grabbed everything solid, and in their haste, toys had been mixed in with the heavy objects.

Marotte was the second wave of attack. As some of the onrushing bogey-men recoiled or dodged the ballistics, he charged into the midst of the mob with Abby's halberd. Each sweep of the heavy wooden pole sent another nightmare roiling away in misty shreds. Groaning and shrieking, the bogeymen stumbled back, withdrawing into shadows.

"Are you spineless?" something shrieked. The faceless woman from the gallery came swooping down from above, trailing her white shroud like a tattered flag. "Return to the fight!" she shouted at the rest of the bogey-men, but not one of them moved back into the middle of the room.

Growling, she rounded on Marotte, who gripped the spear grimly and tried to stare her down. "Don't dare cross the weeping woman," the crea-ture hissed through her stained teeth. Marotte shook his head and swung the spear.

She pounced like a bird of prey, leaping over the wide swing of the weapon, and sank her fleshless jaws into his face. As the skin of his cheek tore, blood spurted into the air. It steamed as it met the cold atmosphere, and Marotte fell with a strangled shriek. La Llorona bore down on him.

And now the Mörkö was at the head of the party, roaring and champing for revenge. A horrified Abby snatched up a handful of cast metal minia-tures to throw, but John clamped his hand over hers. "Mine!" he shouted over the shrieking chaos, and she didn't have the time to think of an alter-native.

A bag man named Torbalan took advantage of the distraction and slipped in like a hunter, seizing Abby's midsection with its bony claws. Flakes of skin sloughed off as the aged chain-mail bit into its hands, yet Torbalan held tight, sinking its claws into the metal links and crushing the breath out of Abby. She tried not to scream, and John rounded on the struggling pair, but the blue giant was leaping at him.

The Mörkö swung one glowing fist at them, but John slipped under the punch like a cat diving for a dropped sardine and jabbed one hand into the monster's stomach. An oversized yellow pencil, sharpened to stakelike precision, buried itself in the half-formed blue flesh. He whooped as the Mörkö writhed and clutched its gut.

"Abby! Go!" John roared above the rising wind. Abby whipped her right hand up, flinging the clutched handful of toys into Torbalan's face. The smell of burning skin mixed with a guttural shriek, and she struggled out of his suddenly slackened grasp and lunged forward, half-falling towards her partner. John gripped her mail shirt, and she dug her fingers into the side of his denim jacket, each holding the other upright as they plunged towards the staircase.

An agonized scream made them halt. "Mal—" Abby began, trying to turn. She could see nothing of their friend, but they could hear him. But the bitter truth was that there was nothing they could do. Once again, John pulled on her arm, and they ran.

Shadows grabbed at their feet. Tentacles snaked and dark, hairy hands clawed at their backs. There were things in the darkness that neither of them had ever seen, and some they had never wanted to see again. Involuntary tears streamed down Abby's face as a flash of teeth nearly snapped one flailing hand off, but the grim-faced John grabbed her arm exactly as she had pulled him out of the cookie jar so many times—she felt the wind on her fingertips, but nothing came to harm. The staircase was just ahead.

Then something hooked itself around John's neck, and he tumbled backwards with a shout. His grip on Abby was torn free, leaving her to watch in horror as he vanished into the swirling darkness.

Fear and dread and confusion were all swept away as Abby flailed for John's hand and could not find it. With a growl, she plunged a hand into her pocket and pulled out the silver crucifix. The darkness roiled and drove back before it.

"I believe in this!" she shouted to the shadows, and those shadows seemed to listen. A hand reached for her ankle, but Abby darted the tiny object towards it and the fingers dissolved into greasy black smoke. "I believe!" she repeated. Her voice steadied as she spoke. "And Harvey believes in himself, and Marotte believes in himself, and Giovanna believes in her friendly bogeyman, and John—John, he believes in *violence!*"

The grasping hands fell back, dissolving into the darkness. The faint glow bleeding through the tiny windows above wavered and grew stronger, and Abby stepped into the patch of light. The edges of the square trembled where the creatures threatened to spill over into it, but Abby's resolve was strengthening with every passing second, and her belief grew steadier as the edges of the crucifix bit into her palm. The silence swept through the cold basement.

"You can't stop us," she breathed, trying to calm herself. "I believe. Harvey believes. Giovanna believes. John believes. And John believes really... *back off!*"

She kicked at a vague hand of darkness that was trying to creep over the line, well aware of how juvenile it was and not caring in the slightest. It felt good to have the upper hand for once. They'd all been running blind, trying to feel their way by instinct alone, ever since this whole mess began: following vague assumptions, smothering themselves in dusty old books and papers, listening in a cold sweat as the numbers of abductions and deaths continued to climb. Kicking and shouting satisfied some childish instinct to have her own back.

"John!" Abby yelled. A tendril made a swipe for her legs, but she slashed at it with the trailing chain and watched in satisfaction as it retreated hastily. "John, come on! You believe in your gun, don't you? It's lousy, it's ineffective, it stovepipes like hell, but it's *yours!*"

For a long moment, the world held its breath. Then the silence was broken: the sharp report of a Desert Eagle, once, twice, three times in quick succession. The darkness convulsed, hands, paws, claws, and skeletal graspings twisting and fading into one another. A fourth gunshot sent the shapes skittering off across the dim floor.

With one final twitch, a bundle of shadow unraveled, dropping a semiconscious John onto the hard concrete. The Englishman was groaning and muttering to himself, sprawled on his side and clutching his ribs as he fell into the square of orange light. His pistol was lying where he had dropped it.

And there was no magazine in the gun.

Abby felt a chill spread across her neck and down the spine as she stared at the empty socket where that small, vital component ought to be. Her partner still clutched it like a lifeline, but as she forced her legs to move her across the cellar floor and bend stiffly to let her kneel by his side, she could smell not a whiff of gunpowder. When she laid a hand on the muzzle, it was stone cold.

"John, where are your spare clips?" Abby asked. She was still unsteady, her heart racing from the thirty seconds of hideous fright that had only just passed, but she mustered enough attitude—always fake a smile with Jimmy, always fake nonchalance with John—to aim a halfhearted glare at the loose pockets of his oversized jacket. He always kept his ammunition in his pockets, fumbling through them whenever he misplaced his cell phone or that fiber-optic novelty pen he liked so much. But there were no magazines. A whiskey miniature, two sheets of straight pins, half a pack of chewing gum, a diving knife, and a corkscrew were there, but no ammunition.

"All out," the man murmured. His head turned this way and that, perhaps looking for something. John looked disoriented and vague, and he shook himself like a wet dog trying to dry himself off. There was a shallow cut above his left eye, and a small drop of blood was just leaking out of the corner of it.

"But—you always have spares. Don't you?" Abby said. She hitched her arm under John's shoulders and tried to hoist him up, grunting a little when they both stumbled against the wall. How could one thin man be so heavy?

John's eyes were glazed and unfocused. "All gone. Everything's gone."

"What, this from the eternal optimist?" she whispered as she hauled on his arm. John stayed plastered against the wall, breathing heavily, as immobile as a sack of clay.

She tugged on him again, but he refused to move. Muttering angrily to herself, Abby grabbed the collar of his jacket and yanked hard, trying to get his attention. The collar tore under her fingers. "Cheap clothes," she commented to the air. Fear was trying to creep back in, but she was riding the wave of surging anger. She glared at the loose threads in her fingers, feeling the roughness in them. Why did John wear this crap?

"We weren't gonna get through alive," John muttered in response. His fingers were fluttering spasmodically against the concrete wall.

Abby gave him a shake. "What the heck is wrong with you, John? Wake up!" Her angry tone was tinged with hysteria now, and she shook him again for good measure. The darkness was creeping back. "John!"

"We won't, Abby." The eyes were beginning to glaze over and the blinking had stopped. Thin lines of blood trickled from the cut downwards, succumbing to gravity but diverting around the raised bone of the eye and sliding down the outer side of his cheek like a boat skirting the edge of an island in midstream. "Chance of survival. None, thanks for asking. Not gonna happen. 'S the way things go. Make an impression, make 'em think when you're gone."

"But you shot them!" Abby insisted, yanking on his lapels and trying to get him to focus on her. There was another cracking noise as the plasticized thread tore. "I heard the shots!"

John almost giggled, even though his eyes were still foggy. "'And if all of you clap your hands three times,'" he singsonged in a bad Japanese accent, "'My gun will be magically filled with bullets!'"

She cracked a smile in spite of the situation, and gently patted his torn collar back into place. "Quoting silly movies? You must be okay. Are you trying to fool me?"

"Wouldn't dream of it," he muttered in response. Abby slipped her arm under his shoulders again and tried hard to lift him, but he seemed to have grown heavier in these last few moments. Now, she couldn't even budge him.

"John," she whispered to him, bending down close to his ear so that nothing else could hear them. She *knew* they were still being watched; she could feel it at the base of her spine, where all her fears tended to hide. "John, listen to me. I need you to move. I need you to get up and walk. They won't let me carry you any more."

"Can't walk," he said vaguely. "Abby, we're gonna die."

"Don't say that."

"Gonna die."

"Don't say that!"

"Well, he's right, isn't he?"

El Cucuy seemed to materialize out of the fog. There they were: the calm red eyes, casting a faint illumination on the thinnish pale face.

"You," she said shakily. Her protective instinct warred with her fatigue and frustration, and protection never stood a chance. "You keep away!"

"You came to confront me, didn't you? Asking to be left be isn't going to do any good at this point in the proceedings." The dead child beckoned, and three huge fur-covered monsters stepped out of the shadows with absolutely no ceremony. Abby bit her lip again when one of them snatched her by the arms. But when they reached for the semi-conscious John, she lashed out with both her feet.

"Leave him alone!" she shrieked. *"Leave him alone!"*

"No," El Cucuy said simply. Another one of the hairy men snatched John up as easily as if he'd been made of paper. The Englishman struggled weakly, but the huge creature gave him a tap on the head and he slumped forward. Abby could feel her heart sink—there was enough strength in one of those fingers to kill any of them. What were they going to do?

"We have the whole collection," El Cucuy continued. "It's time to start."

Chapter Twenty

The sculpture court stood at the heart of the American Art gallery, and showcased the best in nineteenth-century workmanship. Solid, square white pillars supported a second story balcony of fluted columns, and a huge skylight cast a square of yellow light on the floor. Polished surfaces gleamed. And all around them, hundreds of blank eyes watched.

Pallas Athene was there, her limbless upper body perched on a plinth, staring dazedly as if some ambitious hunter had taken to stuffing and mounting the gods of Olympus. Her form was shaped out of white marble, smoothed and turned so expertly that the eye skimmed easily over faint discolorations and hairline cracks. Not far from her was Nadia, the blind flower seller of Pompeii, caught in a moment of fear as she stumbled through the destroyed city with cane in hand. A wind two thousand years gone still whipped her skirts and tangled the girl in motionless cloth.

Across the court, Greek figures gave way to the wild west. A pair of copper Indians stood nobly, poised to shoot an arrow into the sun, ignoring the humans being dragged along.

Beyond the square of light in the center of the court, figures were dim and motionless, picked out in dappled pools of light and shadow. Some were statues, and some were the Family. Some were the shuddering children they clutched. Worn and frightened, the young ones had stopped squirming, and watched the scene with dull, deadened stares. They were ready to witness the scene, and to give life to the new bogeyman legends.

The only bogeys that could be clearly seen were a pair in the center of the lit square, bound in torn strips of blanket. One wore the form of a gray-haired man, the other was the L'uomo Nero that the old woman had described. And huddled at the base of a statue not far from them was Giovanna herself, badly burned and breathing shallowly. It was a sorry scene.

El Cucuy hopped up onto the edge of a bench with a quick birdlike motion. He stood still and calm while Abby and John were hauled forward. Both were pinioned by the grips of two more huge hairy men.

There was a guttural moan from across the court, and a moment later, La Llorona drifted into view. Abby slumped in relief when she saw that the Llorona carried a twitching, bleeding, but definitely living bundle that could only be Marotte. "Thank heavens," she whispered. "John—Mal's alive!"

John's head flopped a little as he struggled to focus his vision, but he nodded to show that he heard her. He was shivering, even though it didn't seem very cold in the sculpture court, and his face was pale.

With a clack of her bloodstained teeth, La Llorona dumped Marotte at his friends' feet. "Fix him," she said.

Their captors released them. Stumbling, Abby sat down by Marotte's head and pressed a hand to his torn face. Her gorge rose as the warm liquid seeped through her fingers. Beside her, John wavered a little as he gripped the sleeve of his torn jacket with shaking fingers and clumsily tore a piece out of the cloth. Fighting the urge to be sick, Abby took it and began to swab the blood from Marotte's skin as carefully as she could. The injuries were ugly: La Llorona's bite marks had barely missed his right eye. Marotte groaned a little and raised a hand to cup his face, and Abby pushed it back down.

There was a rustle, and suddenly, El Cucuy was looking down at the groaning man. "A fine illustration," he said, making the SSR agents flinch a little, "of the impractical human design. Llorona's teeth came very close to severing an important artery."

"Kind of you to tell us," John said flatly. He focused on El Cucuy, one hand on Abby's arm, gripping it for support while remaining seemingly nonchalant. "Make a study of humans, do you?"

"We were born of humans and in humans. It would be imprudent to not know everything about them." El Cucuy gave a little bow to the assembly. "Now. To business, if you wouldn't mind. The humanization of my Family; that I know of. Likewise the old woman. What I do not understand is where you three—four, once we find your djinn—fit into the picture."

Abby and John glanced at each other, and John's grip on her arm tightened. "It's our job," she said loudly, trying to ignore the bloodless feeling in her skin. "We're the Society for the Security of Reality." The words sounded hollow.

"A presumptuous title, isn't it?" El Cucuy commented. "Demon-hunters, then—it's been known to happen. But why look into the affairs of the Family?"

"When thousands of kids disappear in one night," John slurred, "it's going t'attract a bit of interest."

"And your Mörkö gave the game away, smashing through walls left and right." Abby looked back to Marotte, who was still breathing, albeit shallowly. The strip of cloth wasn't very absorbent, but the wound was now clotting and she couldn't do much more. There had been medical supplies in their bags, but those bags were still up in the Arms and Armor gallery.

John rummaged in his pockets and silently handed her the whiskey miniature. El Cucuy watched curiously as Abby poured the whiskey onto the folded scrap of cloth and pressed it to Marotte's face. He groaned and rocked back and forth a little, but his eyes remained closed.

"Will he regain consciousness?" the Family's leader asked, leaning over Marotte.

"That's none of your business, is it?" Abby said tightly.

"Why do you pour intoxicants on his wounds?"

"Why do you want to know?"

El Cucuy hissed a little between his teeth, and the air grew colder around them. "Do you always reply to questions with questions? Answer what is put to you, human."

"Well, we're bloody well not inclined to be friendly now, are we?" John said. "Not what with you kidnapping and murdering and all. So pardon us if we're not going to make the reign of terror any easier on you." Abby elbowed him frantically, gesturing for him to keep quiet, but El Cucuy had already heard.

The dead child turned and shook his head, laughing a little. "And this, brothers," he said to the listening bogeymen, "is what we face every day." He flung out a hand towards the crouching SSR agents, as if showing off the prize of his trophy collection. "This passel of meat is exactly what I was talking about! I see inside their heads, and I know this man's wits are disordered, for he realizes quite well how idiotic it is to insult someone who can tear him apart... and still, arrogance! It's breathtaking, my brothers.

"They are so because they were told not to fear us." El Cucuy's voice was sharp, and the laughter was gone. "If we fail to check this, then there will be more humans crashing into our Homes, attacking our people, talking back, making our brethren small and weak. It happened to the Mörkö, and now they sell toys of him!"

"Don't see why you mind that," John murmured. "'S another form of belief, innit?"

El Cucuy rounded on him. "What did you say?"

"Abby, tell 'im."

"Well... it is a bit like worship," she admitted in spite of herself. Marotte groaned again, and she poured a little more of the whiskey onto his wound. It made sense, in a strange sort of way. "All those little kids?" she repeated. "Kids all across the world, playing with the Mörkö?"

"What?" The dead boy's face showed his confusion, and he snapped the word. "Make sense!"

"You should've listened to your mum," John said. "Abby's one herself, y'know."

"I have no mother! Make yourself plain, you little pest!"

Cold wind ripped through the room, a sudden burst of arctic chill that made them all flinch. El Cucuy's sanity was tenuous at best, and his grip on it was loosening by the second. With an effort, Abby gathered herself.

"Look, you're made in the image of people... why don't you understand that? Little kids play with their toys, and they love them and treat them like best friends. I saw Jimmy do it, when he was little; he had a dinosaur that he dragged everywhere with him. He named it Butter, because it was the only word he knew."

"Belief, you could call it," her friend added. John settled himself painfully onto the concrete, propped his chin in his hands, and aimed a deadly serious stare at the seething Cucuy. "Didn't you wonder why the Mörkö didn't vanish? Sure, he's in a humanish form, but he's not gone. Been stabbed, still here. He's got all the belief he needs—just not the sort you're used to dealing with."

El Cucuy's breath came forth in a venomous hiss. "That's ten times worse! Not simply departure or death, but *betrayal*."

"Oh, get a grip!" John shouted. "He changed. It happens! The world changes, and you're afraid of it!"

"SILENCE!"

John pushed himself to his feet. "Sod that! He changed! And you know what? He'll live! He'll stay alive, in his friendly form, when you're gone and forgotten! He'll be doing kids' parties a thousand years from now, and you'll be a footnote in some grad student's essay. What d'you plan to do about that?"

With the fresh blast of cold came a small figure, hurling itself forward. As if by magic, a red slash opened up across John's face, cutting a diagonal slice over his nose and cheeks. The man staggered slightly, pressing a hand to his face to ease the pain.

"That was a warning," El Cucuy growled. The darkness all around them deepened; within the square of light, bound by the statues, Likho and L'uomo Nero could only watch as he loomed before the cowering humans.

And to their great surprise, John nudged Abby and grinned. "Getting frantic, aren't you? Bit human of you."

The heat sucked from the room as the enormity of the statement struck the bogeymen.

"I WILL NOT BE INSULTED!" El Cucuy roared. Clusters of mists rose up around the form of the child, bleeding into the darkness and whirling around the heads of the captives. His voice was hysterical, and beginning to crack. "I am the dead child, the secondborn! I am the one the children fear the most! Keep your lying mouths shut, or I will have my legions tear you to shreds!"

John's cheek was bleeding, his face was pale. A massive bruise was blooming on Abby's face—souvenir of the brawl in the gallery—and her trembling hands were scratched and torn. Marotte was barely conscious. Anger and adrenaline and fear of death had sustained them this far, and it couldn't carry them much further. But the sight of the little boy, fearsome though he might be, shouting and raging at the grown-ups, activated a far different reaction in Abby.

She reacted like a tired and exasperated mother. Dropping the whiskey bottle, she grabbed El Cucuy by the arm and slapped him as hard as she could.

A hiss of anger ran through the ranks of the bogeymen as El Cucuy rocked backwards, his eyes widened, a red hand print on his cheek. John caught hold of Abby's arm, stumbling a little himself in his effort. "Don't do anything stu—" he began, but the child was already lashing back.

Clawing shadows surrounded them, slashing at their clothes and skin. The monstrous darkness flailed in vain against the ancient mail, but the invisible nails bit freely into faces and hands. Abby stumbled, trying to shield her face with her arms, falling backwards against John's chest. The two of them fell to the ground and curled around each other, covering themselves as best they could, but cold hands were pulling them apart. Skin burned, cloth tore, blood flowed.

In the center of the sculpture court, Likho and L'uomo Nero were jolted to their feet. Trapped within the square, they were helpless; none of the other bogeymen could get in, but neither could they get out. L'uomo Nero hurled himself at the barrier, and was thrown violently back.

"She disciplines the child!" he cried out. "She does as she should! This must not be! Children cannot kill mothers! It is wrong!"

Huddled by the statue of Nadia, Giovanna lifted her ancient head. The ugly red burn had paralyzed half of her face, and one eye was seared shut. Her legs shuddered, and her house dress and scarf were far beyond repair.

"Cucuy!" she shouted, and the sound of her thin voice made every bogeyman turn. El Cucuy rounded on her, and the shadows dispersed. It was in time; three battered humans still breathed outside the square of light. But no gaze was on them; Giovanna was rising to her feet. Watery hazel eyes met burning red ones, and the air seemed to spark between them.

"The way I see it," Giovanna said after a long, tense moment, "things aren't so complicated after all. You've got your job to do, and I've got mine. And there's rules to those jobs. Aren't there."

El Cucuy snarled, making the brass railings ring as his voice thrummed through them. "There are rules, hag. And we enforce them."

Knees trembling, Giovanna clung to Nadia's plinth for support. "Mister Likho," she called out clearly. "I've got a question for you. You punish children that break the rules, don't you?"

The Russian ghost seemed dumbfounded at being addressed, but he turned to answer her. "That's the way it works," he replied.

"And that isn't all of it. Your body makes you what you are, doesn't it?"

"Lady, we're in deep shit, could you please—"

But Giovanna just shook her head and turned a little. The deep-set and blackened eyes gleamed as she faced El Cucuy. "The rule is, bad children are punished. And you've been a bad one," she said softly. "Very bad, to treat an old woman like this."

El Cucuy's nostrils flared as he stared her down. "I do what's necessary, human. They'll believe in us for a thousand years when they see what happens to you."

"But you know what happens to bad little boys, don't you?" Giovanna murmured, almost to herself. "It's all about the form and the rules. Bogeymen have got rules, too. And I'll bet anything you like that half these children haven't done anything wrong. You broke your rules, little one."

"Grandmother-power," El Cucuy snapped. "She's trying to make us uneasy. Don't listen to her!"

"You know what happens, don't you? I think you do." Raising one frail hand, she made a knobbly fist and knocked twice on the plinth of the statue. El Cucuy stormed forward, infuriated and reaching for the old woman's throat, but Giovanna just smiled even more widely. "There are people that come for bad little boys, you know," she said.

Shadowy fingers froze. Red eyes widened in shock as El Cucuy stopped dead. "What did you say?" he hissed.

"I said," the old lady repeated, "that I believe. And I know that bad children are very tasty to some monsters out there."

El Cucuy's nervousness dissolved in amusement. "You really are dimwitted," he said mock-affectionately, lowering his hands. "I don't blame you, granny. Eighty years with only L'uomo Nero for company—no wonder you've gone mad."

Not to be swayed, the old woman knocked again, this time on the marble tile. "Do you hear that?" she murmured. "That's the black man at the door. He comes to take the bad boys away."

"I'm sorry," El Cucuy chuckled, curling his fingers around the knocking hand and gently crushing it in his shadowy grip. "We need the belief. Good night, granny."

"I'm here."

And a wave of fear shuddered through the crowd as they realized that L'uomo Nero was no longer within the square of light.

A shadow loomed over him as El Cucuy reached for Giovanna's throat. "I am here," a voice said, and it was a cold voice, cold like the iron railings in a churchyard and old as the soil of the graves themselves. L'uomo Nero stood tall, face shadowed by the priest's hat, form shrouded in a long coat dusty from the road, the bag in one hand open-mouthed like a hungry leech. "I'm here," he repeated. "And you have been bad."

El Cucuy's mouth opened and shut soundlessly as he gaped at the towering figure in front of him. "You—you—" he managed to squeak. His grip on Giovanna's hand loosened, and the old woman fell on her bottom and crawled backwards, away from him. "You can't have got out!" the child finally burst out. "I thought so carefully—I planned—you were in the—you can't get out! You can't!" His voice faltered. "Stand back, traitor!" he shrieked at last. "I lead this Family! I am your commander!"

"You're a *bad child,*" Giovanna called out. Her voice was hoarse and raspy, but within the folds of wrinkles, the beady eyes were bright and triumphant. El Cucuy rounded on her, but some sort of force seemed to **thrum** through the room and pulled his attention back to the bogeyman staring down at him. "The rules say the Black Man comes for the bad boy."

"I am the leader, and I order you to stand down!" The dead boy's high voice cracked as he stared up at the towering figure of L'uomo Nero. The monster did not move. "I order you! I am your leader! I can have you thrown out of the Family!"

One hand raised the gaping bag, and El Cucuy flinched backwards. "I command you!" he repeated shakily. "Put it down! I command you! Do your duty!"

There was a moment where the world stood still, and then the dark figure let out a breath like the hiss of heat from a boiling pot. "What sort of creature would I be, El Cucuy," it said, "if I did not do my duty?"

"You would be a traitor and an idiot!" El Cucuy roared as best he could. "Do as you're told!"

"Very well," L'uomo Nero murmured. And as the bag went over the boy's head, all El Cucuy could do was scream in rage and frustration.

The bag bulged and jerked, and L'uomo Nero dropped it as quickly as he could. Rents appeared in the worn weave, leaking greenish light from every frayed patch. Something squirmed, and there was a ghastly shriek. Claws bit through the fabric and were dragged back again, leaving behind shredded holes from which poured light and a thick, greasy black smoke.

Then the bag split open. There was a gurgling howl and a figure streamed out in a cloud of smoke, reaching the ceiling in a trice and scattering small bones left and right in its wake. It shuddered when it struck, sending a miniature hand falling from the smoke cloud and landing at Giovanna's feet. The cloths binding Likho melted into the air, and the bogeymen drew back.

Reborn, it was hard to look Bavbav in the eye. The cloud was changing at high speed, morphing and re-shaping and twisting like something seen under a microscope. There were all sorts of suggestions there—hands became paws, paws became claws, claws became things that it hurt the head to look at—but it was jumbled up and constantly re-forming itself. Were there even eyes to meet? There were teeth, teeth that would grab an unfortunate child and crunch the bones with no compunction, but it was hard to spot the gleam of an eye in the smoke and light.

L'uomo Nero stumbled forward and fell onto his knees, almost weeping in fear. "The bag—" he began. "Lord, the bag—"

It will be mended, the billowing creature said. There was no voice to go with the words; instead, the information came in a rush of sensations that flowed into the head. It was like the ghostly voice that L'uomo Nero used, but older. **It will be mended and the only faithful one will be rewarded.**

Likho looked sour when he heard that, but refused to throw himself on the floor for anybody—Bavbav or God or even L'uomo Nero. "And that's it?" he demanded. "What about the jackasses who threw us around? What about the high-minded bastards who tried to kill you *and* me?"

They are seen, Bavbav murmured. **They are seen in small desires, small greed, malice, hate, fear, cowardice. Gifts have been misused. They are taken.** Light flashed, and for a moment the tendrils of smoke were claws again. Far off in the depths of the hall, they could hear a distant scream.

Huddled on the floor, the humans were still alive. They were covered in cuts and bruises. John and Abby were holding fast to each other, trying to shield the badly injured Marotte from any further harm. John's arms were wrapped around Abby's shoulders, and her face was buried in the crook of his neck. She heard the words faintly, but her blood pounded in her ears and the rapid thunder of John's heartbeat seemed to fill the world. She could feel the cold sweat mix with the warmth of the tears that, come another day, he would never admit to shedding.

They were alive. Oh, thank God, they were alive. Fresh bruises flowered like dandelions in the grass, but her hands clutched a real, living person. The warmth of skin and hair seemed like something out of a fairy tale. His hands were trembling where they clutched her shoulders.

Bavbav's voice broke into her thoughts, and slowly, Abby raised her head from John's shoulder. High above them, the cloud gathered—not a cheap gray fog like the formless, spineless Harvey, but a swirling primordial storm. **It is done,** Abby heard him say.

And as for you, Likho, he continued, letting amusement creep into their heads along with his voice, **you too have served in your own way. Your visit to sister Baba Yaga gave to me the ring which helped to bring this end. I will give you the belief and the stewardship of the**

new ones who will arise from their legends. Hombre del Saco, Hastrman, and all the rest will answer to you.

The Russian bogeyman made an incoherent noise and bit his lip in his
hurry to speak. "Eh—thanks—" he finally managed, and the smoke of
Bavbav's form curled and danced in laughter.

And as for these—

The leader of the Family reached out a tendril of smoke—claws, paws,
hand, skeletal grasp—towards the three humans. Abby found herself
unceremoniously shoved back as John stumbled, trying to cover both of
his partners. But the man was unsteady on his feet, and Abby forced herself forward again. "Don't touch us!" she gasped with a conviction she did-
n't feel, brandishing the necklace still curled around one bloodied fist.
They were alive, and she wasn't going to let that be threatened again. She
swung wildly, the silver chain cutting into the white flesh of her hand. "I
have a crucifix, and I believe in it, and I don't believe in you!"

Believe what you will. A gentle puff of smoke curled around the crucifix. **Loud and crude and bitter and unfaithful though you are, you
too were my chosen. Be proud that it was you to whom I brought
the ring.**

Abby took a deep breath. There was no attack, no more flaying claws.
Her hand still trembled, but as the seconds stretched on and there was no
more pain, she lowered it slightly. "You brought it to us?" she said softly.
"Why?"

**Because it is in my power to know you. Abigail Marquise, born to
the name of Teller. You are married, and keep no contact with him.
Your child is not his, but one of a man you knew little when you
were young. He does not know this.**

Her eyes widened. "I—" she began, before choking on her words just as
Likho had. "How did you know that?" she added. "I never told—"

Bavbav's laugh echoed through their minds. **Nobody knows how
much I know.** The smoky hand glided out from the rising cloud and rested itself on Abby's cheek. **Tell me, Abigail who was Teller. What
would you ask from the unknown?**

She had only a moment's worth of hesitation. "Cure Marotte," she said.
Her words echoed hollowly in her ears. "He lost a lot of blood."

There was a burst of surprise from the swirling bogeyman. **Curious.
Humans think often of vengeance; it was thought you would ask
for a death for your husband.**

"I can take care of that myself," Abby muttered.

You would truly kill him?

"No, I wouldn't." She flashed a weak grin at the spirit. "But I'd like to."

Bavbav's motion stilled slightly, though the clouds of drifting blackness still moved. **But to kill or to wish to kill is wrong, and you want it anyway. Has much changed since entering the black man's bag? It was once known that matters such as these were matters of honor, and to be decided as such.**

"They used to be," Abby said dully. "Not any more. Terry and I had our problems, but it wouldn't be right to ask you to kill him. He doesn't deserve to die."

Not as selfless as you would seem, I think. But for your friend I will make a new life. He will awaken weak, but in good health. Bavbav swirled in place, and faces flashed past them. **I suspect I already know what his wish is, and I will grant it. Take care, Abigail who was Teller.**

John Sawyer, the voice said. John flinched backwards, eyeballing the smoky form as best he could and refusing to back down in the face of yet another arrogant bogeyman. A dozen cuts on his face and hands stained his clothes with blood, he was weakened and tired, but if looks could kill.... Against all common sense, Abby reached out, putting a gentle hand on his shoulder. He relaxed, very slightly, and she thought she saw a fresh gleam in the corner of his eyes. It might have been her imagination.

John Sawyer, Bavbav repeated. John still did not speak. **There are things in your brain that were seen, a long time past. Strange. And it is suspected that it is known what you want, John Sawyer. It is granted.**

"Pardon me, your fucking honor," John began, in a pained voice heavy with sarcasm, "but promises aside, you're still a bogeyman, and bogeymen aren't very friendly to us mere mortals. What the fuck's been going on?"

Oh, yes, the great plan. It can be seen all that they did. It was hard to tell, but the voice might have held a hint of sadness. **It was done in our name, but it was against all that our Family should stand for. Rules are in place for a reason.**

"But you can fix it, can't you?" Abby said hurriedly. "Bring them back? Those bogeymen over there—" and she gestured to the crowd of shadows at the edge of the hall "—have taken thousands of children from this country, and some of them are dead! There are kids right here, right now, watching this happen. Can't you fix that?"

It can be made so it had never happened... but it would cause more harm than it would cure. For a moment, the face of an old man looked out at them, blinking pale eyes. **The Family killed without cause. But those that did not deserve death are now alive. It will be granted to all of them a false memory. The human authorities will be summoned, and there will be evidence found to convince them of a kidnapping ring intent on money.**

"You can do that?" Abby said.

Nobody knows.

"But—" She mouthed soundlessly for a moment. "Those that did not deserve death? You're not—you're not bringing them all back?"

Those that deserve, the shadow repeated.

The anger burst out again. "You have the power to fix it all!" she shouted, wiping the tracks of blood and tears from her face and staring up at the whirling form of the bogeyman chieftain. "You can bring them all back! Why are you letting those kids die?"

It was not the work ordained. The face of the old man appeared again and hovered closer.

"You brought back the others!"

All are returned.

"What? But you said—"

Know this, Abigail who was Teller. Though gifts are given, benevolence is not a right. For a moment, the old face flickered and distorted, becoming something hideous. The humans flinched backwards, and the faces dissolved into clouds of smoke again. **You made conclusions. Is it thought that some of the young did deserve to die?**

Abby sputtered. "No, but—"

Then why was it thought so?

"You..." she trailed off into silence for a moment, and then gave the hovering Bavbav the oldest look that had ever appeared on her face.

"And you've got the magic answer to everything, have you?" John's legs were stronger now, and he looked angry.

Be careful, John Sawyer. It is seen that anger will buy you a great deal of trouble.

The cloud came lower, hovering over Marotte, whose breathing was now deep and regular. The crust of blood remained, but the skin underneath it was smooth and unblemished.

There is a name here, Bavbav's thoughts told them. **But a name that will return of its own accord in time. Nothing much is needed in this matter.**

And now, for the black man.

L'uomo Nero was still kneeling in place. Two thin tracks of tears made striped patterns in the dirt and grime ground into his face. For a man or monster who had just won a battle and been relieved of a heavy weight on his shoulders, he looked almost ready to die.

Black man, the voice of Bavbav called. Jerkily, L'uomo Nero clambered to his feet, moving like a puppet whose strings were badly tangled up. **Black man, who was a most loyal follower and protector in two hundred years of darkness. What would you ask for yourself?**

"I ask nothing, lord." The voice was just as it had been before, dull and hoarse and lifeless.

There was a ripple in the strange ethereal form that was Bavbav. **Everyone asks for something. A dear son will not be repaid with nothing for his part in this survival!**

"Then let me go back to my work."

Choose, L'uomo Nero! Choose something that you want made right.

L'uomo Nero stared down at the stained concrete floor. "Lord, you were the voice in my bag for so long. Without your presence, I feel lost... as if something has blinded me. I am freed now, but I cannot make myself so. I wish to be guided awhile longer."

Bavbav's form rippled again, curling around L'uomo Nero until the black-coated man was wreathed in smoke. **It is remembered when you were the terror of a thousand cities,** the master of the Family admonished. **It is remembered, before the time in the bag, that you used to snatch the children away no matter how well they begged. What has happened to the horror, to the legend of the black man?**

"I feel no more guidance. If you will grant a wish of mine, lord—give me someone to lead me."

Still standing against the wall, the SSR agents watched the scene silently. Crouched by Marotte's still form, Abby stared, taking in every detail and storing them away in her head. She could see the thick clouds of black smoke drifting across the floor, towering and spinning themselves into all sorts of shapes. Here was a suggestion of a face, there a shoulder jutted out of the fume before dissolving into nothingness once more.

L'uomo Nero's blank, despairing face, the bare motion as Giovanna breathed slowly—her flowered scarf was gone, and those clothes were destroyed. There she was in the wide shallow darkness of the museum's sculpture hall, with the polished tile cold against her feet and the heavy weight of John Sawyer next to her, his shallow breath warm on her neck, her many cuts and aches pulsing with dull pain. L'uomo Nero faced a choice, and Abby watching as he struggled with it.

Even if he was a protective spirit, a monster, a killer, all the things that she'd seen the bogeymen be—he wasn't trouble. She hoped he would be kindly dealt with, not torn apart like the dead boy had been.

Then Bavbav laughed again, and the horror of the scene drained away as quick as lightning flickering across the sky. **It is known what you want,** the creature said affectionately. **And it is known how to give it to you. L'uomo Nero, black man, look to the girl you walked with.**

She, too, will receive new life. It is believed she will guide you, at least until you learn again how to be the conquering Hannibal.

And in parting, each mortal here is made a promise. He rose in the air, the clouds shaping and billowing around him like massive shadowy wings, and sparks of red light danced across the cold floor, juddering around their feet. **That when you die and come to dust, as all living ones shall, you may have a third choice. Heaven and Hell will await you, but so shall the ranks of my Family. Consider this.**

And with a sweep of the great wings, he dove forward into the ground. The tiled floor groaned, cracking and buckling. Arcs of red and blue and yellow flared through the room, sinking into Giovanna's semiconscious form and playing over the faces of the children. As one, the bogeymen set up a great wail and faded with him.

And as the energy crackled and faded out, the children sank slowly to the floor, minds blank as their memories were rewritten. But Giovanna....

They were watching a life in reverse. The sparse white hair sprouted like a field of wheat, turning a dull brown that nevertheless seemed miraculous after the bareness that had been there before. Wrinkles stretched out and faded as the flesh swelled, while the bulging veins that lurked beneath her papery skin like worms sank out of sight. The skeletal frame blossomed with healthy fat and muscle, and the gusts of wind ripped the last remnants of the flowered scarf from her head.

In seconds, it was over. There, leaning against the wall and breathing heavily, was a figure that John and Abby remembered from a black-and-white photograph. The stern nose and the strange, deep-set brown eyes were still there, but the rest of her seemed to have stepped out of the past. Darkish hair, ruffled and disordered; slightly roughened skin, tanned by time spent out-of-doors in the bright summer sun; square shoulders; straight back, no longer bent by age or arthritis.

Slowly, Giovanna raised a hand to her face, staring at it as if she could not believe what she was seeing. "I... it isn't time for my medicine yet..." she mumbled, then leapt and clutched at her own mouth again. "Is that me?" she whispered. "Blessed Mary, I haven't sounded that way in years...."

John shook his head. "You look fantastic," he mumbled. Giovanna looked up sharply at him and tried to rise from her crouch, but John shook his head. "Don't, please. You're not in the best of shape yourself."

"I've been worse!" she snapped, and for a moment, her voice creaked again. "And you are now too, I'm sorry to say." Bracing herself unsteadily, she rose to her feet, a young woman with an old woman's mind, incongruous in the tattered robe and the sadly ruined dress. Her legs trembled slightly, unaccustomed to her new weight and height. "You don't need to treat me like glass any more, not when you people are the ones that need help."

Giovanna rocked slightly when she walked, but she was quicker than he would have thought an eighty-seven-year-old woman could be. She bent down over Marotte, listening to his heartbeat. "Good and strong. Abigail, you give me a helping hand with this one, and we'll soon have him out. Nice of those bogeys to leave us."

Between them, the two managed to raise the tall man to his feet. Marotte's face twitched, and his eyes flicked open. "Sweet Helen, make me immortal with a kiss," he murmured dozily. "Must it happen so when I am but a half a man?"

"The other half'll be getting a walloping if you don't shut that mouth," Giovanna said firmly, staggering only a little under his weight. Abby nodded gratefully to her, and between the two of them, they managed to help the battered man to his feet. The crust of blood crumbled and fell away, leaving behind only a few streaks of redness. Of the wound there was nothing to be seen.

John, still not very steady himself, stood back a little against the wall and looked around. "What a nightmare," he murmured to himself. But he grinned a little at the sight of Giovanna, Abby, and Marotte.

"Well," he said. "How's it feel to be among the young again?"

"I'll manage," she said as she hauled on his arm. "You, on the other hand, look like you're ready to die any moment. And you, you stay awake, Mister Marotte; there've been enough bodies out of this nightmare already."

Chapter Twenty-One

It was chaos. The children filed out, trudging and shuffling, tired and emotionally drained. Some of them looked dazed in the brilliant flare of the blue-and-red lights, a few were still whimpering and rubbing their eyes, and many were looking around for their parents. A whole squad of ambulances had surrounded the scene, and as each child emerged, they were pulled into the flock of EMTs. Seen from above, it looked like a paramecium engulfing some helpless bit of sustenance.

News anchors were there, of course. The story was being covered with a vengeance, although what exactly the story entailed was still under debate. Fox had it as "Kidnapping Ring Busted," NBC spun it into "Long-Awaited Return of Children to Bereaved Families," CNN added that "At Last the Nightmare is Over," and ABC, straining for a fresh angle, wondered "What Damage Has Been Done to These Young Minds?" Squads of ambulances kept the children corralled, and riot police pulled from their beds took out their tiredness in keeping off the invasive reporters and gawkers.

More information came out by the minute. A list of the places where the children were kept was found in the sculpture court, along with a full confession; the riot police also discovered the site of an explosion in the basement, where the kidnappers had apparently committed a Jonestown-style mass suicide. Some of the authorities on the scene shook their heads, unable to believe that all the loose ends were being tied up so neatly, but the parents streaming in were all too glad to have their children back with no questions asked. Within twenty-four hours, conspiracy theories would be streaming across the Internet, and the incident would remain a touchstone of controversy for years; yet that night, more than one person gave thanks for an unlikely miracle.

Nobody paid attention to the handful of figures who slogged off into the night. In fact, considering the circumstances, one might have thought they were almost invisible.

He was gone again!

It was getting on towards evening on the Sydney waterfront, and one angry bogeyman was standing on the pier, glancing around. No L'uomo.

Groaning, Likho jammed the squashed felt hat onto his head, snapped the end off a cigarillo with exasperated swiftness, stuck it between his teeth, and flicked his fingers. A flame leapt from the end of them and turned the end of the cigarillo into an orange inferno. Likho inhaled, blowing smoke out of his nostrils and letting the routine calm his shattered nerves.

Not four hours before, he and L'uomo Nero had stumbled into the nothingness, slicing their way as far from that damned museum as they could. For a while they had stood there, not speaking, just thinking and rebuilding themselves. Too much had happened, and after their imprisonment, it was a luxury to stand still and not flinch at the shadows. Bavbav was back, and that was food enough for thought.

And he had turned around to retrieve his hat, torn from his head by a gust of wind (damn, it was nice to just go ahead and be solid), and L'uomo had vanished.

Likho remembered the last time he'd gone chasing after his friend. Well, the cat was out of the bag—so to speak—and L'uomo's brains seemed to be coming back to him. They would be finding out just who the black man would be soon enough. Likho was done chasing down insane bogeymen, getting trapped and burned and shouted at.

It was a remarkable feeling of freedom. No more babysitting—his friend could take care of himself. No more El Cucuy, either: the dead boy was frying in whatever circle of hell was reserved for unrepentant manipulative bastards. Bavbav would do unto him what he had done unto others. The legend would be manipulated, and another spirit would step in to take the Cucuy's form and belief. All that would remain would be a cautionary tale about the dangers of getting too big for your boots.

The Russian ghost breathed out a stream of smoke, relaxing for the first time in years. The sun was bright, the wind was brisk, and the slate-green waters of the bay washed against the wood and concrete pilings beneath his feet. Thousands of seagulls streamed across the sky, cawing at each other, while small vessels silhouetted themselves in white and gray, riding the swirling surface of the water. An oil tanker and a commercial tuna fisher were moored further down the wharves, with men scurrying up and down the ladders like ants.

From all Likho could see, there in that peaceful moment, he felt himself thinking that there were worse things to be called than *human*.

She had been old for a long time, and now the world had turned itself upside-down. Dressed in cast-off clothing, she stood on the corner of the street, watching the scurrying crowds. Cellular telephones and strange little white-and-gray radio things were everywhere, and the clothes made her gape in shock.

"This isn't my sort of world," she said to the tall man at her side. "And I think it'll take more than just a bit of fast talking to go back to my old life.

What's left of my family isn't taking me back. There's nothing for me any more, black man."

"But you are young again," the hoarse voice murmured. "Perhaps we can walk again?"

She took his hand. "That's all that's left for me, I think."

The Marquise home was small, one-story, built of sturdy blocks and covered over with carefully scrubbed white siding. The lawn had been manicured, there wasn't an inch of crab grass to be seen anywhere. The front porch had been scrubbed with Lysol, and the paint was fresh.

In the living room, Abby Marquise looked like a statue. At a loss for words, she stood still in the doorway, her eyes red-rimmed and her bandaged hands gripping each other. Jimmy had kicked the coffee table over and was pacing back and forth in a rage, clenching and unclenching his fists in front of him as if trying to grab something invisible out of the air.

"Where do you get off, Mom?" he demanded, wheeling to face her. "Maybe I'm not one of your *team*, but I saw the news. You were at the museum, weren't you?"

Abby bit her lip. "Jimmy, it was important. The kids are back, and—" She straightened her back, and looked him in the eye. "And you don't get to talk to me like that, Jimmy."

She tried to sound brave, but it didn't work. There was a note of pleading in her voice that made her shudder inside. It was thin and frightened, like the voice of the Mörkö when he'd begged not to go into the armor gallery.

"How do I know you weren't involved with those kidnappers? You come home, grab a knife, tell me you might not be back, and then just waltz off without giving a fuckin' damn! I'm not stupid, Mom!" Jimmy kicked at the overturned table again, his worn tennis shoe making a solid *thunk* on the pine planks.

"Look, we can work this out," Abby said cautiously. "The director called earlier—he said the whole staff is getting a bonus and hazard pay. We can order pizza for dinner, call your dad, talk about it when we're both a bit calmer...."

"A bonus for what?" Jimmy's voice rose a little, breaking at the height of its pitch. "Wrangling the aliens? Shaving the wolf man? I don't want to know where you're really getting the money, Mom, but you're one to talk about taking care of yourself!"

"It's good money, Jimmy." Her voice was just a little chilly now. The salt in her tears had left a burning sensation behind, and her eyes felt like they had been boiled in their sockets. "I don't know why you hate the SSR, but they do good work and they pay well. You don't want our water and power turned off, do you?"

"Christ, Mom, get it through your head!" The next kick turned the table over again, leaving it turned turtle with all four legs in the air. "There. Is. No. God. Damned. SSR! You're delusional!" His face was very pale and drawn, staring back at her through the green-dyed tips of his blonde hair. "And you go around ladeedahing all through the day, and me and Dad have to watch you get crazier and talk about your aliens and shit! And you're telling me that *I* need to get help! Shit, Mom, think about it!"

Her head turned, fixing him with an icy stare. "You and Dad. You've been talking to your father about this?"

"One weekend every month, Mom," Jimmy said bitterly. "He says that if you agree to get help, he's not going to make social services do an investigation. 'Exposing a minor to hazardous situations.'"

Something caught in the back of Abby's throat. "And it's that simple?" she said, half to herself. "You'd just have me declared insane? Take everything away?"

"It's been going on too long!" her son yelled. He stamped hard on the ground, making the overturned table judder and vibrate. "Why am I the only one who sees this? *Aliens*, Mom! No such thing! And you think you're—what? Fighting them?"

"Only some of them," she said in a low voice. "Some need help, too."

"End of the line, Mom. End of the fucking line. It's over." He shook his head. "I'll call the hospital, okay? Just stay here. I'll get them to check you out, and they can find out what's going on. They've got brain specialists and shit. They can take care of you. Just stay here."

"Jimmy, I'm not crazy. I can prove it." Abby stepped towards the overturned table, where her purse and car keys had been lying. Her feet felt unsteady under her, and the room seemed to waver. Her eyes burned. "I'll take you to the office. We've got specimens in jars, the traveling ring, the Anthology, everything. Jimmy—give it to me!"

Jimmy had snatched up her purse and snatched the car keys from it. "Sorry, Mom. Dad said I shouldn't let you drive." He shoved the keys into his pocket and pulled out his cell phone. Abby started towards him, and he leapt back and held up his hands warningly. "Don't do it, Mom. Stay back."

"I'm not crazy, Jimmy. I can prove I'm not crazy. Give me the keys, okay?" Abby said.

"Back off, Mom. I don't want to have to hurt you!"

Slapping El Cucuy had been the catalyst. Abby's temper had been under lock and key for so long—restrained by layers of guilt, maternal instinct, obligation, fear, and bleeding-heart pity—but if she could slap a minor deity, then she could control her own son. "James Lawrence Marquise," she said, rolling out each syllable like the tolling of a bell on Judgment Day, "I am your mother and you will listen to me!"

Abby strode forward, the wrath of God in Lane Bryant. Jimmy backed up as she stepped over the coffee table and held out her hand, glowering. "Give me the keys, Jimmy," she ordered. "This ends right now, do you hear me?"

"Not happening!" Jimmy snarled, snatching the keys back out of her reach. They stood there, staring each other down, son towering over mother.

"Jimmy," Abby said through clenched teeth, "Give me the keys. I am not crazy, and I can prove it. What don't you understand about that?"

"Mom—" there was real warning in his voice "—don't try anything stupid. I'm bigger and stronger, and I *will* knock you the fuck out if I have to."

Abby's lip curled. "You're being an idiot, Jimmy. I was nearly killed last night, and I don't need my own son mouthing off about things he's not even going to try to understand! So give me those keys right now, or I am taking them back and grounding you for a month!" To emphasize her point, she made a snatch at the keys in her son's right hand.

The punch came faster than she had expected, right in the stomach. Abby's breath whooshed out as her son's fist sank into her midsection, making her gasp. She doubled up in pain and Jimmy pulled back, his face a mixture of anger and horror.

"I told you!" he shouted, and flung the keys away. "I'm calling 911!"

But it was a poor SSR agent who couldn't recover quickly. Abby, still crouched over her aching stomach, barreled forward and crashed into her son's legs, knocking them both to the floor with her on top. She slapped at the cell phone in his hand, and it skittered across the floor. Jimmy swore and kneed her in the chest, bone impacting bone with a sickening thud, and followed it up with a sharp cut to the face that snapped her head back hard. She rolled sideways, bringing up a hand to block the next punch; when it came, she caught it and twisted hard, nearly dislocating her son's elbow and ending his curse with a shriek of pain.

Then Jimmy kicked again, as hard as he could. His tennis shoe struck Abby sideways across the face, knocking her backwards and almost stunning her. Dizzy with the blow, she raised a hand and touched her lip, wiping away the blood that seemed to be everywhere.

As she tried to raise her head, the front door crashed open. A dark form darted past, and Jimmy let out a high-pitched shriek. Suddenly terrified, Abby heaved herself to her feet, trying to focus on the intruder. A bogeyman? A burglar?

No. John stood in the living room, his face pale and drawn. He looked worse than ever. The slash marks on his face had scabbed over, but the largest had been stitched closed: Abby thought she recognized Dummy's handiwork. His hands were still heavily bruised, and there were dark circles under his eyes. But he stood steadily, implacably, and the Desert Eagle was aimed at her son's head.

Jimmy fell back, gasping with the effort of the fight and pale. "What the fuck do you want?" he demanded shakily. "Get out, or I'm calling the cops!"

A muscle leapt in John's cheek, and Abby thought she recognized that look. His eyes were gleaming with the effort of suppressed rage. "What do I want?" he said in a falsely jaunty tone. "First off, I'd like less of the assault and battery. Your mum's had a hard enough time lately. Abby?"

Abby shook her head dazedly. She knew she must look no better than John. Blood was leaking from her nose, and she could feel new bruises flowering over the ones from the night before. "'ll be okay," she mumbled, clambering unsteadily to her feet. "John, what are you—how did you—"

"Went back to my apartment to sleep, and wouldn't you know, I got a message," John said. "In a dream, of all things."

Her eyes widened. "What? A premonition?"

"Better. Giovanna's killed herself and joined the bogeymen." As Abby gaped in astonishment, John shook his head a little, apparently bemused. "Can't say I'm surprised."

"John, you're joking," she began shakily. "I—didn't Bavbav make her young again?"

He scoffed a little, but there was no malice. "That's all you're worrying about? She's mad for the bogeys—always has been. But better her than you." John's eyes narrowed as he turned his full attention back to Jimmy, who was watching them with a mixed expression of disbelief and horror. "She sent me a message in a dream, said I ought to keep an eye on things here. And it seems it's a fucking good thing I did, too," he continued with brittle brightness. "What's he done now, Abby?"

"He thinks we're crazy," she said, gingerly touching her swollen eye. "He tried to call the hospital, and wouldn't give me the car keys. I don't think he's going to believe anything we say."

"Oh, very funny," Jimmy broke in. "Look, pal, whoever you are, this is breaking and entering. You can leave right now, or you're going to be in serious fucking trouble."

"Son, son," John said, "you've got the wrong person. Your mum's perfectly sane. *I'm* the one with the voices and the issues, and right now, at least half a dozen of 'em are telling me that you're a right foul little git, and that a good telling-off isn't going to do a thing." He cocked the pistol, and the color drained out of Jimmy's face.

"You wouldn't!" Abby hissed, grabbing his arm. "John, if you even *think* about—"

"Of course I wouldn't. Go ahead, Abby, ruin a perfectly good intimidation tactic." John cast his eyes heavenward in exaggerated despair. Mother and son both breathed again. "But that still leaves us with the question," John continued, "of what we're going to do with the little bastard. Custody battles or trouble with social services rather put you off your work. Any suggestions?"

Abby shook her head. Her lower lip was beginning to swell also, and her left eye was definitely purple. "Jimmy?"

"Mom, this is fucked up—you gotta listen to me—" he began.

"Jimmy, please." She moved forward, putting herself between him and the Desert Eagle. Jimmy tensed a little as if preparing to run, but she shook her head again. "Jimmy, you really think I'm crazy. But all I want is to show you that we're not. I'm sorry about the divorce, I'm sorry things aren't going well. I want to make that up." Her voice cracked. "I want to be a good mom. I want to give you everything I can. Oh, God, if it had never happened, I'd be the happiest person in the world." Her heart broke as she steadied herself, looking into her son's widened eyes. How had it come to this? "But first, I have to prove that we're telling the truth," she said softly. You have to meet someone."

At those words, John's smile began to grow.

"I want you to meet the bogeyman, Jimmy." Abby stepped back and slowly, ceremonially, raised her hand and knocked twice on the wall. "Do you hear that?" she said in a quiet voice. "That's him knocking at the door."

"What?" Jimmy said disbelievingly. "Mom, listen to yourself!"

"You didn't listen to your mum, lad," John added. "The bogeymen won't have any of that."

Abby nodded, and knocked again. "There he is."

There was a gargling noise from Jimmy. He had backed up against the wall, pop-eyed. "Mom," he said, "you are really goddamned fucking *sick!*" Abby flinched backwards as his words struck home, and Jimmy slapped the wall angrily. "Sick, sick, fucking sick! You better hope I don't live through whatever the fuck you've got planned, because I am going to get you fucking arrested and locked up for this shit—"

"Now what would Marotte say under these circumstances?" John wondered aloud. "'There are more things on heaven and earth, Horatio, than are dreamt of in your philosophy?'" He grinned mirthlessly at Abby. "Don't tell me I never say anything important, now."

"You're all fucking insane!" Jimmy was shouting. John didn't even bother to shush him. Instead, he looked Abby straight in the eye. *Are you sure?* he mouthed. Abby nodded back at him, and raised a hand to knock again at the wall.

No need. There was a crash as the door blew open, sending a cold wind whistling through the house and bringing with it a stench of wet, dead leaves and crusted mold. There were soft footsteps, muffled by the worn carpet, and a gaunt figure stepped into the room.

He had on a long black coat and a wide-brimmed black hat, like something a Spanish priest might have worn. The brim shadowed his face and tilted down over his eyes, so that the vaguest shapes of a hollow cheekbone and a thin neck disappeared into the gloomy depths of the high collar. From one hand dangled a rough burlap bag.

"Okay, okay, I get it!" Jimmy yelped. Bravado had replaced anger. "Nice! Nice! You get some jackass to dress up, and you think it's gonna scare me—"

Then L'uomo Nero opened the bag, and for a long time afterwards, everything was silent.

Abby was the first to speak again. "Take care of him," she said. There were fresh tears collecting in the corners of her eyes, making them even more puffy and red. "I just want him to realize what was going on. Don't hurt him. Please. Just show him the truth."

"Humans often deceive themselves," the bogeyman said. His voice was steady, and his unclouded eyes shone in the shadow like two chips of onyx. "He does at the heart desire what would be best for all. I will give him the truth, which is what he deserves."

"Without pain?"

"Without pain." There seemed to be a ghost of a smile lurking beneath the shadow of the wide brim. "La Donna Nera is eager to teach him."

And he was gone.

THE END

Stark House Press
CLASSIC MYSTERY AND DARK FANTASY FICTION

1-933586-01-X **Benjamin Appel** Brain Guy / Plunder $19.95

1-933586-26-5 **Benjamin Appel** Sweet Money Girl /
Life and Death of a Tough Guy $19.95

0-9749438-7-8 **Algernon Blackwood** Julian LeVallon /
The Bright Messenger $21.95

1-933586-03-6 **Malcolm Braly** Shake Him Till He Rattles /
It's Cold Out There $19.95

1-933586-10-9 **Gil Brewer** Wild to Possess / A Taste for Sin $19.95

1-933586-20-6 **Gil Brewer** A Devil for O'Shaugnessy /
The Three-Way Split $14.95

1-933586-24-9 **W. R. Burnett** It's Always Four O'Clock / Iron Man $19.95

0-9667848-0-4 **Storm Constantine** Oracle Lips (limited hb) $45.00

1-933586-12-5 **A. S. Fleischman** Look Behind You Lady /
The Venetian Blonde $19.95

1-933568-28-1 **A. S. Fleischman** Danger in Paradise /
Malay Woman $19.95

0-9667848-7-1 **Elisabeth Sanxay Holding** Lady Killer / Miasma $19.95

0-9667848-9-8 **Elisabeth Sanxay Holding** The Death Wish /
Net of Cobwebs $19.95

0-9749438-5-1 **Elisabeth Sanxay Holding** Strange Crime in Bermuda /
Too Many Bottles $19.95

1-933586-16-8 **Elisabeth Sanxay Holding** The Old Battle Ax /
Dark Power $19.95

1-933586-17-6 **Russell James** Underground / Collected Stories $14.95

0-9749438-8-6 **Day Keene** Framed in Guilt / My Flesh is Sweet $19.95

1-933586-21-4 **Mercedes Lambert** Dogtown / Soultown $14.95

1-933586-14-1 **Dan Marlowe/Fletcher Flora/Charles Runyon**
Trio of Gold Medals $15.95

1-933586-02-8 **Stephen Marlowe** Violence is My Business /
Turn Left for Murder $19.95

1-933586-07-9 **Ed by McCarthy & Gorman** Invasion of the
Body Snatchers: A Tribute $17.95

1-933586-09-5 **Margaret Millar** An Air That Kills /
Do Evil in Return $19.95

1-933586-23-0 **Wade Miller** The Killer / Devil on Two Sticks $17.95

0-9749438-0-0 **E. Phillips Oppenheim** Secrets & Sovereigns:
Uncollected Stories $19.95

1-933586-27-3 **E. Phillips Oppenheim** The Amazing Judgment /
Mr. Laxworthy's Adventures $19.95

0-9749438-3-5 **Vin Packer** Something in the Shadows /
Intimate Victims $19.95

0-9749438-6-x **Vin Packer** Damnation of Adam Blessing /
Alone at Night $19.95

1-933586-05-2 **Vin Packer** Whisper His Sin / The Evil Friendship $19.95

1-933586-18-4 **Richard Powell** A Shot in the Dark / Shell Game $14.95

1-933586-19-2 **Bill Pronzini** Snowbound / Games $14.95

0-9667848-8-x **Peter Rabe** The Box / Journey Into Terror $19.95

0-9749438-4-3 **Peter Rabe** Murder Me for Nickels /
Benny Muscles In $19.95

1-933586-00-1 **Peter Rabe** Blood on the Desert /
A House in Naples $19.95

1-933586-11-7 **Peter Rabe** My Lovely Executioner /
Agreement to Kill $19.95

1-933586-22-2 **Peter Rabe** Anatomy of a Killer /
A Shroud for Jesso $14.95

0-9749438-9-4 **Robert J. Randisi** The Ham Reporter /
Disappearance of Penny $19.95

0-9749438-2-7 **Douglas Sanderson** Pure Sweet Hell /
Catch a Fallen Starlet $19.95

1-933586-06-0 **Douglas Sanderson** The Deadly Dames /
A Dum-Dum for the President $19.95

1-933586-29-X **Charlie Stella** Johnny Porno $15.95

1-933586-08-7 **Harry Whittington** A Night for Screaming /
Any Woman He Wanted $19.95

1-933586-25-7 **Harry Whittington** To Find Cora /
Like Mink Like Murder / Body and Passion $19.95

If you are interested in purchasing any of the above books, please send the cover
price plus $3.00 U.S. for the 1st book and $1.00 U.S. for each additional book to:

STARK HOUSE PRESS
2200 O Street, Eureka, CA 95501
707-444-8768
www.starkhousepress.com

Order 3 or more books and take a 10% discount. We accept PayPal payments.
Wholesale discounts available upon request. Contact griffinskye3@sbcglobal.net

COMING SOON FROM

Stark Houae Preaa

Danger in Paradiae / Malay Woman
A. S. Fleischman

1-933586-28-1 **$19.95**

Two south sea, cinematic adventure thrillers, with a new introduction by the author.

"Filled with a colorful cast of characters and wonderful noir dialog." MICHAEL CART, *Booklist*

SUMMER 2010

One for Hell
Jada M. Davis

1-933586-30-3 **$19.95**

The quintessential bad cop novel from 1952.

"A boxcar bum named Willa Ree enters a small town with the intention of picking it clean, and in the process all kinds of secrets and corruption come to light. It's a fine noir story with a powerful ending that Jim Thompson would have been proud to have written." BILL CRIDER'S *Pop Culture Magazine*

FALL 2010

The Silet Wall / The Return of Marvin Palaver
Peter Rabe

1-933586-32-x **$19.95**

Two previously unpublished novels by one of the top noir authors of the 50's and 60's—a serious study of Mafia revenge, and a crazy con from beyond the grave.

"With Rabe, you never know how the plot is going to unfold." MICHAEL SCOTT CAIN, *Rambles*

WINTER 2010

Dead Dolla Don't Talk / Hunt the Killer / Too Hot to Handle
Day Keene

1-933586-33-8 **$21.95**

Three short novels of mystery and suspense from the golden age of the paperback.

"He knew how to tell a story that gripped the reader immediately and held him to the end." BILL PRONZINI

New introduction by David Laurence Wilson.

2011

STARK HOUSE PRESS
www.atarkhouaepreaa.com